CALLIE HILL

New Beginnings
1866-1874

Kathy Meismer Darding

Kathy Meismer Darding

PublishAmerica
Baltimore

Softcover 9781462670758
PUBLISHED BY PUBLISHAMERICA, LLLP
www.publishamerica.com
Baltimore

Printed in the United States of America

To my family with love - Darrell, Andy, Kari, Mom...and Dad.

ACKNOWLEDGEMENTS

Thank you to my readers and proofreaders - Pam Edmonds, my mother, Betty Meismer, and my aunt, Donna Hersemann. They offered very helpful suggestions and caught many mistakes that I read over.

I used *The Woodford County History,* compiled by the Woodford County Sesquicentennial History Committee, published in 1968, especially the section on Clayton Township written by Mrs. Rose Toole, for information on the early history of Clayton Township and Benson, Illinois.

Another source of research was the *Standard Atlas of Woodford County, Illinois*, published in 1920. The fictional Chapmans' land was actually owned by my great-grandfather, Henry Meismer, and then by my grandfather, Joseph Meismer. It was where my father, Bob Meismer and his siblings lived.

I thank everyone who loved the first *Callie Hill* and encouraged me to write the sequel. I hope you enjoy this novel as much and like the "grown up" Callie. Your support has meant so much to me.

To my husband, Darrell, my children, Andy and Kari, and my mother, Betty Meismer, thank you for all your love and support in this adventure. Dad, I know you are with me too.

Chapter 1
1866

Callie Hill stood looking at the two freshly dug graves. She wasn't bothered by the damp March air swirling around her or the dark ominous clouds gathering above her. She was deep in thought. She sat down on the fresh spring grass automatically reaching for Socks, her dog. Socks curled up besides her laying his head on her lap.

"Oh, Socks. I just don't understand. I think I know why God wanted Grandpa Preston. He was old and hadn't felt good for years. He'll be happier in Heaven where he will be whole again. But I can't figure out why God took little Nathaniel before he even took his first breath. Mama Kathleen said God wanted a baby angel and Nathaniel was specially chosen."

Before Callie could think anymore, the skies opened up and the rain came down in a torrent, changing the red Georgia clay on the graves to tiny rivers of mud. Callie stood looking up at the sky.

"Looks like it's going to rain for a while, Socks, guess we'd better hightail it back to the house. Come on, boy, let's run!"

By the time they arrived at the front veranda, both were soaked. Callie's clothes clung to her body and water dripped off her long ash blonde curls. She laughed as Socks shook himself from head to tail, delivering a spray of water at her. She wished she could do the same. She couldn't go into the house yet and drip all over the highly polished pine floors. She would have to stay out here until she was drier. She didn't mind. It was a mild spring day and she wasn't cold.

"Miz Callie, whatcha doin' out here drippin' wet?"

Trudy, Callie's former slave, had opened the front door and stepped out onto the veranda.

"Let me git you sumpin' to dry you off wit." She went back into the house and soon returned with a well worn towel and an old quilt. Callie dried herself off the best she could and then wrapped up in the quilt.

"Trudy, come sit in the swing with me for a while. I'm not ready to go into the house yet. It's not storming, just raining hard."

Callie knew that Trudy, like herself, was afraid of bad storms after a twister hit their plantation, Oak Hill, years ago.

"What on your mind?" Trudy asked, sensing Callie was troubled.

"Oh, I don't know. Lots of things. So much has happened. Everything has changed. Remember when we were little girls and we would sit out here on this swing without a care in the world?"

"I's 'members the time you tooks your clothes off to cool down an' Miz Beulah an' Mammy Sallie caughts you! They was sooo mad, smoke was a'comin' outa their ears!!"

Callie laughed. Trudy could always make her feel better. They had been through a lot together, especially the last few years: Sherman's troops marching from Atlanta to Savannah with a stop at Oak Hill where, luckily, only the outbuildings were burned, the house was spared; James Williams' abduction of Callie and the kind Yankee, Ben Chapman, who had shot and killed him and saved Callie's life; her father, Nathan, and her brother, Samuel, returning from the war; the emancipation of the slaves and subsequent desertion of most of them from Oak Hill; all the physical labor they both had to do now to keep Oak Hill alive and producing; and, now, death, not one, but two.

Preston Hill suffered a massive stroke the end of January and died a day later. Oak Hill was thrown into mourning. Preston had built Oak Hill, planted the cotton fields that produced its wealth, and served as master to his slaves. He was a very loving husband, father, and grandfather. His wife, Beulah, was devastated by his death, but like many steel-boned Southern ladies, she accepted it as a part of the cycle of life. She had prepared herself for just such a day after Preston suffered his first stroke years ago, but it still was a great loss. They had spent forty-six years together side by side building their plantation and raising their son, Nathan, and his children. She would require time to heal. Meanwhile, she was looking forward to the birth of her grandchild, Nathan and Kathleen's baby, to be born around the first of May.

Kathleen made sure Beulah was kept busy getting things ready for the new baby. The two of them scrounged the attic and wardrobes looking for Callie and Samuel's baby clothes. There would be nothing new for the baby as commerce had not yet reached Oak Hill since the end of the war. Nathan wanted to make a trip to Savannah to purchase a layette, but Kathleen wouldn't let him go. He was still healing from war fatigue and, besides, she needed him at her side. She was ecstatic over her first pregnancy, but because of her age, thirty-three, she was afraid of complications.

In her seventh month, the end of February, Kathleen went into premature labor. She knew the baby was coming too early. Lenora and Mammy Sallie, former slaves of the family, did everything they could, but the baby, a boy, was stillborn. Everyone in the Hill household mourned the death of little Nathaniel Preston Hill. He was to be their new face for a new future after the great war. But it was not to be.

Beulah was grief stricken. She had hoped the pain of Preston's death would be eased with a new Hill child. She wanted to see the next generation who would carry on Preston's legacy.

Nathan was lost. He had been so happy with the thought of another son or daughter. He especially wanted a child with Kathleen, his love. Even though Kathleen loved Callie and Samuel as her own, he wanted her to have a child of *her* own.

Samuel was affected, but indifferent. He still had demons of his own to expel from his war experiences.

Callie was devastated. She had been so excited at the prospect of being a big sister and not the baby of the family anymore. She had just come to grips with Preston's death and this was too much. She was comforted by Trudy and Mammy Sallie, both grieving themselves. Their former masters' lives were so intertwined with their own that they felt the same pain as the others.

But the person feeling the most grief and pain was Kathleen. She was a strong willed Irishwoman, but this was just about more than she could bear. She had carried this child for seven months, feeling it move in her womb. She had loved him from the minute she discovered she was expecting. She had dreamed of what his life would be, what she would teach him, what he would teach her. All was gone in an instant. Her baby boy had died without knowing her or his family. She had held his still body until Mammy Sallie took him away. She felt so empty. A hole opened in her heart, never to be filled again. She knew she would never have any more children - she was too old. This had been her one chance to give Nathan a child and she had failed. She took to her bed and stayed there. She refused to see the baby in its little pine coffin that Joseph, the carpenter, built. She refused to walk to the family cemetery east of the house for his burial. She couldn't possibly think of her child buried in the cold wet ground.

For two weeks, Nathan let her stay in her bed and grieve. Then he went to her and pleaded for her to join the world again. Kathleen understood his loss too, and only because of her love for Nathan, did she come out of the shadow of grief into the dim light of healing. By no means was she over her pain, but she was trying. She had to. The rest of the family was depending on her to be strong. She had stood up to a Yankee lieutenant, a murderer, and a land defeated. She could do this and she tried. Only when she was alone did she let her grief wash over her and consume her. She hoped those episodes would lessen with time.

Callie, especially needed her help. Almost thirteen, Callie was still vulnerable and sensitive. Kathleen knew James Williams' taunts, before he was killed, hurt Callie deeply. He had shouted that Callie had killed her mother, Hannah, because Hannah had died hours after Callie was born. Callie had been horrified. Mammy Sallie and Beulah had been at Hannah's death and explained to her this was not the case. Hannah had loved her very much and wanted her very much. Callie had accepted this, but Kathleen knew thoughts still lurked deep inside Callie's head. Of all the members of the family, even Nathan, Kathleen knew she and Callie would grieve for little Nathaniel the longest. So together, they would journey towards an understanding of why God made Nathaniel a baby angel.

* * *

Callie and Trudy stayed out on the swing until the rain lessened and then went into the house. Mammy Sallie spotted them in the front hall.

"Miz Callie Hill! Whatchu doin' in them wet clothes! Mercy, chile! You ketch your death o' cold!" Mammy hurried up to Callie and ushered her towards the stairs. "You gits out of them clothes this very minute. You tryin' to give your Mammy trubble? Trudy you gits up there an' helps her. Hummmpfff. You young'uns goin' be the death of me yet!"

Callie and Trudy started up the stairs laughing at Mammy Sallie's antics. Sallie sometimes forgot they were now old enough to take care of themselves, but they liked the attention anyway.

Callie changed into a dry dress and combed her long hair. She pulled it back away from her face and tied a black ribbon around it at the nape of her neck.

"There, that should do for now. Trudy, I'm going to visit Mama Kathleen. She seemed sad this morning and went back to her room. Papa and Sam are out in the barn where the mare is birthing a new foal, so they may not be back for a while. I'm going to go keep her company."

"Alls right, Miz Callie. Think I's sneaks down to the libery an' reads a book 'fore Miz Beulah or Mammy Sallie puts me to work. This a good day to reads a book. Cain't do nuthin' outside no ways."

Callie smiled. It was so nice now that Trudy could read without worrying about being sold. Before and during the war, she learned to read when Kathleen was Callie's teacher, but no one knew. Eventually Callie, and then Mammy Sallie, found out, but they kept her secret until she was freed. Even then, Preston Hill was leery of her reading.

"That sounds like a good idea, Trudy. Maybe I'll join you later."

Callie walked down the hall to Kathleen and Nathan's room. Kathleen was laying on the chaise in front of the window, staring out at the raindrops running down the panes.

"Mama Kathleen? May I come in?"

Kathleen turned her head towards Callie. "Of course, sweetie. What a pleasant surprise. You know I always have time for you. Anything special on your mind today?"

Kathleen moved her legs and motioned for Callie to come and sit by her on the chaise.

"No, nothing special. Just wanted to see if you were all right. You seemed awfully quiet this morning at breakfast."

Kathleen reached out and stroked Callie's hair. "Where have you been? Your hair's damp. Were you out in this rain?"

Callie didn't know if she should tell Kathleen where she had been or not, but she had never lied to her.

"I was at the cemetery when the rain started and I got soaked. Then Trudy and I were sitting on the porch for a while talking. I just came up to change - Mammy Sallie had a fit that I was wet."

Callie grinned at Kathleen at the last words. Kathleen smiled back and then glanced back out the window again.

"Is his grave all right? The water isn't hurting it, is it? Is he next to Preston?"

Kathleen's questions startled Callie for a moment. She thought before she answered.

"Everything there is fine, Mama Kathleen. Yes, he's next to Grandpa in the cemetery, but we both know they are in Heaven. Nathaniel is our baby angel, right?"

"Yes, Callie. That's true. He was so special God had to have him. He was so beautiful. Looked exactly like your father. Such tiny fingers and toes. Soft silken hair. Think it would have been red like mine. So perfect. Yet........."

Tears had started spilling down Kathleen's cheeks. She didn't wipe them off, letting them run down her neck onto her collar. Callie blinked back her own, not knowing what to say. She reached over and grabbed Kathleen's hand and squeezed it tight.

"Grandpa and Mama Hannah will look after him in Heaven. He will be safe there, Mama Kathleen, and loved."

"I know, sweetie. It's just that I miss him so much." Kathleen shook her head as if to clear her thoughts. She finally reached up to wipe her tears away. She turned towards Callie with a faint smile on her face.

"Thank you so much, Callie dear. I don't know what I would do without you."

She reached over and wrapped her arms around Callie, clinging to her. Callie hugged her tightly, stroking her back. Kathleen broke the embrace and took Callie's face in her hands.

"Callie Hill, what a wonderful young lady you are. We are so blessed to have you, do you know that? I don't think your father or I tell you that enough. You have blossomed into a lovely person even after all that's happened to you."

Callie smiled at Kathleen. "*I'm* the one who's lucky to have you. We can sure thank Uncle John for sending you to Oak Hill to be my teacher, can't we? Otherwise, you and Papa wouldn't have met and gotten married."

"That's true. We owe a lot to Caroline and John. I'm hoping we can go visit them in Savannah this summer. Their last letter said they were back there cleaning their house after the Yankees moved out and would soon be ready for visitors. It would do us all good to get away from Oak Hill for a little while, don't you think?"

"I love to go to Savannah. I haven't seen Victoria since they brought us the chickens. Remember how excited we were to get them? Now we have lots of eggs and fried chicken again."

Kathleen laughed. "Yes, Belle was pretty happy when she butchered those first fryers. Said she almost forgot how to make her special fried chicken!"

Callie was happy to see the color return to Kathleen's face and her dark green eyes sparkle, if only for a minute.

"It sure tasted good, I remember that," Callie laughed.

They were interrupted by a knock at the door. It was Mammy Sallie.

"Miz Kathleen, Masta Nathan at the back door drippin' wet wantin' to know if ya'll wants to see the new baby colt. He said it standin' sucklin its mama an' is a sight to see."

Kathleen looked at Callie and they both answered at once, "Of course. Tell him we'll be right there."

* * *

As April arrived at Oak Hill, the inhabitants were more hopeful of a return to some sense of normalcy in their lives. Everyone knew, though, that life as they knew it would never be the same. Too much had happened during the war years.

Oak Hill was better off than most plantations. Preston and Nathan had the foresight to liquidate their assets into gold and silver currency, which they buried in the cemetery. Still, Nathan was reluctant to spend that money, hoping to get Oak Hill back to being self-sufficient first. He wanted to keep the cache as an emergency fund. The South was very unstable under the military occupation of the North and anything could happen.

The family members that were able, and former slaves, Trudy, her mother, Dinah, Joseph, William, and Malindy made up the work force. Beulah, Mammy Sallie, and Belle kept the house; Lenora watched over the former slave quarters and took care of any injuries or illnesses. Everyone else was used to rebuild the buildings, work the cotton fields, take care of the livestock, and maintain the kitchen garden.

Nathan was determined to get a cotton crop in the ground this year. Planting began in earnest that April. Instead of thousands of acres planted, only twenty was cleared, plowed, and seeded. They just didn't have enough manpower to do any more. But it was a start. They also plowed up several acres to grow corn for the animals. They all worked from early dawn to dusk, falling into their beds after eating the evening meal.

On April 23rd, Callie celebrated her thirteenth birthday. She told everyone she was now too old for presents, but no one listened. Nathan and Kathleen gave her Hannah's ivory toiletry set, Samuel parted with one of his favorite books, Beulah gave her a pair of her earrings, Trudy made her a new petticoat out of old sheets, and Mammy and Belle made her a delicious cake. Callie dressed up for dinner that night in Hannah's sky blue gown and had Mammy Sallie fix her ash blonde hair into a chignon. Nathan still couldn't get over the transformation in his daughter. She looked so like her mother then. Luckily for Callie, she hadn't grown too much this year in height, but her shape was changing. Her waist was narrowing, her hips spreading, and her bosom growing. Still, Hannah's old dresses fit her and didn't need to be altered.

The next day, it was back to work. The work crew trekked off to the timber to fell some trees. The compound still needed a proper stable for the remaining horses. The small newly built barn was bursting at the seams with new foals and calves. The trees were sawed into crude boards at the site and those were hauled back to the grounds where the men sawed them again into thinner boards, then planed them smooth. It was a labor intensive process that took weeks to complete. But at the end, a new stable rose on the site of the old. Callie's little pony, Rumpel, was one of the first occupants and whinnied his approval immediately.

Several of the old slave cabins were torn down, and this lumber was used to build a new hog shed and fence. Pork was a staple on the family dining table, so the hogs were treated almost royally.

The kitchen garden sprouted fresh greens which the family gratefully consumed after months of eating dried or canned vegetables. Callie and Trudy went around the grounds collecting young dandelion greens, which Belle would turn into delicious salads.

The family had learned to eat their food supply sparingly, rationing it out until the gardens and fields produced. They were lucky this year as it was a perfect spring for growing.

Callie and Trudy were carefully hoeing the weeds around the tender new lettuce shoots in the garden when Callie suddenly stopped.

"Trudy, do you remember what we used to do on a day like this? We would eat a huge breakfast with bacon, sausage, eggs, grits, potatoes, and cornbread. Then we would go to the schoolroom and Mama Kathleen would teach me, and you, to read or do our numbers. Then we would go to lunch and have cold pork, ham, biscuits, gravy, pickled vegetables, and other good things, and then we would go laze on the swing or out under the big oak tree on an old quilt. Or I would go ride Rumpel and later Daisy. Then we would go eat a big dinner of fried chicken, mashed potatoes, sweet potatoes, ham, cornbread, beans, salads. Out on the veranda we would go to enjoy the night air and talk about everything and anything. What happened to those days, Trudy?"

"The big war came, Miz Callie, an' changed everythin'. One thin' nice now, tho', is that I's free. Not a slave no mo'. Don' 'long to nobody but myse'f."

"I know, Trudy, and I think that is a good thing, as long as you decide to stay here at Oak Hill with me."

"Don' plan on goin' nowhere else, Miz Callie. I's home rights here at Oak Hill, jes' like you."

Callie stopped her musings and went back to hoeing. Yes, things had certainly changed at Oak Hill.

* * *

One person who was having a very difficult time with the change in his life was Samuel Hill. Samuel had been very eager to fight for the Confederacy, enlisting even before his eighteenth birthday. The death of his cousin Andrew Whitson during the battle of Fort Pulaski in 1862 fueled his desire for revenge against the North.

Samuel was injured during the Battle of Gettysburg and captured in the Battle of Kennesaw Mountain. He spent the rest of the war as a prisoner at Camp Douglas near Chicago, Illinois. These events in Samuel's life had hardened him into a resentful person, sometimes to the extent that those who loved him hardly recognized him. They didn't say much, knowing he needed time to heal from what he had been through. All tried to be cheerful and understanding, hoping to see the old Samuel appear soon.

Samuel knew his family wouldn't understand the real reason why he was so sullen. It wasn't because of what he had suffered during the war, but because he wasn't able to fight to the end like his father and others. He was embarrassed he had been captured during the battle and spent the rest of the war in the North where he couldn't do anything to help the Confederacy. His honor had been compromised. He had done nothing to help Oak Hill survive, the *women* had done that. He couldn't even save his own sister's life. A Yankee, of all people, had done that! In his eyes, his sense of Southern honor and chivalry was gone. He was just the same as any white trash or darkie now. Here he was working like a common field hand trying to grow enough food to keep from starving. It just wasn't right! People in the North weren't suffering now like the South was. They weren't groveling, eking out a living. Their land was untouched by the ravages of war. No one had burned their homes and stolen their dignity.

Sometimes, these thoughts in Samuel's head seethed for days. He really couldn't understand his father. Nathan never complained or said anything negative about their current situation. He never brought up why they were now on the level of common farmers. He always brought out the positive - the house was saved, they were all alive, safe, and together. Well, maybe they were, but they sure weren't the same family as they had been before the North invaded them.

Samuel still loved Oak Hill with all his heart, as he had as a child. But he wanted it back the way it used to be. He didn't even have time now to sit and watch the Spanish moss on the live oaks wave in the breeze, or listen to the darkies sing in rhythm while they weeded the cotton. He missed the activity in the Quarters. Now only Joseph, Dinah, William, Lenora, and Malindy lived there.

Now *he* was the one weeding the cotton. How did this happen? Where had the South gone wrong? Would it ever be like it used to be?

Samuel kept all these thoughts to himself, but Nathan knew his son was troubled. He just didn't know how to fix him. He, himself, was dealing with images from the war, but he had Kathleen to soothe him at night when he woke up screaming. He now had an overpowering drive to return Oak Hill to its pre-war glory, especially since the death of his father. This took precedence over all his troubles and was what kept him going. He only wished his son had something to drive his demons away.

Callie also knew something was haunting Samuel. She tried to get him to talk about what was bothering him, but she was just met with a scowl and then he walked away. She had never seen her brother act this way and felt helpless as to what to do. It seemed easier to just leave him alone until he worked things out for himself.

The only person who could break through to Samuel was Mammy Sallie. She knew "her Samuel." She left him alone when he seemed in another world, and talked to him when he was present in this one. She knew something had happened to him during his days in the prison camp and sooner or later he would tell her about it. Until then, she would wait and be there when he needed her.

* * *

The hot, humid summer days were spent toiling on the land. It was imperative to the Hills that the food grown would be on the table now and in the future. Nathan was obsessed to have a small cotton crop to sell. He watched over the young growing plants as if they were his children. Second only to the cotton was the corn crop. He was determined to reap enough corn for the livestock to offset buying any. He wanted to save what money they had for necessities not produced on Oak Hill.

The family was fortunate this summer because there was just enough rain and sun for the crops to flourish in the red Georgia clay. Callie and Trudy were very proud gardeners as the kitchen garden produced an abundance of greens and vegetables. They had an outstanding potato and yam crop this year. The fruit trees were laden with ripening apples, peaches, apricots, and pears. The Hills would be eating very well this winter.

* * *

As soon as the mail resumed in Georgia after the war ended, Nathan had sent a letter to Mr. Benjamin Chapman of Woodford County, Illinois:

Dear Mr. Chapman,

There are no words to express my thanks to you for saving my daughter, Callie, from James Williams. My wife has relayed to me your heroic endeavors that day. If you hadn't stayed behind to watch Williams, I would be mourning the death of my little girl.

If there is ever ANYTHING that I could possibly do for you, please, please let me know. I wish there was some way now that I could repay you, but I don't know how. How do you repay someone for the life of their child?

I will pray for you and your family every day that you remain healthy and safe. That is the best I can do.

If you are ever in our parts again, please come and visit us. I am anxious to meet you, Mr. Chapman. Thank you again for all you have done for my Callie.

Forever indebted,

Nathan Hill

It was many months later when a letter arrived at Oak Hill. It was addressed to Callie. Callie was very curious when she came in from feeding the horses and found it on the front table.

She turned the envelope over and over before she finally opened it.She pulled out several sheets of paper and began to read:

June 17, 1866

Dear Miss Hill:

I don't really know how to begin this letter, but I'll try. I received one from your father thanking me for saving your life in '64. I don't feel like I did anything out of the ordinary. You were in trouble and I took care of the trouble-maker. He was a bad one, anyway.

I'm mighty glad your pa made it back home to you. Did your brother too?

I thought maybe you would like to know what happened after I left your place that day. Your ma gave me that horse and after I buried Williams, I raced back to my unit. No one seemed to have missed me. When they saw the horse, they just assumed I had been "foraging" a little longer. No one ever said a thing about Williams, no one cared. We went on towards Savannah where we were quartered for several weeks.

General Sherman then had us go north to South Carolina where he followed the same warfare as in Georgia. I was really sick of it by then and tried not to participate, especially in the burnings. Since I now had a horse, my life was much easier, no more foot marching. For this I am very grateful to your ma. She wouldn't have had to give me the horse. Please thank her for me.

We went through South Carolina and then to North Carolina. By then Lee had surrendered at Appomattox and the war was over. I have to say, I was very sad to learn of Abraham Lincoln's death. It hit us soldiers real hard. It was so sad when we had the big revues of the armies in May at Washington, D.C. It just didn't seem right to not have Lincoln there to see us march past.

I had to leave your horse - I named him Chief - with the army. We all boarded trains and were sent home.

For me, home is on the Illinois prairie in Woodford County. My folks and my sister, who's about your age, live on a farm in Clayton Township. Pa has about 160 acres in the southeast quarter of the section. He hires out to help farm it, but not all is tilled. Some is pasture for our cattle, horses, and sheep.

I sure was glad to get back home in one piece. Not all our neighbors survived and some came back maimed. My best buddy, Leroy, was killed at Cold Harbor and I didn't know it until I got back home.

Give my regards to your family. I would like to meet the rest of them some day.

Yours in peace,

Ben Chapman

Callie read the letter again, not knowing exactly what to think. It was nice of Mr. Chapman to write to her, but she wasn't sure why he had. She decided to show the letter to Nathan and Kathleen. It seemed more appropriate for them to read it than her.

After reading the letter, Kathleen looked at Callie and said, "Why, Callie, this is a very nice letter from Mr. Chapman. What is your problem with it?"

"Why is he writing to me, Mama Kathleen? Papa was the one who wrote to him. I would think he would write back to him, not me."

"Well, *you* were the one he saved. Maybe he feels more connected to you because of that. He hasn't even met Nathan. And, there might still be some feelings about him being a Yankee and your father fighting for the Confederacy. Maybe he felt Nathan would hold some grudge against him for ransacking and burning Oak Hill, too. Writing to you was probably the least of many evils. He must be a nice enough man, though, to write back at all. Don't you think so?"

"I guess so. What do you think, Papa?"

"I agree with Kathleen, Callie. I think it was very nice of him to write to you. If it weren't for him, you probably wouldn't be here." At that Nathan reached over and hugged Callie hard. "I think you should answer his letter. Let him know how things are around here and what you've been doing. Since he farms, he will understand what we are doing too. You have that in common, no matter if it is in Georgia or Illinois."

"But he never had slaves."

"And, according to the outcome of the war, we don't either." Nathan frowned at Callie. He was recalling that Congress had passed the Thirteenth Amendment last December making slavery unconstitutional, one result of all the fighting.

"Then I'll write him a letter back. I should really thank him myself anyway. I didn't get much of a chance that day, as he left in a hurry."

Thus, began the correspondence between Callie Hill and Benjamin Chapman.

CHAPTER 2
1867

Ben Chapman stood on the front porch of his family's prairie house and gazed out at the sunset. It was a beautiful one tonight. Streaks of magenta pink turning to fiery orange and then to flaming red spread out across the aqua blue sky. Puffy white clouds were scattered about the colors. He breathed a deep sigh. At the moment he was content. All the chores had been done and it was time to go in and eat with the rest of the family. He relished this time of the night when he stood on the porch all alone looking out at the landscape. During all the fighting of the past years, he never thought he would be able to do this again. He considered himself blessed. So many of his comrades lay in graves in the South or hobbled on one leg or managed with one arm.

"Benjamin, time to eat." His mother, Abigail, broke his reverie.

"Be right in, Ma." He gave one more look at the sky, now dimming with the setting sun and walked into the house.

* * *

Henry Chapman, Ben's father, immigrated from England in the early 1830s. He made his way across the eastern half of the United States to the state of Illinois. At first he settled along the banks of the Illinois River in Spring Bay Township, Woodford County, leading a bachelor's life. Then in 1842 he met and married Abigail Schneider from near-by Partridge Township and his life changed radically.

The newlyweds decided to strike out on their own and moved a little distance east into what would later become Clayton Township. There they purchased acreage and started farming the land. Two years later, Abigail miscarried three months into her pregnancy. She was pleased when a year later she was once again expecting and delivered a healthy baby boy, Benjamin Henry Chapman.

Abigail suffered two more miscarriages after Ben's birth. She and Henry thought Ben was to be their only child, but when Ben was seven, Abigail gave birth to a healthy baby girl, Emma Abigail, who Ben adored.

One more pregnancy and one more miscarriage decided that Abigail and Henry would have no more offspring; therefore they doted on their two living children.

Henry eventually purchased 160 acres in the Southeast Quarter of Section 34 in Clayton Township. As the land grew, so did the work. Henry hired several live-in workers to help with the farm. Ben and Emma grew up with Slim, Gus, and Ed thinking they were family. All three were confirmed bachelors, or so they said. Gus eventually met and married Eunice Corbin from Linn Township, next door to Clayton, and started a family of his own there.

Henry only farmed about half of his land, the rest being used as grazing for the livestock. The land was extremely fertile, black, rich loamy soil. Corn grew like a weed, along with oats and wheat. Bountiful harvests came from the gardens. The Chapmans ate well. Ben and Emma grew up healthy and strong.

When the War Between the States started, the family was busy worried about the spring plantings. Charleston, South Carolina seemed too far away for them to be concerned. Ben was only sixteen and Henry considered himself too old, so there was no worry about them going off to war.

However, the market for their grain was disrupted by the war. They usually took their harvest to Peoria and sent it down the Illinois River to the Mississippi River to New Orleans. The war changed that. Now their crops were sent via the Illinois Central Railroad to Chicago and out through the Great Lakes, which cost them more money for the shipping. While the closure of the Mississippi River temporarily unhinged farm markets, the crop prices consistently rose. Henry plowed up more acreage to plant in grain. The family and hired hands were busier than ever.

In July of 1863, after reaching the age of eighteen, Ben was drafted into the Union army. Henry wanted to pay the $300 to find a substitute for him, but Ben was unwavering about serving his country. He was also anxious to get off the farm for a while and see the rest of the country. To an eighteen year old, the war sounded exciting. His father knew better, but since Ben was of age, he couldn't stop him.

Abigail had a fit. Her only son was going off to fight a war in the faraway South, putting himself in danger, but her protests fell on deaf ears, and Ben went off to war just when he was needed the most on the farm.

Ben was assigned to the Union Army of the Tennessee fresh from the victory of Vicksburg. He then participated in the campaigns in Tennessee and Georgia, culminating in Sherman's March to the Sea. It was then that he arrived at Oak Hill and saved Callie Hill's life.

Ben thought about Callie and her family frequently after he arrived back in Clayton Township. He was even more intrigued when he received the letter from Nathan Hill. He hadn't said anything to his family about his army service so their interest was also piqued when the letter arrived from Georgia. Ben told them what had happened at Oak Hill that day in December of 1864. He sugar coated some of the rough spots, not wanting his family to know he was participating in the "foraging." They accepted his rendition for what it was worth and never questioned him again.

For some reason, he felt he had to contact Callie to see how she was doing. He wondered how her family was faring. He knew times were really tough in the South, unlike the boom they were experiencing in post-war Illinois. That was why he finally put pen to paper and wrote to her, hoping she would write back in return. She did.

* * *

In the spring, Oak Hill was recovering slowly. This year Nathan planted more acres in cotton, a few more in corn, and a few in oats. The former slave gardens were tilled up and more vegetables were planted there.

Several more of their former slaves returned, unhappy with their current lives. Nathan accepted them back gratefully, needing their hands to help with the work. They moved back into their former cabins and set up house. Nathan would give them shelter and food and if they performed well, a silver coin at the end of the year.

* * *

At dinner one night in the early summer, Nathan turned to Callie. "How would you like to go to Savannah and visit Uncle John and

Aunt Caroline? They are back in their house in town and asked us to visit."

"Oh, Papa, I would love to go! I haven't been there in such a long time. It will be good to see Savannah again."

"Well, I think just you and Kathleen and I will go. I need to discuss some things with John, and I think you ladies deserve a rest from all the hard work you've been doing. A change of pace and scenery will do you good."

Callie knew he was talking about Kathleen who had observed the birthday of little Nathaniel several months ago. She had been very melancholy for weeks. A trip to Savannah to see the Whitsons and also her family would cheer her up.

"When will we go, Papa? Soon?"

"I think in two weeks, Callie. That should give you girls time to get things packed and ready. Be sure and take your better dresses. Caroline wrote that some people are hosting parties again in the city. It will give you a chance to show off."

"Papa! I don't have anything to show off!" But Callie was excited about having someone else besides the family see her dressed up and looking older.

"Can Trudy come too?"

"You'll have to ask her if she wants to. I know Caroline wouldn't mind."

"Sam, why aren't you going?" Callie turned to her brother who was very quiet this evening.

"Someone has to stay here at Oak Hill. Besides, I'm not anxious to go back to Savannah. Father and I were just there not too long ago. Most of my friends there were killed in the war or have moved away. Things have changed there for me, Callie. There are Yankee soldiers all around and that just brings bad thoughts for me. I'm happier here at Oak Hill with Grandma and Mammy Sallie."

"I understand, Sam. But I'll miss you while we are gone." Callie thought how things had changed. Usually, Samuel was the one going away and she was the one left behind.

Kathleen smiled at Callie as if reading her mind. "You and Victoria will have a wonderful time, Callie. Caroline said in her letter the young people are starting to socialize again, so you will get a glance of Savannah society. This time you can participate more. We will have to make sure your dresses still fit. Maybe we can even have Dinah modify one of your mother's old ball gowns. I'm sure there will be a ball while we are there."

"Do you think so, Mama Kathleen? Let's go up to the attic tomorrow and see what's there. This will be so much fun!" Callie couldn't wait to go ask Trudy if she wanted to go along.

* * *

Trudy didn't want to go to Savannah. Callie couldn't believe it. "Why don't you want to come, Trudy. It will be lots of fun."

"Fun for *you*. Won's be fun for *me*. What's I's 'posed to do whiles you out gallivantin aroun all dressed up goin' to balls? Ain't nobody goin' let Trudy in the door. 'Sides, them darkies at Miz Caroline's uppity. Thinks me an' Mammy was country darkies. No, I's ain't goin', Miz Callie. You's goes an' tells me all 'bout it when you gits back to Oak Hill. 'Sides, somebody gots to take care of Socks an' Rumpel."

Callie thought for a minute about telling Trudy she *had* to come, but now that Trudy was free, she could do what she wanted. Callie also knew Trudy was right. She wouldn't be able to attend any of the events with her and have any fun. She was better off staying at Oak Hill.

Callie did ask Mammy Sallie if she would go along and do her hair and help her dress while they were in Savannah.

"Miz Callie, I's gittin' too ole to travel to Sava'na any mores. These ole bones cain't take a trip like that no mores. You jes' has to let's Dora do your hair an' he'ps you gits ready. You's big gal now, you should he'ps yourse'f anyways." Mammy frowned at Callie, who suddenly felt uncomfortable.

"You're right, Mammy. I can take care of myself. But I will miss you." She reached over and gave Mammy a hug.

"I's guess you miz your ole Mammy," Sallie chuckled. "Buts you's be fine."

* * *

After all their chores were done, Callie and Kathleen spent the rest of their time trying to get some facsimile of a wardrobe together. Unlike Nathan, whose clothes were just fine, theirs would have to be reworked and updated somewhat. Callie's dresses especially needed altering. She hadn't grown any in height or weight, but her shape had changed again. Her waist was tiny, her hips flared a little, but her bosom was bigger. Her two dresses, the sky blue one and the green print one, both had to have a gusset added in the back to accommodate her bigger chest. Otherwise they were both fine to take.

Kathleen mended some rips and tears on her dresses, added some lace to the bottom of the frayed hems, and turned down the cuffs and sleeves so as not to show the wear. Her midnight blue gown had seen better days, but she made it presentable enough to attend a ball.

Callie needed a ball gown. After rummaging through the attic, they found a gown of Hannah's. It fit Callie everywhere but the bust. Dinah added a gusset down the back and it fit perfectly. Callie loved the dress. It was made entirely of pale green organza. The neckline was off the shoulder, low, scooped, and showed cleavage. The sleeves were tiny and capped just below the shoulder. The wide skirt had rows and rows and rows of organza ruffles, from the waist to the hem. It was beautiful.

Callie was admiring herself in the mirror. "Oh, Mama Kathleen, it is so pretty."

"No, Callie, *you* are so pretty in the dress. You must wear Hannah's pearl earrings and I have the perfect necklace for you. Wait here just a minute while I go find it."

Callie turned and twisted in front of the mirror, still not believing it was actually her in the reflection.

"Here, Callie, let me put this on you. My mother brought this from Ireland and gave it to me when I was about your age."

Kathleen fastened a necklace around Callie's throat that was a simple pendant containing an emerald stone hanging from a gold herringbone chain.

"There, that's absolutely perfect. Look how the green matches the color of your dress."

Callie agreed. "Thank you, Mama Kathleen. It is beautiful, but are you sure you don't want to wear it yourself?"

"No, no, no. It's perfect with this dress. I want you to wear it, sweetie. You will be the 'belle of the ball!'"

Callie could hardly wait until they got to Savannah so she could really show off her "new" clothes.

* * *

The trip to Savannah would be much different than the ones Callie took before. They had no carriage - the Yankees had burned it - so they had to travel in their wagon along with their trunks. Also, there would be no plantations along the way where they would spend the night. They had been burned and their owners gone. It would be a night under the stars or a night of constant traveling. They elected the latter, unless an inn had sprung up lately.

Nathan enlisted Judah, a returned slave, to drive for them. Jed, their former driver, had disappeared with the Yankees and hadn't been seen since. Nathan, unbeknownst to Kathleen and Callie, was going to purchase a new carriage while in the city. It would be delivered to Oak Hill when finished.

The wagon was packed with their trunks on one side and then feather beds were laid at one end for them to sleep on along the way. Judah and Nathan would sit on the front bench to steer the horses. Another bench was added behind them inside the wagon bed for Callie and Kathleen. It was not going to be a comfortable ride. Still Callie was excited to be going. She hadn't been to Savannah since Andrew Whitson's funeral five years ago. This would be a much happier visit.

After receiving a big basket from Belle packed with all sorts of food for their trip, they left Oak Hill bound for Savannah. Callie looked at Kathleen, who already had color in her cheeks from excitement. Traveling the way they were, though uncomfortable, was adventurous. But not for long.

The bench became very hard, especially when the wagon hit ruts or holes in the road and Callie and Kathleen bounced. At first it was funny, but then hurtful. Finally, Callie had enough and went and lay down on the beds in the back. Even though the sun was beating down on her, she slept.

When she awoke, she was surprised to see Kathleen lying beside her. "I couldn't stand it any more either, Callie. My backside is probably all bruised by now!"

They both laughed, causing Nathan to turn around and ask what was so funny. They laughed even more. Nathan didn't mind, he was glad to hear his wife laugh again.

It wasn't long before they pulled over to a shady creek to eat some of the food Belle had sent them. It felt good to be on the ground again and walk around, but before long they were back on their way. The two women decided to try it once more on the bench, this time padding it with some of the comforters they had brought along. This helped somewhat. At least they lasted longer on the bench than before.

As the dusk turned to twilight, the stars started appearing in the clear night sky.

"Oh, Mama Kathleen, look at all the stars! They are so bright tonight. Doesn't it look like you can just reach out and touch them?" Callie was lying on her back on the bed again, as was Kathleen.

"It is a beautiful night, Callie. You can just smell the sweetness in the air, can't you? Just beautiful."

Just as Kathleen uttered those words, two men jumped out of the ditch beside the road startling the horses. Judah had a hard time bringing the pair to a stop. Callie and Kathleen peeked over the rim of the wagon bed. Kathleen put her finger to her lips and nodded to Callie to be quiet. The men had white hoods over their faces and brandished guns.

One of them shouted at Judah, "What you doin' here darkie? Git off that wagon and put your sorry behind on the ground here."

Nathan stood up. "This man is working for me. Leave him be, and let us pass."

"You sure, mister, this man ain't hijackin' this here wagon an' stealin' it? You sure he ain't makin' you come along with him as a hostage? 'Cause we can take real good care of him if he is."

"Yes, I'm sure. He is my employee. Now let us pass."

"You got anything in that there wagon worth anything? Me an' my partner here would like to take a little look an' make sure you ain't got any contraband in there. We's take a look around in there."

"NO, you won't!" Nathan shouted. "This is my property and mine alone and you will not be touching anything in there."

At that, Nathan reached under the bench and pulled out his rifle, cocked it, and aimed at one of the men. Judah did the same, aiming at the other. The two hooded men stood still.

"No need to get upset, mister. We's jus' makin' sure you ain't bein' kidnapped or something worse. Don't get all excited. Lots of darkies come this road who cause trouble. We take care of them so folks are safe around these parts."

"That may be well and good, but we don't need your help, so please put your weapons down and let us pass."

The men dropped their arms with the pistols and walked back toward the ditch. "Go on, mister. We won't bother you unless we've reason too."

Nathan had Judah start up the horses again and they trotted along the road quickly. Kathleen and Callie braced themselves so they wouldn't bounce out of the wagon bed. Nathan kept his rifle trained on the men by the ditch until they were out of sight.

"Keep down, Kathleen, until I'm sure they aren't following us." Nathan still had his rifle pointed at the road behind them.

"Who are those men, Nathan?"

"I imagine they are part of the new group that John wrote about. Call themselves the Ku Klux Klan. They hide their faces and come out at night to terrorize darkies and Northern sypathizers. What a cowardly bunch! Preying on the innocent and not even showing their faces!"

"I's shore glad you here, Masta Nathan," said Judah, who was still shaking from the encounter. "I's 'fraid I's be one dead darkie if'n you not here wit dese rifles. Dem bad men, bad men. Could o' hurt Miz Kathleen an' Miz Callie too. Good t'ing dey's in de back of de wagon. Uh-huh, bad bad men. Hopes we don' sees no more o' dem de res' o' de way."

"You're right, Judah. No sleep for either one of us. We will both have to be on alert. If you get sleepy, just let me know. I'll take over long enough for you to get a few winks."

"Yessir. Ain't sleepy now, dat's fo' shore. Dem men put de fear in me. I's stays 'wake de res' of de way now. Sleeps when we gits to Masta John's an' Miz Caroline's. No sir, not sleepy now."

Callie and Kathleen were wide awake too. After they were some distance from where the men were, Callie was still shivering. Kathleen, too, was quite shaken. They were both thinking would their lives ever be without the threat of violence again? At least Nathan was there this time to protect them.

* * *

The Hills arrived in Savannah in the late morning after traveling all night. They were very grateful and relieved to finally pull up to the Whitson's mansion on the corner of Gordon and Barnard Streets. The travelers were very weary, but glad to reach their destination unharmed; only frightened.

John and Caroline Whitson's red brick Georgian mansion still stood proudly by Chatham Square. It needed a new coat of white paint on the pillars and trim, but was still very impressive from the street.

Judah guided the wagon through the rod iron gates and up to the extensive front veranda. It wasn't long before the massive front door was opened and John, Caroline, and Victoria came out into the blazing sunlight.

"Greetings! Welcome back to Savannah! Oh, it so good to see you again!" Caroline rushed up to Kathleen and then Callie, giving them hugs while she was talking.

John reached Nathan and pumped his hand in a tight grasp, then proceeded to greet the women with embraces. Victoria hugged everyone. It was a warm welcome from all there.

"Do come in, it is quite warm out here and the house is much cooler. Have your driver take the wagon to the stables, Nathan, and we'll get some help to unload it. Won't you be glad when you have a carriage again?"

Kathleen and Callie laughed. "Yes," said Kathleen. "Our backsides are pretty sore from all the bouncing. It wasn't much better laying down, either."

Caroline laughed. "I hope everything else was all right."

"Well, actually.........." Nathan turned to John and then described the encounter with the hooded men.

"I was somewhat afraid of that," John said. "I've heard that group is getting more and more daring and unfortunately, larger. We can talk about it later, Nathan." He indicated he didn't want the women to hear. "Now let's get you settled into the house."

Callie felt like she was back in familiar surroundings. The house had not changed during its occupation by the Union surgeons. There were deeper scratches on the polished floors where army boots had walked, some of the furniture was stained, but overall the house looked much the same. She and Victoria headed upstairs to Victoria's room. Callie once again thought she had entered a fairy land with all the pink rosebuds in the room.

"Victoria, I'm so glad your room stayed the same. I love all the pretty rosebuds in here."

"Really? I think I've outgrown them. I would like something more sophisticated now. This still looks like a child's room and I'm fifteen! I'm no longer a child. But Mother says it may be a while before I can redecorate. We need to save our money and spend it wisely as things are so chaotic in the country still. So, once again, I can blame the war for ruining my life!"

Callie just laughed and said, "Oh, Victoria, your life isn't ruined. It's just beginning."

* * *

Victoria was right about the country still being chaotic. The Radical Republicans in Congress wanted to punish the South for seceding and fighting the war. President Andrew Johnson wanted to follow Lincoln's more conciliatory path; however, he wanted to exclude the ex-slaves. At Johnson's urgings, every southern state except Tennessee rejected the 14th Amendment to the Constitution, which guaranteed basic civil rights to all citizens, including the ex-slaves. As a result, a huge rift developed between Congress and the President.

Congress passed the Reconstruction Act of 1867 that swept away all the regimes President Johnson had set up, put the former Confederate states back under military control, and called for the ratification of new state constitutional conventions. It required these new state constitutions to include Negro suffrage and disqualified former Confederate leaders from holding office. Under this new law, Georgia became part of the Third Military District along with Alabama and Florida. This further infuriated southerners.

John and Nathan were discussing this very issue when Caroline and Kathleen joined them in the drawing room after a delicious meal. Both men rose to their feet as the women entered the room. Caroline was carrying a tray with coffee and condiments.

"Would you men like to join us in some coffee? It's the real thing. I finally found some in the market. It's taken two years for coffee to return to Savannah. And, I have some white sugar and real cream. Such luxuries!" Caroline sighed and then laughed.

"I'd like some, dear wife," grinned John. "We can't let good coffee go to waste, now can we? Nathan, help yourself."

All four adults sat quietly enjoying the taste of real coffee again after many years of substituting other ingredients for it.

"I was just about to approach Nathan with our investment opportunity, Caroline. Now Kathleen can listen too."

"What's that, John? A scheme of yours?"

"No, no. This is a solid investment. As you may already know, a charter was granted last year to the Savannah, Skidaway, and Seaboard Railroad to build rails connecting Thunderbolt, Isle of Hope, and Skidaway Island."

"Yes, I'd heard of that. That's an excellent idea. May even attract more people from the North to come here and spend money as tourists."

"Yes, well, I've been offered a share in another newly organized rail company, Central of Georgia, to rebuild the rails from here to Atlanta. If that goes well, it will branch out to other states. I've checked it out thoroughly. All involved are very reputable men who want to see our state grow again and prosper. Railroads will be front and center if we are to do just that. It was very evident during the war that we were handicapped by the North having so many more lines than we had. I thought you might want to join in this adventure. I know it will be very profitable for both of us."

Nathan sat back in his chair and looked at Kathleen. "That sounds very tempting, John. I know the rails are going to be important to the South regaining commerce again. How much money are we talking about?"

"Several hundred. If you don't want a full share, we can split it. I'm going to buy several. I think it's a really good deal and I want to get in on it at the ground level."

Again Nathan looked at Kathleen. "I can't give you my answer right now, John. I'll have to think about it and talk it over with the rest of the family. But it does sound like a sound investment. Thank you so much for thinking of us. I'll let you know after we get back to Oak Hill and I can talk to Mother and Samuel, but right now I can tell you, I'm very interested." Kathleen nodded her head in agreement.

"On a different subject," John continued "what are you going to do about working your land? Are you going to hire the darkies, sell off parcels, or just let it lay fallow? I've been puzzling over what to do at Magnolia Grove."

"I don't know. I haven't come up with a solution yet. I know I have to plant much more cotton - the market is growing and the price will be higher - but I need laborers. The family and what slaves have come back just can't do the physical work. Do you have any suggestions?"

"You're right about the price of cotton. At the Cotton Exchange we are already seeing it sky rocket. The northern mills are hungry for southern cotton again, as is Europe. I've heard some of the planters talk about share cropping."

"What's that, John?" Kathleen asked interestedly.

"We planters let some of our ex-slaves 'rent' a section of our land. They work the ground and plant the crops. In exchange, we receive some portion of that crop, a half or a third, at the end of the year. They get the rest. They live on their plot and grow cash crops, mainly cotton. People that I've talked to who are doing it say it works out just fine."

"Hmmmm……that does sound like a plausible solution to our problem. John, you've given us a lot to think about." Nathan stretched and yawned. "Think it's time to get some sleep now. Kathleen, you have a busy day tomorrow, don't you? "

"Yes, I'm going over to see Mother and Father in the morning. Then I'd like to take Callie shopping in the afternoon. She needs some new shoes and various other things."

Nathan turned back to John. "If you don't mind, John, I'd like to meet with some of the other railroad investors while we're here. Do you think you could arrange a meeting?"

"I'll work on it first thing tomorrow, Nathan. This could be the beginning of a wonderful future."

* * *

After being in Savannah for little over a week, Callie sat at a desk in the Whitson's library writing:

Dear Ben,

I have so much to tell you that I don't know how to start. Please bear with me if I start to ramble. First of all, we are in Savannah staying at Uncle John and Aunt Caroline's house. I am having so much fun. I almost had forgotten what fun is.

Anyway our trip here was not uneventful. Two men accosted us on the road at night wearing hoods and carrying guns. I think they wanted to harm Judah, our darkie, who was helping Papa drive the wagon. Papa said they probably wanted to rob us too, but he and Judah stopped them with their rifles. Mama Kathleen and I were in the back of the wagon lying down and were really frightened, as you can imagine. But all ended well.

We have been doing so many things during the day. Mama Kathleen and I went shopping at the City Market - do you remember it? It was very bustling and crowded. But a very sad and frightening incident happened while we were there. First, I must say I was surprised to see so many Yankee soldiers still here. That and so many darkies wandering about begging. But back to what we witnessed.

An older white woman was trying to cross one of the crowded streets while carrying her purchases. No one seemed to be paying much attention to her and wouldn't get out of her way. Then a well dressed darkie came to her rescue and took her arm and picked up her packages and helped her across. Almost instantly there were three white men, slovenly dressed, around the darkie. They shouted at him asking him how he dare touch a white woman. No amount of explanation by him or by the woman calmed the men down. Then suddenly one of them pulled out a pistol and shot the darkie in the head! It was awful. People were screaming and running. Mama Kathleen and I were standing quite a distance from the fracas, but everyone seemed to run in our direction. Evidently, the murders ran the other way and weren't caught. The poor darkie lay dead in the street until finally some Yankees came and carried him away.

When we told Uncle John about this, he said, unfortunately, it was becoming common place. Whites, especially poor whites, were blaming the darkies on everything bad that happened because of the war. Like the men that stopped us on the road, many are joining the group called the Ku Klux Klan, whose mission is to rid the area of the darkies. They also are terrorizing Yankees who have come south to make money. They call them "carpetbaggers."

I don't know how people can be so mean. I would certainly hate to see Trudy or Mammy Sallie hurt just because they were darkies. It's a good thing they both decided not to come. They were right. It's awful. Ben, you can be glad you are back safe at your house far away from all this madness.

Mama Kathleen and I had made most of our purchases before the incident so we immediately left to go back to Uncle John and Aunt Caroline's. I must say, though, that until that happened we were having a wonderful time. We bought shoes for both of us - work ones. And calicos to make some much needed work dresses for all the women at Oak Hill. Papa told us he thought the cotton crop this year would be good, but to still pinch our pennies! We did. It was fun bargaining with all the merchants to get the best deals.

I need to close as I am supposed to take a nap before the Gardenia Ball tonight. That's right - I'm going to my first ball!! It's at the

Marshall House. Do you remember it? It was the hotel that was used as a hospital for you Yankees after you arrived here. Victoria and her friends are going too. I am SO excited. I have a beautiful dress - not a new one, it belonged to my Mama Hannah - but new to me. Dinah reworked it to fit me. I think it's beautiful. I know you probably think I'm being silly, but it will be so fun to finally be grown up enough to attend a ball. I'll write you later to let you know how the night went.

I hope all is fine in Illinois and I look forward to hearing from you again. I enjoy reading your letters so much.

Your friend,
Callie

"Callie! Callie! Where are you?" Victoria was shouting up and down the great hallway.

"I'm in the library, Victoria."

"What are you doing in here? We have to rest now before we get ready for tonight."

"Yes, I know. I'm finishing a letter to Ben, the Yankee who saved my life. We have been writing back and forth for a while now."

"Really? How intriguing! What do you write about?"

"Oh, different things. What we do during the day. About our families. I was telling him about my trip here."

"Hmmmm. How old is this Ben?"

"He's eight years older than me, so I guess around twenty-two."

"Ahh, an older man!"

"Not that much so. Anyway, what are you getting at?"

"I think Ben might be your beau!"

Callie burst out laughing. "My beau? How could he be my beau when he lives thousands of miles away? Really, Victoria. He's just a friend that I write to, like I do you sometimes. It's really interesting to hear about his life, though. Sometimes it is so different from mine and then again sometimes it is so much the same. Anyway, I owe him a lot for killing that evil James Williams."

Victoria shrugged. "If you say so….. Well, we'd better get upstairs and rest or Mother won't let us go tonight."

"I'm too excited to rest, Victoria, aren't you?"

"Yes, but we must at least lie down."

"All right then, let's go. I just can't wait to get all dressed up. Just think, Victoria, we're going to a ball!"

The two girls laughed and joined arms as they went up the stairs to Victoria's room where they laid down on the soft feather mattress and closed their eyes trying to sleep.

* * *

Of course, half the fun of going *to* the ball was getting ready *for* the ball. Callie and Victoria had Dora fix their hair up in an intrical style, and then donned their corsets, chemises, drawers, hoops, petticoats, and finally, gowns. The finishing touches were their jewels. The emerald pendant and pearl earrings for Callie and an ivory cameo on a pink ribbon and earrings to match for Victoria.

Callie had on her pale green gown and Victoria was dressed in a pale pink silk with a tulle skirt. They stood together in front of Victoria's floor length mirror.

"Victoria, we look like the rosebuds on your wall!" Callie smiled into the mirror.

"We do, don't we - me the pink and you the green!"

"I think we look very nice as rosebuds," Callie laughed. "Even if I am in a reworked gown and borrowed jewels."

"Well, my gown is an old one of Susan's that was reworked too. And, I borrowed Mother's cameos."

"By the way, are Susan and Joshua attending the ball tonight?"

Victoria looked at Callie with a shocked look on her face. "Of course not, silly! Susan is as big as a cow. Expecting women don't go out in public! Mother says she thinks Susan will have twins this time - she is so huge. It certainly has helped Joshua with the baby, or babies, coming. It's given him something to look forward to."

"I…hope…..she has healthy babies."

"Oh, I forgot about your little brother. I'm sorry, Callie."

"That's all right. Kathleen is the one who mourns the most. But this trip to Savannah has done wonders for her. It's so nice to see her cheeks rosy and her eyes sparkle again."

"Which reminds me, we'd better get going or they might all leave without us!"

Callie and Victoria floated down the grand staircase and were greeted by their parents below.

"My goodness. Look at our little flowers, all grown up. Here's your finishing touch." Caroline put a freshly picked gardenia in each of their hair, behind their ear.

"Oh, Aunt Caroline, you are too nice!"

Nathan and John looked at their daughters, seemingly all grown up, going to their first ball. They seemed dumbstruck.

"Ladies, I think your fathers know what beautiful young woman you are. Look at them, they're both speechless." Kathleen and Caroline smiled at their spouses. Both John and Nathan blushed.

Finally, John cleared his throat. "Well, it is amazing what a transformation you girls can make. I don't know what happened to little Victoria and Callie. Who are these beautiful ladies in front of me?"

It was Callie and Victoria's turn to blush. Then they each went to their father and gave him a hug. Caroline and Kathleen looked at one another and winked. They understood the bond between father and daughter quite well.

"Let's get going. I can't wait any longer to see what a ball is like," said Callie putting her arm through Nathan and Kathleen's. "My carriage awaits!"

Laughing, they all went out the door onto the veranda in the sweet night air perfumed with roses and gardenias. They were going in two carriages. There wasn't enough room in one to accommodate four ladies' hoop skirts.

The Hills and the Whitsons got out of their carriages at 123 East Broughton Street in front of the magnificent Marshall House with its twelve foot high rod iron fence. They walked through the gates anxious to see how the House had been transformed for the ball.

The Marshall House was the first hotel in Savannah, much needed as the city grew. In fact, the Hills had already stayed there during

Andrew Whitson's funeral. However, after the fall of Savannah to the Union army, the House had been used as a hospital for Yankee soldiers. The last soldiers to leave was just two years ago. Efforts had been underway to return the House back to its former glory.

The families walked through the front door and stood in line to be admitted and announced. Callie and Victoria were getting more and more nervous as they approached their turns.

Finally the gentleman said, "John Whitson with his wife, Caroline, and daughter, Victoria from Savannah. Visting the Whitson family, Nathan Hill with his wife, Kathleen, and daughter, Callista from Oak Hill."

They all nodded their heads as people in the room looked their direction. Then they stepped into the ballroom itself. Callie could only gaze and stare. The large room was lined with sconces filled with candles which gave off a radiant glow of light. There were gardenias everywhere - on the tables, the railings, the doorways, the orchestra box. They perfumed the air with their spicy, sweet fragrance.

The floor had been sanded and polished to a high gloss, but if one looked carefully, the dents and scratches from many Union boots could be seen. The walls had been freshly painted a soft green, the color of Callie's gown. There was a table on one wall with leaded crystal punch bowls filled with a delicious looking drink. Dainty little cookies were piled high on polished silver trays lined up one after the other, invitingly.

"Callie, close your mouth," whispered Victoria in Callie's ear. "People are staring."

Callie automatically closed her mouth, not realizing it was open. "I'm sorry, Victoria, but I've never seen anything like this before. It's beautiful!"

"It is, isn't it? Who would have imagined this was a hospital not too long ago. Oh, look, there's Fanny Smythe. You remember her, don't you? And there's Martha Norris, Joshua's sister, with her fiancé. Come on, let's go visit. We need to fill our dance cards too."

Callie looked at Nathan and Kathleen, who nudged her along. "Go, have fun, Callie. We'll be fine. Enjoy yourself!"

Victoria pulled Callie's hand and off she went into a maze of color and flowers. She remembered back to when she was in Savannah for all the festivities of Susan and Joshua's wedding. She had especially enjoyed the party at the Norris's when all the women's gowns were twirling in a swirl of colors. Now she would be part of that picture instead of watching from the sideline.

The group of girls they joined quickly enlarged with young men. The chatty girls suddenly became demure, coquettish, young ladies. The boys were signing dance cards for the rest of the evening.

Most of these young men missed out on the fighting, but many had lost brothers and fathers to the war. There were several single men who had been in the conflict and they proudly wore their Confederate uniforms tonight, complete with new bright sashes. There were others who had engaged in the battles, and now were suffering from their wounds. Many had missing limbs or still suffered from internal injuries.

Nathan looked at all the young people. Kathleen saw him focus on the men in uniform.

"What happened to your uniform, darling?"

"Mine simply wore out. These men never saw battle or theirs would be gone too. They probably worked for officers behind the scenes and never stepped foot on the fields."

"Well, dear, it takes many people to run a war. It doesn't make them less patriotic." Kathleen had detected a disgusted tone to Nathan's voice. She changed the subject. "Look at Callie. She's having the time of her life! I wonder who that good looking man she's dancing with is.

"I don't know, but I'm going to find out. He'd better behave himself."

"Nathan, quit frowning. She's having fun. She has to grow up sometime, you know. You can't keep her isolated at Oak Hill all her life."

"I know. I just can't believe my baby girl is growing up and the way that boy is looking at her bothers me."

"Isn't that the way you look at me?"

"Yes, and that's why it bothers me!"

Kathleen burst into giggles. "Come on, papa bear, let's go mingle ourselves. Callie is just fine. She has a good head on her shoulders."

"She's only fourteen!"

Kathleen laughed again. "Nathan Hill! You're sounding like an old man! Let's go get some punch and then dance ourselves."

Nathan looked at his wife. He hadn't seen her this happy in a long long time. He didn't even get the punch. He took her in his arms and led her in a waltz.

* * *

The young man Callie was dancing with was Daniel Moore. He had shyly approached her in the group of girls and asked if he may be on her dance card. Of course, she said yes. She didn't realize until later that he had filled all her slots.

She was very quiet when they started dancing. She was concentrating on the steps, just like Beulah and Kathleen had taught her. Daniel was a very good dancer and led her easily. The music ended, he bowed, and she curtsied.

"Would you like some punch, Miss Hill? I hear it's quite delicious."

"Yes, please, Mr. Moore. I think I'll go stand by the window over there and get some air."

It wasn't long before Daniel came back with two cups of punch. Callie sipped hers slowly, although she wanted to guzzle it down, she was so thirsty. Daniel also sipped at his. They stood there for a while before he spoke.

"Miss Hill, I have been quite struck with your beauty since the first time I saw you."

Callie was taken aback, but remembered her manners. "Thank you, when was that? I don't recall meeting you until tonight."

"It was at Susan and Joshua Norris's wedding. I was only nine years old at the time, but when I saw you coming down that aisle tossing rose petals, I thought you were so beautiful."

"My goodness, I wasn't quite seven years old then! Were you at the reception later?"

"Yes. Apparently, I didn't make much of an impression on you. We played together with the other children there."

"Hmmmm. No, I don't recall."

"Then I saw you two years later at Andrew's funeral."

"That was a very sad time for my family."

"Yes, ours too. My brother was also killed at Fort Pulaski. His funeral was two days after Andrew's."

"I'm so sorry. My brother, Sam, and my father both survived the war. Sam was in a prison camp in Illinois. Our plantation, except our house, was burned by Sherman's men."

"You must have been very scared."

"Yes, it was a harrowing experience, one I never want to go through again."

Daniel saw that the conversation was taking a gloomy turn. "Well, Miss Hill, let's toast to better times for the South. May she rise again!"

"Please call me Callie, Mr. Moore."

"Only if you call me Daniel...........Callie."

"Agreed."

"Shall we return to the dance floor, Callie? This is a lovely waltz they're playing."

"Yes, let's, Daniel."

* * *

The rest of the evening was a blur to Callie. She danced and danced until her feet hurt, and then she danced some more. She and Daniel mingled with the other young people there, but Daniel was her only dance partner for the evening. Before she knew it, the ball was over and she was back in the carriage with Nathan and Kathleen.

She sank into the seat and sighed heavily. "I've never had such a wonderful time in my life, but my feet hurt soooo bad and I'm sooooo tired!"

Nathan smiled at his daughter. "Sweetie, I'm glad you had such a good time at your first ball. That young gentleman seemed to monopolize all your dances. I was lucky to dance once with my baby girl."

"Papa! I introduced you to Daniel. He seems to be very nice."

"Yes, he does. He asked me if he could see you again while we are at John and Caroline's. I think you are too young, but Kathleen said it should be your decision."

Callie looked at her father with surprise. "He asked to see me again? He asked to see me? He really asked to see me? Doesn't that mean he must like me?"

Kathleen reached over and squeezed Callie's hand. "Of course that means he likes you, Callie. I don't know why you are so surprised. You are a beautiful, intelligent, well-mannered young southern lady. If he hadn't filled out your entire dance card, every young man at the ball would have danced with you. Didn't you see all of them watching you?"

Callie just looked at her. "They were watching me?"

Nathan took her other hand. "Callie, dear, I hate to admit it, but you were the 'belle of the ball.'"

Callie smiled and laid her head on her father's shoulder. "Well, I don't know what to say. Oh … Papa…. yes, I do want to see Daniel Moore again while we are here. I liked him too."

* * *

While Callie and family were in Savannah, Samuel was indulging in some much needed soul searching at Oak Hill. He was finding himself alone in his thoughts without interruptions. Mammy and Beulah stayed in the house, William and Malindy and the other former slaves did their work, but left him alone. He tended to all his chores and then found time to spend by himself. He started taking long rides in the late afternoons on Daisy, Callie's horse. He could lose himself in the splendor of the nature around him.

Trotting down the oak-lined lane towards the road invigorated him more than anything else had done for a long time. He seemed to gather strength from the strong tall oaks. Out on the road, he passed many creatures, birds, mice, insects, and living things. Everything seemed to be teeming with life, new life. A life Samuel wanted to be a part of again, but wasn't sure how. During the time he spent at Camp Douglas, something had died in him, and he was having a hard time finding it again, but riding Daisy on a beautiful early summer day seemed to clear his head.

Mammy Sallie and Beulah began to see subtle changes in Samuel.

For one, he looked much healthier. His skin lost its pallor, the dark circles under his eyes were less noticeable, and he had gained weight. He was less moody and sullen. They thought maybe Samuel was finally healing.

Samuel himself noticed the changes, but something was holding him back emotionally. He still felt he had compromised his honor by surrendering to the enemy at Kennesaw.

After riding one day, he returned to see Mammy Sallie sitting on the front steps fanning her. Mammy Sallie was getting older, but she still seemed the same Mammy to Samuel. She was the one constant in his life that never seemed to change.

He rode Daisy up to the veranda. "Mammy, I'm going to rub Daisy down and put her in the corral, and then I'll come back and join you."

"I's be here, Masta Samuel, I's be here. Takin' a lil res'."

Samuel rode Daisy down to the new stables, took off the saddle, rubbed her down, brushed her, and gave her some oats and water. All the while thinking, "I always had some stable hand do this for me before........well, those days are over."

He walked back up to the house and sat down next to Mammy. They sat there for several minutes, neither one speaking. Mammy finally broke the silence.

"Masta Samuel, I's knows you since Miz Hannah birth'd you an' I knows when sumpin' is wrong wit you. I's been waitin' for you to works it all out in your head. I's thinks maybe you has since your papa been gone to Savannah. You seems diff'ent, more at res'. Does ole Mammy has it right?"

Samuel looked at that kind, wrinkled, brown face that had been such a pillar in his life. Always loving him, always caring for him, always worrying about him, always there. Those dark brown eyes started filling with tears as Samuel stared into them.

"Mammy........" It was all he could get out before he dissolved into tears of his own and laid his head on Mammy's breast. She instantly cradled him in her arms and rocked him as she had done so many times when he was a child. Samuel sobbed, heaving sobs.

"There, there, it all rights, Masta Samuel. You's jes' let it alls out.

Let your Mammy help you." She started humming a lullaby she used to sing to him and Callie when they went to bed. It calmed him and he stopped sobbing. He looked at Mammy with embarrassment.

"I'm..I'm.. sorry, Mammy. I don't know what came over me. I'm so sorry." He sat up straight and wiped his face with his handkerchief. He was too ashamed to look at her.

Mammy grabbed his chin and forced him to face her. "Now, you lissens to me, Masta Samuel. You's got nuttin' to be 'shames 'bout. I's your *Mammy*! I's loves you like my own. You an'me gots a 'pecial bond. Now, you jes' tells Mammy what's been botherin' you since you comes back from the war."

Samuel looked at her and started talking. He told her about the battles, about the prison camp, how disgraced he felt, how he had let the family down, the country down, Georgia down. He told her about the men he knew who had died honorably, who had wounds and lived honorably. He had neither. He told her how he felt belittled doing the work the slaves used to do, how he missed his old life. He told her how inadequate he felt for not being able to save Callie from James Williams. If he hadn't surrendered, maybe he could have fought harder for Oak Hill, even been there to drive the Yankees away.

Mammy listened without speaking. She let Samuel talk until no more words came out of his mouth. Then she grabbed both of his hands in hers and held them tight.

"Now, you looks at me, Samuel Hill. You done all you coulds do in that awful war. It neber was to be." Samuel turned his head away. "Looks at me, Samuel. I's been a slave all my life, now I's free. I's free, but I's still here. I's here 'cause I's wants to be. You's still here 'cause God wants you to be. He an' Miz Hannah puts you in that prison to keeps you alive so you can comes back here. They's gots plans for you."

"You gits all that nonsense outta your head 'bout honor. Honor don't makes a man. *You* makes yourse'f a man, Masta Samuel. You's already a good man. Your family an' Mammy sees that. You's jes' has to believe it yourse'f. An' you will, you will. You's figure outs what you goin' do. You smart, Masta Samuel. Use your head for figurin' outs good things, not 'bout things you cain't change no more."

"Now, 'bout doin' all this work 'round here that us darkies did. Cain't help you wit that. Jes' knows don' hurt you none to git your hands dirty! Work makes you stronger, not weak. Maybe now you 'preciate all us darkies more, 'pecially your Mammy!" Mammy Sallie cackled and grabbed Samuel's head. She planted a big kiss on his forehead. Samuel rewarded her with a brilliant smile.

"I's shore do loves you, Masta Samuel. An' I's thinks maybe my ole Masta Samuel cames back today."

"I love you too, Mammy Sallie. Yes, I think I almost might be myself again. Thank you so much for listening to me and talking to me. I feel so much better now. I think I can tackle my problems better now."

"That's what Mammy's are for, son. That's what Mammy's are for." She put her arms around Samuel's shoulders and squeezed him hard.

* * *

Callie, Nathan, and Kathleen said their good-byes to the Whitsons and traveled back to Oak Hill. This time their journey was not interrupted, although all were uneasy about possible encounters. Callie lay on the bed in the wagon playing back the trip in her head, looking at the bright stars shining above her. She sighed contentedly. She had the most wonderful time of her entire life.

Daniel had come to visit her several times after the ball. Each time, Nathan made sure there was someone near-by to chaperone. However, Daniel was the perfect gentleman. He made Callie feel so special. When they parted, they promised to write to one another, and Daniel said he would try to make a trip to Oak Hill in the fall to see her, if Nathan approved.

Callie couldn't wait to tell Trudy about her visit to Savannah, especially about the ball. When Oak Hill's lane came into sight, she sat up practically bouncing with excitement.

"Mama Kathleen, I don't think I can wait another second to tell Trudy about Daniel! And, the ball, and all of Victoria's friends! I had such a wonderful time in Savannah. I'm so glad I got to go with you and Papa."

"I am too, Callie. We all had a good time. It was just what I needed - a little journey away from everything. Now we can get back to work with more of a purpose."

As the wagon approached the front veranda, Samuel was coming from the stables. He saw them, ran to the front door, and shouted that they were back. Soon Beulah, Mammy Sallie, and Trudy appeared on the porch. Everyone was greeted all around.

Callie couldn't stop talking until she had told Trudy everything she had done. She saved the part about Daniel calling on her until the end. Then Trudy's eyes grew quite large.

"You's means you's gots a beau now, Miz Callie?"

Callie demurely lowered her eyes. "Well, I don't know if he's a *real* beau. Papa said I'm too young to have a beau. But we did become *very* good friends and he wants to visit me here at Oak Hill. Isn't that exciting, Trudy!"

"Guess so." Trudy lowered her eyes and looked at her feet.

Callie grabbed Trudy's hand and squeezed it. "Daniel has nothing to do with our friendship, Trudy. You know you will always be important to me. Now, get that frown off your face and help me unpack. You should have seen how I looked at the ball…….."

The two girls walked hand in hand into the house, Callie chattering all the way. The adults stood looking at them, smiling, remembering when they, too, were young and going to balls.

Nathan turned to Samuel. "Looks like everything is just fine here, son. You did a good job while we were gone. We have a lot to talk about at dinner tonight, something your Uncle John proposed to me."

Samuel grinned at his father. "Yes, Father, we have a lot to discuss. I made a lot of discoveries about myself while you were gone."

"From the looks of you, they were all good ones. Welcome back to the world, Samuel. Welcome back." Nathan grabbed his son by the shoulders and hugged him hard. When he broke away, Samuel saw tears in the corners of his father's eyes.

"It's good to be back, Father."

* * *

At dinner that evening after everyone had rested and was refreshed, Nathan brought up the issue of the investment in the railroad.

"This concerns everyone in this family, so I thought it should be a family decision," he began. "John thinks it is a good investment - not too risky. I tend to agree. The South is going to *have* to rebuild existing rails and build new rails to compete with the North, if we are to have any kind of commerce at all. One of the reasons the North was successful in the war was their abundance of railways. They could ship supplies and troops faster than we could. Lincoln also started a transcontinental railroad that will join the two coasts. Rail travel is definitely the wave of the future and I think we should jump aboard. But I wanted everyone's approval before I inform John. After all, you have all worked very hard here at Oak Hill to save the money we have, and I don't want to just throw it away."

Beulah was the first to speak. "Nathan, are we talking about a large sum of money? Will we have enough left to cover our expenses here?"

"John, said it can be several hundred, several thousand, however much we want to spend. He also said we can split shares with him to start with if we are leary. I'm inclined to start with a few hundred and then, if all go well, invest more. I'm sure we can afford to spend that, Mother. Oak Hill is doing better every year and once again becoming self-sufficient. Oh, while I'm thinking of it, John also told us about a new system of farming the land. It's called share croppping. We let our former servants live on the acreage and farm it. We purchase the seeds and materials for them. Then when the harvest is in, they give us back our share and keep theirs. It will put the land back in use and we will still receive moneys for it."

"Wait, Nathan, I can only think of one thing at a time." Beulah held up her hand for Nathan to stop. "Let's decide the railroad investment first. I say, let's do it. Your father and I wouldn't have Oak Hill if we hadn't taken a risk along the way. I think it would be a sound, logical investment. Count me in."

"Thank you, Mother. Samuel, what do you think? You've been pretty quiet."

"Just thinking things over, Father. I agree with Grandma. If Uncle

John thinks it's a good way to make more money, then it must be. I trust his judgment, and yours. You kept telling me the North would win the war because they had more railways and industry than we did and you were right. The South needs to enter this new age and we should be a part of it. Count my vote as a yes."

"Good." Nathan turned to Callie. "Baby girl, how about you? What do you think?"

Callie looked surprised. "I..I..I.... don't know. I guess it's a good thing. Why are you asking me, Papa?"

Nathan's eyes sparkled and his grin filled his entire face. "Well, if my baby girl is old enough to be called on by a young gentleman, then I guess she's old enough to participate in family decisions."

Callie's face turned bright pink and she looked down at her hands folded in her lap. "Papa, you're making fun of me!" Then she raised her face up and looked right into her father's eyes, her own now dancing with mirth. "I guess I *am* old enough now to make family decisions and my answer is yes, let's do it. If we make more money, I can have more ball gowns and go to Savannah and dance!"

Everyone at the table erupted in laughter, including Callie. "I think that's enough decision making tonight," Nathan laughed. "We can talk about the share cropping at another time. Oh, it's good to be back home, isn't it Kathleen? We can sleep in our own bed tonight!" He reached over and patted his wife's hand.

Kathleen returned his smile and stood up to help clear the table. It was *very* good to be back home.

CHAPTER 3
1868

Raymond Carswell meandered on his rented roan horse along the road northwest of Savannah. "Sherman did a fine job on these folks," he thought as he rode along. All he saw were burned out buildings and brick chimneys standing alone on the bleak landscape. Scraggly weeds and thorny vines were growing where once beautiful mansions stood. Now the land was barren and scarred, except for the occasional burst of color from an old camellia bush planted years ago when life was more carefree.

Raymond wasn't paying too much attention to the landscape, though. His thoughts were on planning a new scam to make money. His brain was clicking like a clock, discarding one elicit scheme after another. There had to be something this carpetbagger could do to make some easy money.

Raymond Carswell never had an easy life. When he was a young boy, his father, Artie, had moved his young family to Cincinnati, Ohio, in hopes of finding work along the river. Instead, he found whiskey. When he drank, he became a different man - mean, surly, violent. He would beat Raymond's mousy mother for no reason at all. Then he would turn to the young boy. Raymond learned at an early age to run fast and hide from his father. Artie would be too drunk to chase after him, so Raymond would be safe until his father passed out. Then his mother would come and find him and together they would cry and plot how they could escape.

They didn't go soon enough. One night Artie came home from the tavern weaving and cursing. His mother sat in the small rocking chair darning socks by the light of the fire. Raymond was at her feet, trying to read a ragged, old book. They both knew the minute Artie walked through the door that the night would not end well for the two of them.

He started cursing, yelling for something to eat. When Raymond's mother didn't move fast enough, he hit her hard across her face with the back of his hand. She stumbled backwards toward the fire with the darning still in her clutches. Artie came after her again, this time hitting her with his fist. She fell unconscious next to the burning logs, the darning catching fire beside her. Quickly, the orange flames licked at her skirt and then engulfed her body.

Raymond and Artie stood gaping at the sight. Neither one could move to save her. Artie turned and looked at Raymond. "Now see what ya have done to your ma, you lazy, no count lad? Ya killed her, burnt her to a crisp. Why ya little no, good….." Artie lunged toward Raymond. Being younger, though, Raymond was quicker.

Thinking he could do nothing more for his mother, he thought only of surviving himself. He ran out of the cabin as fast as he could and kept running until he was out of breath. He stopped and listened. If his father had followed him, he couldn't hear him. He was sure Artie would have passed out by now. Raymond looked around, but didn't even know where he was.

He started running again. And he kept running for the rest of his life. And, now he was in Georgia. He had heard after the war ended there was money to be made in the recovering South for those smart enough and devious enough to find it. Well, he certainly was devious enough. He had survived for thirty years now on his own and it was about time for him to strike it rich. He couldn't think of anyone who deserved it better.

Raymond chuckled to himself at the thought. Of course, he deserved it. He had survived his drunk of a father; his marriage to a whiny, shrill, ugly woman - one which he was coerced into by her father at the end of a shotgun; his evasion of the draft during the war by hiding out in the hills of northern Kentucky; and escaping a tar and feathering at the last village he occupied. Yes, he was ready for a change in his life and Georgia would be it. It was ripe for the picking.

He had some cash from the last poker game he played. Good thing no one discovered he had cheated. Now he just had to figure out how to parley that cash into more, legally or illegally.

Raymond felt a cold gust of wind which broke his daydreaming. He turned up the collar of his newly purchased bright green and yellow plaid coat.

Raymond wasn't a particularly handsome man. He looked older than his thirty-five years. He had a ruddy complexion marked with pox scars. He sported a full beard and moustache to cover up those scars. His auburn hair was collar length, slicked back from his forehead with oily pomade. Under his bushy eyebrows was a pair of very small dark brown eyes. They were deep set and darted constantly.

He was of medium build and looked uncomfortable as he rode the horse with his carpetbag valise tied to the pummel of the saddle. He looked like he was up to no good and he was.

Raymond heard in Savannah how poorly the planters were faring. Their lands were lying fallow as there was no labor force to work them. Those who had stayed were trying to eke out an existence on their once bountiful lands. As he rode along, his conniving brain settled on a possible scam.

He would offer to buy some of their acreage, put down a small down payment, promise to pay the rest monthly, get the deed, and then turn around and resell it for a profit to some of the scalawags now eagerly looking for land. Of course, he wouldn't pay the planter the balance of the money owed; he would just leave the area like he had done many times before. The owner would be too embarrassed to try to find him. Anyway, by that time he would be long gone.

Wouldn't the former aristocratic southern planter be surprised to find a scalawag now owned his land, and a carpetbagger had instigated the deal? Hah! It was perfect! Even better would be to find a grieving war widow and steal the land right from under her. He was going to *love* Georgia!

* * *

Callie was sitting on her bed reading again her latest letter from Ben. Their harvest had been quite good, he was very pleased. His father took some of the money and built a new kitchen onto the back of the house for Abigail and purchased a fancy new cook stove. That was her Christmas present. The family had attended some get-togethers for the holidays with the neighbors and near-by family. They had put up a Christmas tree this year and decorated it with popped corn, dried fruit, wheat wreaths, and candles. It was his job to sit with the bucket of sand to douse the lit candles if one of the branches caught fire. Emma was very excited to be asked by a young man to go to a church Christmas party. Abigail had made her a new dress to wear. She looked very pretty in it. He thought she had a good time at the affair.

Ben had enclosed a small gift for Callie. He hoped she enjoyed it and had a good Christmas too.

Callie didn't receive the letter until after the first of the year. Now as she read it again, she reached over to touch the small brown, tortoise shell comb Ben had sent her. She thought it was beautiful. She would wear it in her hair tonight at dinner.

Then she put Ben's letter down and picked up the latest one from Daniel. He spoke of her beauty and how much he missed her. He apologized again for not being able to visit her last fall, but family issues kept him in Savannah. He would try to come this winter. His words were very flowery, not straightforward like Ben's. But he, too, had included a gift. Inside, wrapped in a fine linen white handkerchief, was a pair of earrings - tiny, fine gold chains with a small oval piece of green jade dangling at the end. They were very pretty. She would wear them tonight also.

"You readin' them letters, agin?" Trudy came into the room and flopped down on her bed on the floor. "I's tired! Helped Miz Kathleen move some of the books in the lib'ary. Then we dusts alls of them. An' you jes' been sittin' up here readin' those letters agin. Miz Callie, I swears, you silly 'bout them two beaus!"

Callie flashed a look at Trudy. "They aren't my *beaus*! We're just friends."

"Uh-huh. Pritty good frien's to send you presents, I'd say. Don' see nobody sendin' Trudy no combs or earrin's. Yep, they's beaus."

"They are *not* beaus. They both live too far away, especially Ben. And, I haven't seen Daniel since last summer. I'd hardly call him a beau. And, I haven't seen Ben since I was twelve, for heaven's sake. We just enjoy writing to each other. I didn't send either one of them a gift. I don't know why they did me. But I can hardly send them back now, can I? That would be rude. I've written to both of them thanking them and that will be that. Quit looking at me that way, Trudy. You know me better than anyone. Do I look like a person with two beaus?"

Trudy started laughing as she eyed Callie. Callie had on her work calico skirt, an ill fitting muslin blouse, and work shoes. Her hair was braided into two braids which hung on her shoulders.

"No, you don' looks like someone wit *any* beaus rights now, I's agree, but when you gits all dolled up in them fancy dresses an' has Mammy do your hair, you looks mighty fine then. *Then*, you could has some beaus."

Callie started laughing along with Trudy. "Oh, Trudy, you always make me laugh. You are my only true friend. I don't know what I would do without you. Don't you ever go and get a beau."

Trudy put her hands on her hips. "Me! You sees any fine lookin' darkie mens 'round here? I don' thinks I's ever fines me someone to jump the broom wit. Nobody 'round."

"Oh, someday, a handsome man will come here and sweep you off your feet and you'll jump the broom and have lots and lots of children."

"Miz Callie, you dreamin'. You dreamin'. I's goin' back outside an' feeds them chickens. You comin' too?"

"Of course. The rooster would miss me if I didn't come, wouldn't he?"

* * *

Since most of the houses were few and far between along the road from Savannah, Raymond Carswell decided he'd better pay more attention and find a place where he could stay for the night. He didn't relish sleeping out in the open. He heard about the men terrorizing free slaves and carpetbaggers, which really unnerved him. He carried a pistol, but was reluctant to use it - he was not adept at using firearms.

He rode for a few more hours and just about dusk saw a lane lined with live oaks that looked inviting. Even if the plantation was abandoned, he'd surely be able to find somewhere to hole up for the night.

As he continued on the lane, his spirits rose, for it looked like there was a house at the end that was intact. Also, there was livestock and plowed fields. It looked like he had picked the right place. He just hoped the people inside would be hospitable.

Raymond rode up to the front veranda and dismounted, tying his horse to the hitching post there. He looked around again and saw no one about. Maybe they had all gone inside since the sun was setting. "Well," he thought, "nothing ventured, nothing gained," and pounded on the front door. He waited. No one seemed to be coming so he pounded again, harder this time.

Finally, the door opened a fraction and a pair of dark brown eyes peered out of the opening.

"I'm sorry to bother you, Ma'am, but I seem to be caught on my journey without any shelter for the evening. Could you perhaps provide me with a roof over my head? I've money to pay for it." Raymond spoke rapidly before the door closed.

"Jes' a minute, Mista. Waits here."

The door shut and he could hear the brown-eyed person retreating to another part of the house. It wasn't long before the door opened again, wider this time, to show a man standing there.

"Sir, may I be of assistance?" Nathan asked.

"Thank you, yes. I'm lookin' for a place to stay the night. I'm rather cautious about sleepin' under the stars, for I've heard there are hooligans roamin' the countryside. I will gladly pay, sir."

"I can put you up in one of our old cabins, if that suits you. It's clean and somewhat comfortable. Do you have any need of some nourishment? My family is dining now and we are willing to share with you."

"That would be most appreciated, sir. I haven't eaten all day. And, yes, the cabin will be fine. Thank you for your hospitality."

"Please, come in. I'm Nathan Hill and this is our home, Oak Hill."

Nathan led Raymond into the house to the dining room. Everyone at the table turned to see who their guest was going to be. When Beulah and Kathleen saw Raymond's attire, they raised their eyebrows and gave Nathan an inquiring look. Nathan just shrugged his shoulders slightly.

"I'm so sorry; I didn't get your name."

"Raymond. Raymond Carswell. I apologize for interruptin' your meal, but, my, somethin' smells mighty fine."

Kathleen spoke. "Please, Mr. Carswell, do sit down. Mammy Sallie will bring you a plate of Belle's good food."

Raymond looked at the lovely woman who had just spoken to him. She was a real beauty, that red hair was tempting. Nathan pulled up a chair next to his and Raymond sat down. He looked around the table. An older woman, a young man, and a pretty young girl had stopped eating to stare at him as he sat down. The older woman looked very disapprovingly in his direction.

"I'm, sorry, Mr. Carswell. Let me introduce the rest of my family. My wife, Kathleen, my mother, Mrs. Hill, my son, Samuel, and my daughter, Callie."

"Pleased to meet all of you. I certainly appreciate your kindness. Not everyone would let a stranger join them for a meal."

"We understand the perils of traveling these days, Mr. Carswell. Our home is open to those desiring protection. When I was making my way back to Oak Hill after the war ended, I relied on kind strangers to feed and shelter me. I feel this is one way to repay all of them." Nathan looked Raymond straight in the eyes, conveying by his look that he expected Raymond to behave himself.

Mammy Sallie arrived with Raymond's plate of food. "My, this looks delicious." He took a big forkful of sweet potatoes. "Mmmmm. This is so tasty." And, then realizing just how hungry he was, he dove into the food with relish.

Kathleen broke the silence of everyone watching Raymond eat, "Where are you from, Mr. Carswell?"

Raymond swallowed his mouthful of roast pork and turned to Kathleen. "I'm from Ohio, Ma'am, but I've been all over. Never really settled in one place before. I'm thinkin' I kind of like the looks of Georgia. Might just decide to stay in the state for a while. I'm headed to Atlanta - heard there's lots of opportunities there."

"What do you do, sir?" Beulah had a tone to her voice that Raymond didn't like.

"A little of this and a little of that, Ma'am. I can do just about anything, but right now; I'm interested in acquirin' some land. 'Bout time I put some roots down. Think I'd like to buy my own little piece of Georgia. Do you know if anybody is sellin' around here?"

"We know of no one in this area," Samuel answered Raymond. "Perhaps you will have some luck in Atlanta."

"Seems I've passed lots of empty lands around here. Surely, some of the owners would be willin' to sell some acres. Better than lettin' the land ly fallow. Heard it's hard to farm now with no slave labor. Think somebody would like to make some money instead of just havin' weeds take over."

By this time, Raymond had finished his meal and leaned back in his chair. He toyed with the water glass in front of him. It was then that he really noticed Callie. He couldn't believe he hadn't looked at her until now. What a beauty! She must be around sixteen or seventeen, maybe a little younger. That hair and those eyes. Raymond caught himself staring. That wouldn't do. Her father would kick him out the door so fast…….. But she was a real looker. He forced himself to look at Samuel, who had been answering him.

Raymond looked at him blankly. "I'm sorry, sir. I didn't hear what you just said. Ears must be full of dust."

"I said, most people around here aren't willing to sell their land because it is their heritage. Even if it's not being used now, it will be in the future. Other labor will be found and the South will once again be the place where cotton is king."

"If you say so, sir. Just an observation of mine." Raymond realized he was upsetting his hosts. It was too soon for him to be trying out his scheme. He could wait. "I must say, this was a wonderful meal and I enjoyed the conversation, but Mr. Hill, if you would kindly show me my cabin, I think I will turn in for the night. I have been riding all day and I'm plumb wore out. Oh, do you have a place for my mount?"

"Your horse has already been taken care of. William fed and watered him and he is in our stable."

"Well, thank you again, sir."

Nathan got up from the table as did Raymond. He bowed to the women and then followed Nathan out the door to the former slave cabin.

"I'm sure you will be comfortable here tonight. I'll see you in the morning." Nathan turned to leave.

"Wait, Mr. Hill. Here's the money I said I'd pay you for the cabin. And, I'll probably get up early and leave to make Atlanta before nightfall."

"I don't want your money, Mr. Carswell. As I said, I like to think I'm repaying all those who took me in. Did you serve in the war, Mr. Carswell?"

"No, I didn't, sir."

"Ah, I thought not, otherwise you would understand. William will have your horse ready in the morning too. Good night, Mr. Carswell. Nice meeting you." Nathan left to go back to the main house.

Raymond called after him, "Good-night, Mr. Hill. Thank you again."

Nathan raised his hand and vanished into the dark.

"Well, well, Raymond, you sure found a good place here. Guess won't have to go to Atlanta after all. Looks like Mr. Hill and his family have some money left over after the war. Gotta be someplace. Lots of land here too. They aren't sufferin' like the other places around here. Hmmm....wonder what their story is. Mighty fine looking wife too and that girl............"

* * *

Nathan went back into the house and straight to the dining room where his family was still sitting at the table. They turned and looked at him with questions on their faces.

"What on earth possessed you to allow that man into our home, son?" Beulah demanded. "He looked like some vile creature that crawled out from a swamp. Ooooo...he made my skin crawl."

"Mine, too, Beulah, but I understand why Nathan chose to be hospitable. Let's just hope tomorrow he's on his way to Atlanta, never to be seen by us again." Kathleen pushed back her chair to rise.

"Well, I didn't like the way he looked at me," Callie ventured. "I felt like I didn't have any clothes on."

At her comment, Nathan's face clouded. "I *shouldn't* have let him in. I'm sorry, baby girl. I'll make sure you never see Raymond Carswell again. Put him out of your mind. My fault, I was trying to be charitable. I will have to be more careful in the future." Nathan looked at Kathleen. "I'll stay up tonight to make sure Mr. Carswell remains in the cabin *all* night."

"I'll help you, Father, we can take shifts."

"Thank you, Samuel. That will be fine. Callie, when you and Trudy go to bed, make sure you lock your door. Don't be afraid. Just being cautious. Kathleen and Mother, lock yours also. Samuel and I will stay downstairs and keep watch. Again, I'm sorry I brought this situation into our home."

Kathleen walked over to Nathan and stroked his arm. "It's all right, dear. We'll survive." She looked at Callie. "Come on, Callie. Let's clean up this table and then go into the back parlor and sew."

* * *

Raymond stretched out on the cot in the slave cabin, his mind spinning. He would have to be very careful around the Hills. They were of the old South, thinking they were still high and mighty. He would leave tomorrow on the pretext of going to Atlanta, but he wouldn't go far. Then he would return and see if he could get something out of this family. If nothing else, he might have some fun with that fine looking girl.

He rose early in the morning to find his horse saddled up and ready to go. He was surprised to see Nathan Hill sitting out on the veranda. It was a chilly day, with gray skies blocking out the rising sun.

"Well, good morning, Mr. Hill. I'm surprised to see you."

"I thought you might like to take some of Belle's biscuits with you for breakfast." Nathan walked down the steps with the biscuits wrapped in a fresh white napkin. He extended them to Raymond.

"Thank you kindly. They will surely taste mighty fine. Give my compliments to the cook." Raymond started toward Nathan to take the biscuits. He stopped when he saw the look in Nathan's eyes. They had narrowed and looked hard and dangerous.

"I think it would be to your advantage to continue to Atlanta, Mr.

Carswell, in case you had any ideas of staying in this area. There's nothing here for you, nothing at all. So just keep going on down this road." He handed Raymond the biscuits.

Raymond took them and stared at Nathan. "Reckon nobody needs to tell me where I can and can't go, sir. I'm plannin' on Atlanta, but my plans could change. Nice to meet you and thanks again for the shelter and food."

Raymond awkwardly mounted his horse, pulled the reins to turn the horse towards the lane, and kicked it in the sides to make it trot. When the horse jerked into motion, Raymond almost fell off. It was all Nathan could do to keep from laughing. Raymond recovered and set off down the lane, bouncing on the saddle as he went.

Nathan watched until he could no longer see Carswell and then turned and went back into the house for breakfast.

* * *

Raymond slowed the horse down to a walk after exiting Oak Hill's lane. He was seething with anger. How dare that man tell him what to do! Well, he'd see about what he could do to Nathan Hill. Again, his mind started churning out plans. He was so deep in thought, he almost missed the next plantation.

This one had no house, only chimneys standing against the dull gray sky, but there seemed to be evidence of people living there. Maybe he'd just stop to say hello and check it out. He turned the horse onto the path by the former slave cabins. There was a fire going in front of one of them.

"Halloow, Halloow.....anybody here?" Raymond searched the area. An older woman opened the door of the cabin and stuck her head out. She saw Raymond and shut the door again. Soon, another young woman poked her head out, followed by another. Finally, an old man hobbled out into the open and limped over to Raymond sitting atop his horse.

"What you want, stranger?" The old gentleman looked up at Raymond with red watery eyes. The women ventured out of the cabin and were staring at Raymond now.

"Just need to water my horse and myself, if you can direct me to your well, sir. Could I stand by your fire for a few minutes as well? It's chilly out here today and my bones are cold."

"Guess so." He turned to one of the woman. "Lizzy, go fetch a pail of water for this man's horse and a dipper for him."

Raymond dismounted from the horse and went to stand over by the fire. It was then he noticed the older woman had a shotgun in her hands. Looked like these folks weren't going to be so friendly.

"Fire feels good," Raymond said looking around. "Looks like the Yankees didn't do you any favors during the war."

"No sir, they burnt our house to the ground and took darn near everything else we had with them. Never touched the Quarters, though. Guess they was teaching us a lesson. Starting all over again, just like back in the '30s. I'm too old to do that, but you do what you have to. Gotta take care of the women here. Their pa died in the battle of Kennesaw. Good man, my son." The old man's eyes teared up. He wiped them with a dirty handkerchief. "Aren't you a Yank, sir?"

Raymond was hesitant to answer with the shotgun present. "Well, I'm from the North, but southern Ohio, so I had sympathies with the South. Didn't fight in the war for either side. Hope to settle down in Georgia now. Seems my kind of place."

Lizzy arrived with the water and the dipper. "Thank you, Ma'am." Raymond sipped at the water gratefully. He looked around at the barren fields.

"What are your plans for your place, Mr.......?"

"Montgomery. Elijah Montgomery."

"Raymond Carswell, sir." Raymond held out his hand. Elijah shook it uncomfortably.

"This here is my daughter-in-law, Almina, and her daughters, Lizzy and Jenny. Can't say we have plans, except to stay alive. All our darkies left with the Yanks."

"I was just at your neighbors up the road, the Hills. They graciously gave me shelter for the night. They seem to be doin' pretty well."

"That right? We don't see much of anybody anymore. Miss Kathleen and Miss Callie rode down here a few times with some food, other than that we don't see much of them. Figured they had their own work to do. Heard the Yanks didn't burn their house, though, just the outbuldings."

"You, know, Mr. Montgomery, after ridin' through this area, I'm thinkin' I might like to stay for a while. Looks like you could use some help around here. Think we could come to some sort of agreement? I'd help you out and you'd let me stay here in one of the cabins. Give me a chance to look around for some property. Think I'd like to buy some land here and have my own place."

"Well, hmmmmm, well.... Now, sir, let me go discuss this with the women. You just stay here by the fire." Elijah walked over to where the women were standing. There was a lot of discussion. Raymond could tell the old man was in favor, the women were not. He smiled at them when they looked his direction. The older woman was definitely against it, but it seemed the old man was winning his case.

Elijah walked back over to Raymond. "Sir, we'll give it a try. If it don't work out, then you'll have to move on. And, you'll have *nothing* to do with the women folk. We'll put you in the far cabin; you'll cook your own meals and eat there. I'll get you started on what needs to be done, like clearing some of these fields again. It's hard, hard work. Sure you up to it?"

"I think I can handle it, sir. If you're satisfied with my work, maybe we could agree to a percentage of the crop?"

"I'll think about it. Lizzy and Jenny will get your cabin cleaned out and you'd better change them fancy clothes and start to work. No time like the present."

Raymond beamed. His scheme was started. "I'll be ready right fast, Mr. Montgomery. I won't disappoint you."

"Well, then, welcome to Pine Wood, or what's left of it."

* * *

Dear Ben,

I'm sorry I haven't written for a while, we have been busy plowing, planting, weeding, etc. Although spring is my favorite time of the year, it also involves the most work, as you surely know.

Papa has decided to sharecrop some of our lands. He told William, one of our former servants, to spread the word that any person who wants to farm his own land to get in touch with him. We've had a few takers. Papa gives them 40 acres to start, the seed, some equipment, and builds a cabin for them to live in. In return, they work the land and then sell the crop - they pay Papa back for the seed, etc. and a certain percentage of the profit - the rest they keep. Papa said we will try it and see how it goes. At least our lands will be worked again instead of lying empty.

I had my 15th birthday last week. I think I'm getting too old to celebrate, but my family doesn't think so. Belle made my favorite cake, and I received many lovely presents.

My friend Daniel, from Savannah, came and visited before my birthday. He only stayed for 2 nights, that's all Papa would allow. He's the first guest I've ever had.

We had an interesting visitor in mid-winter. A man, who Grandma called a carpetbagger, showed up one night. He quite unsettled me. Papa let him stay in one of the old cabins and then he left. We hope to never see him again. As Grandma said, "he made my skin crawl." He reminded me of James Williams, Ben. Hopefully, I won't need you to rescue me again!

I keep forgetting to tell you - Papa and Uncle John have invested in a new railroad and maybe, just maybe, we will be able to take a trip north to check out other railroads. If, and it's a big if, we do, we might come to Illinois. I'm hoping we can make it near your home. Papa would so like to meet you and thank you in person for saving me. Wouldn't that be nice if we could meet face to face again? I think so. I'll let you know if anything happens on that front. It's still in the "maybe" stage.

I'd better close; Trudy is outside calling from below my window about something. Please write and tell me about all your spring activities.

Your friend,
Callie
May 2, 1868.

"Trudy! What do you want?" Callie leaned out the window of her room where she had been writing to Ben. "What's wrong?"

Trudy looked up at Callie's head hanging from the window sill, her blonde braids blowing in the breeze. "Nuttin', jes' seein' if you was up there. It too nice a day to stays inside. Come on out. We's can takes Socks for a walk."

Callie turned her head. She saw Socks laying several feet away. When Trudy mentioned his name and "walk," his tail started wagging vigorously. Callie smiled.

"I'll be right down. I just have to address this letter to Ben." She folded the letter carefully, making sure first the ink had dried and then wrote Ben's address on the front of an envelope. She blew on the ink, drying it faster. She inserted the letter into the envelope, took her candle, lit it, dripped some of the wax on the back of the envelope, pressed it with a seal she had, and waited until the wax had hardened, sealing the envelope shut. She carried it downstairs to the library where she found a stamp and put it on the desk to be mailed. Then she walked to the front entry and out the door to the veranda where Trudy stood with Socks.

It was a luscious May day where everything stood out clearer than ever. The greens were greener, the pinks more pink, the reds, redder, the yellows more vibrant, the lavenders, softer, and the sky a brilliant shade of blue. White puffy clouds were scattered across the vast horizon. Callie took a deep breath. It was a wonderful day to be alive and take a walk with her friend and dog.

* * *

Callie did not know yet that, on her birthday, the governorship and the state senate, which were now controlled by the Republicans, had approved a new constitution for the state of Georgia. Also, unprecedented, thirty-two blacks were elected to the legislature.

This fact, alone, irritated the growing Ku Klux Klan, who now targeted Republican and black leaders, many falling as their victims. The Klan rode at night, covering their faces and bodies with white sheets. They would roust their victims out of their homes, torture them, and then, usually, lynch them. Many lawmen were either a part of the Klan or too afraid to arrest them, thus, fear reigned among the black population once again.

In Washington, D.C., President Andrew Johnson was having his own problems. He was involved in a lengthy political battle between himself and the "Radical Republicans." These members of Congress wanted a harsher, stricter reconstruction of the South.

Everything came to a head in February when the House of Representatives, for the first time in history, impeached President Johnson. After a three month trial in the Senate, on May 16, 1868, the president escaped removal from office by one vote.

It was no surprise when five days later in Chicago, the Republicans nominated Ulysses S. Grant as their candidate for the presidency in the upcoming election, passing over the incumbent Johnson. Speaker of the House of Representatives, Schuyler Colfax, received the vice presidential nomination.

Grant was an extremely popular person in the North, being seen as the man who won the war, but his campaign slogan would be "let us have peace." This was hard for the southerners to believe, since Grant and Colfax's views were with the Radical Republicans, who supported stricter reconstruction. They also supported black suffrage, which was contrary to what most southerners believed.

Tammany Hall in New York City hosted the Democratic convention from July 4 to July 9. After numerous ballots, Horatio Seymor, former governor of New York, was nominated as their presidential candidate. He very reluctantly accepted. Francis Blair, Jr., an ex-Union Army officer, was their choice for vice president.

The Democratic platform was for a peaceful reconstruction of the South, much like Lincoln had in mind. This was more in line with the South's version of how they wanted to once again be part of the nation.

An interesting presidential election was forecast for November, the first since the country was once again united.

* * *

Ben Chapman was sitting on the front porch enjoying the pleasant early July evening. He could smell the sweet fragrance of the lavender phlox blooming next to the porch, while he watched the first stars of the night appear in the darkening sky.

Ben was confused. In his hand he held Callie's latest letter. He had read it several times. Thoughts were swirling around in his head. Why was he so intrigued by this young girl, whom he had only seen for a few minutes nearly four years ago? Why had he continued to write to her? Why had he sent her a gift for Christmas? Well, that one he could answer. When he saw the tortoise comb in the shop in Metamora, he instantly thought of her long blonde hair and knew it would be perfect for her. He wondered what Callie looked like now that she was older. He knew Emma had really changed from twelve to sixteen - she went from a girl to a young woman. He assumed Callie had done the same. Her letters certainly didn't sound like a young girl's anymore.

And, just who was this "Daniel" she mentioned? Was he a beau? He must be if he stayed at her house. But, evidently, her father hadn't approved. Why did he feel upset about Callie mentioning another man in her life? Was he actually jealous? Why?

He knew by heart the part in the letter of the Hills possibly coming to Illinois. Why did he feel excited about that? Why was he hoping against hope they came to Clayton Township? He knew, partly. He wanted to see Callie again, to see how she had changed, to see those beautiful eyes again, that flowing blonde hair.

Here he was, twenty-three years old, dreaming of a girl eight years younger, only fifteen! One who he hadn't seen in almost four years! Yet, he felt he knew her through her letters. She seemed to be, well…. relaxed when she wrote him. So natural. Her letters sounded like she was sitting next to him talking. He could picture everything she wrote about in his head. Maybe that's why this mention of "Daniel" bothered him. He could see him courting Callie, dallying with her innocence. Maybe breaking her heart. It bothered him.

Many in the area were starting to talk about him. It was evident Josie Miller had her cap set on him. She flirted with him whenever they were in the same place. Eyebrows were raised and people gossiped. Josie didn't care, Ben knew that. He knew she wanted him, and nothing was going to stop her, except Ben himself. He didn't know why he didn't return her feelings. Josie was pretty. She was smart. She was a hard worker. She just wasn't Callie. Oh, goodness! Had he really thought that? What was *wrong* with him?

He put his head in his hands, then looked up and shook it, trying to shake the thoughts out of his mind. He looked up at the night sky now filled with twinkling bright stars. Was Callie looking at the same stars? Was she thinking of him? Or was she thinking of "Daniel?"

* * *

Callie was indeed looking up at the same night sky as Ben, but she wasn't thinking of him. She was out on the porch swing with Trudy. The day had been very hot and the heat in their room had driven them outside. They sat looking up at the dark sky filling with the faraway stars. Socks was asleep at their feet, snoring softly.

"Oh, Trudy, isn't it a beautiful night? Just look at all the stars. Do you ever wonder how they got there or what else is up there besides Heaven?" Callie had scrunched down in the swing in order to see the stars better.

"Mmmmm....sometimes. Mostly don' care. Kind o' pritty t'night, tho'. Hope it cools down some, don' wanna sleeps out here t'night."

"It seems to be getting cooler. Our room should be all right in a little while. The breeze is picking up a bit and it's coming in the direction of our windows. But let's stay a little longer. It's so nice here. Listen, you can hear the crickets chirping. Mama Kathleen says they make the sound by rubbing their legs on their bodies. Isn't that odd?"

"Mmmmm...don' like crickets. They jump an' scare Trudy. Don' like any bugs." Trudy shivered.

Callie laughed. "Silly, they can't hurt you. You're much bigger than they are."

"Why's you so happy t'night? You prac'cally bubblin' like a brook? You git anudder letter from Ben or Daniel?"

"No, I don't know why I'm feeling so good. Must be the night air, the stars, the smell of the grass, you next to me, Socks snoring.......I don't know. I just feel good! I feel like someone is thinking of me and wishing me well. Does that sound silly?"

"Guess not. Better to feel goods than bads. Maybe one of your beaus *is* thinkin' 'bout you."

"Trudy, for the upteenth time, they are NOT my beaus!! Now, don't ruin my good mood." Callie smiled at her friend and Trudy laughed.

* * *

It had been quite a while since the Hills had a surprise, but several weeks later one came up the lane. Early in the morning as Kathleen was sweeping the front veranda, she looked up to see a most unusual sight. Callie and Trudy, who were tending to the weeds in the garden, heard the noise and stopped to investigate.

"Beulah, come here!" Kathleen ran to the front door shouting at her mother-in-law. "Callie, come!" she yelled towards the garden, but Callie and Trudy were already on their way.

By the time they arrived, Kathleen was standing with her broom in her hand and her mouth wide open. There stopped by the front mounting step was a beautiful carriage. It was shiny, dark emerald green with bright gold trim around the doors, front and back, with black wheels trimmed in the same gold. On either side of the driver's seat were two shiny brass lanterns. There was a storage area on the top and in the back. Pulling it were a pair of lovely matched bay horses. Behind it, attached by a rope was another horse, this one a saddled roan.

No one was in the carriage - it was empty. The driver jumped off his seat and hitched the horses to the post near-by.

"You Mrs. Hill, Ma'am? Mrs. Nathan Hill?"

Kathleen stammered, "Yes....yes... I am." She turned to Beulah, "This is Mrs. Preston Hill."

"Pleasure to meet you both. I'm Jim Jackson. I was supposed to deliver this here carriage last week, but somethin' came up and I got delayed. Sure hope y'all enjoy it." He turned to go get the horse in the back.

"Wait, wait...." Kathleen said, "I know nothing about this. Are you saying this is *our* carriage? There must be some mistake. My husband has said nothing about a new carriage. Can you wait a few minutes until I find him? Please, come sit on the porch." She turned to Callie and Trudy. "Girls, go get Mr....umm... Jackson something to drink. I'm going to find Nathan."

"He and Samuel are down by the barn, I think, Kathleen," said Beulah. "At least that's where they said they would be."

"Right. I'll be right back. Excuse me."

Kathleen lifted her skirts and ran towards the barn. Callie and Trudy went to the kitchen and then to the well to get Mr. Jackson a cool drink of water. Beulah directed him to sit on the porch in the shade.

Kathleen reached the barn. "Nathan! Nathan! Where are you? Samuel!"

Both men appeared at the door of the barn. "What's wrong, Kathleen? Is someone hurt?"

"No, Nathan, nothing like that. There is a man here with a brand new beautiful carriage and he said it's ours. Is there a mistake or did you order a carriage?" Kathleen looked at her husband with apprehension.

"Is it a dark green carriage?" Nathan's eyes twinkled and a grin turned up the sides of his mouth. "Is it the very same color as your beautiful eyes?"

Kathleen looked at her husband with a stunned expression on her face. He looked like he was about to explode with pleasure. "Why, yes....it is dark green. And, yes...." she looked down coquettishly, "I guess that is the color of my eyes. What have you done, dear husband?" She looked up into Nathan's eyes, smiling now.

"Well...... I thought maybe the next time we go to Savannah, you can ride in a little more comfort than the back of a wagon, so I commissioned a new carriage to be made. It's taken a lot longer than I thought it would, though. I......."

He couldn't finish because Kathleen had thrown herself into his arms and was clinging to his neck, covering his face with kisses. Samuel burst into laughter. "Guess she's surprised, Father."

Kathleen had forgotten about Samuel being there and quickly disengaged herself from Nathan. She blushed, looked down at the ground, and started smoothing her skirt. "I'm .....sorry... Samuel. I was so excited I forgot myself."

Nathan and Samuel both chuckled, causing her to turn even redder. "Oh, you two, stop it!" She joined them in their laughter. "Let's go see our new carriage. I left poor Mr. Jackson with Beulah."

The trio walked back up to the house where Mr. Jackson was being entertained by Beulah, Callie, and Trudy.

"Mr. Jackson, I see my carriage is finally here. Mind if I look it over to see if it's what I ordered?" Nathan reached the front steps and stuck out his hand for Jackson to shake.

"Yes, sir, Mr. Hill. Take a good look. I'm sure you will be satisfied."

"Kathleen, come look inside, while I inspect the outside." Kathleen opened the door and climbed inside the roomy carriage. There were two facing seats easily wide enough for three people on each side, six altogether, and plenty of leg room in between. The seats were of a soft, supple, black leather with tufting on the backs. It smelled of the new leather. Kathleen leaned back against the seat and took a deep breath. It was beautiful.

She opened the door. "Callie, Samuel, Beulah, come see. We will all fit in it with plenty of room." The three climbed inside and marveled at the roominess and the opulence of the interior.

Nathan finished his inspection of the exterior and peeked inside. "Everything satisfactory in here?" He was met with nods of approval and smiles.

"It's the prettiest carriage I've ever seen, Papa," said Callie. "It will be much nicer to ride in than the wagon and it's bigger than our old one the Yankees burned."

"It's lovely, son, but I'm sure it cost plenty." Beulah lifted her eyebrows up, looking at Nathan questioningly.

"Yes, Mother, it wasn't cheap, but I got a really good deal and with the extra money from our railroad investment, we can well afford it."

"Very well, then." Beulah rubbed her hand on the soft leather, luxuriating in the feel of it.

"Do the horses stay too, Papa?"

"Yes, Callie, the bays do, but Mr. Jackson will ride the roan back to Savannah. The Hills can't have unmatched horses pulling this new carriage, now can they?" Nathan's voice dripped with sarcasm. Then he laughed that deep laugh Callie loved. "You, baby girl, can even name them. Think about it for a while. You and Trudy put your heads together and come up with something unique."

"All right, Papa." Callie jumped out of the carriage and went to pet the horses. They whinnied at the attention and stamped their hooves impatiently.

"Well, Mr. Jackson, since everything has met our approval, I guess you can be on your way back to the city, unless you'd like to stay here for the night."

"Thank you, Mr. Hill, but no, I'd best be on my way. I can move much faster without the carriage now. Should reach Savannah not long after nightfall."

"Be careful, Mr. Jackson. There are still ruffians and riff-raff on the road, especially at dusk. We encountered them not long ago. Are you armed?"

"Oh, yes, sir. Have to be now-a-days." He mounted the roan. "Thank you again, sir, for your business. I hope you enjoy your new carriage." And then he turned the roan and started trotting down the lane.

"Well, now we will just have to build a carriage house to put this new one in," said Samuel. He turned to look at Nathan. "You made more work for us, Father."

Nathan grinned. "Yes, I guess I did. For now, I think we can fit it into the barn at the far end. We can attend to the new house when the weather gets cooler. Come on, help me unhitch the horses and get them to the stable."

"Wait, Nathan," said Kathleen as she walked back towards the carriage. "May we have a ride in it first? Just a short one?"

"Yes!" said Callie. "Come on, there's room for all of us. Papa you drive. Trudy, you and I will sit on the side with Mama Kathleen. Sam, you and Grandma sit on the other side. Oh, let's go get Mammy Sallie. She will fit too."

"Mammy's resting, Callie. I don't think she's feeling herself this morning." Beulah said as she stepped back up to the carriage and sat down.

"Oh, I hope she's all right. Well, I guess we can give her a ride some other time," Callie said disappointedly. Then she stuck her head out the window and shouted, "Let's get going, then, driver! Onward!"

Nathan picked up the reins and pulled on the harnesses of the beautiful new horses. "Giddyup! Let's go!" They turned around and started down the lane, the passengers smiling broadly. The real test would be when they turned onto the road. As they continued, they all marveled at how smooth the ride was.

"Aahhh," sighed Kathleen laying her head back against the tufted seat. "Now *this* is luxury! And, much easier on our backsides too, Callie!"

* * *

Georgia suffered another setback in their reconstruction on September 19th. The Georgia state legislature took it upon themselves to expell twenty-eight newly elected members because they were at least one-eighth Negro. One of the men who was expelled, Philip Joiner, led a twenty-five mile march from Albany to Camilla, along with several hundred blacks and a few white men. They were going to attend a Republican rally at the Camilla Courthouse.

Many whites, who were against the rally, were stationed around the courthouse. When the marchers arrived, the whites opened fire, killing a dozen of the marchers and injuring thirty or more. On the return to Albany many more marchers were assaulted by whites along the way.

When word reached the Republicans in Congress at the Capitol, they were apalled by the violence of the "Camilla Massacre." As a result, once again, Georgia was required to undergo military rule and her representatives and senators were denied their seats in Congress.

News of the "Massacre" did not reach Oak Hill until early October. Samuel had taken a trip to Atlanta where he learned of the incident. Tensions were very high in the new state capitol. No black was safe on the streets of Atlanta or any other city or town in Georgia. They had already been suffering from the "black codes" passed by the state legislature two years ago, which stated ex-slaves who had no steady employment could be arrested and ordered to pay fines. Prisoners who couldn't pay the fines, which were most of them, were hired out as virtual slaves again. The black population was also prevented from buying land, receiving fair wages, voting, serving on juries, or testifying against whites. Slavery had returned to Georgia, only in a different form.

The national election in November proved how important the black vote was. Ulysses S. Grant became the eighteenth president by a slim popular vote, but a large electoral vote. The difference in the popular vote was the 500,000 black votes cast for the Republican. The Radical Republicans carried all states in the South, except Georgia and Louisiana, and all the Northern states. Mississippi, Texas, and Virginia could not participate in the election because they were still not re-admitted to the Union.

The popular general would now have to continue to reconstruct the South, of which he had so viligantly destroyed.

CHAPTER 4
1869

"I can't stand it anymore! Let's GO!" Callie was standing with Trudy and Victoria by the front door. She had been pacing for some time now, waiting on the adults. Victoria and Trudy just watched her and shrugged their shoulders.

"I'm anxious, too, Callie, but you can't hurry Mother. She's on her own schedule anymore. Besides, we have plenty of time. We won't miss the train."

"Can't Uncle John speed Aunt Caroline up just a *little* bit?" Callie began fidgeting with her new bonnet's ribbons and looked up the stairs again, wishing her aunt and uncle to appear. Instead her father and Kathleen were coming down the steps.

"Are we ready to go now, Papa? Is Aunt Caroline coming behind you?"

"Just a moment, baby girl. Caroline still has some items to put in her satchel. Take a breath and relax. We have plenty of time to get to Swainsboro."

"Ohhhhh........." Callie turned to Trudy. "I just don't think I can wait another minute! I've been thinking of this trip for weeks, months really. Now that I'm finally going, I have to wait! Mmmphhh...."

Callie gritted her teeth and paced again up and down the entry way hall. She had on her brand new dark blue, light wool traveling dress, bonnet, and shoes. Her long blonde curls were tucked into a neat bun at the nape of her neck, just low enough for the new bonnet to sit on.

"Miz Callie, you ain't makin' Miz Caroline move any faster by shoutin' an' pacin'. Settle yourse'f down, now. Y'all have plen'y o' time."

"I know, Trudy, but I just want to get started. We've been planning for this trip so long, that I just *want to go!*"

Indeed, the Hill family had been planning this trip for a long time. They were going North with the Whitsons to observe Northern railroads, farmlands, and industries. It took so long to plan the journey because many obstacles had to be crossed before Nathan felt secure enough to leave Oak Hill for an extended period of time. They would be absent from the plantation for at least two months. He hated to leave Samuel with all the responsibilities, but his son had insisted. Samuel was not anxious to return to Chicago, where he had spent almost two years at Camp Douglas. He was very content to oversee Oak Hill while Nathan was gone.

Beulah, also, had no desire to travel. She was getting older, almost seventy, and felt she couldn't keep up with the others physically. She was happiest doing her needlework, reading, or reminiscing with Mammy Sallie.

It was decided then that Samuel and Beulah would stay behind with the workers to tend to Oak Hill. Trudy was also being left at the plantation. Callie had begged, pleaded, and threatened her, but Trudy was adamant. She didn't want to go and now Callie couldn't make her. She had no desire to be the only darkie traveling with whites, even if she thought of them as her family. Trudy had heard of all the murders and beatings of blacks in the southern cities and towns. She was going to stay at Oak Hill where she knew she would be safe. Besides, she knew Callie. Once they arrived at their destinations along the way, Callie would ignore her, especially since Victoria was going too. No, Trudy wasn't putting herself in that position. She was staying home.

The Whitsons had arrived two days earlier with many trunks and boxes packed in their wagon. Victoria was just as excited as Callie to go on this trip, as she, too, had never ventured out of Georgia. The two girls giggled and talked into the night, leaving Trudy out of much of the conversation. This only reinforced Trudy's decision to stay at Oak Hill.

Callie heard John and Caroline talking as they descended the stairs. "*Finally!*" she whispered loudly in Trudy's ear. "Now, maybe we can get going."

"I's knows why you's so wantin' to go, Miz Callie. Sooner you's gits goin', the sooner you's gits to sees Mista Ben!" Trudy chuckled as Callie's face turned beet red.

"That's just not true, Trudy Hill! I have never ridden on a train before or even been farther than Savannah. I'm just very excited to be going somewhere." Callie stuck out her lower lip and glared at Trudy.

"Uh-huh. That's what you's says, but that's not the whole truf. You been wantin' to sees Mista Ben for a long times now 'cuz he's your beau."

Callie stared at Trudy with a deep frown on her face and her eyes were like daggers. "Oh, Trudy! You exasperate me so!" Then she turned and faced Victoria who was giggling at Callie's expense. "Not you, too, Victoria. Oh, both of you......."

"Is something the matter, Callie, dear?" Caroline had reached the foyer and was smoothing her hair before she donned her bonnet.

Callie smiled sweetly at her aunt. "No, Aunt Caroline, I'm just really anxious to get going. We've been waiting on you."

"Yes, I know. I apologize. I was dilly-dalling and lost track of the time. But, I'm ready now. Let's go to the carriages." She turned, "Kathleen, we are all ready now, aren't we?"

"I think so. We've already said our good-byes, but I'll tell Beulah we're leaving so they can see us off." She left for the back of the house. Soon Samuel, Beulah, and Mammy Sallie appeared.

The Hills hugged each other one last time and then descended down the veranda steps and out to the waiting carriages. Callie would be riding with Victoria in the Whitson's carriage so they could chatter. Both girls hurriedly climbed into their seats. It was then that Callie remembered she hadn't properly told Trudy good-bye.

"Wait just a minute, Uncle John." She climbed back out and ran back up the veranda steps where Trudy sat sadly on the swing. When she saw Callie, her face lit up in a huge smile.

"Trudy, Trudy, I'm sorry, you know how excited I get." Callie embraced her friend tightly. "I will miss you terribly. I'll try to write, and I promise I will bring you something special from everyplace we go."

"I's miss you's too, Miz Callie. Now, goes has funs an' tell Mista Ben I thinks of him." Trudy's black eyes sparkled with mischief.

"Oh, Trudy...........you're mean!!" One more quick hug and Callie hurried back to her seat in the carriage. "Good-bye, Grandma,

bye Sam, bye Mammy, good-bye, Trudy! See you in a couple months!"
And then the carriages started down the lane and Callie was off to her
great adventure.

* * *

Raymond Carswell had his morning coffee cup in his hand and
since it was a nice day, he decided to walk down the lane to see if
the new drainage ditch was working. He and Jenny had spent several
days digging in the hard red earth to route the water from in front of
the cabins.

He heard the horses and carriages before he saw them, and decided
to move closer to the road to see who was coming by. He stayed in the
shadows of the live oaks so as not to be seen.

The first vehicle was a handsome dark green carriage pulled by a
matched set of bay horses. Their harnesses were highly polished brass
that reflected the morning sunlight. He briefly caught a glimpse of
the occupants through the glass windows. He thought he recognized
Kathleen Hill, her copper hair peeking out of her bonnet. Yes, he was
certain it was her.

He raised his eyebrows and smiled a devilish grin. The Hills must
have come into even more money to have such a fancy, expensive
carriage. He wondered where they were off to. He stayed in his place,
hearing more activity on the road.

The next carriage was black, larger than the Hills, and pulled by
a pair of sleek black horses. The trim on this carriage was silver,
sparkling in the sun. The horses pranced, displaying their fancy mane
braids and rich harnesses of gleaming silver.

Carswell inhaled sharply. This was a very wealthy person's
carriage. Who could this be? They had to be traveling with the Hills.
Then he caught a glimpse of Callie Hill. He knew it was her, tendrils
of her ash blonde hair poked out from under her dark blue bonnet.
Even from here, he could see her brown eyes. She was seated next
to a girl who was very attractive also. About the same age, only with
brown hair curling out of her bonnet. Across from them was seated a
man and a woman Carswell guessed to be approximately the same age
as Nathan and Kathleen Hill. Maybe they were friends or relatives.

Whoever they were, they had to be very rich.

Following the carriages were two wagons piled high with trunks, satchels, and boxes. Wherever these people were going, it looked like they would be gone for quite a while. Raymond's cunning mind stored all this information. Maybe he should make a little visit to Oak Hill to check out what was going on there. Just to be neighborly. He chuckled to himself at this turn of events and then walked back to his cabin, whistling cheerfully as he went.

* * *

The carriages and wagons arrived at the newly built train depot in Swainsboro. There the passengers left their carriages and the wagons were unloaded. The drivers of all the vehicles turned around and headed back to Oak Hill.

Belle had packed a big basket of food for the travelers which they now distributed on one of the tables inside the station. Cold thinly sliced pork on tender biscuits, tasty fried chicken, hard boiled eggs, pickled beets, bread and butter pickles, corn relish, canned peaches, and rice pudding were but a few of the goodies from the basket.

They all ate heartily as this would be their last home cooked food for a while. From now on they would be eating restaurant or railroad food.

Callie and Victoria were still too excited to eat much. They watched the people sitting in the station, the workmen, and the other people arriving. The train was supposedly on schedule and would be arriving in a little over an hour. The girls could hardly wait.

"Ladies, you'd better eat some of this delicious food Belle sent," Nathan said as he chewed on a chicken leg. "Might be the last decent food we eat for a long time."

"Oh, Nathan, you know we will be dining at excellent restaurants along the way." Caroline smiled at him. "That's the fun of traveling, isn't it - to have new experiences? I'm sure the Yankees have good cooks too. But, he's right, girls, you really should eat something now. We don't know when will be the next time we eat. Probably not until we get to Atlanta tonight."

"I think we will have enough left from the basket to take aboard in case some of us get hungry later," said Kathleen. "Belle really sent a lot of food - enough for another meal, I think. But, Callie, you and Victoria should eat a little more - better to ride on a full stomach."

Callie and Victoria each shrugged their shoulders and reached for a pork filled biscuit. It was really tasty. They both giggled as they ate one and took a piece of chicken too. Belle's food was just too good.

It wasn't long before they heard the chugging of the locomotive, the hissing of the released steam, and the long whistle of the approaching train. Callie felt her stomach lurch with excitement. She turned towards Kathleen with a brilliant smile on her face, her cheeks flushed.

"It's here! The train is finally here!" Callie had to shout to be heard above the commotion.

Kathleen nodded her head and smiled also. She, too, was looking forward to this trip. She had just observed little Nathaniel's birth and death last week for the third year. She pictured him as a strong, chubby three year old with Nathan's eyes and her hair. Yes, this journey was exactly what she needed.

"Alllllllll aabooarrddd!" The conductor stood on the steps leading to the passenger car and cried out. "Alllllllll aabooarrdd!!"

"All right, ladies first," said John as he stood by the steps and helped Caroline, Kathleen, Victoria, and, finally, Callie up the steps to the car. Then he and Nathan boarded.

Callie didn't really know what to expect when she entered the passenger car, but she was terribly disappointed. There were no seats, only benches, long enough to hold two people with a long aisle in between. The windows were smeared and dirty with dust making it impossible to see out. It was also chillier in the car than outside. She shivered. The other passengers looked somewhat seedy. There were no other females, only men, rough looking men.

She saw Victoria had the same look of disappointment, as did Caroline and Kathleen. Nathan let out a long sigh and quickly grabbed Kathleen and Callie's arms. John did the same with Caroline and Victoria.

Under his breath, Nathan whispered to Kathleen, "Looks like we were put on a pretty rough car. The other people at the station didn't look like this. Maybe John and I should request the other car."

Before Kathleen could answer, the conductor stuck his head in, and as if reading Nathan's mind said, "All cars filled up, take your seats please. The baggage has been loaded and we're ready to roll."

"I guess we'd better find seats then," Kathleen whispered to Nathan. "Let Caroline and I sit together, you and John sit with the girls."

"Good idea. Come on, baby girl, you sit with your papa today."

John and Victoria followed the Hills' lead. There was no argument from the girls. They were perfectly content being with their fathers. In fact, Callie slipped her arm through Nathan's and sat as close to him as she could. She hoped it was a short ride to Macon where they would change trains.

The train started chugging and finally lurched forward with a motion that nearly knocked Callie and Nathan off their bench. They both recovered and laughed. Their journey had begun.

* * *

After sitting on the hard benches for over three hours, the train pulled into the depot at Macon. Callie could hardly wait to get off and stretch. Her back hurt, her legs cramped, and she had a terrible headache from all the cigar smoke in the car. The rocking of the train had made her sleepy, but it was impossible to doze off. Just when she would put her head on Nathan's shoulder, the train would pitch and jerk her awake. The rest of the family suffered the same troubles; so needless to say, none of the family members came off the train in a congenial mood.

"My goodness, that was an experience!" Caroline said as they all walked toward the station. "Did you notice that man who had the corn cob pipe and the beard that reached his belly? And, what about the one with no teeth dressed in an old Confederate uniform? But the one that gave me the willies was the dapper one with the goatee and the skinny moustache who was all dressed up. He kept looking at Kathleen and me and winking. Then he'd smile and nod his head at us. Ooooh, I hate men like that! They think any female will bow down before them."

"No worry about you bowing to any man, my dear," John said affectionately, "unless you're about to punch them in the gut!" He started laughing.

"Oh, John, you're terrible!" But Caroline couldn't help chuckling along with him as did the others.

"Well, I for one am very glad to get off that train. My backside is so sore, I may not be able to sit down ever again. Those benches were harder than our wagon bench, Mama Kathleen. We should have brought some kind of padding along."

Kathleen laughed and her green eyes sparkled. "Yes, we should have, Callie. Well, let's hope our next car is better. Aren't we taking the Central, Nathan, *our* railroad?"

"Yes, let's hope it's more comfortable, or John and I will have to either sell our shares, or complain loudly to the board and president. Unfortunately, we won't be able to control the caliber of the passengers."

The travelers walked around the station to get the kinks out of their muscles and then settled down outside at a table. Kathleen produced the basket of food and Belle's creations were devoured.

As they ate, they marveled at all the activity around them. Macon was fast becoming a transportation hub of Georgia. Sherman had bypassed the city, so it was still mainly intact. They had several hours before their train arrived so they decided to walk around the area.

Walking north on Cherry Street, they saw the Judge Asa Holt house, the only home damaged during the Battle of Dunlap Hill in 1864. The Union army launched cannon fire into Macon from across the river, hoping to free thousands of Federal prisoners of war held there. One cannonball struck the left column of the house and crashed into the inside of the home, landing on the hall floor.

Macon was the site of the Confederate arsenal, so Union attempts to enter the city were rebuffed. That was one of the reasons General Sherman bypassed the city and instead ransacked Milledgeville, then the state capitol.

"Look at that beautiful home, John." Caroline was pointing to a three story red brick house with a white cupola on the top. "It's quite different than the typical Southern home, isn't it?"

"Do you like it, Caroline?" asked Kathleen.

"Yes, I think I do, but I much prefer our grand verandas and columns. This one looks dainty, don't you think? I do like the cupola, though."

"It does look dainty, but look how large it is. It goes deep into the lot. Rather deceiving. Maybe it's the new look of the future," Kathleen answered her.

They continued their walk, marveling at the gracious homes lining the streets, until they returned to the station. Refreshed from their walk and their stomachs full, they all were ready for the next link on their journey - Atlanta.

* * *

They arrived in Atlanta almost four hours later. The passenger car was somewhat more comfortable. The benches at least had back rests so one had some support, but still no padding. The train made several stops at small towns along the way to pick up passengers and freight, finally pulling into the Atlanta station around seven o'clock in the evening. The cars were unloaded as the passengers got off the train, stretching stiff muscles from sitting so long on the hard seats.

"John, we'd better hire one of the transfer coaches over there to take our baggage to the hotel. We can hail a hack to take us."

"I'll take care of that, Nathan. You take the ladies in the cab and I'll join you at the Old Orchard Inn."

"Good idea. Come on, ladies, let's find a cabbie and get ourselves checked in for the evening. The Old Orchard has an excellent dining room, I've been told. Once we've found our rooms, we can get some dinner."

The women and Nathan found a hack easily and were on their way to the hotel. It was dark so Callie couldn't really see anything along the way; however, she could make out the outlines of many new buildings under construction.

Since Confederate General John Bell Hood burned most of Atlanta before he retreated from the city and Union General William Sherman set fire to the rest when he left for his March to the Sea, Atlanta was rising from the ashes as a brand new city. Those who had the foresight, and the money, invested heavily in the new structures housing the recently created businesses in the city. Many of them were northern carpetbaggers and southern scalawags, but no matter, the city was once again vibrant and alive.

The Hills and Whitsons were staying in a brand new inn, just having opened three months ago. The Old Orchard Inn was small and intimate, but beautiful. As they entered the lobby of the inn, Callie and Victoria were impressed by the simple aesthetics of the décor. Everything was crisp, shiny, neat, and clean.

The families had reserved two suites next to one another. Since Callie had stayed at the Marshall House in Savannah, she expected the rooms to look much the same. They were not. The Old Orchard Inn's rooms were large, comfortable, and opulently furnished. She and Kathleen both gasped as they entered the rooms.

"My, Nathan, this is beautiful! I didn't expect anything this grand!" Kathleen's hand went to her mouth in surprise. She circled the room looking at everything in it.

"This is really nice, Papa," Callie echoed as she followed her stepmother around the room. "Really nice." She turned to her father and smiled that wonderful smile he so loved.

"Only the best for my two girls," Nathan grinned.

"But, isn't it expensive, dear? Can we afford this?"

"Yes, Kathleen, it is a little high, but remember, we are officially on a 'business' trip, so part of it is being paid by the railroad company. So don't worry - just enjoy it."

"How long will we be in Atlanta, Papa?"

"A few days, baby girl. John and I will attend to some business and you ladies can sightsee, and dare I say...shop."

There was a knock at the door. Their luggage had arrived just in time for them to change from their traveling clothes to ones suited for dining. They met the Whitsons in the hallway and proceeded to the dining room.

"Well, now let our adventures in eating get under way," Caroline said as she scanned the menu. "Ooooh, this looks inviting. Leg of mutton with caper sauce. Mmmm. Or chicken with egg sauce. How about the beef tongue in onion sauce?"

Callie and Victoria were both making faces. Caroline looked up from the menu and laughed. "Not to your liking, girls? You need to be open to new tastes. How bad could pickled pork and spinach be?" She raised her eyebrows and tried not to smile.

Everyone else at the table was chuckling. "Well, I think I'm going to order good old roast chicken with the boiled Irish potatoes," said Kathleen. "I have to make my ancestors happy. The green apple pie sounds good for dessert. How about you, Callie? Find anything you like?"

"Hmmm. Think I'll be like you, Mama Kathleen, only I'm going to order the ham with sweet potatoes. I see they have pound cake on the menu - I'll try it, but I doubt it can be as delicious as Belle's."

"Oh, I can see you two are going to be boring diners." Caroline put down her menu. "I guess I'll be the bold one. I'm going to try the beef tongue in onion sauce with hominy. And, then maybe mince pie for dessert. John, want to join in my adventure?"

"No, Caroline. Think I'll stick with what I like - roast beef with mashed potatoes. But I will be brave and try the sago pudding for dessert."

"Victoria, Nathan, what about your choice? Going to be dull or exciting?"

"Sorry, Mother, I'm going to be dull and order the same as Callie."

"Me, too, Caroline. I'm going with roast pork, sweet potatoes, and the apple pie."

"Oh, y'all too dreary! You need to broaden your experiences, take chances, try something new!!

"Well, let's see how your beef tongue turns out and then maybe the next time, I'll join you," laughed John.

Their food came and everyone enjoyed their dinner, except Caroline. She finally admitted the beef tongue had a bad texture and the onion sauce was too strong, but the hominy and pie were good. John felt sorry for her and shared some of his roast beef with her, adding maybe she had learned her lesson for being "bold."

The travelers were having a good time, but Callie started yawning and then Victoria, so it was decided to retire for the night. It had been a long, but splendid day.

The days in Atlanta sped by. The women shopped at the new dress shops, shoe stores, and millineries. Callie, at first, was very disconcerted to find the city still occupied by Yankees. Union soldiers were everywhere. She found she still flinched whenever a blue uniformed man approached her. It immediately brought back memories of the Yankees at Oak Hill. But, then she would tell herself Ben was also a Yankee and he had saved her. Still, it was upsetting.

Callie looked through the shops to find Trudy something from Atlanta and finally purchased a handkerchief with the city's name embroidered on the edge. Callie thought Trudy would love it. She also bought one for herself. Kathleen decided on a black cotton shawl for Beulah and a dark red one for Mammy Sallie. Caroline and Victoria also purchased mementos of the city to take home.

It was time to once again board the train to travel north. Their next stop would be Chattanooga, Tennessee where they would change trains and then journey on to Knoxville. Callie was excited to finally be beyond the state of Georgia. She had no idea what to expect.

* * *

Trudy missed Callie more than she thought she would. Beulah let her stay in Callie's room this time; before when Callie was gone, she had to go to Dinah's cabin. Still, Trudy didn't sleep in Callie's nice feather bed, but chose her own straw mattress on the floor.

Trudy, now sixteen going on seventeen, had matured into an attractive young woman. She was of medium height, but lanky in build. Her skin was the color of light brown sugar with a bronze sheen. She usually wore her hair in corn rows or tiny braids, sometimes with a kerchief tied around her head, sometimes with a turban. Her eyes were large and very dark brown, almost black, with long thick black lashes. It was her smile that made her pretty. Her teeth were perfectly formed and brilliantly white. When she smiled her entire face lit up and almost glowed.

Today, Trudy didn't feel much like smiling. It was a dismal early

March day, cloudless, gray, damp, and dreary. And, she missed Callie. Today she regretted not going on the big trip north. She imagined all the fun Callie and Victoria were having along the way. Trudy sighed a long, exasperated sigh.

She had been walking aimlessly around the main floor of the house looking out one window after another. Mammy Sallie finally saw her gazing out the library window.

"What the matter wit you, Trudy Hill? Missin' Miz Callie? Wishin' you'd gone too?"

Trudy turned at the sound of Mammy's voice. "Lil bit, Mammy, lil bit. But pro'bly bes'. When Miz Callie gits 'round Miz Vic'oria, she change. Likes she don' even knows Trudy no more."

"I's knows, Trudy. White fo'ks like that. Even Miz Callie, but she don' knows she do it."

"I's knows. That's the hard part. Hopes she don' change too much after goin' north. Hopes she still loves me when she gits back."

"Don' worries, Trudy, Miz Callie always loves you. Sometimes, she jes' forgits."

"Uh-huh. You rights, Mammy. You rights."

Trudy was still staring out the window when she noticed movement. Someone was walking around the house towards the back door. She and Mammy instantly heard the knocking.

"Now who coulds be knockin' at the back door this time of day?" Mammy ambled off to see who was there. Trudy, curious, followed her.

Mammy slightly opened the door and there was a young black man standing with his battered hat in his hand.

"Ma'am, would this be the Hill plan'ation?"

Mammy had the door open only a crack. "Yes, it be. Who wants to know?"

"I's do, Ma'am. I's Caleb Jones. I's likes to talks to the masta if'n I could."

Mammy looked at Caleb from the top of his bare head to the bottom of his worn shoes. "What's you wants from the masta, Mista Jones? We's alreadys hired 'nuf darkies to work 'round here, don' need no more."

"I's don' wants to be hired, Ma'am." Caleb looked Mammy straight in the eyes. "I's wants to gits some land to sharecrop. Heard Mista Hill lettin' some of his land out that way. I's gots money an' now I's wants some land of my own. Now, is the masta here or nots?"

Mammy was rather taken aback by the tone of Caleb's voice, but opened the door wider. "Masta Nathan not heres, but Masta Samuel out in the barn. The calves is bein' born. He mighty busy rights now, maybe you comes back later."

"No, Ma'am. I's waits out heres 'til he comes. I's comes a long way an' I's waits."

"Might be nears sundown 'fore he gits back up here."

"He gotta eats, don' he? Shorely comin' 'round noon to eats? I's waits."

"All right, you waits out heres on the back po'ch, Mista Caleb Jones, but don' 'pects nuttin' from me."

"Yes, Ma'am. Thanks you. I's be jes' fine out here waitin'." At that, Caleb sat his tall, lean body down on the back porch step and rested his head against the cold bricks and waited.

Mammy Sallie shut the door and turned to Trudy who was right behind her. "Now, what's you thinks 'bout that? That youn' man out theres waitin' for Masta Samuel. Says he want to sharecrop."

"Yes, I's heard, Mammy. Where you thinks he from? Says he comes a longs way. How he heards 'bout Oak Hill? Think I's jes' go outs there an' find out."

Trudy straightened herself up, smoothed her kerchief and skirt, pinched her cheeks for color and opened the back door. Caleb was still sitting on the porch step, holding his hat in his hands, gazing out at the buildings surrounding the house. When he heard the door open, he looked and saw Trudy come out. He quickly stood up.

Trudy walked down the steps and faced him before she said anything. She stared at him with her black eyes, checking him out. He was tall, taller than she was, and thin. His arms seemed too long for the rest of him. His skin was like rich coffee, but had an ocher cast to it. He was bald, not one hair on his head. He looked a few years older than herself. He was not looking at the ground, but staring right back into her eyes.

"Likes what you sees?"

Trudy involuntarily twitched at the sound of his voice. It was a deep voice. She didn't say anything, still staring.

"I's aks agin. You likes what you sees? You been lookin' long 'nuf."

Trudy didn't quite know what to say, but she thought Caleb Jones was pretty sure of himself. She liked that.

"Well?" Caleb shrugged his shoulders and smiled at Trudy, showing lots of teeth.

Trudy flashed him her best smile, lighting up her entire face. "Guess y'all do." She walked back to the steps, swishing her skirt, and calmly sat down. Caleb sat beside her. "I's Trudy Hill."

"Caleb Jones."

"I's heard."

"Guess you lives here?"

"Uh-huh. All my life. I's belonged to Miz Callie 'til the war free me. Where you froms?"

"I's from 'round Jonesboro. Big plantation there. I brung there when I's a lil boy, so don' 'members no place else. Works wits the carpenter, Ol' Abel. Then whens the war come, masta puts me in the cotton fields. Hard, hard work, but learns hows to plant an' weed' an' harvest. Now want my *own* land to plant an' weed an' harvest. My *own* cotton. Saves my money. Works in 'tlanta buildin'. But not safe there no more. Whites killin' darkies for no reason. I's sets out this direc'ion an' heards 'long the way Masta Hill lettin' land for sharecroppin'. Likes to do that an' gits started on my new life."

As Caleb was talking, Trudy could see his eyes focusing out in the horizon. It was as if he was seeing his new life out there somewhere, just out of reach. Then he turned to her and she could see in his face the determination to build this new life for himself. She stared into those dark brown eyes and for a second lost herself in his dream. She shivered, not from cold, but excitement. Trudy had never seen such eyes. Caleb Jones was quite unique and worth getting to know.

* * *

Callie's head fell forward as her eyes closed and she momentarily slept. The movement of her head jerked her back awake, but the motion of the train and the clickety-clack sound of the rails put her right back to sleep. This was repeated several times before Nathan finally put his arm around her and laid her head on his shoulder. Kathleen was asleep on his other side in the same manner.

They had been on the train from Knoxville for several hours and wouldn't arrive at the Williamsburg station for a couple more. The train traveled more slowly now that they were in the hills of northern Tennessee and southern Kentucky. They would be spending the night in Williamsburg, Kentucky and, hopefully, eating a decent meal. Their lunch at the depot between Chattanooga and Knoxville was awful. Nathan's stomach was starting to rumble now from hunger. He laid his head on the back of the seat and tried to sleep also.

The train slowly pulled into the station at Williamsburg. The Whitsons and the Hills gathered their belongings and left the car. There was a transfer coach waiting to take them to the one and only hotel in the small town.

"Have a nice evening, ma'ams, sirs. This here's a nice little town," the conductor said as he helped them down the steps.

"I just want to stretch out in a nice bed and sleep," said Callie yawning. "Who ever thought traveling could be so tiring."

"I agree," said Victoria, stretching. "I feel like I've been working all day."

"Since when do you 'work?'" asked John, grinning mischieviously.

"Oh, Father, you know what I mean!"

Soon they were at the hotel across from the courthouse square. It was small, but very clean and comfortable. Their rooms were plain, but had the feather beds Callie longed for. After changing from their dusty traveling clothes, they all proceeded to the small restaurant inside the hotel. They were only serving fried chicken, mashed potatoes with cream gravy, green beans, and biscuits, but that suited the travelers just fine.

While drinking their coffee, Nathan asked the waiter if the town was known for anything famous.

"Well, sir, we've been here since the early 1800s, only by a different name. We got some springs that are notable. But, see that courthouse lawn over there?" He pointed to across the street. "Had us a battle there back in '63 with the Yanks. Just a skirmish, but Col. Scott, Confederate, drove back an Ohio infantry. You a Reb, sir? You fight the Yanks?"

Nathan nodded in the affirmative. "As a matter of fact, I fought in some battles in Tennessee, but my company never made it into Kentucky."

"Glad to meet your acquaintance, sir, and thank you for serving in the Confederate Army, may it rest in peace."

Nathan had never encountered this reaction. He just nodded his head in thanks.

However, the conversation and gesture was not lost on the rest of the party at the table. Callie, for the first time, realized what her father had done in the war. She looked at him with a different perspective.

John cleared his throat as an awkward silence followed the waiter's remarks. "Nathan, I guess none of us really know what you went through during the war. You and all of those who fought for our Lost Cause. I, too, am proud of your service. I'm sorry it's coming so late. Forgive me."

"John, please, you're embarrassing me. Actually, it's a time in my life I don't particularily want to remember. So, let's just drink our coffee and then try out those feather beds. We have an early departure tomorrow morning."

At dawn the next day, Callie reluctantly left her nice soft feather bed, washed, dressed, and went with the others to the station to once again board the train. Their journey today would end in Lexington, Kentucky, where they would be staying for two days.

* * *

Callie watched the darkening skies outside the small train window. In the hills, a murky mist was swirling around the rounded tops, hiding them. The train chugged along, braving the approaching storm.

It struck suddenly and intensely. Streaks of hot white lightning shot through the sinister looking skies, followed by an earsplitting clap of thunder, heard even above the sound of the engine.

Victoria, who had been napping, screamed at the reverberation. "What was that?" Her question was lost as another streak lit up the skies, followed by another deafening roar.

Then came the winds. They buffeted the passenger car from the west, the side the families were sitting, rocking it on the tracks. Instantly, the heavens opened up in a deluge of water. The winds were blowing the downpour horizontally against the car, blocking any view of the outside. The passengers were surrounded by nature's chaos, held hostage in the car by the weather.

Callie was shaking. She was reliving the terrible twister that hit Oak Hill when she was younger. Victoria was just plain frightened.

"Come on ladies, it's just a little thunderstorm. It just sounds worse because we are at a higher elevation." John tried to mollify the party, but even he had an anxious look on his face.

The train had slowed down considerably to avoid being blown off the tracks. As it was creeping along, the rain continued to splatter against the car, making it impossible to view the turmoil in the skies.

The conductor appeared at the doorway. "Please remain in your seats. The engineer is navigating the rails splendidly and we will be out of this storm soon. Stay calm. You are in very capable hands. No need to worry or get upset."

He just got the words out of his mouth when a strong gust of wind struck the car and knocked him to his knees. The conductor got back to his feet. "Again, please remain seated. I think I will go find my seat." He smiled weakly. "There is no need for concern. This railroad has weathered many storms, stronger than this one." At that he left to sit down.

"Nathan, what are we to do?" Kathleen tugged at her husband's sleeve.

"What the conductor said, dear. There isn't much we can do, except pray. I'm sure he's right. They have experienced engineers who know what to do in a storm like this. We just need to get through it."

Another shot of lightning, followed by a tremendous bang of thunder shook the car and rattled the contents. Callie's eyes were as big as saucers and she was still shivering.

"Papa, I'm really scared. Is this like the twister at Oak Hill? Will this car stay on the track? Are we going to die?"

"Callie, please. Take some deep breaths. No, we are not going to die. We will stay on the tracks. Everything will be fine. From what I can see, the sky doesn't look like it did during the twister - it doesn't have that funny green color. Please, sweetie, hold on to my hand and everything will be fine."

Callie clasped Nathan's hand very tightly, took some deep breaths, and calmed down a little. With her other hand, she grasped Kathleen's and squeezed it hard. John and Caroline were doing the same with Victoria. The families sat that way in the wind-rocked car, trying to glimpse out the rain streaked windows, as the train slowly inched out of the storm.

* * *

The train finally limped into Lexington several hours behind schedule. The passengers gladly got off the car. Callie felt like kissing the ground, it felt so good to be on solid land once again. Experiencing such a storm from her house was bad enough, but to have it occur while on a moving car was terrible.

"Oh, I'm so happy to be off that car," Kathleen sighed as they gathered around the station waiting for their baggage to be unloaded. "That was quite a ride. One I hope to never experience again."

"I agree, Kathleen, that was not an enjoyable experience," Caroline said as she watched the workmen start unloading the baggage car. "But I must say, I'm proud of how our families behaved. There was no screaming and wailing as some of the others in the car did. And, I know everyone was frightened. Must be our 'proper Southern upbringing.' Hah! I think we might have been too afraid to speak!"

Everyone smiled and agreed; thankful the experience was behind them. The men found a transfer coach and soon they were on their way to the hotel.

During their stay in Lexington they toured the city seeing the childhood home of Mary Todd Lincoln, the residences of John Breckinridge, who John and Nathan had voted for in the presidential election of 1860, and the famous Confederate general, John Morgan. They also took a buggy ride on a wonderfully warm early spring day to visit Henry Clay's estate, Ashland. A picnic lunch was enjoyed along the way in a beautiful grove of maple trees, where the branches were just beginning to fill with their tender green leaves. Early wildflowers were poking their buds towards the bright sunshine, opening their petals to its warmth.

They all agreed Lexington earned its nickname as the "Athens of the South." It was a beautiful city. But, soon, they were back on the train bound for Cincinnati, Ohio - the first city of the North.

* * *

There was no other word to describe it - Ben Chapman was giddy. Callie Hill was coming to Clayton Township. He never dreamed this would happen, even when she mentioned in her letters that a trip north was in the making. Now, she had written that they left the last week of February and were headed to Chicago. When she arrived there, she would write and give him an approximate day when they would be in the township. The travelers were going to stay in Bloomington and just she and her parents would be coming to see the Chapmans. Nathan particularily wanted a tour of Henry and Ben's farm.

After receiving her last letter detailing the trip, Ben tried to keep his emotions in check, but he just couldn't help smiling every time he thought of her. This new happiness didn't go unnoticed. Emma teased him incessantly, his mother and father looked at him questioningly, and Josie was perplexed.

Every day he would read Callie's letter telling of their itinerary until he had it memorized. Today she would be in Knoxville - tomorrow, Williamsburg, and so on. He counted down the days until she would arrive in Illinois and then Chicago. They were staying there for two weeks and then heading back south, along the way stopping at the Chapman farm. He didn't know if he could wait much longer.

Ben had discussed the visit with his parents, of course, to get their permission for the Hills to stop. Henry was pleased to know someone wanted to tour his farm, so he was taking great pains to make sure everything was in excellent shape. They had not begun the spring planting yet, but they did have winter wheat growing and the pastures were doing well. He would also show off his newly purchased equipment.

Abigail and Emma were busy cleaning the house, putting up new curtains, and making new rag rugs for the floors. Ben was not the only member of the family who was excited about the visit, but he had other reasons to anticipate their arrival - Callie.

He had pictured her so many times in his mind and now he was actually going to see her in person again. His heart raced at the thought. Maybe she still looked like the young girl he had saved, or maybe she had changed completely. Maybe once she saw him, she would be disappointed and not have anything else to do with him. Maybe he would feel that way about her, but he didn't think so. Maybe she would be appalled at his home; after all, she lived on a plantation. Maybe…maybe….maybe…

* * *

Callie and her family were enjoying a wonderful breakfast at the Burnett House in Cincinnati. She was having her usual cornbread with butter and honey, but was also eating something new to her - an omelet. She was enjoying it immensely.

Victoria was cutting a waffle into tiny bites and savoring each one, along with her corned beef hash - another dish new to her palate.

The men were wolfing down beefsteaks, fried potatoes, grits, and buttered toast. Caroline and Kathleen were delicately eating fried mush and ham.

"Mmmm….this omelet is really really good, Papa. Mama Kathleen, we must remember it and tell Belle how to prepare it. I think it has cheese and onions in it."

"I'm glad you like it Callie. Yes, we can bring it to Belle's attention."

"See, this is what I mean by gaining new experiences in eating," Caroline jumped in.

"Like your beef tongue in onion gravy?" chuckled John. "That seemed to be quite a new experience for your tastebuds."

Caroline looked at her husband with disgust. "John, sometimes you totally exasperate me! At least I *tried* something different. Your 'tastebuds' must be very bored."

Everyone laughed at the couple and then finished their meal. They were staying in the southern Ohio city for several days. John and Nathan, once again, were attending to business while the ladies were free to do what they wanted.

The women hired a carriage to take them on a tour of the city. They learned Cincinnati had several nicknames, "Porkopolis," "City of Seven Hills," and "Queen City of the West." They learned quickly why "Porkopolis" was appropriate.

"What is that dreadful smell?" Caroline asked the driver as they passed by some buildings near the river.

"Meat packing factories, Ma'am. Where all the hogs end up sooner or later around here."

Caroline and Kathleen held their linen handkerchiefs under their noses so as to not breathe in the disgusting odor. "Please, hurry out of this area before we get sick," Caroline directed. "How can you people stand that stink?"

"Guess we just get used to it, Ma'am."

The driver took them to the parts of the city where the German and Irish immigrants lived. They decided to have lunch at a nice looking Irish pub. Kathleen felt right at home with the dishes offered and the familiar speech in the pub. Caroline declared it another wonderful adventure. Victoria and Callie felt very grown up to be patronizing a pub.

It was well known to southerners that the city was a prominent spot on the Underground Railroad before the war, and that many slaves had made their way to the North by crossing the Ohio River into Cincinnati. It was also home to the many slave catchers who then brought the errant property back to their masters.

"I always wondered what happened to Josiah," Kathleen said as she was looking at a row of shops. "He was so angry and fierce about his freedom. I wonder if he could be living here today."

"Whatever made you think of him, Kathleen?" Caroline looked at her with her eyebrows raised.

"I'm not sure. I guess I saw that darkie over there by that shop and I thought he resembled Josiah. Actually, I often wonder what happened to all the slaves that left Oak Hill after the Yankees came. I hope they are all happy and doing well. Don't you ever think about yours?"

"We didn't lose that many. Since Sherman missed Magnolia Grove, there wasn't the opportunity for our darkies to go with the army. We did have some younger ones leave, but most of the others stayed."

"Odd how our lives changed so, isn't it? I think our families are lucky we adapted so well. I hear others are still living in the past and can't get over the Confederacy's defeat."

"Yes, but our husbands were smart to look to the future even before the war to save our moneys. I think we can all thank Preston for that."

"You're right, Caroline. Well, I think I'm ready to go back to the hotel and freshen up before dinner. How about the rest of you?"

"Me, too, Mama Kathleen. I think I smell like all those hogs!"

The others laughed with Callie and instructed the driver to deliver them to their hotel.

The passengers were pleasantly surprised a few days later when they boarded the train car for Indianapolis, Indiana. Their now familiar benches were replaced with leather chairs. Not soft, upholstered chairs, but a real chair with a seat and a back. They were surprisingly very comfortable. They had also purchased, for several greenback dollars, small baskets of food at the Cincinnati station in case there were delays or they became hungry.

As the engine pulled out of the station, Nathan turned to Callie, "Now, we are really going to be in the northern country, Callie, so pay attention and see if you notice any differences in the geography and, when we stop, in the people. I need an extra pair of eyes to see why the North is much more industrialized, even in their farming, than we are.

"I'll try, Papa." But Callie was really thinking, her heart racing, "I'm that much closer to seeing Ben."

* * *

It didn't take the Hills and the Whitsons long to see a difference between the North and South as far as railroad travel. They noticed right away the car they were riding in was of higher quality and the traveling was faster and smoother. As they left Ohio and entered Indiana, they saw many factories and businesses along the way. When the train would pull into a depot, it was nicer than the ones they had encountered in the South. The food was better, as well as the over-all atmosphere. They also noticed the passengers themselves were better dressed and well mannered.

Callie and Victoria were seated together looking out at the countryside. The gentle hills of Ohio had become smaller and they were entering into the flat prairie lands of Indiana.

"I wonder what Chicago will be like, Victoria. Papa said it is a big city, bigger than Atlanta or Cincinnati. Sam said it was always very cold or very hot while he was in prison there. Poor Sam. That must have been terrible."

Victoria didn't want to talk about Samuel being in prison. It was too depressing. "Callie, how are you doing with your shopping so far? Have you found things for Trudy like you said you would?"

"Oh, yes. I got the handkerchief in Atlanta, a little toy horse from Lexington, and a china pig from Cincinnati. I didn't have time to buy anything from our other stops. I'll have to get her something from Indianapolis. I think Papa said we will be staying there a day. Maybe there will be a shop close to our hotel. How about you, have you bought things you wanted?"

"Yes, but I've been purchasing things for *me*!! Didn't you see that lovely new pink silk bonnet I got in Cincinnati? I can't wait to show it off in Savannah. None of the other girls will have a 'northern' bonnet! I'm glad I listened to Mother and took along an empty trunk. I'm beginning to fill it up. Haven't you bought anything for yourself?"

"Just a few things - some ribbons for my hair, a new pair of gloves, some slippers."

"Are you going to wear the ribbons when you see Ben? Aren't you getting excited about seeing him again?"

"Yes, I have to admit, I am."

"I know I would be. How romantic - after all these years.....falling in love through letter writing..........." Victoria held her hands against her face and fluttered her eyelashes.

"*Victoria*, no one has said anything about 'falling in love!' Good gracious! You're as bad as Trudy! We are just friends who write to one another occasionally." But despite herself, Callie started blushing. She turned her head so Victoria would not see.

"Yes, but you're forgetting.....he just happened to also save your life. That would make him more than 'just a friend' in my book. That makes him very close to you, I would say."

"Well..... I don't know. I just know I'm anxious to see him." Callie's heart rate accelerated as she thought of the moment she and Ben would meet each other again. She had been playing the scenario in her mind all during the long train rides. But it would still be weeks before it came to fruition.

"Do you know what we will be doing in Indianapolis?" Victoria decided to change the subject. "I hope it is a civilized city. We are in the North now, you know. I wonder how we will be treated. Do you think they will know we were Confederates?"

Callie looked at her in exasperation. "Victoria, all we have to do is open our mouths and speak and everyone will know we are southerners. We have that southern accent, don't you know? Haven't you ever spoken to a Yankee? They don't talk like we do."

"Yes, why of course, I've spoken to Yankees, but only when I've had too. I suppose you are right. We do have a more genteel, lilting way of speaking. They sound so harsh, clipped, and twangy. Not very pleasant to the ear, actually. They seem to be in a hurry to get out what they want to say, too. Always speaking so fast, it's hard to understand them. Really, I don't think Yankees are very refined."

"I'm sure there are Yankees who have good manners and etiquette just the same as us," Callie answered, staring out the window. "You probably just haven't met them yet."

"Hmmm.....we'll see. I'll be on the look out now that we are in 'Yankee-land.' It will give me something else to do. See anything interesting out that window, Callie? You seem pretty intent on looking out there."

"Well, the land has changed from being somewhat hilly to being flat. And, look at all the tall grass - prairie grass, Papa says. The land under it is supposed to be very black and rich. That's why the farmers here can grow corn, wheat, and other crops so well; where as our red soil is good for cotton and tobacco."

"My goodness, Callie, I didn't know you were such an expert on agriculture!"

"Well, Victoria, I've learned a lot these last several years when we were rebuilding Oak Hill. It's strange. I've always loved the land, but now I enjoy *working* the land. Besides, that's what this trip is about. We are supposed to be observing industries and farming to see how we can apply what we see back home."

"You mean this journey isn't for us to have fun, eat, shop, and see new things?"

Victoria tilted her head and looked down her nose at Callie, smiling sarcastically. Then she laughed loudly, as did Callie.

It wasn't long before Callie noticed the beginnings of the city of Indianapolis from her window seat. The train started slowing down as it approached the station. This station was different from the rest, though. The engine pulled under a huge brick train shed where there were many railroad lines meeting.

Like most small cities of the time, Indianapolis had the problem of each competing railroad line having its own station in different parts of the city. This left much confusion and inconvenience for the passengers. Sixteen years prior, the city solved its problem by connecting all the lines to one place, a union station. However, there were still safety issues as passengers had to cross tracks to get inside the station.

The Hills and Whitsons were almost frantic as they left the train car and stepped out onto all the railroad tracks in front of them, with trains arriving constantly.

"Hold my hand, Kathleen, and watch where you step. Callie, take Kathleen's hand and be careful also." Nathan was trying to navigate the tracks to the station.

"Nathan, this is awful! Don't let go!" Kathleen clutched her husband's hand tightly as they heard another engine enter the shed.

"Papa! My ears are hurting! There's too much noise!" Callie was grimacing but didn't dare let go of Kathleen's hand to cover her ears.

Finally, the families made it into safety. "Goodness, that was an adventure, wasn't it?" Caroline said as she brushed off the dust from her traveling skirt. "I think they need a better system of accommodating their passengers."

"Yes, but the idea of all the lines meeting in one place is marvelous," John echoed as he was looking around. "Quite ingenious."

"I agree, John. Something we need to take back with us and present to our board of directors. Come, let's get ourselves together and find a coach to the Concordia House." Nathan led the way as the weary travelers looked forward to a nice hot dinner and pillowy feather beds.

After a day of shopping and a visit to the city market, the families were once again on the train. Tomorrow evening they should be at their destination - Chicago, Illinois.

* * *

They had only been on the rails for over an hour when the passengers noticed a darkening in the skies. "Oh, no," thought Callie, "here comes another storm." But nothing happened - yet. They all had their eyes to the ominous looking clouds fearing the worst. Still no precipitation or storm. Eventually, they were all lulled into thinking maybe it was just an overcast day.

The train stopped at a small town where the travelers ate a quick lunch of vegetable soup, bacon and cabbage, and apple pie for seventy-five cents each. The food was satisfying and tasty.

When they boarded again, each person's eyes were focused on the gray skies above, which were even darker now. They also were aware of a dramatic drop in temperature.

"Papa, what do you think is going to happen? Is it going to storm or just rain?"

"I don't know, Callie," Nathan answered as he gazed at the threatening clouds. "I've heard weather on the prairie is unpredictable. We'll just hope we can get past these clouds before they decide to open up."

The train car hadn't gone much further before the skies did open up, but it wasn't rain. It was sleet - freezing rain. It first pelted the car with tiny pings and bounced off. Then it sounded like rain, but one could see the drops. The southern passengers were amazed by the ice drops.

"I've never seen anything like this," Kathleen said as she was looking out the window. "Look. Sometimes it looks like rain, but then you can see it bounce on the ground. It's not like snow, its little balls and drops of ice. Wonderous."

"It certainly is different, "added Caroline, "but I wonder what affect it will have on our traveling. Can we keep going in this, John?"

"I'm sure we can, dear. Just relax."

The train did proceed at its current pace for another half an hour or more and then began to slow down. The conductor came to the car.

"Ladies and gentleman, as you may have surmised, we are in the midst of an ice storm. The tracks ahead are coated with ice and will be quite hazardous. We are going to try to make it to our next stop, which is Danville, Illinois. After that will depend on the weather. But I don't see you making it to Chicago tonight. There are facilities in Danville that will accommodate you for tonight or how ever long we will be held up. Sorry, but we can't control the weather. It's one of those mid-March freak storms that sometimes happen on the prairie. We appreciate your patience."

"Well, isn't this something," said Caroline after the conductor left. "I hope this doesn't conflict with any of our bookings in Chicago."

"It will be all right, dear. Nathan and I will have the rail dispatcher telegraph ahead and tell our hotel what has happened. They probably will already know if this storm is there also. We'll manage. Just a little bump in the road."

The train gradually made its way into the Wabash Station in Danville. It was late in the afternoon, but it felt like late at night. As the passengers got off the train, they were met with another surprise. The temperature was hovering around the freezing mark and the wind was howling, making it even colder.

Callie took one step off the train and was buffeted by a gust of wind. The pellets of ice struck her hard in the face. "Ouch! This hurts!" She turned her face to avoid the pelting, but it was everywhere. Then she took several steps toward the station and nearly lost her footing. The decking was as slick as glass. It took all her balance to avoid falling.

Nathan finally came to her rescue, sliding towards her, and grabbing her arm. "Callie, stand still. Then take small steps, sliding a little. There, now you have it. I have to help Kathleen."

By sliding and taking baby steps, the group arrived safely within the walls of the station. By this time, they were giggling over their predicament.

"I'm sure glad we don't have ice storms at home," Callie told Victoria. "Isn't this awful?"

"I feel like I've been battered and blown," answered Victoria. "And, I'm freezing. Let's move over to the stove and get warmed up while we wait on a carriage."

They had to wait quite a while before a cab arrived. The horse didn't like being out in this weather either. The six squished into one cab and the horse gingerly picked his way to the Aetna Hotel on the corner of Vermilion and North Streets, where the families would be staying the night.

Once inside the hotel, the travelers felt more at ease. They looked around at the fairly new Aetna Hotel.

"Why, this is quite nice, John. It has a 'Parisian' feel to it. Really lovely." Caroline was eyeing every inch of the lobby.

"How would you know what 'Parisian' is, Caroline? We've never been to Paris."

"Well, I read and look at periodicals, dear, and believe me, this is 'Parisian.' I'm just surprised this modern look is out here in the middle of nowhere."

"Actually, Caroline, I think this city has been here for a while," said Nathan. "When I checked us in, the clerk told me the place is somewhat famous for its connection to President Lincoln."

"Really, well, that's interesting. I guess we *are* in his home state now. I wonder if there are still people here that knew him personally."

"Oh, I'm sure there are. It hasn't been that long ago. The clerk also told me that the grand opening here was the same night Lincoln was assassinated. When word reached Danville, everyone fell into mourning. He said the city was the last Illinois town Lincoln saw on his way to Washington, D.C. to be inaugurated."

"Nathan, dear, did he seem upset that we are from the South?" Kathleen looked at her husband, her forehead creased with concern.

"He didn't seem to be, Kathleen, but one never knows. We really should be careful now that we are in the North. I know there are still bad feelings. We want to keep a low profile and not antagonize anyone. I think it will be different in Chicago since it's such a big city, but we'd better be cautious in these smaller communities."

"I agree, Nathan," said John. "One doesn't want to stir up any unnecessary trouble."

"Really, Father, what kind of trouble could *we* get into? We aren't soldiers or politicians, just traveling families." Victoria looked at John with an exasperated look on her face.

"We just need to be cautious, Victoria, and go out of our way to be cordial and co-operative. That's all I meant. One just never knows. We are in unchartered territory now. We have no idea how these people react to former enemies. Just be careful."

The two families ended up spending two nights in Danville because the storm was affecting the rails to the north. They didn't stray too far from the hotel, eating most of their meals there. The second day, the ice was melting so they ventured out into the street. They ended up eating lunch at the McCormack House and learned this was where Lincoln stayed when he was in town. They were very polite, but the waiter seemed to cringe when he heard their southern accent. They didn't linger there very long.

It seemed everywhere they walked downtown they were reminded of President Lincoln. He had a law office in the Barnum Building across from the courthouse where he practiced law; he visited the Old Red Seminary for magic lantern shows; he attended church services at the Presbyterian Church; he told stories and bought writing supplies at Woodbury's Drug Store, where next door was Lincoln Hall, named for the President. A few blocks away he slept at Doctor and Mrs. William Fithian's house while campaigning for the Illinois Senate; he had Thanksgiving dinner with his friends, Oscar and Elizabeth

Harmon, at their little farm on East Main Street. They were amazed at all the references to the deceased President, who was felled by a Virginian's bullet. On the third day, they were more than ready to once again board the train and head north to their destination.

* * *

When the weary travelers finally arrived at the Tremont House in Chicago, there was mail waiting for both families. Nathan had a letter from Samuel and Callie was surprised to receive letters from Trudy and Ben. She stole away for some privacy and then ripped Ben's letter open, quickly scanned it, and then settled into a comfortable chair and read it leisurely.

"March 10, 1869

Dearest Callie,

I hope you have safely arrived in Chicago. We have had some strange weather this spring, so hope it didn't affect your travels.

I'm anxious to know how you like Illinois and Chicago. I've only been there once when I went with Pa to look at the latest farm equipment. It's too big for a farmer like me, I was ready to get back home, but hope you enjoy it.

I know you will write and tell me when you think you will be in Clayton Township. Callie, my family is very excited to meet you and your parents. Ma said you must stay with us at the house. There are no hotels near enough to accommodate you. Pa says you have to stay for at least one night and two days - longer if you like - in order to see everything. He's very excited about showing off our place to your father. Do you think you can stay here at least that long?

We love having visitors, so tell your parents not to fret about putting us out or anything. You are all very welcome to stay. In fact, Ma and Pa insist *you stay! So no arguing about that!*

We have lots planned to keep everyone busy. And, Ma is a really good cook, especially at baking pies. Emma is very anxious to meet you, too, as you both are about the same age, I think she's a year older than you.

I'm sure you will have lots to tell me about your journey when you arrive. Until then I remain..

Your 'Yankee' friend,
   Ben
   Postscript: Enclosed are directions to our farm from Bloomington."

Callie laid the letter down and smiled contentedly. Ben had called her "Dearest." He'd never done that before. Then she thought, "I will be staying in Ben's house! But what if Papa and Mama Kathleen won't do that? Oh, dear. What if they won't go there at all now? No, they will go. Papa wants to meet Ben. Oh, I don't think I can wait much longer to see him!" She flew out of her chair to find Kathleen and show her Ben's letter. Kathleen would make sure Nathan would stay. She surely would.

Nathan opened the thick envelope containing Samuel's letter and sat down to read it.

"March 8, 1869
Dear Father and family,
   If you are reading this, it means you are in Chicago safe and sound. We are all well at Oak Hill. Grandma is complaining of some aches and pains, as is Mammy Sallie, but otherwise, all healthy. We had several calves birthed and we should be getting a foal any day from one of the mares. No rain, weather has been comfortable, just a little cool. We miss all of you. It seems quiet around the house when Callie is not here.
   Father, several days after you left, we had a surprise, an unwelcome, visitor - Raymond Carswell - remember him? The carpetbagger we let spend the night? Well, it seems he didn't go to Atlanta as he originally planned, but is living at the Montgomery's. Apparently, old Elijah let him stay there and help out.
   He really never said what he wanted - 'Just being neighborly.' But he sure was looking around. I tried to keep him in one place, but he kept asking about this and that like he was really interested and wanted to use our ideas to help the Montgomerys. Don't worry, I was very careful and cut his visit as short as I could. Funny, he never asked where you were - like he knew you were gone. I will keep an extra eye on him and have told the same to our workers. Something about that man just isn't right.

Another interesting thing. A darkie named Caleb Jones arrived one day wanting to sharecrop. He had been living in Atlanta, working as a carpenter, but had come from a plantation by Jonesboro. He was very determined to pay me for his land so I gave him forty acres by the northwest field. He went and built himself a cabin right away and set to work on the land.

But he's been asking if I need any carpenter work done. Joseph said he needs help as he isn't getting any younger, so Caleb has been spending a lot of time around the house. I think part of that is due to Trudy. It seems the two have struck up a 'friendship.' Trudy seems very happy these days. I think she wrote to Callie, so maybe her letter will explain more.

Tell Callie Rumpel and Socks are fine. Socks spends most of his time with Trudy or lying on the front porch. Rumpel is content in the stables, but I take him out for walks every day.

I hope your journey has been enjoyable and also informational. I don't envy your travels, though, I'm very content here at home. Give my love to Kathleen and Callie, Uncle John, Aunt Caroline, and Victoria.

Your loving son,
Samuel"

Nathan put down the letter and sat thinking. What on earth did Carswell want? Samuel was probably right - something was not right about that man. There was nothing Nathan could do now, but when they got back, he was going to get to the bottom of this.

From the laughter and giggles coming from Callie, he assumed she was reading Trudy's letter. It always warmed his heart when he heard his daughter laugh. She had been through so much in her young life. He went over to where she and Kathleen were sitting.

"What are you ladies laughing about over here?"

"Oh, Papa, we are reading Trudy's letter. She is so funny. She's telling me all about a new sharecropper, Caleb Jones, and trying not to sound like she is friendly with him. I'm sure she doesn't want me teasing her about having a beau, like she does me, but it sure sounds like that's what he is. She even helped him with his cabin. Does that sound like my Trudy? Caleb Jones must be a fine man to win over Trudy. I can't wait to meet him. And, speaking of meeting someone......Papa, I got a letter from Ben, and his parents have invited us to spend the night or even more so we can see all of their farm, and he said it's not an imposition because they love having visitors, and his mother is a really good cook, and there aren't any hotels for us to stay in, and .....Papa, do you think we could stay there?" Callie looked down at her hands, waiting for Nathan's answer.

"Whoa, Callie. Did you say they want us all to stay in their home overnight? I thought we were just going to stay for a few hours so I could thank Ben for his heroism and then we'd leave. Isn't that what you thought, Kathleen?"

Callie didn't see her father wink at Kathleen or his eyes twinkle with mischief. Kathleen looked at Callie and saw the longing in her face and couldn't join in Nathan's teasing.

"Nathan, the poor girl is suffering, don't tease her! Of course, we'll stay, Callie. We wouldn't want to hurt the Chapman's feelings by not accepting their offer of hospitality. Besides, we came to look at northern farms, so what better way to see them than to stay on one. Isn't that right, Nathan?" Kathleen looked up at her husband with a look that said "be nice."

"I guess you're right, dear wife. It wouldn't be very cordial of us to turn down their invitation."

"You mean we can stay there, Papa? Truly? Oh, thank you, Papa, thank you!" Callie ran to Nathan and threw her arms around him. "Thank you so much!"

* * *

The weeks in Chicago couldn't go fast enough for Callie, but they did fly by. The families enjoyed touring the city and looking at all the sights.

One day they drove a carriage to a pier on Lake Michigan. Callie was awestruck at the vastness of the water.

"Papa, I've never seen so much water in one place! I can't even see land ahead. Look how the sun is shining on the surface! It must be magic!"

Nathan looked at his daughter's face. It was lit up in amazement as she gazed at the lake. "Callie, I forget, we've never taken you to Tybee Island to see the ocean, have we? Next time we are in Savannah we must do that. It's more impressive than this."

"Yes, Nathan, we must take her there. I can have a picnic lunch made up and we can all spend the day at the beach," Caroline said. "I'm surprised we've never done that before. I guess we always had something else to do."

"Well, if the ocean is better than this, I definitely want to see it. Can we go down and walk in the sand a little ways?"

"Go ahead, sweetie, enjoy yourself."

Callie and Victoria walked down to the shoreline, Callie picking up some sand as she went. She turned around and shouted, "Papa, do we have anything I could put this sand in? I want to take some back for Trudy."

They all rummaged through what was in the carriage and John came up with a box that had contained some chocolates. "I think this will work, Callie. Here."

"Thank you, Uncle John, it's perfect. Trudy won't believe me when I tell her about this lake's beach unless I have some evidence."

On other days the group enjoyed visiting the Academy of Science Museum, a new activity for all of them, and the Lincoln Park Zoological Gardens, another new experience. The women went to the acclaimed shop of Field & Leiter & Company, where they were amazed at the selection of new fashions and other items. Here Callie and Kathleen both purchased new gabardine skirts and lacy cotton petticoats. Around the corner was a brand new millinery shop where all four ladies purchased new bonnets in the latest styles.

They also enjoyed dining at the restaurants the city offered, from elegant ones to small cafes. They tasted some of the best beefsteak they'd ever eaten and even tried some new items such as codfish balls, broiled salmon, and fried lake trout, which were declared delicious.

John and Nathan spent a great deal of their time meeting with businessmen concerning the railroads and also observing new feats of construction. One thing that impressed both was the raising of the city that had occurred earlier to accommodate the brick sewer system. Some buildings were raised as much as ten feet.

Another novelty was the construction of an underground water tunnel from the shore to far out into the lake to eliminate sewage and one, still under construction, beneath the Chicago River for land traffic.

Both gentlemen thoroughly enjoyed going to the Chicago Board of Trade, learning much about the futures and options exchange for commodities. John, especially, was enthralled and determined to use this knowledge at the Cotton Exchange.

Soon the two weeks were gone and the travelers were once again boarding a train, this time to Bloomington, Illinois. They were on a brand new Pullman car, one which even sported a dining car. Their lunch was going to be served *on* the train, although Callie swore she wasn't going to be able to eat a mouthful. She was just too excited. In one more day, she would be seeing Ben.

* * *

"Can't this horse go any faster?" Callie said to no one in particular. She was perched on the edge of her seat in the carriage and in frustration leaned back against the soft leather. "I don't think we'll ever get there. Are you sure we're going the right way? Are we following Ben's directions?"

"Yes, sweetie, we're going the right way. It takes a while to go thirty miles, you know that. We'll be there in a couple hours. Just sit back and enjoy the ride. Look at all the ground around here - it's so flat. No wonder it's easier to farm here - they only have to plow up the prairie grass. No trees or rocks to hinder the plow. And, look at how black that soil is. Quite a contrast to our Georgia red." Nathan was gazing out the carriage window at the fertile fields before him.

"It is a different landscape isn't it, dear? I'm so glad we can see it closer than from the train windows. It even has a different smell - loamy and earthy, don't you think?"

"Yes, Kathleen, you're right. Even the smell is different. What do you think, Callie?"

"I think this horse is going slower. We may never get to Ben's!"

The driver pulled the horse over to a watering trough as they entered the town of El Paso. "Need to rest and water the horse for a few minutes. You can get a good meal over at that new restaurant in the meantime."

Callie looked at the driver stunned. "We aren't hungry! Let's keep going! That horse isn't tired, he hasn't gone far or fast enough. He's had a drink, now let's get back on the road."

"Sorry, Miss, but old Jimmy has to rest a bit and so do I. Do you good to stretch your legs and walk around too. Might as well eat - I'm gonna." And, at that the driver tended to the horse and walked toward the restaurant.

"Well.........I never.....Papa, do something! Make him come back!"

"No, Callie, he's right. Come on, let's see what's on the menu. We'll get to the Chapman's soon enough, don't worry."

"Hmmpphhh....." Callie trudged after Nathan and Kathleen into the small building where they had a quick meal. She ate as fast as she could, finishing before the others, and then walked back to the carriage and got in. She pouted there until the driver came with her parents and they started out again.

"Don't worry, Miss, we only got 'bout ten to twelve miles to go. Be there in a little over an hour."

"Can't you at least make him trot some of the time? Does he have to walk?"

"Jimmy ain't a young horse, Miss, got to go at his own speed."

"Oh, for goodness sake." Then Callie whispered to her father, "Papa, you should have found a faster horse to hire." Nathan laughed, making her all the more annoyed.

* * *

Ben Chapman had done his chores for the morning, ate lunch, did the midday tasks, and now was waiting. Surely, they would be here today. Callie had written they should be in Bloomington on the 27th or 28th and would be leaving the next morning to come to Clayton. He had waited all day yesterday for them to arrive, staying up late in case they may have had a late start. He thought maybe they had spent the night in El Paso or Panola and would arrive early, but they didn't. Now all he could do was watch the lane and see if they were coming.

"You gonna sit out here and do nothing until they come, son?" Abigail questioned her son, who was sitting tensely on the front porch. "Watching a pot doesn't make it boil."

"I know, Ma, but seems they should be getting here pretty soon. I hope nothing happened or they got lost or something."

Abigail shaded her eyes from the midday sun, shining brightly on this beautiful late March day. "Think I see something over yonder, Ben. Can you make it out?"

Ben squinted his eyes toward the east. A carriage! It had to be Callie!

"Ma! It has to be them! Hurry, go get Pa so he can clean up a bit before they get here. Tell Emma too! I'm going down the lane to meet them."

"Settle down, son. We aren't meetin' the King and Queen of England, are we? 'Cause if we are, I'd better put on my best dress." Abigail smiled at her son.

"Oh, Ma……….." Ben blushed. "I'm just excited, that's all."

"I know, Benjamin, she's important to you. Don't worry, everything will be fine. We'll just *pretend* they're the King and Queen of England!" Abigail laughed at her own joke. "Come on, no need to meet them out at the lane. Stay here with me. You don't want to appear too anxious, you know."

The Chapman family had convened on the front porch just as the hired carriage pulled up to the hitching post. The driver got down and opened the door. Out came Nathan Hill, who in turn helped his wife Kathleen and then Callie. Ben was watching, afraid to say anything.

Callie turned to face the people on the porch and smiled, but her eyes were on Ben only. Ben drew in a quick sharp breath. She was beautiful. No, she was exquisite. And, she was walking toward him.

Her face was almost glowing. Her pale complexion was flawless, her cheeks, heightened with excitement, were a rosy pink. Her blonde hair was tucked into a bun at the nape of her neck, but the curls had loosened during their travels, especially around her face. She wore a new blue bonnet perched forward above her eyebrows. Her lips were perfectly formed and were a dark pink; they were parted in a brilliant smile, showing even white teeth.

She was walking forward with a gliding motion. Her body was petite, lean, shapely. She was full busted with a tiny waist and rounded hips. She wore a dark blue traveling suit that showed off her womanly curves. But it was Callie's large eyes that tugged at Ben's soul. They were a deep, dusky brown with tiny flecks of gold, outlined with dark thick lashes and framed by perfectly arched brows. And, they were looking right at him.

He reached out for her hand to help her up the steps. Her hand was trembling with anticipation. He looked into those brown eyes, now brimming with expectation.

"Why, Miss Callie Hill, so we meet again."

"Yes, Mr. Benjamin Chapman, it seems so."

* * *

The minute Ben touched Callie's hand she relaxed. It was as if she had known him all her life. He held her hand firmly and didn't let go. She smiled at him thinking what a handsome man he was.

Ben Chapman was several inches taller than her and very muscular in build. Since their encounter at Oak Hill, Ben had matured into a very good looking young man. Light sable brown hair framed a smooth shaven face that now radiated happiness. He had small dark tan freckles sprinkled across a finely chiseled nose, under which were full sensuous lips. His eyes were a deep, teal blue, elliptical in shape, fringed with short brown lashes and heavy eyebrows.

Callie couldn't stop looking at him and smiling. Ben couldn't stop looking at her and smiling. And, neither wanted to let go of the other's hand. They stood there like that, holding hands for several minutes, neither one talking or even acknowledging that anyone else was there besides themselves. Finally, Nathan loudly cleared his throat.

"Callie, please come and meet Ben's parents and sister, our hosts for the evening." Callie slowly turned towards her father as if in a trance and then looked back at Ben.

"Callie, dear, remember your manners," Kathleen said somewhat impatiently.

"Benjamin, you too need to remember your manners," said Abigail.

Callie and Ben blinked as if to break the spell they were under. Ben dropped her hand, but put his palm in the small of her back and led her over to where their parents and Emma were.

"Yes, forgive me, Ma. Mr. Hill, I'm so pleased to finally meet you. Mrs. Hill, it's nice to see you again under better circumstances."

Callie was hoping against hope that he wouldn't remove his hand. It felt like it just fit there. He didn't.

"I'm so happy to meet you both, Mr. and Mrs. Chapman. I've heard so much about you, I feel like I already know you. And, Emma, I think we have so much in common. It will be wonderful to talk to you."

"Please, let's get you settled in your rooms so you can freshen up, then we can eat and visit. Emma, take Callie to your room. Callie, I hope you don't mind sharing with Emma." Abigail turned to Callie, still standing with Ben.

"Oh, no, not at all. It will give us a chance to get acquainted." Emma started to go to the door, but Callie didn't follow.

"Mr. and Mrs......"

"Please, Nathan and Kathleen, Mrs. Chapman," Kathleen interrupted.

"Only if you call us Henry and Abigail," Henry smiled.

"Done."

"Please, Nathan and Kathleen, you will have Ben's room. He will bunk with the hired hands tonight."

Nathan and Kathleen, led by Abigail and Emma started through the front door. Nathan stopped. "Callie, come on, let's freshen up and then you can talk to Ben. Come on, sweetie."

Callie was thinking, "I don't want to go, Papa, because then Ben will take his hand from my back and I like it there." But, instead she stepped forward towards her father. Ben led her through the door and then removed his hand as she went with Emma into her room. He looked lost, as did Callie.

While their guests were changing clothes and freshening up,

Abigail and Emma took charge in the kitchen producing the evening meal. Henry and Ben did their chores, returning in time to clean up and join the others. Abigail cooked a feast: fried chicken with milk gravy and mashed potatoes, canned green beans, buttered carrots from the cellar, creamed corn, pickled beets, head cheese, dill pickles, hard boiled eggs, just baked bread, and, for dessert, warm bread pudding with buttered whiskey sauce.

"Abigail, everything is just delicious," Kathleen complimented her hostess. "I'm curious about this....what did you call it.....head cheese? It doesn't seem like cheese at all."

"It's not, but that's what my German relatives call it. It's the head of the hog cooked, then the meat is shredded, vinegar and spices are added to the fat from the boiling, and then it sets until it's gelled."

"Well, I think it's very tasty. I'll have to have our cook, Belle, try to duplicate it. Don't you like it, Callie?"

"What? Oh, yes, everything is very good, but I'm sorry, I guess I'm just not that hungry." She looked at her plate and realized she hadn't eaten hardly anything. She had spent her time staring at Ben across the table.

"Why, Ben, you haven't eaten much tonight. You feelin' all right, son?" Abigail exchanged knowing glances with Kathleen, both of them aware of the reason for their children's lack of appetite.

"I'm fine, Ma. Just not that hungry. Guess I didn't work up an appetite today."

"Well, I'll put this left over chicken in the ice box on the back porch and if anyone gets hungry later, it's there for the eatin.'"

Nathan pushed back his chair a little from the table and looked in Ben's direction across the table. "I must say, Ben, how truly grateful I am to you. There is no way we can ever repay you for what you did for Callie at Oak Hill. God only knows what would have happened if you hadn't stayed behind that day. You are a hero in our family's eyes. You saved my baby girl and for that, I will be forever indebted to you. Henry and Abigail, thank you for raising a son who cares for others and doesn't go against his principles. The Lord put him at Oak Hill at the right time, but you put him on this earth. We are indebted to you also."

Ben looked back at Nathan. "Thank you for your kind words, sir. I'm sure glad I was at Oak Hill at the right time too." Ben turned to look at Callie, his eyes softening. "I'd be mighty unhappy now if anything had happened to Callie that day."

Callie felt Ben's eyes boring into her soul. She looked at him with such affection that Nathan was shocked. He started to say something, but Kathleen nudged his knee under the table. She gave him her "be still" look.

"Nathan," said Henry. "Let's go take a walk around the farm and let the women folk clean up in here. Would you like a shot of schnapps to take with us? Abigail's kin introduced it to me long ago. It helps settle the stomach after a big meal."

When the two men left, Kathleen said, "Abigail, why don't you and I clean up in here and let the young people go out on the porch and get acquainted? It seems to be a nice evening."

"Think that's a good idea, Kathleen. Ben, you take your sister and Callie outside. Try not to bore them."

"All right, Ma. Come on ladies. Let's not pass up a chance to get out of work."

The three young people walked back out to the front porch and settled in the chairs there. Ben moved his chair as close to Callie's as he could. Emma sat across from the two of them.

"It is a lovely evening isn't it?" Callie looked out across the flat prairie just starting to show patches of green.

"Pretty nice for late March. Sometimes we've had blizzards this time of the year," Emma said.

Ben was in a rocker and he rocked slowly, never taking his eyes off Callie. This did not go unnoticed by Emma. "Ben, you gonna say anything or are you just goin' to keep starin' at Callie?"

Ben looked at his sister, his face turning red in the early setting sun. "Just waitin' for a chance to get a word in with you two girls." He smiled, at Callie, not Emma.

Both of the young women laughed. "Well, now's your chance, brother." But then Ben just grinned, "Can't think of anything to say!"

Again they all chuckled.

Then all three started conversing about everything and anything that concerned people their ages: education, work, fashions, travel, socials………

Henry and Nathan arrived after their walk and went into the house where Abigail and Kathleen were visiting in the parlor. The night air grew cooler as the sun set, casting a faint pinkish glow on the land. The stars started poking out of the gray blue sky and a three-quarter moon became visible. Finally, Abigail stuck her head out the front door and said the adults were going to bed and she expected the young ones to follow.

Callie didn't want to leave Ben. She looked at him with her saddest expression. "Can't we stay just a few minutes more? It's so nice out here."

"Well, you two can stay, but I'm goin' to bed." Emma yawned and stretched her arms above her head. "Don't be long, Callie. Ma will come and get you and she can be pretty fierce, can't she, Ben?"

Ben laughed. "Ma's about as dangerous as a newborn kitten. She just *thinks* she's fierce."

"Just a few minutes more, then?" Callie pleaded.

"I'll catch her if she starts out here," Emma smiled. "I think you two need to talk." She left them alone on the porch in the darkness with only the moonlight and the stars.

Finally alone, the two didn't know what to say or do. Ben finally broke the silence. "I know this sounds ridiculous, but I've been waiting for this day so long that now I don't know what to say. I've planned a speech, but it doesn't seem important now. What is important is that you are here now, with me. Emma's right, if Ma finds we're alone, she'll come get us, so we better speak fast if we have anything important to say."

"Callie, there is one thing that's been bothering me that I'd like to straighten out. Is Daniel your beau back in Georgia?"

"Daniel? Daniel Moore? Why on earth would you ask me that?"

"Well, you wrote once that he spent some time at Oak Hill with you and I assumed….."

"Heavens, no! You know what that Daniel Moore did? I thought he *might* be my beau because we had such a good time in Savannah, but when he came to visit me he really changed. No one at Oak Hill would leave us alone, but one day we went to the stables. I guess everyone thought someone would be there, but William wasn't so we were by ourselves. The first thing Daniel did was to push me up against Rumpel's stall and try to kiss me on my lips! He didn't ask or anything. Just grabbed me. Well, I wasn't going to let him do that to me without my permission so….." Callie looked Ben straight in his eyes, which were now very close to hers, "I *slapped* him. Right across the mouth. He called me a name, a bad one I think, and left. I haven't heard from him since, but Victoria says he's courting Fanny Smythe."

Ben couldn't believe his good fortune. "Then he isn't your beau?"

Callie looked at Ben and cocked her head. "Didn't I just say I *slapped* him? No, he's not my beau!"

Ben decided to take a chance. "Do you have any beaus?"

Callie grinned a devilish grin and said in a saucy voice, "No, but I *might* have one in Illinois if he's willing."

Ben was taken aback, but just for a second. "Oh, I think he's more than willing, Miss Hill, more than willing." He gathered Callie's hands in his and stared into those deep brown eyes. "Miss Callie Hill, would you permit me to kiss you right now because I have a powerful urge to and I surely don't want to get smacked."

"Oh, Ben, you may kiss me any time you please. But if it's now, hurry before your mother comes."

Ben reached up and cradled her face with his hands, gently touching her face. He was memorizing every little part of that perfect face. Callie couldn't stand the intensity of his eyes on her, she shyly lowered hers. Ben tilted her chin up and softly brushed his lips against hers. She opened her eyes and smiled. She then eagerly pressed her mouth against his in a long sweet kiss.

"Benjamin Chapman!!" Abigail was opening the front door. Ben and Callie quickly broke their embrace and moved their chairs apart.

"Yes, Ma, what is it?"

"You get yourself down to Slim's cabin so Miss Callie can get to bed. I imagine she's plumb wore out from all her travelin'." Abigail walked out onto the porch. "Where's Emma?"

"In bed, Ma. Callie and I just wanted to spend a little more time out here. It's a grand night."

They heard Abigail mutter, "I'll deal with Emma tomorrow, she knows better." Then louder, "Well, tell Callie good-night, son, and scoot. Come on, Callie, I'll take you to Emma's room."

Callie had no choice but to leave with Abigail. She turned, "Good-night, Ben. See you in the morning."

"Good-night, Miss Hill. Sleep well."

Callie stepped into the house, but didn't feel the floor. She was so happy she was walking on air.

* * *

Callie was happy to see Ben early the next morning at the breakfast table. They looked at each other somewhat sheepishly, knowing their secret. It would be hard to find some time alone today as the Chapmans had a full day planned for their visitors.

Henry looked across the table at Nathan with his coffee cup in his hand. "Nathan, you really should stay another night. There's no way I can show you everything this morning. You can get up early tomorrow and Ben and I can drive you back to Bloomington."

Before she could stop herself, Callie blurted, "Papa! Please, let's stay another night!" She realized what she said was out of turn and looked down at the napkin in her lap, her face turning a lovely shade of red. She raised her eyes, fringed with the dark lashes. "I'm sorry. It's just that there is so much to see here. We *did* come to observe northern farm life, Papa, and what better way to experience it? You wouldn't want to have to rush to get it all in, would you? The Chapmans are very gracious to ask us to stay another day, don't you think?" Callie batted her lashes at her father keeping her face lowered.

"You make a good point, Callie. But you forget we left Uncle John and Aunt Caroline in Bloomington. They will be expecting us tonight."

"No, Nathan, they won't." Kathleen looked at her husband next to her. "I told Caroline we could be delayed a day or two and for them not to worry."

"Well then, Henry, it seems everything is taken care of, so if you don't mind, I guess you have us for another day."

"Wonderful! I've been wanting to demonstrate my new equipment and try it out myself. Let's finish up here and then head to the barns."

Callie exchanged glances with Kathleen and mouthed "thank you" to her step-mother. Kathleen just nodded her head knowingly and smiled.

Henry and Nathan finished eating Abigail's hearty breakfast and left. They went past the stables to the large barn where Henry kept his equipment. He had just purchased a new spring-tooth harrow for seedbed preparation. It was pulled behind a team of horses and loosened the soil before planting the crops. He also had a sulky cast iron plow made by John Deere that was used to break up the tough prairie grass in preparation for planting. It also was pulled by horses as the driver sat in a sulky. But, Henry's pride and joy was his two horse corn planter. The corn field was marked on a grid and the corn kernel was planted at each intersection. A knotted wire activated the seeding mechanism to drop the kernel into the ground.

Nathan was very impressed with the planter. "I wonder if this could be adapted to plant our cotton seeds. It would certainly make our planting easier and faster. Henry, could I borrow some paper and pencil to make a sketch? I know this is something John and I need to look into."

"Certainly, Nathan, but I can tell you who to contact. The inventor and manufacturer is George Brown from Aledo, Illinois. That's over on the west side of the state close to the Mississippi."

"Well, I wish I would have known that sooner. We could have changed our route to include it. I'll have to be satisfied with taking my own sketches and perhaps writing to Mr. Brown. Thank you so much for showing me this, Henry, it's been the most helpful item I've seen on our trip."

While the men were inspecting Henry's new equipment, Ben was completing his daily chores as fast as he could. He presented himself back at the house in record time.

"Why, Benjamin, that's the quickest I think you've ever finished your work," Abigail said as she cocked her head and smiled at her son. "Must be some reason for hurryin' so."

"Yes, Ma. I thought I'd take Callie for a buggy ride around the farm and maybe take a picnic lunch to eat down by the creek. There's still some chicken left over from last night, isn't there?"

"Well, now, Ben, I don't think it's quite proper for a man your age to be alone with a girl her age. Don't imagine her folks would appreciate that either."

"But, Ma.......we can take Emma along. Would that be 'proper' enough for you?"

"Don't get sassy with me, son. Yes, if your sister wants to go along, that would be fine. But she has to stay with you two all the time, not like she did last night scootin' off to bed and leavin' you and Miss Callie alone on the porch."

"Oh, Ma. You know nothing's goin' to happen. I'm a gentleman and Callie is certainly a lady. But, you know, Ma, I've got feelin's for her and she does for me too. I guess by us meetin' like we did and then writin' to each other all these years, we feel like we already know each other. Kind of sweet on her, Ma. You gotta admit, she's awful pretty too."

Abigail stood in front of her son, her arms akimbo on her hips. She frowned, then grinned, and then laughed. "I'm not blind, Benjamin, and I may be old, but not *that* old! Kathleen knows too. All right, you go have your picnic, but Emma's goin' along to make sure no mischief happens."

"Thanks, Ma! I'll go get things ready and then surprise Callie...........and Emma."

* * *

The azure sky was cloudless on this last day of March and the air was infused with the smell of rich soil, new grasses, and early wildflowers. Callie thought she was in a dream as the chestnut colored horse trotted along the dusty road. She was squeezed into the buggy with Ben in the center, driving, and she and Emma on either side. Emma said they would have to leave their hoops at home or they wouldn't fit in the buggy. She was right. But, oh, how wonderful it was to be so very close to Ben! It felt like their arms, hips, and legs were joined together. The heat radiated from one body to the other. She almost trembled from the experience.

Emma was chattering away about something along the way, but Callie wasn't paying attention. All her thoughts were focused on the body next to hers. When they arrived at the timber near the creek bank, she was disappointed to leave the buggy. Ben helped her out and held her hand as they walked down to the grassy area where Emma was laying an old quilt on the ground.

"This is one of our favorite places for a picnic," Emma was saying. "We come here often in mid spring. When we have a nice rain and then some hot days, we come to hunt morels. Ma says when the asparagus is up, so are the morels."

Emma finally had Callie's attention. "Morels? What are those?"

"You've never had morels? They're a spongy mushroom that we fry up in eggs and butter. Mmmmmm…..makes my mouth water just thinking about them. Won't be too much longer either. It's fun to find them too."

"Sounds interesting." Callie was distracted by Ben bringing the picnic basket over and then sitting beside her as he passed out the chicken. They sat that way until each person had their share of the chicken, licking their fingers when done.

"Now is a good time to relax, don't you think, ladies? Beautiful day, bright sunshine, cool breeze……….makes a man sleepy."

Callie playfully swatted Ben's arm. "Don't you dare go to sleep on me, Ben Chapman! I'm leaving tomorrow so we have to make every minute count. Why don't we go for a walk? That will wake you up. Come on, Emma."

"You two go ahead. Think I'll take Ben's advice and have myself a little nap." She stretched, yawned, and then grinned at her brother. "But as far as Ma knows, I never left your side."

"Bless you, little sister. Come on, Callie, let's explore the creek."

Callie didn't hesitate. She blew Emma an imaginary kiss for thanks, then grabbed Ben's offered hand and followed him along the bank. They went far enough away so as not to be heard by Emma and then found an old log to sit on.

"Callie, I just had to be alone with you again." Ben took both of her hands in his. "I…..I…..I'm sorry…..I don't know how to say this right. I don't want to scare you."

"Well, you're scaring me now, Ben. What's wrong?"

"Nothing is wrong. Oh…..I just want to say……I just want………."

Callie pulled his hands holding hers towards her, leaned towards him, and gently kissed his lips. Then she leaned back and smiled coquettishly. "Is that what you want?"

Ben was surprised and sat for a few seconds stunned. "No…I mean….yes….oh, Callie, I want nothing more than to just be with you." And, then he took her in his arms, holding her tightly. He whispered into her ear, "I don't want you to leave, ever." He pulled away, with his hands on her shoulders and looked deeply into those wonderful brown eyes, now glistening with tears. "Callie Hill, I think I'm in love with you and I don't know what to do about it."

"I do, Benjamin Chapman. Kiss me again, longer this time." Callie eagerly offered her lips. He couldn't refuse. Her lips molded to his as if they always belonged together. He pulled away once more, his face unsmiling.

"Callie, how do you feel? About me…I mean…"

Callie became very somber as she looked into Ben's hopeful teal eyes and measured her words carefully. "I think I have loved you from the moment you rescued me from that evil James Williams, Ben. You are my 'knight in shining armor.' After we started writing to each other, I knew we were destined to be together somehow."

Then Callie grinned. "But don't *ever* tell Trudy or Victoria. They have teased me forever of having you as a beau and I kept denying it because I never dreamed I'd ever see you again. I'm not dreaming now, am I? Because if I am, I don't want to ever wake up!"

"No, dear Callie. You're not dreaming. I'm right here." Ben embraced her once again. "And, you're right. Somehow we will be together……..somehow."

"BEN!! CALLIE!" Emma called from behind them. "I think it's

time to get back or we will all be in trouble."

"Coming, Emma! We'll be right there." Ben gave Callie another quick peck on her lips and helped her off the log. They walked back to the picnic area hand in hand, gazing at each other as they walked.

* * *

The rest of the afternoon flew by too fast for Callie. Ben had to do his afternoon chores so she and Emma sat on the front porch chatting. Abigail and Kathleen joined them before long and then the men returned from their touring. Henry had given Nathan demonstrations of his new harrow, plow, and planter. Nathan was obviously very excited by what he had witnessed.

"I tell you, Kathleen, it's too bad John isn't here to see these mechanisms work. They will surely cut down on the labor at our plantations. A machine can do the work several men do, isn't that right, Henry?"

"Yep, it sure makes things go a little faster. And, the sooner the plantin's done, the faster the corn grows and the sooner the harvest's done. Think inventors will eventually find ways to use only machines to farm."

"Really, Henry? That seems far into the future, though. Long after we're gone."

"Maybe not, Nathan. Seems lots of things were learned in the war that can be made into something good. Machines will be one, I think. Instead of usin' machines to kill one another, they can be used to help us."

"I hope you're right, Henry. We need something good to come out of the war."

Ben had arrived too. "I hope so too, Mr. Hill. But meeting your family, even the way I did, has been a good thing from the war for me." He looked over at Callie who was sitting in a rocking chair and smiled widely. Callie returned it with one of her own.

Nathan and everyone else there, could not help but fall silent at the intensity of the two young people's unabashed gaze of each other. Abigail broke the silence.

"Well, I think I'd better get supper started. Hope you folks like pork ribs, mashed potatoes, and sauerkraut. Kathleen and I picked some new dandelion greens this afternoon, so I'll wilt those. Got some canned apples to stew too."

Henry smiled at his wife. "Sounds like a good German supper tonight. One of my favorites. You folks are in for a real treat."

"Sounds delicious," answered Kathleen rising from her chair. "Just tell me how to help, Abigail."

"No help needed, but I'd enjoy some company in the kitchen."

When Kathleen left to follow Abigail, Ben sat in her vacated chair next to Callie. It was like there was no one else around as the two quietly talked and frequently laughed. Everyone else thought it best to ignore them and carried on their own conversations.

After the evening meal, which the Hills pronounced better than anything they had eaten on the trip, the families moved to the front parlor since the night had turned too chilly to be outside. Even though they had just met yesterday, they talked and chuckled as if they had known each other for years. It was surprising to them they had so much in common while living so far apart. It wasn't North against South, but farmer with farmer, woman with woman, and family with family. The Hills and the Chapmans were thoroughly enjoying each other's company.

Finally, it was time for the evening chores and then off to bed. The Hills were leaving early the next morning. Henry and Ben were driving them in the Chapman's carriage back to Bloomington.

Ben left to do the chores, but told Callie to wait for him, as he would return when he was done. She told her parents she wanted to stay up a little longer to tell Ben good-night. Nathan wasn't too happy, but Kathleen told him she would stay with her.

As they sat waiting for Ben, Kathleen took Callie's hand and squeezed it. "You really like Ben, don't you Callie?"

"Oh, Mama Kathleen, I think it's more than 'liking' him, I love him! I want to be with him all the time. I feel empty when he's out of my sight. But what am I to do? We're leaving tomorrow and I may never see him again!" Tears started gathering in the corners of Callie's brown eyes and gently ran down her cheeks.

Kathleen brushed the tears away with her fingers. "Callie, dear, please don't be too upset. In matters of the heart, things have a way of working out. You and Ben can correspond again. And, who knows, maybe he can journey to Oak Hill. The rails will continue to improve and travel will be easier. If it's truly love, you both will find a way to be together. Also, remember you are still only fifteen...."

"Almost sixteen."

"Yes, almost sixteen, which is still very young and he is much older....."

"Only eight years."

"Yes, but still eight years is quite a bit........"

"Papa's older than you by more than that."

"Yes, I guess you're right. I'm just saying.......maybe time apart could be a good thing. Then you both will know if you're really meant to be together."

"Oh, we're meant to be together, Mama Kathleen. He saved my life and now he has my heart. We know it. We both know it. We *will* be together.......somehow."

Kathleen embraced Callie and whispered in her ear. "I just don't want that heart to ever be broken."

"It won't. Not by Ben. I know that."

Kathleen sat back and looked at her with a slight smile on her face. "You've always been stubborn and usually get what you want, Callie, so I believe maybe you and Ben will be together some day. And, if you promise me you will behave, I'll leave you two alone when he comes back. I can sit in the kitchen for a little while, but not too long or your father will worry."

"Mama Kathleen, I love you so much! Thank you! You know I will behave."

They heard the front door open and Ben came into the parlor again. Kathleen stood up and smoothed her skirt. "Excuse me, but I have something to do before I retire for the night. Take good care of our girl, Benjamin." Kathleen looked sternly at Ben and started for the door.

"Don't you worry none, Mrs. Hill. Callie is very precious to me too." Ben walked over to the settee where Callie was sitting. "Would you like some company?"

"Of course." Callie noticed Ben had something in his hand. "What do you have there?"

"Just a little something for a person I'm particularily fond of."

"Hmmmmm......I wonder who that is? Oh, quit teasing me, Ben, I know it's for me!"

"Ha! What if I told you it was for Emma?"

"Then I'd be very disappointed." Callie made a sad sad face.

"All right, here. Yes, it is for you and I hope you like it. I was going to send it to you for your birthday, but since you are here and your birthday is only weeks away, I thought you might like to have it early."

He handed Callie a small box wrapped in a piece of muslin. She tried not to open it too fast, but couldn't help herself. She ripped off the muslin and then opened a beautiful navy blue velvet box. Inside was a small oval gold locket, engraved with tiny flowers and vines. She carefully picked it up out of the box and held it in her hand.

"Oh my goodness, Ben, this is so beautiful!"

"Open it up."

Callie carefully pried open the locket with her fingernail. Inside was a miniature daguerreotype of Ben. "Oh, my, how wonderful! Now I can always have you close to my heart."

"That's exactly what I thought when I had the picture taken in Peoria after I saw the locket. You like it then?"

"I love it, Ben. Thank you so much. I will wear it every day."

"I didn't get a chain, but the clerk said ladies have been wearing them with ribbons."

"That's perfect, because I bought some new ribbons on our trip." Callie looked shyly at Ben. "I have something for you too that I had made in Chicago, but it's in Emma's room. I was going to give it to you tomorrow, but I'll go and get it now."

She stood up and walked quietly out of the room. Ben felt lonely already without her next to him. She reappeared with a small dark green silk pouch closed with a black cord drawstring, which she handed to Ben. "I hope you like it."

Ben opened the drawstring and felt inside the pouch. He pulled out a round, gold pocket watch etched with scrolls. Attached to it was a braided ash blonde fob. He stared at it for several seconds.

"Callie, is this your hair?" He was holding up the watch fob.

"Yes, I had some cut from the back - you can't even tell - and the jeweler made it into a fob. Then I saw the watch and just knew it was for you, so I bought both. Do you like them?"

"Do I like them? They're wonderful! But the watch must have been expensive." Ben frowned at the thought.

"Papa said it is worth every penny because you saved my life, and he's right, Ben. I wouldn't be here with you now if you hadn't saved me. The watch is just a small token of my appreciation, but the fob is from my heart. I hope you will think of me when you use it."

"Callie.....Callie........I am already missing you so."

"Well, we will have these mementoes to remember each other." Callie sighed. "But it's not as good as really being together, is it? I miss you already too."

Then the two found themselves in each others arms and finally, in a desperate kiss. The tears flowed silently down Callie's cheeks until Ben tasted their saltiness. The embrace was broken and they spent the next minutes in silence until they heard Kathleen walking toward the parlor.

She cleared her throat and stood outside the doorway. "Callie, I think it's time you come to bed now."

"Yes, Mama Kathleen," Callie said in a small voice. "I'll be right there." She caressed Ben's jaw line once more and stood up. "Thank you for the lovely locket and picture, Ben." Then she whispered softly, "I love you."

Ben stroked her arm as he stood up beside her. "I love you too, Callie Hill. I will remember you every day until we are together again."

"Good-night, Ben."

"Good-night, Callie."

* * *

The ride back to Bloomington in the morning was a heartbreaking one for Callie and Ben. They knew they needed to savor these last few hours together, but yet dreaded the time when they would part.

Henry was driving with Nathan at his side, talking farming all the way. Kathleen sat in the carriage with Callie and Ben, trying to keep their spirits raised. She spoke of how efficient the railroads were becoming and how much faster a trip would be in the future. She told them the mail was also speeding up because of the rails carrying it. But still they looked at her with long, unhappy faces.

Kathleen overlooked their holding hands and gazing at each other. She finally gave up on trying to converse with them and the interior of the carriage fell silent.

Abigail had packed a basket of snacks so midway into the trip, Henry pulled over at a grassy shaded spot where he rested the horses and the passengers stretched their legs. Callie and Ben separated themselves from the others where they could confide in each other privately.

"I will write to you every day, Callie, and save my money for a trip to Oak Hill."

"I'll write every day too, Ben. Papa seems so fascinated with your farm that maybe we will come back again soon."

"Don't worry, we will see each other again. I will make it happen." Ben hesitated and looked directly into Callie's eyes. "There is one thing that worries me, though."

"What could that be?"

"There isn't any chance that you will see Daniel again is there? Or find another beau?"

"Benjamin! Of course not! My heart belongs to you now. No one else can take it from you, I promise. I can ask the same of you. Is there anyone else that you could give your heart?"

"No, no one. Why do you think I'm not already spoken for? Most men my age are married with children, but I've waited for you. I knew you were the one for me."

"We were meant for each other, Ben, right from the start. You're right. We will make it happen. I know we will be together.........and soon."

"Let's get back in the carriage and get going," Henry announced. "We need to be on our way so Ben and I get back before dark."

The rest of the journey was bittersweet for the passengers inside the carriage. Even Kathleen was morose for the two young lovers. She understood completely what it was like to be apart from the one you loved.

Before long the travelers arrived at the outskirts of Bloomington. Callie's stomach churned at the finality of saying good-bye to Ben. She grasped his hand in urgency. By the time they pulled up to the hotel door, she was almost sick. But she took some deep breaths and looked at Ben intensely, memorizing every feature of his face. He was doing the same to her.

As the Hills were getting out of the carriage, the hotel door opened and the Whitsons came out. They were on their way to a late lunch. Greetings and introductions were made with Victoria smirking at Callie and Ben. Callie ignored her for the time being. She was too upset at telling Ben good-bye.

Finally, after some small talk, it was time for the Chapman men to depart. Kathleen and Nathan said their farewells with profuse thanks for the last two days of hospitality and extended the same to Henry and his family. Callie and Ben stood slightly apart watching the others walk away.

"Come on, Ben. We've got to hightail it back home before your ma gets to missin' us." Henry climbed back up to the driver's seat and gathered the reins of the horses.

"Well, Callie, I guess this is it. It's not good-bye, but until we meet again." Ben held her hand in his and raised it to his lips, brushing the back of it.

Callie threw all caution away and threw herself into Ben's arms, wrapping hers around his neck and kissing him passionately on his lips. Even though Ben was caught off guard, he responded ardently.

"CALLISTA HILL!!!" Nathan bellowed at Callie. Kathleen jerked his arm as he started towards the couple. He turned and glared at her.

"Leave them be, Nathan, leave them be." The look in Kathleen's eyes stopped him in his tracks.

Henry turned around from the carriage to see what the commotion was and saw his son kissing Callie. "BENJAMIN!!"

Ben and Callie finally realized they were the center of attention of their families and also other people who were walking on the street. They broke their embrace. Both of their faces were wet with tears.

"I have to go, Callie. I love you."

"I love you too, Ben."

Ben ran and jumped up on the seat beside his father who was scowling at him. "Not now, Pa. Let's just go."

The carriage pulled away. Callie hopelessly watched it travel farther and farther away from her, tears streaming down her face. She didn't care that everyone was staring at her. She finally turned to Kathleen with such a look of loss that Kathleen gathered her into her arms and led her into the hotel. Over her shoulder she said, "I'll take care of her. The rest of you do something else instead of gawking at her."

As the two women went through the door, even Caroline was at a loss for words. John looked at Nathan, "What on earth happened on that farm, Nathan?"

Nathan looked at him with a blank expression on his face. "I don't know. We really enjoyed ourselves, and I learned so many things. I guess I was oblivious as to what was going on between Callie and Ben."

"Well, something surely is," said Caroline. Turning to Victoria she asked, "Do you know anything about this?"

"I know she really wanted to see him. She kept saying he was just a friend, not a beau, but it looks like it's a lot more than that doesn't it?"

"I would say so. Well, Nathan, guess we're going to have a lovesick girl on our hands for a while. Come on Victoria, John, let's get something to eat. Nathan, I think you'd better tend to your girl."

"I think you're right, Caroline. Excuse me, please. We'll see you later at dinner. John, I have so many things to discuss with you."

* * *

Callie later would remember very little about the trip back to Oak

Hill until they arrived at Nashville, Tennessee. She knew they stopped in Springfield where they walked by Abraham Lincoln's home. She remembered viewing the Mississippi River in St. Louis, but Cape Girardeau, Missouri was a blur.

In Nashville, Nathan took them all to the battlefield where he had fought the Federals. He even showed them the spot where he lost his great horse, Chester.

Nathan stood on the field gazing out at the area. A lost look filled his eyes. Kathleen was standing with him, as was Callie and the Whitsons.

"So many died here, so many….and now I often wonder why……. What did we accomplish? And, look at what we all lost………… Especially our families…. Young Andrew gone………Joshua crippled…..Samuel tormented….was it worth it all?"

No one answered Nathan's questions. They stood there in silence mourning those who had sacrificed their lives for the Cause. But it was here, on the battlefield, that Callie finally regained her senses. Yes, she had to say good-bye to Ben, but he was still alive. They had a chance at a future. Not like those who perished on this field leaving loved ones behind, like the Whitsons, who would never see that person again.

She shook her head as if to clear out the sad thoughts. Kathleen saw her. "Are you all right, Callie?"

"Yes, Mama Kathleen. I'm fine. I'm sorry I have been such a burden lately. I'll be better now."

Kathleen smiled. "You know you will see Ben again, don't you?"

"Yes. Yes, I do. We have our future ahead of us and I can't wait to see it."

* * *

The train pulled into the station at Chattanooga just as the sun was setting in the west. The families got off to view an amazing sunset framed against the Appalachian Mountains, now speckled with blooming dogwoods. They hired a transport to take them to the Cruchfield House where they would be staying the next two nights. As they registered, there was another letter from Samuel waiting for

Nathan:

"Dear Father and family,

We are all well. Grandma is recuperating from a bout with the ague. Lenora and Mammy Sallie are taking good care of her.

The plantation is running well. I have help with William and Caleb. Malindy and Trudy are taking care of the garden.

The reason I am writing again before you arrive home, Father, is to warn you that we have had several more visits from Raymond Carswell. I want you to be especially careful when you pass the Montgomery place because that is where he is living. He's not happy with me and I don't want you to be unaware of a possible confrontation with him. I don't want to scare you, because nothing will probably happen, but I want you to be aware of the situation.

He keeps offering me money for the land adjoining Elijah's and I keep telling him it's not for sale. He exploded the last time saying he knew I sold land to a 'no 'count darkie from Atlanta' (Caleb) and insisted I sell land to him. I explained Caleb is sharecropping, not out right owning the land. Carswell isn't interested in sharecropping, he wants to buy it. Also, I told him I will not make any transactions like that without your presence and that he would just have to wait. He stormed off that day and then came back the next week all nice and pleasant. He apologized for his behavior and said he would wait until you returned. But all the time he was here he kept tactfully asking questions that referred to our finances. And, I have a hard time keeping him corralled in one place. He wanders around like he's looking for something hidden. He also always inquires about Callie, which bothers me the most. He's a very strange man, Father, and I don't trust him as far as I could throw him.

We can discuss this more once you are home, but, as I said, I want you to be aware of what's happening and take extra precautions.

We have all enjoyed your letters from your travels. It sounds like your trip has been most productive. I'm sure Callie will have a different perspective than you do, so we are anxious to hear from her too.

We have missed all of you and hope you will enjoy the rest of your

journey and arrive home safely in a few weeks.
  Your loving son,
  Samuel
  March 22, 1869"
Nathan handed the letter to Kathleen, but not Callie. "What do you make of this?"

Kathleen quickly perused the pages. "I knew that man was trouble the minute you let him in our house. I'm surprised he hasn't already caused some ruckus with us not being there. Evidently, Samuel is handling him well. I guess we will just have to see what happens. You'd better tell John and Caroline so they won't be caught unawares if something does happen near the Montgomery place on our way home." Kathleen handed Nathan the letter back.

"Yes, you're right. It always seems to be something, doesn't it?" Nathan sighed heavily.

"That's life, dear. That's life."

* * *

As the tired travelers crossed the border into Georgia, they were all very anxious to finally return home. It had been a wonderful journey, but they were all ready to get back to their normal lives. All, except Callie. She dreamed of being with Ben; however, she had to admit, she too, was eager to return to Oak Hill. She had so much to tell Trudy, she didn't know where she would begin.

As the train pulled into Atlanta, the families once again looked forward to staying at the opulent Old Orchard Inn. The Hills slept well that night in the soft feather beds, knowing tomorrow night they would be in their own beds.

Very early the next morning, they boarded the train to Macon and then Swainsboro for the final leg of their journey. Callie didn't even mind the awful seats on the car to Swainsboro. The closer they got to Oak Hill, the more anxious she became.

Victoria was seated next to her this time. "Well, Callie, I think we had a wonderful, wonderful trip, don't you?"

"Yes, Victoria. It certainly has been grand."

"You haven't said much about Ben Chapman, Callie." Victoria

raised her eyebrows quizzically and looked at Callie with a wry grin.

"Well, I'd like to keep that private, Victoria. It's between me and Ben."

"Oh, come on. What really happened at Ben's farm? I can keep a secret!"

"No, I'd rather keep it to myself."

"You certainly kept that good-bye kiss to yourself! Everyone on the street saw you fling yourself at him and kiss him. It was quite a spectacle, Callie!"

Callie started blushing at the thought of that kiss. "Yes, I guess I did. It was just really hard to leave him. I didn't think of everyone else there, just that we were going to be apart."

"Don't tell me that he isn't your beau *now*! And, he's much more than just a friend."

"That's true. He is my beau, but he's still my friend. He's very special to me, Victoria, very special."

"The way he kissed you back, I guess he thinks you're pretty special too."

"Yes, yes he does."

"So are you going to get married?"

Callie turned and looked at Victoria. "We haven't discussed that. I'm only going to be sixteen. Besides, I don't think that's any of *your* business!"

"Well!" Victoria turned away from Callie and spent the rest of the trip looking out the window.

* * *

Later that evening the travelers left the train at Swainsboro and climbed into their awaiting carriages for the trip to Oak Hill. The four adults were very apprehensive as they would be driving past the Montgomery plantation in the dark of night. Callie and Victoria were each traveling with their parents, as Victoria was still in a huff about Callie's reluctance to share the details of the days in Clayton Township with her.

Nathan and John were on the edge of their seats, trying to peer into the dark, starless night for any sign of an aggressor. The drivers also rode with their pistols cocked and rifles loaded beside them. As they neared the Montgomery farm, the tension was thick. But they passed by with no sign of trouble.

Finally, the live oak trees with the Spanish moss swaying in the slight breeze came into view.

"Callie, wake up, baby girl! We're home!"

Callie opened her sleep heavy eyes and saw the tall, strong oaks. "Oh, Papa, it feels good to be home again!"

The two carriages and the wagons loaded with trunks and boxes turned down the long lane with their passengers glimpsing the large white manor at its end. The families were startled to see the house ablaze with light at this time of the night and especially surprised to see Beulah, Samuel, Mammy Sallie, and Trudy on the front veranda to greet them.

What a reunion they had! The travelers were so happy to have taken their long journey, but also so elated to return to their home.

* * *

Raymond Carswell was in the thicket near the road, concealed in the darkness. He saw the carriages and wagons go by. He saw the silhouettes of the drivers with guns in their hands. He saw the outlines of Nathan and John peering anxiously out of the carriage windows. He had no intentions of doing anything..........yet. He obviously was outnumbered and would be stupid to attack the families now. He wasn't a violent man anyway. He would get what he wanted. He wanted Oak Hill......and Callie Hill ....and he knew how he would get both. He was a patient man.

CHAPTER 5
1870

"No! You will NOT jump the broom, Trudy Hill! You will have a proper wedding. I won't hear another word about it. You are my best friend, almost my sister, and I will not have you get married by jumping over any broom. We will get a minister here and you and Caleb will be married at Oak Hill. Your mama will make you a beautiful wedding dress and I will be your bridesmaid and that's that."

"But, Miz Callie, Caleb wants to gits married at his cabin, our new home, an' he wants to jumps the broom. That's the way alls us fo'ks gits married."

"Not any more, Trudy. You are no longer a slave, you're free. And, since you're free, you have to be married in a proper, legal way. Besides, it's your wedding, not Caleb's. Everyone knows you do what the bride wants, not the groom!"

Callie thought for a minute and then sighed. "Well, if he *insists*, maybe you can do both. We can have the ceremony with the minister and at the end you can jump over a broom, if that will make him happy. But the wedding will take place here on the grounds and *not* at his cabin. This is your home; this is where you will get married. He has no choice on that matter, Trudy."

"Maybes you better tells him that, Miz Callie, 'cause he pritty strong 'bout jumpin' the broom at his cabin. He don' want no big show an' lots o' people."

"I *will* tell him that and it won't be a 'big show.' Just your family here at Oak Hill. Now, that's settled. Let's go find Dinah and figure out a dress for you and me and then find Mama Kathleen to find the perfect spot for the wedding.............." Callie grabbed Trudy's hand and off they went to plan Trudy's wedding.

* * *

It was almost a year since Callie returned from her long journey north. It didn't take her long to re-acclimate herself to life at Oak Hill, but she missed Ben desperately. They both kept their word - they wrote to each other every day, sometimes more. They poured out their love to one another on paper, along with what was happening in their lives.

Ben wrote he was sure he could save enough money for a trip to Oak Hill this year after the fall harvest. Nathan helped his cause by acquiring free passes from his railroad for those legs of his journey. Now all the young lovers had to do was wait.

* * *

Trudy and Caleb had informed the Hills of their wish to marry soon after they returned from the North, but Caleb wanted to wait until the following year to make sure he could support Trudy with the money from his share of the harvest. He worked very hard, with Trudy's help, to plow, plant, cultivate, and finally harvest his first cotton, corn, and wheat crops.

Nathan had "loaned" him a milking cow, a mule, some chickens, and several sows. Caleb vowed to pay him back once his livestock started reproducing. Nathan marveled at what a hard worker Caleb was. He tended to his own crops and livestock and then came and worked for him and Samuel, for which they paid him very little. Caleb never complained. He wasn't afraid of hard work to get the kind of life he wanted for himself and Trudy.

Finally, after last fall's harvest, he had some money in his pocket even after paying Nathan for his share of the crops and some of the livestock. Caleb felt it was time to marry the woman he loved and start a family of his own. However, Trudy didn't want to get married in the fall or winter. She was set on a spring wedding as was the custom of most southerners. That suited Caleb fine if it was before the planting began and if they jumped the broom at his, soon to be their, cabin. He liked the Hills fine, and they were more than fair to him, but he didn't want them involved in this union other than being guests. He hadn't counted on Callie's reaction to the site of the marriage and the ceremony.

"Miz Callie says I's part of the family, Caleb, an' I's needs to gits married at Oak Hill 'cause it my home. An', that's all the truf. She says we needs a proper preacher so it's alls legal an' then we can still jumps the broom after the preacher done. She says we needs to do that 'cause we's be free now, not slaves no longer. That's the truf too, Caleb."

Trudy was sitting next to Caleb on the front steps to his cabin, casually stroking his arm as she talked. "Thinks she right, Caleb, I's d'serves a real weddin' jes' like other free fo'ks. Won' be nuttin' fancy. Jes' us an' my family at Oak Hill. Then Miz Callie says we's has Belle fix up sumpin' to eat an' that's it." She looked up at him with her dark eyes and smiled.

Caleb frowned. He didn't think he could fight both Trudy *and* Callie, but he really didn't want a big celebration, especially with white folks.

"I's don' knows, Trudy. Seems like Miz Callie makin' it her weddin' 'stead o' ours. You really wants a preacher an' gits married at the big house?"

"Lawd! Miz Callie already plan her weddin' to Mista Ben an' it ain't nuttin' like mine! No, sireee. Caleb, I's really wants a proper weddin'. I's really do. Guess me an' Miz Callie played weddin' when we was li'l an' now we's goin' gits to do it for real." She flashed that brilliant smile that Caleb loved.

"Well, then, guess we's do it your way. Weddin' at the big house wit the white fo'k. But only 'cause I's loves you so much, Miz Trudy Hill. Only 'cause I's loves you."

"I's knows, Caleb, 'cause I's loves you too. Cain't hardly wait no longer to be your wife." Trudy lifted her face up to Caleb's and kissed him lightly on the lips.

He wrapped his arms around her, hugging her tightly. "I's cain't hardly wait neither."

* * *

It was a perfect day for a wedding. The early spring flowers were standing tall in the slight breeze and the new green grass lent a fresh smell to the air. The sky was clear except for a few white billowy clouds casting their shadows on the festivities at Oak Hill.

"Trudy, turn around now so I can get a good look at you." Trudy obediently turned to face Callie where she was scrutinized from the top of her head to the tip of her toes.

Callie sighed loudly. "Well, Trudy, I have to say. You are a beautiful, beautiful bride. Your mama did a wonderful job on that dress. It is sooooo pretty and you look like a princess in it. Wait until Caleb sees you walking out onto the porch. His eyes will pop right out of his head!"

Trudy giggled. "You thinks so, Miz Callie? He been so nervous 'bout this weddin'. Hope he shows up."

"He's already here, Trudy, no need to worry about that. Samuel and Papa have him in the back parlor making sure he looks fine too. Papa gave him one of his old suits to wear, so maybe *your* eyes will pop out when you see him."

Trudy giggled again. "You looks mighty pritty too, Miz Callie. Shore am glad you's my bridesmaid. Needs you there when I's takes my vows to Caleb."

Callie did a twirl in her new dress. "Thank you, Miss Trudy. I'm glad I'm your bridesmaid too." Then Callie turned serious. She took Trudy's hands in hers and looked her right in the eyes.

"Trudy, just because you're marrying Caleb doesn't mean you won't still be an important part of my life, does it? Because if it does, I won't let you out of this room! We'll still love each other and see each other all the time, won't we? Won't we, Trudy?"

"Of course, Miz Callie. You ain't gittin' rid of ole Trudy that fas'. I's still loves you an' sees you, jes' like before. Only won' be sleepin' in your room wits you no more. Be sleepin' wit my husband!"

"I will miss you at night, Trudy, but I know you will be so happy with Caleb. Soooo, let's get you ready to walk down the stairs and out to the porch so we can get you married!"

Callie and Trudy gave each other one last long hug and then proceeded to the front veranda where the ceremony would be held. When they arrived at the bottom of the stairs, Mammy Sallie met them with two bouquets of daffodils and a single rose for their hair. Nathan was also there to escort Trudy out to the veranda where Caleb was waiting for her.

At the front door, Callie turned back to Trudy, "Don't forget to smile!" Then she opened the door leading the small procession. The guests were already seated in chairs and when Callie opened the door, they all stood in anticipation of the bride. Callie smiled at Samuel, Kathleen, Beulah, Mammy Sallie, Dinah, William, Malindy, Belle, Lenora, and Joseph as she walked towards the minister standing next to Caleb. She went and took her place opposite Caleb.

Trudy took Nathan's arm and together they walked towards the minister. Trudy was not only smiling, she was beaming. Caleb's eyes did indeed almost pop out of his head when he saw his bride. Callie chuckled to herself at his reaction.

The ceremony was short, but beautiful. After the minister pronounced them husband and wife, Trudy and Caleb gleefully jumped over a broom laid down by Dinah. A table on the front lawn was loaded with Belle's goodies, including a two tiered wedding cake. It was a perfect wedding for Trudy and Caleb who slyly snuck away to their cabin to be alone in their happiness.

Callie saw them leave and thought to herself, "Soon that will be me and Ben, I hope. They are so happy and we will be too. I just know it." She sighed contentedly and then helped Kathleen and Dinah clean up.

When Callie went to bed that night, she felt so alone. She missed Trudy. She thought she was old enough now to sleep by herself, but she missed her friend, who had slept with her since she was four years old. Socks was snoring lightly on the floor next to her. She got out of bed and picked up the sleeping dog and placed him in the bed. He woke up and looked at his mistress skeptically.

"Tonight you get to sleep in the bed with me, Socks, just like you used to do when you were a puppy. If that mean old James Williams hadn't knocked you on the head, you'd still be able to jump up here. But tonight I'm missing Trudy and you'll just have to do."

Callie got back into the bed and lay down. Socks snuggled up next to her stomach like he used to and let out a long sigh. Callie smiled. She wrapped her arms around her dog and went to sleep.

* * *

"Come on, Daisy. Let's go see how the newlyweds are doing."

Callie mounted her horse at the stables and started trotting toward the lane. It had been a little more than a week since Trudy and Caleb's wedding. Callie had seen Trudy since then, but hadn't seen their cabin. Trudy and Dinah had been hard at work putting a woman's touch to the small home.

The Jones's cabin wasn't too far from Oak Hill, just a nice ride for Callie on a beautiful early April day. She felt the spring sun warm her shoulders as she slowed Daisy to a walk. The air was sweet and she inhaled deeply. She was daydreaming of Ben doing exactly the same thing right now and therefore, didn't notice she was not alone on the road.

Raymond Carswell was a short distance behind her, plodding along on his old nag. He had seen her leave the entrance to Oak Hill and although he wasn't going her direction, he changed his plan and decided to follow her.

He was close enough to see her slender figure on the side saddle swaying in perfect harmony with the motion of her horse. She looked very graceful and confident on her mount. Much more than he did.

Raymond wondered where she was going all alone. Probably not too far. He'd just follow her for a ways and see what she was up to. Maybe, if he had a chance, he would catch up with her and have a neighborly chat. No harm in that. In fact, that is exactly what he would do. He spurred his horse in the sides and urged him forward.

Callie finally woke from her daydream and heard the horse behind her. She looked over her shoulder to see who it was and was suddenly frightened when she recognized Carswell. She froze for a second not knowing what to do - flee or speak to him politely. Carswell decided for her as he was approaching rapidly and was soon at her side.

"Afternoon, Miss Hill. Lovely day, isn't it?" Raymond doffed his hat to her as he pulled his horse up beside Daisy. "What brings you out on such a grand afternoon?"

Callie was flustered, still wondering what to do. She could feel her face redden. Carswell saw her discomfort and confusion and felt satisfied.

"Cat got your tongue, Miss Hill?" he asked.

"No, I'm sorry, Mr. Carswell, you startled me."

"I apologize, Ma'am. I assumed you heard me behind you."

"No, I guess I was thinking."

"And, what would you be botherin' your pretty head about?"

"I don't think that's any concern of yours, sir. Now, if you don't mind, I'd like to get going to my destination." Callie tried to spur Daisy forward, but Carswell had her boxed in.

"Maybe I could ride along with you to keep you company. Not really that safe out here for a single lady, like you, to be ridin' alone."

"I assure you, I'm perfectly fine. I'm not going much further anyway. Please let me pass."

Raymond was starting to get agitated. "Do you think I'm not good enough to be a ridin' companion?"

Callie looked at him and flushed more. She didn't like the look on his face. "No...no....nothing like that. I expected to have some time to myself. I enjoy riding Daisy alone so I can think without any interruptions. It has nothing to do with you."

Raymond's face softened, but he eyes remained hard and steely. "Well, I'm glad to hear that. I wouldn't like to think you feel I'm beneath you somehow. You know, I've been workin' hard at the Montgomerys and Elijah has awarded me with parcels of land. I own much of his plantation now. It seems no one heard what happened to his brother, Hector, so there aren't any heirs except the women and they don't count. I've got plans to start the lumber mill back up soon too, just need a little more capital. Would like to buy the land around it that your family owns, but your brother won't sell it to me, neither will your pa. Do you know why, Miss Hill?"

"No..no... I don't. But Papa won't sell any of Oak Hill."

"Oh, but he has. He's sold to those no 'count sharecroppers - darkies, all of them. But won't sell to me - a white man. What you think about that?"

"I know he hasn't sold the land, the sharecroppers only work the land and then split the earnings from it with us."

"That so? I think different."

Callie tried once more to leave. "Well, it's been nice talking to you,

Mr. Carswell, but I really must be going. My friend is expecting me any minute now and will wonder where I am if I'm late."

Raymond smiled devilishly. "That so? Goin' to see your darkie friend that just got married?"

Callie was caught off guard. "How did you know that?"

"Oh, I know lots of things that's goin' on in our neck of the woods, Miss Hill. More than you know."

Callie didn't like what Carswell did next. He looked her in the eyes and then deliberately lowered his eyes down her body, stopping on her bosom and smiling. She felt the blood rush to her face angrily. Carswell slowly raised his eyes back to her now crimson face.

"Lot more than you know. Good day, Miss Hill. Have a nice visit with your darkie friend. Tell your pa I said hello." He turned his horse around and kicked it into a trot. Doffing his hat once more, he left Callie, laughing loudly as he went. An evil, wicked laugh.

Callie started shaking. She couldn't control herself. She was angry, scared, and frustrated. She felt like she had been violated with Carswell's eyes, just like she did the first time she saw him. She felt naked and exposed. Then her anger at him flared and she stopped shivering. How dare he treat her that way! How dare he threaten her!

"Come on, Daisy, let's get to Trudy's before he comes back." She urged Daisy into a full gallop and sped to Trudy's cabin, calming down along the way.

* * *

The Hills celebrated Callie's seventeenth birthday and Kathleen and Nathan's ninth anniversary in April, then it was on to the hard work of plowing, planting, and tending to the crops and gardens, hoping for a bountiful reward.

The sweet warm spring became a hot, arid summer. The sun beat down from the sky relentlessly, scorching the Georgia red earth. The winds blew constantly, a hot dry wind. No rain fell from the cloudless blue sky and the parched crops and gardens suffered.

Fine red dust was everywhere. It filled the air, choking anyone who ventured outdoors. It sifted into the house and coated the furniture and floors. The animals were covered with it, the grounds were covered with it, the buildings were covered with it. The landscape and everything on it turned dusty red.

Everyone was irritated. Tempers were short. Movement was restricted. Life slowed to a bare minimum and boredom set in.

Then for three glorious days in early July, it rained. Not a downpour, but a steady all day rain. The dying crops sucked up the moisture and slowly began to unfurl their withered leaves. The dust settled. The wells were full again. Cordiality returned and apologies were accepted. Life returned to normal.

* * *

"Samuel, we need to go over the ledgers tonight after we're done eating. Since the rain, it's seems the crops are starting over. I'm afraid the yield will not be good this year - their growth has been stunted. And, if we don't get more rain......" Nathan addressed his son across the dining table as he reached for another biscuit.

"I know, Father. I've observed the same thing. This will not be a good year."

"We will have to rely on the money from the railroad to get us by this year. I'm also concerned for all our sharecroppers. They, too, will suffer."

Callie's ears perked up. "Does that mean Trudy and Caleb will be poor?"

"They may be all right. I'm sure Caleb has a little money saved. Besides, I will always make sure Trudy is provided for."

"Good." Callie sighed. "I wonder if the drought was in Illinois. Ben hasn't mentioned it in his letters. I hope they have a good harvest and a quick one. That means he will get here earlier in November. I don't think I can wait much longer."

Nathan frowned. Kathleen gave him a look, so he didn't say anything. Samuel decided to change the subject completely.

"Well, folks, I have something I want to discuss with everyone and I guess now is as good a time as ever." He looked at everyone at the table now with inquisitive looks on their faces. He had their attention.

"As you know, Georgia was recently officially readmitted to the Union after ratifying the fifteenth amendment to the Constitution.

Granted, we are the last Confederate state to be readmitted, but now it's done. I believe the Republicans in the General Assembly will be voted out of office this year and Governor Bullock will be impeached. It will be a chance for the Democrats to get back in control and I want to be one of them."

"What? What do you mean, Samuel?" Nathan looked at his son.

"I want to run for state senator from our district as a Democrat, and I know I can win. I've wanted to do something for Georgia since I came back from the war, and I believe this is how to do it. Come November I will be elected and in January I will be sworn in."

"My goodness, that's wonderful, Samuel!" Beulah was the first to speak. "I think you will make an excellent senator. Good for you!"

The others, in turn, added their own expressions of agreement, except Callie. "Doesn't that mean you will have to live in Atlanta?"

"Only during the time the legislature is in session, which is a couple of months out of the year. I'll still be here to help Father with Oak Hill when he needs me."

"Then, I think it is a wonderful idea, Sam. How can we help you win?"

"We'll figure that out when the campaign really starts in September. So everybody will help?"

There was a resounding "yes" from all at the table, beaming at Samuel. They were so proud of him. He had found his niche at last.

* * *

Ben sat in his favorite chair on the front porch re-reading Callie's latest letter. The light was dimming as the sun set in the west casting brilliant streaks of crimson and orange across the sky.

"My darling Ben,

We are still suffering from the drought. It did rain yesterday, but only enough to wet the dust. All our plants in the garden have withered. Nothing is producing. We will have to buy food for the winter in Savannah, Papa said. The cotton crop is awful. Scrawny little plants with a tiny tuft of cotton on them. Papa said it's hardly going to be worth harvesting. Even if we have a good rain, it is too late in the season for the plants to revive.

I feel so sorry for Caleb. He has worked so hard and now his crops are dying from the heat. Trudy does her best to cheer him up, but he doesn't listen to her. He's even taken to carrying water from the almost dried up creek to douse the vegetables in Trudy's garden. He wants to be very independent. Papa told him not to worry, he would take care of them, but Caleb stomped away mad, saying he could take care of his family himself. I can understand, but I don't want Trudy to be hurting just because Caleb is too proud to take our help.

I'm glad the drought hasn't come to Illinois and your crops are doing well. That means you will be able to come and see me sooner! You have all your train tickets, now, don't you? I can hardly wait. It's been too long since we last saw one another, Ben. You know how much I miss you and love you.

I think about you the first thing in the morning and the last thing before I fall asleep. And, all times in between!! I'm sighing now, just thinking of being in your arms. I long for that, Ben. Sometimes, I even ache. Oh, I must stop this, or I will be weeping!

I wore the earrings you sent for my birthday to Sunday dinner last week. Mama Kathleen noticed and said once again she couldn't believe how well they match my locket. Now I can hold you in my heart and in my ears!!! Haha! Seriously, they are really beautiful and I can't wait until you can see them on me in person. Not too much longer, darling. Just a few months. I can feel your lips on mine already. Until then.........

I love you,
Callie
August 3, 1870"

Ben leaned back against the chair and stared out at the now darkening sky. He missed Callie so much! She said it right - he ached for her. His life revolved around thinking of her, planning to see her, asking her to marry him, and making a life for them. He had a speech all ready to deliver to Nathan, asking for his daughter's hand in marriage. He had a special ring purchased to give to Callie to pledge his love. He knew what he was going to say to her when he proposed. He was more than ready, but he still had to wait months before he could put his plan in motion. Until then, he ached, he longed, and he yearned.

He brought her letter to his lips and gently kissed it. He placed it back in the envelope, stood up, walked to his room, and placed it in the box with all the rest of her letters. Then he undressed and climbed into his empty bed.

* * *

"Oh, Trudy, I'm so glad you came today. I've missed you this week." Callie hugged Trudy who had just entered the house. Then she stood back and looked at her friend.

"What's wrong? You don't look so good. Are you sick?"

"I's don' knows, Miz Callie. Sometimes I's is an' sometimes I's ain't. This morning I's was. Feels so tired an' poorly one days an' bedder the nex'. Gits dizzy an' has to sets down an 'fore I's knows it, I's 'sleep. Sometimes I's fixin' Caleb's breakfast an' I's has to go outside an' gits sick. Cain't seems to stand smellin' eggs cookin' no more. I's don' knows, I's jes' don' knows."

"Well, I know. We're going to take you to Lenora right this minute. She will know what's wrong and fix you right up. Come on."

"Lez take Socks too. Ain't seen him much lately. Kind o' miss him."

"Certainly. Socks! Socks! Come on boy, let's go for a walk." Socks came slowly out of the back parlor wagging his tail. He went to Trudy and started licking her offered hand. She rewarded him with lots of scratches.

The two girls and the dog started off towards the former slave quarters where Lenora still had her cabin. They found her sitting on her front porch rocking in her chair, with a mortar and pestle on her lap. She was grinding herbs for one of her medicinal concoctions.

"Well, lookie here. Ain't seen Miz Trudy for a spell. How's you likes bein' a married lady?"

"Likes it jes' fine, Lenora, but ain't been feelin' too good lately." Trudy proceeded to tell Lenora her symptoms.

"Uh-huh. You been bleedin' e'ery month since you married Caleb?"

"At first, but not nows."

"Uh-huh." Lenora placed her hand on Trudy's belly. "Thinks you goin' be havin' a baby, Miz Trudy. Whatch you thinks 'bout that?"

"A baby! Oh, Trudy, that's wonderful!" Callie grabbed Trudy and hugged her.

Trudy just looked at Lenora incredulously. "Whatch you mean? How I's git's a baby in there?"

"My oh my, chile. Didn' nobody ever tells you how you gits babies?"

Both girls shook their heads no.

"Miz Callie, didn' nobody tells you neither?" Callie shook her head no again.

"Hmmm. Well, guess up to ol' Lenora to tell you youn' uns hows babies is made. Trudy, you knows when you lays wit Caleb?"

Trudy looked down at her lap bashfully and grinned. "Yes, Ma'am."

"That's when you tryin' to makes a baby."

Trudy's head popped up and she had a surprised look on her face. "That makes a baby?"

"Uh-huh. Chance e'ery time, but don' always take."

Callie looked perplexed. "What do you mean, 'lay with Caleb'? What are you talking about?"

Trudy giggled. "You, know, Miz Callie. When we lays t'gedder at night in bed. We's loves each other."

"I know that, Trudy, but what do you do that would make a baby?"

Trudy rolled her eyes in exasperation and looked to Lenora for help.

"When a man an' a woman loves each odder, Miz Callie, they comes t'gedder, their bodies comes t'gedder." Lenora looked at Callie's face to see if she understood her. "You know, kind o' like when the an'mals mate."

"You mean the way the sheep come together? And the pigs? People come together like that too?"

Both women nodded their heads vigorously up and down.

"Oh..........Oh? ....OH!..... I *think* I see now! You mean you...... and he......and then......?"

"Yes!" Both women exclaimed at once and Callie's face lit up with understanding.

"Hmmm……then you like it?"

Lenora smiled broadly. "If'n it wits a man you loves."

"Well, I love Ben so that will be wonderful! I'd love to have Ben's babies! Trudy, this so exciting! But you're so lucky, because now *you're* having Caleb's baby! I'm so happy for you! Now you must listen to Lenora because I'm sure she can tell you how to have a healthy baby, isn't that right, Lenora?"

Lenora shook her head yes and proceeded to tell Trudy what to do and not do during her pregnancy. "An', don' worries, I's be here to helps you when that baby 'cides to be born."

Trudy frowned. "Think that gonna really hurt, right Lenora?"

"Yes it do, but when you holds that li'l babe in your arms, you don' 'member that pain at all."

"But look what happin to Miz Kathleen. Her baby born dead."

"Sometimes, the good Lawd wants angels. We cain't help that none, Trudy. But you youn' an' you strong so you should has no trubbles birthin' a fine baby. You jes' lissen to me an' all will be fine."

"You ever has a baby, Lenora?" Trudy asked.

"Had me two li'l boys." Lenora got a faraway, poignant look in her black eyes.

"I didn't know that, Lenora. I don't remember any of your children."

"Nebber did heres at Oak Hill, Miz Callie. Had my chiles 'fore Masta Preston buys me. Lived on a li'l farm, jes' me an' my man an' my boys. Missus teached me 'bout med'cines, but I's couldn't saves her life when she done gots sick. When she dies, Masta blames me an' takes me away from my chiles an' my husband. Sells me in Sav'nnah to Masta Preston. Nebber sees my Isaac an' Isaiah 'gin. Nebber sees my man, Tom, neither." Lenora had tears streaming down her face.

Callie stood up and went to Lenora, throwing her arms around her neck. "Oh, Lenora, I'm so sorry. That's terrible."

"That the way us slaves lived, Miz Callie. Always wonderin' when we be sold an' leaves our home an' family. Jes' the way things was. Glad now Trudy won' nebber has to worry 'bout leavin' her babe an' Caleb, 'cause now we alls be free. Thank the Lawd Almighty!"

Lenora raised her tear stained face to the sky.

Callie wiped Lenora's wet tears off the wrinkled brown face with her hands. "Yes, I'm glad you are all free now too. I love all our Oak Hill people, and I'm very glad some of them came back, but I'm glad you're all free now."

"Way the Lawd meant it to be, Miz Callie. Jes' took too long for whites to figures it alls out. If'n theys had, we nebber had that bad, bad war."

The three sat for a few moments in silence, remembering. Then Callie decided to change the subject back to Trudy's happy event.

"When will Trudy have her baby, Lenora? Can you tell?"

"When las' time you bleeds, Trudy?"

"After plantin' time, I's thinks. Maybe li'l later."

"Well, lez sees........." Lenora started counting on her fingers. "My guess is early winter, maybes Feb'a'y. That be 'bout right."

"Oh, Trudy, we can take care of the baby during the winter. It will be so much fun!"

Trudy frowned. "Miz Callie, 'members, this babe be me an' Caleb's, an' *we* takes care of it."

"Well, of course. But I can be its 'Aunt Callie,' can't I?"

Trudy smiled. "Shore you can, 'Aunt Callie,' shore you can."

Callie turned back to Lenora. "Lenora, can you tell if Trudy will have twins?"

"Twins! I's don' wants no two babies at one time, Miz Callie!"

"Well, Susan did, remember? Aunt Caroline says they're a real handful now, but Carrie and Annie, along with Andy have helped Joshua recover so much. Can you tell, Lenora?"

"Nots now, but maybes later if'n Trudy git a real big belly. Sometimes, you can feels two babes movin' in the belly 'fore theys born."

Trudy's eyes were getting larger at every word Lenora said. "You means I's will feels my babe in my belly 'fore it be birthed?"

"Oh, yes, if'n it a healthy babe. It keeps you up at nights kickin' an' squirmin' around in there." Lenora pointed to Trudy's belly. Trudy looked down at Lenora's finger and then back up at Callie and Lenora.

"This havin' a baby gonna be something mighty 'pecial."

Callie and Lenora nodded their heads in agreement. Callie laughed out loud at Trudy's reaction.

"We'll be on our way now, Lenora. Thank you for all your help, and I'm truly sorry about your family." Callie gave the old black woman another hug.

"Me too," Trudy added. "I's be seein' you 'gin soon."

The two girls left Lenora's cabin hand in hand, Socks trailing behind.

* * *

Samuel began his campaign before the harvest began. He attended meetings, gatherings, social events, barbeques, dances, but he knew he would be the next state senator from Oak Hill's district. He had no opposition. Once everyone knew Samuel Hill, a Confederate veteran, was running as a Democrat, no one else ventured to oppose him - either as a fellow Democrat or a Republican.

Republicans were now scarce as the native whites once again were gaining control in the state capitol. The scalawags were being driven out of office - either legally or illegally. The elected blacks suffered the same fate, even worse - many ended up at the end of a hanging noose.

Samuel continued to attend events even though his election was insured. He wanted to know what the people in his district were most interested in and how he could help them once he was sworn into the state legislature. He wanted to be a caring, concerned, honest senator; not a corrupt, dishonest, shady politician. He sincerely wanted to aid his constituents and help them through the throes of reconstruction.

His family at Oak Hill was very proud of him and they knew he would make an excellent state senator. Sometimes they went with him as he traveled around the district making speeches and meeting people. Callie and Kathleen's only complaint was they would not be allowed to vote for him.

"Someday we will get to vote, Mama Kathleen. It's just not fair that we don't already. I don't understand it. We are just as smart as men, maybe more so. I *know* I'm just as smart as some men. Maybe now that Sam will be a senator, he can do something to help get women the right to vote in Georgia."

"Let's hope so Callie. You're right. Women understand politics just as well as men. I've always said the world would be a better place if women ran it. I know for sure there would never be any wars."

* * *

The harvest, as predicted, was very meager. There just hadn't been enough rain. Nathan took what cotton bales he had to Savannah to sell at the Cotton Exchange, but even John couldn't help him get a decent price. He begrudgingly spent that money on food supplies. No luxuries or extras this year.

Caleb was depressed. No matter what Trudy did to cheer him up, she couldn't. He was too worried about supporting her and the baby. He had to use what little savings they had to purchase food too. He took to hunting game, something he wasn't very good at, but learned how quickly to put meat on the table. Nathan had loaned him a rifle. He would be one of few blacks to be armed.

The only person who was not anxious about the disappointing harvest was Callie. She was completely focused on Ben's upcoming visit to worry about what came out of the land. It consumed her even more as November approached. She could hardly stand the waiting.

* * *

"Callie, I was thinking......what if we invited the Whitsons and the Norrises to Oak Hill to meet Benjamin?"

"But, Mama Kathleen, Ben's only going to be here a little over two weeks and I don't really want to share him with anybody else."

"Callie, that's selfish! We could have a barbeque - roast one of the hogs. The Savannah folk wouldn't have to stay the entire time - just a few days. I think it would be nice for Ben to meet the rest of your family. You can show him off."

"Do we have enough money to have a barbeque? Papa said the harvest was awful, so awful that we couldn't get anything new this year."

"Oh, I think he will be fine with what I have planned. We haven't seen John and Caroline and their family for a while and have never seen Susan's twins."

"Well......I guess it would be all right, if Papa agrees. But no longer than a few days. I know the time will go too fast anyway."

Kathleen smiled and thought, "ahhhh, young love………."

* * *

"Papa! Papa! I can't see the train car! Where is it?" Callie was tugging at Nathan's hand pulling him through the throng of people gathered at the Swainsboro station.

"It hasn't arrived yet, Callie. Settle down." Nathan grabbed his daughter by her shoulders and turned her toward him. "Now, catch your breath and breathe. I told you, this wasn't Ben's car. His is to arrive in a few more minutes, after this one has unloaded. How could you forget?"

Callie shook her head to clear it. "I don't know. When I heard the whistle, I just ran."

"Another thing. When Ben does get here, I don't want you making a scene in public, or private for that matter. I know you *say* you love each other...."

"We *do* love each other!"

"Yes, but you don't have to *show* that to the entire world. It just isn't proper, Callie! You'll just have to control your feelings."

Callie frowned. "I'll try, Papa, but I haven't seen him for *such* a long time."

"I know, baby girl, but if you say you are in love, you have to act grown up."

Again, Callie frowned. "I *am* grown up! I'm old enough to know I've loved Ben for a long time now."

Nathan didn't want to have this conversation, but he also did not want his daughter to make a spectacle of herself the way she did in Bloomington, Illinois when she had to say good-bye to Ben.

"All right, Callie, all right......Let's not dwell on this……….Just try to control yourself, that's all I'm asking."

Callie smiled, flashing her brilliant white teeth. "All right, Papa, I will." Then under her breath she said, "But I don't think it will work."

Callie stopped to look around. The crowd was thinning as the passengers left the station. Soon the next train would be arriving and Ben would be on it.

She didn't have much longer to wait. She heard the whistle and saw the steam billowing out of the locomotive. The noise was deafening. She held her hands over her ears to dampen it. Then she looked at Nathan standing beside her and grinned.

He looked at his beautiful daughter, so full of life and so happy, and smiled back. He didn't know Ben Chapman that well, but he trusted Callie, and she wanted Ben. Ben was making a great effort to come and see her, so maybe he was in love with her after all. Time would tell.

The train pulled into the station and amidst screeches and hissings, it stopped. Callie could hardly stand it. As the conductor opened the passenger car, she ran forward, Nathan right behind her.

"Just a minute, Miss, "the conductor stopped her, "have to let the passengers have some room to get off. Back up, please."

Callie obeyed, looking anxiously at the opened door. One by one the passengers got off the car. Each time, Callie held her breath. When she saw it wasn't Ben, she'd exhale.

"Where is he, Papa? Are you sure this is the right train?"

"Yes, not everybody is off yet, Callie. Settle down."

Then she saw a hand reach out to the railing by the door and she knew it was Ben's hand. She looked up as the rest of him appeared.

"BEN! BEN! Here I am!!"

All thoughts of Nathan's warning flew out of her head. Before Ben's feet even touched the ground, she ran to him, flinging her arms around him, practically knocking him down.

"MISS, please get out of the way!" The conductor pulled Callie, along with Ben to the side of the car. "Gracious!"

Callie didn't care. All she knew was that she was in Ben's arms and looking into those teal eyes. She never even heard Nathan behind her or the din of the rest of the passengers.

"Oh, Ben……..you're finally here." She laid her head on his shoulder and sighed.

Ben finally spoke. "That was some greeting, Callie. You almost tackled me to the ground!"

She looked up into his eyes now twinkling with mischief. Then she realized she had done exactly what her father told her not to do.

"Oh, my goodness, I'm sorry, Ben......I ...I.....I was just so excited to see you.....I....oh my." She pulled away and smoothed her cape and skirt, looking down at her shoes.

Ben laughed. "I survived. Besides, that's the best greeting I've ever had. I think we'd better move away from the track before the conductor yells at you again. Your father doesn't look too happy either."

They walked over to where Nathan was standing, his forehead creased in a deep frown.

"Callie.....you're lucky you didn't get hurt."

"Sorry, Papa, I just couldn't help myself."

"Mr. Hill, nice to see you again." Ben extended his hand and Nathan shook it. "No harm done. Callie was just a little overly excited, I think."

"Apparently. Well, I hope your travels went well, Benjamin. Did everything I send you help?"

"Oh, yes, everything went very smoothly. Thank you for all your help. I think I'd better gather my baggage now and then we can get away from this crowd."

"Good. Callie, you wait right here and I'll have Judah bring the carriage around."

"Yes, Papa."

Nathan turned and winked at Ben. "Think she's calmed down now."

"Seems so, Mr. Hill."

* * *

It was an awkward ride home from Swainsboro for Nathan. He was seated across from Callie and Ben who never took their eyes off one another. He finally gave up having any sort of conversation with either one of them. It made him uncomfortable to see his daughter look at another man in that manner, yet he knew she was old enough to have romantic feelings. Still it was unsettling.

Callie was so happy. She still couldn't believe Ben was sitting next to her - sitting so closely next to her. He hadn't changed much from last year. He still looked like she remembered - maybe he had filled out a little more and his hair was a little shorter, but otherwise, he was her Ben.

She loved looking into his eyes. They were staring back at her now and they were full of affection. Her own were brimming with tears of joy. She sighed contentedly.

"Callie, sweetie, are you all right?" Nathan heard her sigh.

"Oh, Papa, I've never been better."

"Hmm. Won't be much longer before we're back home. You can rest from your trip, Ben. I know traveling is tiresome."

"I'm fine, Mr. Hill. I caught a few winks on the train." Ben looked out the window of the carriage. "These parts look different from what I remember. 'Course, it's been six years since I was here before. Goodness, it doesn't seem like it could be that long ago."

"I know what you mean. Sometimes the war seems like it was yesterday and sometimes it seems like decades have past. The South is still fighting the war, Ben, only in a different manner. Georgia just rejoined the Union this summer. Folks around here still believe in the Confederacy and there's no love lost on Yankees."

"Are you tryin' to tell me to be careful while I'm here? I wasn't plannin on leaving Oak Hill. Besides, I already met with some prejudice when the train crossed the Mason-Dixie line. I know exactly what you mean. I suppose it was somewhat the same when you came north. People have long memories, I guess."

"Yes, I guess they do. No matter. I'm glad you made it here safely."

"Me too, Ben." Callie leaned her head on Ben's shoulder.

Ben looked down at that lovely blonde head. He couldn't believe he was actually here either. It had taken a lot of extra work to save up for the trip, but it was worth it. He had Callie on his shoulder. He couldn't wait to talk to Nathan so he could propose and give her the ring he had purchased months ago. He smiled thinking about it.

"You're happy too, aren't you?" Callie smiled up at him.

"Very much."

* * *

The carriage approached the lane going into Oak Hill. Ben looked out the window and suddenly six years vanished before his eyes. He was overcome with emotion seeing the plantation again. Tears gathered suddenly and he blinked to hold them back. He became restless, fidgetting in his seat.

"Ben, is something wrong?" Callie looked at him with concern and then saw the tears trickling down his cheeks.

"Benjamin............what's wrong?" Nathan leaned forward wondering what had happened.

Ben couldn't speak. He waved his hand trying to regain his composure. "Give......minute...." He took his handkerchief out of his pocket and wiped his face.

Callie and Nathan looked at him apprehensively. "Sorry.....don't quite know what happened......when I saw this place again........... brought back too many memories........destruction.........death....... bodies mangled..........bad memories.....Sorry....."

Nathan got a faraway look in his eyes. "I know exactly what you mean. I felt the same way when I stood on the battlefield at Nashville last year."

"But, sir .....you didn't destroy people's homes ......and property ...like we did in Sherman's army. I ...remember waiting outside Oak Hill ....at dawn that day thinking, 'not again.' We burned ....so many places and looted ....so many farms. That day I vowed ...not to participate if I could help it. I swear, sir.....I never lifted a finger here at Oak Hill. I watched Williams ...the whole time. But, then ...I never did anything to stop anyone either. I ...deeply regret that."

"But, Ben, you were a soldier. You had to do what you were ordered, isn't that right, Papa? Just like you did."

"That's right, Callie, but when Sherman marched through Georgia, the war changed. He destroyed the Southern people, not just the army. We still are recovering five years later and it will take many more years yet."

Callie, Ben, and Nathan sat in silence as the carriage continued towards the house. Callie finally spoke, "Well, I think we should leave the past in the past. We are all Americans once again and that should be that. I know it's hard. I still hate seeing Yankees in uniforms after what they did to Oak Hill. Sorry, Ben....but I have memories too. But, now at least our families get along and maybe someday the rest of the country will too."

Nathan looked at his daughter, marveling. "Callie, you really have grown up. I guess our future will depend on young people like you and Ben, and if the rest of them are like you two, then maybe our country does have a bright future."

"Thank you, Papa. Now.....if you two gentleman will help me out, I will welcome Ben to Oak Hill properly."

* * *

Callie was right about one thing. Her time with Ben at Oak Hill was going by much too quickly. Kathleen had planned the barbeque for a few days after his arrival. The Whitsons and the Norrises descended on Oak Hill and the socializing began in earnest.

Everyone was also celebrating Samuel's election as state senator. Even though he had run unopposed, he garnered many votes, which made him feel significant.

The house took on a totally different feel with so many people visiting, especially the young children. Mammy Sallie and Beulah excused themselves several times as they just didn't have the patience any more to deal with youngsters, even though Andy, Carrie, and Annie were well behaved.

Belle enlisted everyone's help to cook all the food for the visitors. Joseph dug a pit outside the smokehouse where the hog would be roasted. The unlucky swine was killed, gutted, and laid on glowing coals, then covered with leaves and then the earth. It cooked that way for several days, tantalizing the guests with the smell of roasted pork.

Meanwhile, inside the kitchen, food was baked, boiled, fried, and roasted. One would have never known it had been a bad harvest year. Finally, the hog and all the trimmings were ready to perfection and the barbeque began. The families and the former slaves feasted on the glistening pork, sweet potatoes, cornbreads, puddings, gravies, vegetables, and everything else. It was a festive, happy time.

Callie clung to Ben's arm during the barbeque. He hardly had time to get acquainted with the visiting relatives, but they all seemed to accept him, even if he was a Yankee. Victoria especially approved. She started flirting with him right away until Callie put a stop to it. Callie didn't care if Victoria was upset with her, she had no business batting her eyelashes and flashing playful smiles at Callie's beau. Callie needn't have worried.

Unbeknownst to Callie, and before the Savannah relatives arrived, Ben had sought out Nathan and asked him for Callie's hand in marriage. Nathan was not surprised, but did have many questions for Ben. What concerned him the most was Ben assumed he and Callie would live in Illinois. Nathan understood completely this was expected - the wife followed the husband wherever he went. He knew he and Hannah would live at Oak Hill, not her home in Savannah. The same was true with Kathleen. But he never really considered Callie leaving her home and living so far away. However, he gave Ben his permission for he knew how much Callie loved him and wanted to be with him. They would have to work out the living arrangements themselves.

After all the food had been eaten at the barbeque and people started napping, Ben whispered in Callie's ear, "Can we sneak away someplace private. I need to talk to you."

Callie's stomach churned. Something must be wrong. But she nodded her head yes and led Ben outside to the big oak tree in the front lawn. They sat down on the rod iron chairs that were there.

"What's the matter, Ben? Is something wrong?"

"No, something is very right." Then Ben got out of his chair and bent before Callie on one knee. He grabbed her hand and squeezed it. Again, Callie's stomach reeled, only this time in excitement.

"Callie Hill, you know how much I love you and want you in my life. I can't imagine another day without you in it. Would you please give me the pleasure of being my wife?"

Callie was stunned. She hadn't expect this proposal so soon and especially with everyone visiting at Oak Hill. She didn't know what to say, she was so overcome.

"Callie? Do you want to marry me?" Ben looked at her with a

worried expression on his face.

She blinked. "Of course, I want to marry you! I'm sorry....I'm just surprised.....of course, I'll marry you.....of course!"

She tried to lean forward to kiss Ben, but he pulled back. "Wait, I have another surprise for you." He reached into his back pocket as Callie watched, curiously. He pulled out a small black square box. He gave it to Callie. "Open it."

She took the box and slowly opened it. Inside was a beautiful ring. A gold band holding a perfectly cut oval opal on six thin prongs. The gem's iridescence gleamed at her. She lifted her eyes to Ben's. "It's too beautiful, Ben. It's too perfect."

"It's meant to be, Callie. Perfect. Just like our love. A sign of our perfect love." He took the ring and slipped it on her left ring finger. It fit, as he knew it would. Then he pulled her up with his hand and gingerly touched her face, gazing into her deep brown eyes, now filling with tears. He leaned down and melded her lips with his own. She eagerly responded, wrapping her arms around his neck.

Finally, breaking the embrace, Callie could speak. "Ben, I love you so much, but have you talked to Papa? Does he know we will be married?"

"Of course, I did. He gave me his permission to marry his 'baby girl.'"

"Oh, then, I'm so happy!! We're going to be married!! I'm going to be a bride!! We're going to be together forever and ever! Ben, thank you! And, the ring is so pretty." Callie extended her hand to look at the ring more closely.

Ben hugged her again, then picked her up and twirled her around and around. Both were laughing gaily until they fell to the ground giggling. "I love you so much," they both said at the same time and then started laughing again.

Callie sat up, brushing herself off. She grabbed Ben's hand. "Come on, let's go tell everyone! I can't wait to tell Trudy and Victoria!"

"Whoa, just a minute. Can't we stay here a little longer? I want to have a little more time with my new fiancée."

Callie looked at Ben. "Of course, but after we're married we will have all the time in the world."

"There is something important we need to discuss, Callie. I hope you know that we will be living in Clayton Township in Illinois. That's where I make my living so that's where we will live."

Callie blanched. "Oh....I ...I...never really thought about that. You mean I will have to leave Oak Hill forever? I....I....don't know, Ben." She lay on her back on the hard ground and looked up at the leaves on the old oak. "Leave Oak Hill........it's the only home I've known. I love Oak Hill." She thought silently, her brain in a tizzy. Ben stared at that beautiful face, now concentrating on this new concept.

"I know it will be such a sacrifice for you to leave your family and home, but, Callie, I already have a farm back in Illinois. Pa gave me forty acres when he heard I was goin' to propose to you and when I get back, I'll build us a house on part of it and start farmin' the rest. He will loan me his machinery until I can afford my own. It's all set up, Callie. I'm a Midwestern farmer, not a Southern one. I don't know how to grow cotton. Besides, I don't fit in here. I'm a Yankee........a Yankee soldier who came through here destroyin' this land. Don't you see the way Samuel and Joshua look at me? They still regard me as the enemy. And, I don't blame them. Do you understand?"

"Yes, I do. I also know that a wife is supposed to follow her husband. Grandma did, my Mama Hannah did and so did Mama Kathleen, in a way. I guess I just never really thought about it, Ben." Callie sighed deeply. "Right now I can't think. I just know I love you and want to be with you. I guess it doesn't matter where as long as we are together."

"Then........you'll still marry me, even if means leavin' Oak Hill?"

"Yes, it does. I'd probably follow you to the ends of the earth, Ben Chapman."

Ben leaned over and found Callie's lips again. "There, it's sealed with a kiss. You can't change your mind."

"Oh, Ben, I do love you so............." She reached up and brought his lips to hers again. The sweet soft kiss turned into one more strong and urgent. Callie suddenly pulled away. "Ben, stop, I feel like I will faint!"

Ben looked at her intensely, but with his eyes twinkling. "Why,

Miss Hill. Have you turned into a shy southern belle? You're already layin' on the ground, how could you possibly faint?"

"Oh my. I shouldn't be lying on the ground. That's not proper for a southern lady in the accompaniment of a gentleman. What will Grandma think?" Callie's brown eyes also sparkled with mischief. "Of course, I am now betrothed to that gentleman, does that make a difference?"

"Certainly." Ben began kissing Callie again, but less passionately.

"Although I'm enjoying this, I think maybe we'd better get up before someone sees us. Nap time should be over soon. One more kiss and then let's go tell everyone our good news."

"All right, Miss Hill." Ben gave her one more quick peck and then got up and helped Callie to her feet. They brushed off their clothes and hand in hand started for the house.

Callie couldn't wait. She pulled Ben's hand as she started running for the veranda calling out, "Everybody, everybody, Ben asked me to marry him!! We're going to get married!!"

If anyone was still asleep, they quickly woke up. Word spread throughout the house and everyone gathered on the veranda to congratulate the couple. Callie was hugged until she felt squished.

Trudy was beaming with happiness for her. Victoria was gracious, but not excited. Samuel was happy, but leary. The Whitsons and the Norrises were polite, but reserved, although Caroline was very happy for her. Mammy Sallie cried tears of joy for her girl and exclaimed she hoped she lived long enough to see her "prop'ly married." Beulah was happy for the couple, as she had witnessed Ben's act of heroism when he shot James Williams. Nathan and Katleen already knew of Ben's proposal, but they were elated also - Kathleen more than Nathan.

Callie's face radiated happiness as she showed off the new opal ring. "Must have been a better corn crop year than cotton," Samuel whispered to his father.

Nathan smiled. "Must have. Look how happy she is, Samuel. I can't believe she's old enough to get married and leave us."

Samuel looked at Nathan in alarm. "What do you mean 'leave

us'?"

"She'll be living in Illinois with her husband. You hadn't already thought of that?"

"I...I....guess not. This will take some getting used to. I never thought of Callie as anywhere but here."

"Me neither, but Kathleen assures me it will all work out for the best." Nathan grinned. "'Bout time you found yourself a mate, Samuel. You're about the same age as Ben."

Despite himself, Samuel blushed. "Yes, I know. I've thought of it, but haven't acted upon it yet. I'm going to concentrate on serving the people of this district in the General Assembly and if something happens, it happens."

"Don't wait too long. No one should spend their life alone."

"I won't."

* * *

Later that evening after all the excitement had died down, Nathan and Kathleen were lying in bed talking. "I just can't seem to grasp the fact that Callie will be getting married." Nathan sat up and pounded his pillow.

"She's in love, Nathan. She's grown up."

"I know, but it just seem so......so....*sudden*."

"But, it's not, you know."

"They've only seen each other *twice*, Kathleen, *twice*."

"I know, but you don't understand, dear husband. All these years they've been corresponding, they *know* each other, probably better than most young couples. When they were together last year, they just immediately knew they were meant for one another."

Nathan sighed deeply. "I don't want to lose my daughter."

Kathleen smiled, as she knew this was what was really bothering her husband. "You won't 'lose' her, Nathan. She'll always be your 'baby girl.' But 'baby girls' grow up. Don't you think my parents felt the same way when I came here and then married you?"

Nathan laughed and his eyes twinkled. "I think your parents were delighted to see you were marrying such a handsome fellow!!"

Kathleen picked up the feather pillow and hit Nathan with it, laughing as she did so. "Ohhhh…..you're terrible!"

Nathan fell back chuckling. Kathleen looked so beautiful when she was flustered. Her skin glowed; her red curls seemed on fire. He grabbed her and held her tight.

"Kathleen, marrying you was one of the best things that has happened to me. I thank God above every day for bringing you into my life."

Kathleen smiled. "Now, that's better, husband. And, I'm sure Callie and Ben feel the same way. You have to admit, it was a rather exceptional way they met - Ben saving her life. I would say the Lord had something to do with that."

"Yes…I guess I would. Oh, Kathleen, what would I do without you? You always have the right answers to my problems."

Kathleen giggled. "No, I don't. I'm just your conscience - that little voice in your head. You don't always listen to it, but you listen to me - I've trained you well!!"

"Hah! Now, woman, you've done it!" Nathan picked up his pillow and pelted Kathleen until feathers flew out. Both were laughing so hard, they had to stop to gasp for breath. Then they fell into each others arms.

* * *

The Whitsons and Norrises left for Savannah and life at Oak Hill returned to normal. Normal for everyone except Ben and Callie. They spent as much time alone as Nathan would allow them. At first, he balked at them being together without a chaperone, but Kathleen reminded him she *lived* with him during their courtship. She also brought up the subject of their long horseback rides together, alone, and they weren't even engaged. Nathan sputtered and fumed, but had to admit his wife was right. Even though Beulah and Mammy Sallie objected, the young couple received permission to be alone as long as they stayed on the plantation.

Nathan received a shock one evening after dinner when Callie and Ben asked to see him privately in the library.

They had no sooner entered the room when Callie blurted, "Papa, Ben and I want to get married before he goes back to Illinois. We can have a simple ceremony here on Tuesday and then I can pack up most of my things and you can ship the rest later."

"WHAT!! No, Callie, no! That's too soon.....too fast. What are you thinking? You just can't leave like that (Nathan snapped his fingers). I won't let you! Ben, what about your folks? Don't you want them to be at your wedding? They will be hurt. No, no wedding now."

Ben and Callie looked at one another in surprise. They hadn't anticipated this reaction. Callie started to speak but Ben shook his head. Nathan was too distressed to argue with.

"Mr. Hill. I'm sorry we have upset you. We thought you might have already considered we would be married before I leave."

"Well, I certainly have not! It never entered my mind! Callie is still only seventeen. I still have some say in her life and now is not the time for her to get married."

"Why not, Papa? When would be a good time?"

"Well.....because...because.....you're still only seventeen. Ben's folks aren't here. It won't give you time to prepare to leave. Christmas is coming, don't you want to spend it with us? Samuel will be going to Atlanta........I don't know....lots of reasons why. A good time? After you are eighteen....when we've had time to think about this and prepare for it. Don't you want a lovely wedding, Callie? Better than .....say... Trudy had? Something like ...Susan's? It's an important day, an important life event. Don't you want it to be special?"

"Papa, just becoming Ben's wife will be special enough for me."

Ben frowned. "Callie, I think maybe your father is right."

Callie turned and looked at him incredulously. "What do you mean?"

"Well, it is a special event in our lives. I want you to have a beautiful wedding day. Maybe my folks would like to be here to see me become your husband."

Nathan sighed heavily in relief. "At least one of you has some sense."

"Papa! I have sense. It makes sense for Ben not to make another trip here - it's a long way. If we get married now, I can just go with him. We can be together. I don't want to be apart from him again."

Tears were forming in the corners of Callie's eyes as she looked pleadingly at her father.

Nathan looked away from her. He knew how she could manipulate him with her tears. "Let me get Kathleen and we'll discuss this with her. She has a good head on her shoulders."

Nathan left the couple alone in the library and went to find his wife. He needed to have her on his side to present a united front. Callie would listen to Kathleen.

"Ben, why on earth did you agree with Papa? I want to get married now!"

"I know, Callie, but what he said made sense too. I just want you to be happy and not regret anything later. We've waited this long - a little longer won't hurt. Besides, I don't have our house built yet. We could move in with Ma and Pa and Emma, but it would be crowded. We wouldn't have much privacy………."

Callie thought. There was some truth to that. But she didn't want Ben to leave again without her. Besides, she didn't want to have a lot of time to think about leaving her family and Oak Hill. She knew that was going to be so difficult. But, if she really thought about it……she knew she did want a special wedding - not a quick ceremony. Even before Trudy and Caleb got married, she had been planning her own wedding.

Nathan and Kathleen entered the library interrupting her thoughts. "Nathan has told me what you two want to do. I'm surprised, Callie. I thought you would want to involve your family and friends and Ben's family in the wedding. Aren't you being a little selfish?"

"But, Mama Kathleen, I want to go with Ben. I don't want to leave him again." Callie grabbed Ben's hand and squeezed it tight.

"Ben, what do you think?"

"Well, I was all for gettin married before I leave until Mr. Hill pointed out some things I hadn't thought of. Maybe it would be better if we waited until things could be planned properly."

Callie shot Ben a furious look with her deep brown eyes. "Ben!"

He turned to her. "It's true, Callie. We love each other, that won't change. Let's think about this."

Kathleen looked at both of them. "Here's what I think. Callie, you should wait until you are eighteen to make your father happy. And, you need to give us some time to get used to you leaving. You should have a beautiful wedding. I've never regretted the lovely ceremony your father and I had. It will mean something to you later. Give us all a chance to see you as a beautiful bride. Let your grandmother and I have the pleasure of planning your trousseau, wedding dress, and the reception. You're our only girl, so we want it to be special, not rushed. The Savannah relatives just left. I know they will want to be here. Don't deprive Ben's family either. He's their only son."

Callie pouted. She knew she was out numbered now, and, in her heart, she knew she agreed with Kathleen. "Well, then, just when *can* we get married?"

Nathan spoke up. "How's this for a compromise? After you turn eighteen....."

Callie interrupted. "We will get married on my eighteenth birthday then, Papa."

Nathan stammered......"I...thought....maybe after the harvest season was over.......next year at this time."

"A WHOLE YEAR! NO! I won't wait that long! Will we, Ben?" Callie looked at Ben with a scowl.

"A year does seem like a long time, sir. Maybe before that?"

"We will get married April 23, 1871 *on* my birthday. Planting season won't have begun in earnest yet then, Papa, and Ben and I can get back in time to plant *our* crops. His family will be able to come then too, as will Uncle John and Aunt Caroline and their family. That should give us plenty of time to plan a wedding, Mama Kathleen. Does everyone agree?"

Callie looked at each person sternly, daring them to oppose her. Finally, Nathan chuckled. "Do you see what you're in for, Ben? She can be quite forceful at times."

Ben smiled and looked at Callie, who was now tapping her foot impatiently. "Yes, sir, but that's one reason I love her."

"Well, then I guess that settles it. April 23rd it will be. I think you two are showing us you are mature enough to make wise decisions.

Congratulations!" Nathan hugged Callie and shook Ben's hand. Somehow from the look in Nathan's eyes, Callie wondered if she had really "won" this argument.

* * *

The rest of the time Ben was at Oak Hill flew by in a blur, and before they knew it, the young couple was once again saying good-bye at the train station. However, they now knew this would be the last time farewells were needed. Still, Callie clung to Ben until he stepped onto the passenger car.

"Only a few more months, Callie.........just a few more months!" Ben shouted as he boarded.

"A few more months, Ben.......a few more months!"

"I love you, Callie!"

"I love you, Ben!"

The other people boarding the train had to smile at the young lovers so sincere and so romantic.

It was a quiet ride back to Oak Hill. Callie's head was spinning. Spinning with wedding plans. She and Ben had agreed he and his family would arrive at Oak Hill at least two weeks before the wedding. That would give everybody time to get re-acquainted and prepare for the ceremony.

Ben and Callie decided they wanted to be married under the live-oak tree where Ben proposed. If it rained, which it didn't dare, they would have the ceremony on the front veranda or in the front parlor.

Callie looked up at her father across from her in the carriage. "Oh, Papa, I hate to say it, but I think you were right to make Ben and me wait until my birthday to get married. There must be thousands of things I need to do before then!"

Nathan smiled at his daughter and nodded his head in agreement. She was so happy, but how was he *ever* going to let her leave?

CHAPTER 6
1871

February 10, 1871

My darling,
Ben! You will never believe where I am writing this letter! Atlanta!!
I have so much to tell you, I don't know where to begin. But the most
important first: I miss you and love you so much. I can hardly wait
another two months before you arrive.

Now, for my big news. Sam is GETTING MARRIED! Can you
believe that? We can't, but here we are for his wedding. Here's the
story:

Sam left for Atlanta right after Christmas to find a place to stay while
he's there for the General Assembly. Another senator immediately
befriended him and invited him to a small get-acquainted social at
one of the older senator's homes. He was introduced to the hostess,
the older senator's daughter, and as Sam says, "It was love at first
sight!" They saw one another every night and last week he asked her
to marry him! Oh, her name is Laura Ricketts. Anyway, she wanted to
get married right away. I don't know why. Maybe she thought Sam was
such a good catch, she didn't want to risk losing him to someone else
in Atlanta. So, here we are at the Old Orchard Inn again preparing
for the wedding tomorrow.

Obviously, it will be a very small affair. Laura's mother died a
couple years ago and she has no other family besides her father. The
wedding will be in their home on Peachtree Street and that's where
she and Sam will live while he's at the General Assembly.

We met her and Mr. Ricketts for the first time last night. She seems
like a lovely girl - I think she is 20 - pretty, light brown hair and eyes,
trim figure. We just arrived yesterday because Grandma and Mammy
Sallie *came too! Mammy Sallie said she didn't care how much her old*
bones hurt, she was going to see Master Samuel get married. And, of
course, Grandma wasn't going to miss it either.

They were both so much fun to watch on the train, Ben. Mammy Sallie's eyes became as big as saucers when the train started forward. I thought I would die laughing. And, Grandma was trying so hard not to show she was excited. Mama Kathleen and I caught the giggles and couldn't stop!

Papa is somewhat concerned that Sam is rushing into this marriage too fast, but Mama Kathleen reminded him Sam is a grown man and can make his own decisions now. I think Papa is sad because he is "losing" both his children to others and it's making him feel old.

He won't really "lose" Sam because he and Laura will be coming to Oak Hill to live as soon as the General Assembly is finished next month. All in time for our wedding! So I guess I will have to add Laura to my bridesmaids list as she will be my new "sister."

Can you believe all this? I can't. Sam has always been so practical, not rash at all. Well, I think he was pretty rash when he enlisted in the army, but that was long ago. Anyway, I hope he and Laura are very happy - just like you and me. I will write to you again after the wedding tomorrow night. I'm going to bed early so I have plenty of rest for the big day tomorrow.

All my love,
Callie

* * *

Laura Ricketts sat in front of her vanity mirror slowly brushing her light brown hair, her eyes staring vacantly at her reflection. A knock on the door brought her back to the present.

"May I come in, dear?"

"Of course, Father. The door is unlocked."

Lester Ricketts entered the room, closing the door behind him. "How are you holding up?"

"I'm fine, Father. Just fine." Laura continued brushing her hair with deliberate strokes.

"You don't have to go through with this tomorrow."

"Yes…yes, I do. Mother's inheritance is gone and we don't have enough money to keep this house. I won't have our home taken from us. Besides, Samuel seems like a nice man. He's not bad looking, except for the scars on his face. He said he received those wounds at Gettysburg. His family seems nice. But most important of all, he has money. And, he's hopelessly in love with me." She looked at her father in the mirror, meeting his eyes and laid down her brush.

"You sound so cynical, dear. There should be other options to our predicament."

"You haven't thought of any, have you, Father? This is our only chance. The tax collector is knocking on the door waiting to take the house."

Laura stood up and walked to the window of her bedroom looking out to the street below. "There is one inconvenience, though. I will have to move to the country when the Assembly is recessed. What will you do while I'm there?"

"I'll be fine. Mammy Jane will take care of me. I'll come to visit you and you will come here. Samuel can't expect you to stay put on that farm all the time."

"I hope not, but he was very adamant about living at Oak Hill instead of Atlanta. Said that land is in his blood. That's what he fought for in the war." Laura sighed. "I just hope it's a decent place or else I will go crazy."

"Well, his family seems nice enough."

"Yes, and his sister will be leaving after her marriage in April, so I won't have to cope with her. His step-mother seems all right. The two older women probably won't be a problem, although he certainly is close to his mammy. I didn't want any darkies at the wedding, but he insisted that if she wanted to come, she could. Oh, well. I'll survive. I always do." Laura turned and looked at her father. "You'd better get to bed, Father. It will be a big day tomorrow. Be a good actor for me."

Lester grimaced. "Laura......."

"What, Father? Am I being too cold for you? Too much like mother?"

"No...no.....I just wish there was something else we could do."

"There isn't, so we....or I....will have to live with it. Who knows? Maybe Samuel Hill will make a wonderful husband and we will live happily ever after." Laura smiled scornfully.

"Laura...dear..."

"Good night, Father. I need my sleep before my wedding day." Laura went to her bed and pulled the coverlet down.

"Yes... of course....good night, dear, and....thank you." Lester turned towards the door.

"You are quite welcome, Father. Sleep well." Her bedroom door closed softly as Lester entered the hall.

* * *

The Hills arrived early at the Ricketts' home the next morning where they were served coffee, tea, scones, and muffins, all from a highly polished silver set. Samuel couldn't eat anything, he was too nervous.

"Callie, are you sure I look all right? Am I missing anything?"

"Do you have the wedding band?"

"Yes, in my pocket right here." Samuel felt for the ring. "It's here, right here."

"That's all you need, isn't it?"

"Guess so."

"Sam, are you sure you want to do this? Shouldn't you and Laura take a little more time to get to know one another?"

"Look who's talking!! How long have you known Ben?"

"Actually, we've 'known' each other for over six years. But we've only *known* each other for two. Remember, though, we found each other through our letters, so it's almost like being with each other all that time."

Samuel looked nervously around the parlor. "I guess that works for you. Laura and I didn't need a lot of time to know we were meant for one another. Probably like when you saw Ben in Illinois - you just knew. We just knew." He glanced around the room again and out into the foyer. "I wonder where she is. Has anyone seen her father?"

"She's getting ready, silly! Papa saw Mr. Ricketts when we came in. They went into the back somewhere talking. Settle down, Sam. I've never seen you like this."

"Well, it isn't every day that a person gets married, Callie!"

The judge who was performing the ceremony entered the parlor.

"I think we are about to begin if everyone would take their places, please."

Samuel walked anxiously over to his place by the judge, turned toward his family in the chairs, and waited for his bride. He noticed Mammy Sallie had tears trickling down her wrinkled brown cheeks. He hoped they were tears of joy.

He could hear Laura and her father descending the stairs and walking across the foyer to the parlor. When she entered the room with her father, she stared straight ahead at Samuel and gave him a half smile.

She was very pale, accentuated by the dark cranberry ensemble she wore. Her dress was of velvet, in the new fashion of a straight front and fullness in the back. The bodice had a tight fitting waist and long sleeves trimmed in mauve lace at her wrists. The front of the bodice had many tiny pleats running vertically from the square neckline to the waist. The neckline was also edged in the mauve lace. The skirt swept back, elaborately draped over an underskirt heavily trimmed with tiny pleats and mauve lace.

Laura had, that morning, cut her hair in the new daring fashion of curled bangs. The curls were achieved by placing an iron wand in the flames of a fire to heat it and then applying it to the hair. Above the newly curled bangs she wore a headpiece of fresh camellias intertwined with the mauve lace. On her neck she wore her mother's strand of pearls and the matching earrings adorned her ear lobes.

Samuel thought she was stunningly beautiful. When she reached him and the judge, she quickly disengaged her father's arm and turned to Samuel with determination in her eyes. If Samuel had looked closely, he would have also detected fear in those hazel eyes, but his own were so full of love and joy at his good fortune to be marrying this lovely creature that he missed it.

The ceremony was very short and in a few minutes, Laura became Mrs. Samuel Preston Hill. The couple went into the foyer to receive congratulations from their families.

Callie didn't know whether to hug her new sister-in-law or not, but Laura's step back when Callie approached told her a hug was not going to be appropriate. "Laura, you look absolutely beautiful. I love your new hairstyle too. I would never be so courageous as to cut my hair like that, but it is very becoming on you."

"Thank you, Callie. I just decided this morning that I was starting a new life, so I wanted a new look."

"Well, I hope you and Samuel will be very happy in this new life. I look forward to having you join us at Oak Hill."

"Yes…..I'm looking forward to it too, although, I've never lived in the country. I guess it will be a new adventure."

"I know what you mean. It's going to be very hard for me to leave Oak Hill and move to Illinois after my marriage. But living with Ben will make everything all worth it. Being with the person you love is what is important, isn't it?"

"Yes…..yes….I guess it is. At least I hope it is."

Callie felt that was a strange answer, but she just smiled and turned to her brother who gave her a huge hug, practically squeezing the breath from her.

"Callie, I am *so* happy!!" He reached for Laura's arm. "My wife! It will take some time to get used to that. We are *married*, darling, you are my *wife!*"

Laura suddenly grew paler. "Yes, Samuel, we are. Now if you will excuse me, I want to go see if the table is prepared for lunch."

"Of course, dear." Laura picked up her skirts and left for the dining room, but instead went around to the back parlor where she went in and closed and locked the door. She fell onto the settee, her hands covering her face, trying to compose herself. What had she done? How was she going to pretend she loved a person she didn't? What was she going to do tonight, their wedding night? What on earth was she going to do at that blasted plantation?

She cursed her father who had unwisely invested all their money in a corrupt venture. How could he do that to her, his only child? Thank goodness, her mother was not here to witness this, but then again, if she were here, it wouldn't be happening.

Mary Stuart Ricketts was a cold, calculating woman. So she was very surprised when Lester Ricketts swept her off her feet. When the infatuation with him was finally over, she found herself married and expecting a child. After the birth of Laura, she informed Lester she was not having any more children and banned him from her bed. Mary also informed him *she* was taking over the family's finances as he seemed to make one bad investment after another. Laura was taken care of by Mammy Jane and saw little of her mother.

Mary found hope in her husband's future when, surprisingly, he showed an aptitude for politics. She made sure they entertained in circles that would benefit and finance his campaigns. Although, a state senator's wages were small, many bribes and grafts came his way, allowing them to live in a stylish fashion. Plus, she began making wise investments in the new businesses in Atlanta, once the capital moved there from Millidgeville. This money was put into a special account for Laura's future.

When Mary lay dying of pneumonia two years ago, she informed Laura of this special fund. It was for Laura and Laura alone, not her father. It would give Laura independence - she would not have to depend on a man for money. However, after Mary's death, Lester found out about the account and through various corrupt friends of his, he had it transferred into his holdings.

Lester then proceeded to lose all his money through bad investments with some of his political cronies. He and Laura barely had enough to live on although they had to keep up appearances. Finally, the tax assessor told him new taxes had been levied by the mayor of Atlanta and it was time to pay up or the house would be seized by the city.

Lester had to approach his daughter and inform her of their predicament. Laura graciously offered to pay the taxes out of her mother's inheritance to her. Lester then had to confess he had already spent that money and more. While her father was telling her this news, Laura sat calmly, but her mind was in chaos. Only one idea kept returning to her thoughts, "I must marry a man with money." Thus, Samuel Hill became her target the night he entered the Ricketts' house. He was a willing participant.

And, now as Laura sat in her back parlor, she realized what she had done. What would her mother do now? Laura dried her tears and breathed deeply. Mother would make the best of the situation and definitely have the upper hand. So would Laura. Getting the money from Samuel would be easy, the rest would be hard......maybe. Samuel adored her. He would do whatever she asked. She would see to that.

She stood up, more composed and resolved. She walked out of the room and back into the foyer to join her new husband who had missed her presence so. She smiled politely, nodded, conversed, all the while screaming inside her head.

* * *

Callie was seated next to Kathleen on the train journeying back to Oak Hill from Atlanta. She was staring out the window blankly thinking of Sam and Laura's wedding. She didn't want her and Ben's wedding to be like that. She wanted it to be warm, loving, and family oriented and........fun. Not stuffy, cold, and mechanical like Laura and Sam's was. But, Sam didn't seem to notice. He seemed to completely lose his senses over Laura. Callie sighed. She hoped he made a good decision.

Kathleen heard Callie's sigh. "Everything all right, Callie?"

"Yes, just thinking about the wedding. Do you think Laura seemed very happy?"

"Well...I guess so. We don't know her well so we don't know what she's like when she's happy. She did seem a little.......stilted to me, though. Maybe it was just nerves and meeting all of us."

"Maybe."

"Callie, speaking of weddings, when are you going to have Dinah start your dress? You should have done it before now. She'll be busy with Trudy and her baby soon."

"Well........I haven't because I wanted to talk to you first. I've been doing a lot of thinking about this and.........if you wouldn't mind........I'd ....like to wear yours."

Kathleen looked astounded. "What? If you don't want a dress of your own, why don't you wear your mother's?"

Callie smiled at her. "That's why I want to wear yours. I want to wear my mother's wedding dress."

"But...." Kathleen didn't know what to say. "But...I mean your mother, Hannah, Callie."

"I know what you mean, but I mean my Mama *Kathleen*." Callie turned on the bench so she could face Kathleen. "*You* are the only mother I've ever known. You are the one who takes care of me when I'm sick, talks to me when I'm upset, smoothes things over with Papa when he disagrees with me. You taught me to read and write, and it was you who protected me when the Yankees were here. *You*, Mama Kathleen, are my mother, and I want to be married in my mother's wedding gown."

Tears of joy were streaming down Kathleen's face. "I don't know what to say, sweetie.......I'm honored.....I love being your 'mother'.......you know that. I love you....but don't you think it would be more appropriate to wear your *real* mother's dress?"

"I'm trying to tell you that *you are my real mother!* Mama Hannah gave birth to me, but *you* are the one who raised me." Callie took Kathleen's hands in hers and squeezed them. "And, from now on, you are no longer 'Mama Kathleen.' You are just plain 'Mama.' Now..... can I *please* wear your wedding gown when Ben and I are married?"

Kathleen smiled broadly through her tears. "Of course, of course......but what will Beulah think? And, your father?"

"They will think I'm a beautiful bride in a beautiful dress."

"Callie, you are so sweet....but I still think Hannah should be represented somehow and you should have something of your own too."

Callie thought for a moment and then her eyes glimmered with an idea. "I'll wear Mama Hannah's veil. And, then, if you don't mind ....maybe....I'll have Dinah make the skirt on your dress in the new style, like Laura's. Does that sound like a good idea, *Mama*?"

Kathleen grinned, "I think that is absolutely perfect. What a wonder you are, my child.......my *daughter*. I am so happy for you, but I will miss you so much." She reached over and hugged Callie tight.

Then the tears slid down Callie's cheeks as she embraced Kathleen. "I know, I will miss you terribly too."

They were interrupted by Nathan who thought something was

amiss and had left his seat to investigate. "Something wrong, ladies?"

Both turned towards him, wiping their tears with their hands. "Of course not, Papa, everything couldn't be better. Right, *Mama*?"

"Right, *daughter*. Everything is fine, wonderful, superb!"

"Then why are the two of you crying?"

Callie and Kathleen looked at one another and burst into laughter, further baffling Nathan.

"A man would never understand, dear. Only us women. Now go back to your seat and take care of Mammy and your mother. My daughter and I are just fine here."

"All right, if you say so…….." Nathan walked back to his seat, shaking his head in confusion.

* * *

While the Hill family was in Atlanta, Nathan had entrusted the care and protection of Oak Hill to Caleb and Trudy. He insisted they move to the premises to keep an eye out for Raymond Carswell as well as other would be intruders. He asked them to stay in the house, but Caleb refused. They would stay in a cabin and he, Joseph, and William would take turns guarding the grounds at night.

Trudy was very happy to be back at Oak Hill and near Lenora. She was sure the time of delivering her child was near. At least she hoped it was, for she had gained much weight and was terribly uncomfortable.

When the carriage arrived back at Oak Hill, Callie leapt out to find her friend and tell her all about the wedding. Nathan spotted Caleb and went to speak to him, but already knew by looking around that nothing of any consequence had happened. Kathleen helped Beulah and Mammy Sallie out of the carriage and into the house.

Callie finally found Trudy in Lenora's cabin, flat on her back on Lenora's bed. Lenora was nowhere to be seen.

"Trudy! Trudy! Is something wrong? Is the baby coming?"

"Miz Callie, so glad you's back from the weddin'. Don' know if'n the babe comin' or not, but I's been feelin' poorly."

"Where's Lenora? Why isn't she here with you?"

"She wents to gits some root or sumpin to make me feels bedder to git this chile born. Don' know. How was Masta Samuel's weddin'?

Is Miz Laura pritty?"

"I can tell you about the wedding later, Trudy. I'm worried about you right now. I'll go see if I can find Lenora. Where's your mother?"

"Don' know. I's been layin' heres sleepin', so don' know where ev'rybody is. Tells me 'bout the weddin', Miz Callie. Gives me sumpin else to think 'bout."

"All right." Callie proceeded to describe the wedding ceremony and tell Trudy about her feelings toward Laura. She looked at Trudy and realized she was asleep. That was not like Trudy at all. Callie left to find Dinah or Lenora.

Lenora was located down the path from the cabins lumbering along at her usual pace.

"Lenora! Where have you been? Why aren't you helping Trudy?"

"Well, hello, Miz Callie. Glad you's back. How was Masta Samuel's weddin'? Did he gits himse'f a pritty gal?"

"The wedding was fine. I'm worried about Trudy, Lenora. She's in your cabin all by herself. What's wrong with her? Is the baby coming?"

"Settles down, Miz Callie. Trudy fine. Thinks that babe might be comin' real soon. She needs rest now to be ready. Don' you worries none. Ole Lenora take good care of that Trudy gal. Bring that chile into this new worl' an' it be *free*. First chile born heres *free*."

"You're sure Trudy is all right? She didn't seem so to me."

"You ain't nebber seen a woman right 'fore she gives birth, now has you, Miz Callie?"

"Well.....no.... I haven't. You wouldn't let me in Mama's room when she had little Nathaniel."

"Then, you don' knows an' I's does. So, don' worries none. Trudy be fine. Jes' lez her rest now."

"All right......but you promise me you will get me if anything happens. I want to be there when Trudy has her baby. Surely, I can be of some help."

"I's gits you, but don' think you be much help." Lenora chuckled. "Birthin' ain't too pritty a sight. But when that lil chile cries it fi'st breaf, that a mighty pritty sound."

"Just send someone to get me if I'm not already there. Promise, Lenora?"

"I's promise, Miz Callie."

* * *

Callie didn't have long to wait. After unpacking her things, visiting Rumpel, and scratching Socks, she decided to visit Trudy once more. This time she *knew* Trudy was about to have the baby. She heard Trudy screaming before she reached Lenora's cabin. Thank goodness, Lenora was in the cabin bent over Trudy when Callie entered.

"The baby's coming, isn't it, Lenora?"

"Yes, Miz Callie. I's reckon it is. But it be a long times, yet. We's jes' gittin' started."

"Should I go get Caleb and Dinah?"

"You can finds them an' tell 'em the babe is on its way, but it be some time yet."

"All right, I'll go tell them." Callie didn't want to admit it, but Trudy's screaming was upsetting her and she was glad to leave.

She found Caleb with her father and when he heard the news, he raced back to the cabin to be with Trudy. Dinah was with Kathleen and she too left to be with her daughter.

"Aren't you going to be with Trudy, Callie?" Kathleen asked her. Callie was standing with her watching Dinah leave, not knowing quite what she wanted to do.

"I want to, Mama, but she was screaming so. She must be in so much pain. I don't know if I can watch her be like that."

A shadow passed over Kathleen's eyes as she remembered her pregnancy and birth of Nathaniel. "Go to her, Callie. Hold her hand. Wipe her brow with cool water. Murmur encouragement. She's in pain now, but when the child is born, she will be so happy she'll forget the pain. Go to your friend. Help her."

Callie looked at Kathleen. "Oh, Mama…..I'm so sorry. I forgot for a moment. Please forgive me."

"Nothing to forgive, dear. I wasn't meant to have little Nathaniel. He's in a better place now. Go to Trudy….go."

Callie turned to leave as Kathleen brushed the tears off her cheeks.

* * *

"Caleb Jones! You gits yourse'f outa here rights now!" Dinah was shooing Caleb out the door as Callie arrived.

"But that my chile bein' born in there. I's wants to be wit my Trudy. She needs me!'

"No, she don'. This is womin's work. No men in there. Now you jes' goes back up to the big house an' waits wit Sallie. We's lez you knows when the chile comes. Now shoo!" Dinah gave Caleb a final push.

"Miz Callie, you can comes in, but thinks you might wants not too. Ain't a pritty sight an' might scares you from havin' chiles o' your own."

"I'll be fine, Dinah. I want to see Trudy. If she doesn't want me here, I'll go." Callie entered the tiny cabin where Trudy lay on the bed with Lenora beside her, humming a calming tune.

"Miz Callie, I's so glad you cames back. Come…come sits over here. Talks to me." Trudy raised up and motioned for Callie to sit on the other side of the bed.

"Are you sure, Trudy? I don't want to bother you."

"Ain't no bother. Sit. Ohhhhhhh……!"

Lenora looked up. "'Nudder pain, Trudy?"

Trudy just nodded. "Worser than the last."

"Uh-huh. You res' when theys goes away, chile. Pritty soon theys come faster."

Trudy rolled her big brown eyes. Callie reached out and grabbed one of Trudy's hands and held it.

"You're going to be a wonderful mother, Trudy. Just focus on that beautiful baby you're about to have. Do you want a boy or a girl?"

Trudy looked at Callie gratefully. "I's wants a lil gal, but Caleb wants a boy. Don' matter none, long as it's all right. Ohhhh….. Here comes 'nudder one, Lenora. Ohhhhhh….."

"Breathe, Trudy. Don' hold your breaf. There now. That good. Gittin' closer nows. That good."

Callie had paled when Trudy clenched her hand so hard she thought her bones were broke. When the contraction was over, Trudy released her grip.

"Can I's have a sip o' water, Lenora? Feelin' mighty thirsty."

"Jes' a sip."

"I'll get it." Callie volunteered and jumped off the bed and went to the ewer on the washstand. She poured a little water into the tin cup and brought it back over to Trudy, who sipped it thirstily.

"That 'nuf, gal. Too much makes you sick."

"Ohhhh……again! Ohhhh…….. Ohhhh….. It bad! Ohhh…"

Callie held her hands over her ears. She couldn't stand to hear Trudy scream in so much pain. She went to the door and stepped outside in the fresh cool air. Sitting on the step was Caleb with his head in his hands.

"She dyin', Miz Callie, I's knows it. My Trudy gal dyin'.'" Tears were running down his face.

"No she's not, Caleb. She's having a baby. I think most women sound like that when they give birth."

Caleb turned to look at her with his tear stained face. "You thinks so? I neber heared no womin gives birth 'fore. Must hurts real bad."

"Yes, that's what I've been told. But Lenora says no matter how much pain there is, you forget all about it once you hold that baby in your arms. Don't you worry, Caleb. Trudy is young and strong and she will be just fine……..so will your baby."

"Ohhhhhh….owwwwwww……ohhhhh…..Miz Callie! Comes back!" Trudy was yelling.

"Coming, Trudy!" Callie ran back into the cabin. "I'm here." Callie went over and sat on the edge of the bed again.

"Miz Callie, if'n I's dies havin' this baby, I wants you to takes care o' it an' Caleb."

"Trudy Jones!! You are not going to die!"

"Jes' in case. Promise me." Trudy looked up at Callie with pleading eyes.

"I promise, but I don't need to. You will be fine, the baby will be fine, and you and Caleb will have a wonderful family to raise. Look at me Trudy. Listen to what I'm saying. You are going to have a healthy baby and you will take care of it until it is grown."

Trudy's eyes glazed over, then her face contorted with pain. "Ohhhhhh......owwww.....it hurts so bad!"

Lenora got up, felt Trudy's belly. "Miz Callie, raise her up an' sits 'hind her so she can leans agin you. That's right. Now, Trudy. Trudy! Looks at me! When I says you push, you push hard an' we gits this babe out."

Trudy looked at Lenora but wasn't focusing. Lenora grabbed her face and forced her to look at her. "Now, Trudy. NOW! PUSH!"

"Uhhhhh.....ohhhh....." Trudy sounded like no human Callie had ever heard, but she stayed where she was, helping to hold Trudy's shoulders straight.

"Good! Now push agin........HARD!"

Trudy obeyed. She fell back against Callie, exhausted.

"One mores time. PUSH! PUSH!"

Trudy did and suddenly there was a baby in Lenora's hands. Callie screamed with joy. "It's here, Trudy, your baby is born! Oh, Trudy, it's here!" Callie didn't realize that she was sobbing and laughing at the same time.

Lenora held up the baby with a big smile on her face too. "Mir'cle of life, Miz Callie. Trudy Jones, you's gots yourse'f a mighty fine baby gal! Lez me cut the cord an' then you holds her."

Trudy turned to Callie. "Did she say a gal? I's gots my gal, Miz Callie? Allelujah!"

Lenora placed the now crying child on Trudy's stomach. "She bootiful. She so pritty. She my gal. My baby gal." And then Trudy fell asleep, exhausted from the birth.

"Miz Callie, you goes tells Caleb he a papa to a fine gal. Tells him the mama is fine too, jes' tired. Then you brings him in here to see his gals."

Callie did as told. When she and Caleb entered the cabin, Lenora had the baby girl swaddled in a blanket and Trudy was arranged on the bed with the sheets pulled up, still sleeping.

Caleb walked over to Lenora. "They's both fine, Caleb. Here, holds your lil gal. She a pritty one. I's seen ugly babes, but she's a fine lookin' one."

Caleb gingerly took the baby from Lenora and hesitantly touched her little hand. He grinned from ear to ear through his tears and looked at Callie and Lenora. "She gots hands! Teeny hands!"

Callie and Lenora burst out laughing. "'Course she gots hands. Feet….arms.. legs…toes…..She gots eve'ythin'!" Lenora unwrapped the blanket so Caleb could see for himself. He just glowed with happiness.

Trudy moaned and then slowly woke up. She concentrated on Caleb with the baby and smiled. He went to her side and knelt down by the bed showing her their child.

Lenora motioned to Callie. "Come on, Miz Callie. These two needs to be 'lone." Callie nodded in agreement and she and Lenora stepped outside allowing the new family to bond.

Callie exhaled a big sigh of relief and hugged the old woman. "That was amazing, Lenora. Thank you for letting me stay to see it. What a miracle!"

* * *

Trudy was sitting up in bed with the baby girl nursing at her breast. Callie was pacing purposefully across the worn pine floor of Lenora's cabin and Caleb was rocking leisurely in Lenora's chair.

"Trudy, you just can't make up a name."

"Yes, I's cans. I's cans do whatever I's wants. Ain't that so, Caleb?"

Caleb nodded in agreement. "I's named her Liberty, an' Trudy names her Caludy."

"But 'Caludy' isn't even a word, Trudy. You know that!"

"Is a new word. 'Cal' for Caleb an' Miz Callie, 'udy' for Trudy. Caludy! Liberty Caludy Jones. I's thinks that a pritty name. "'Cept we callin' her Libby."

"Well, I can understand naming her Liberty - she's the first free darkie born at Oak Hill, and I like the name Libby, but Caludy? I'll have to think about that."

"You shoulds feels good 'bout it, Miz Callie. I's givin' part o' your name to her 'cause you such a 'portant part o' my life."

Callie suddenly stood still, shocked. "Oh, good heavens, Trudy. Where has my brain been? Of course, I'm honored. I'm so sorry……

..I didn't even think of it that way. I just thought it sounded odd…….
Forgive me? Liberty 'Libby' Caludy Jones. A perfect name for this
beautiful baby girl. It's a wonderful name, Trudy. Thank you so much
for making me a part of it."

Trudy chuckled. "Thought you sees it that way." She removed
Libby from her breast and held her up to Callie. "Here, Aunt Callie,
holds Miz Jones for me while I's gits myse'f backs togeder."

Callie took the little bundle and tenderly rocked her in her arms.
Libby Caludy just looked back at her with big brown eyes and waved
her tiny hands in the air.

"She's just too precious, Trudy. Look at her eyelashes. They are so
long and dark. And, that little nose. And, she smells so good." Callie
brought Libby up to her face and kissed her smooth cheeks. "She's
just so perfect."

"Looks like you gots a way wit chiles, Miz Callie," Caleb said.
"Be havin' your own after you an' Mista Ben gits wed. Libby be good
practice for you."

Callie looked at Caleb and was suddenly very serious. "I truly hope
Ben and I have children, Caleb. Especially if they are as sweet as this
one. Libby is a beautiful sign of your love for each other. I would like
nothing better than for Ben and I to have that too."

"All my screamin' an' yellin' didn' scare you from havin' your own
babes, Miz Callie?"

"Well……..a little. But not when you get a baby like this in the
end, Trudy. She's worth it all, isn't she?"

"Yes, ma'am. Worth it all. Funny, don' even 'member most. Jes'
her comin' out an' Lenora puttin' her in my arms. Best feelin' I's ever
ever had."

Libby let out a little cry. The three laughed. "Guess she's glad to be
here too," giggled Callie as she cuddled the baby even more.

* * *

Raymond Carswell happened to be on the road between Oak Hill
and the Jones's cabin when he noticed Callie Hill riding ahead of him.
He was certain it was her - he could tell by the straight back and the
way she handled her horse.

He followed her at a distance, not wanting her to know he was there. He saw her turn into the lane to the cabin, dismount, and enter the little house. He waited for several minutes, then decided to leave. But he marked the time of day.

The next day, he was again waiting to see if Callie would appear at the same time. She did. Again he followed her and watched her enter the cabin. This time he waited to see how long she stayed. He hid himself and his horse in the brush across from the house.

After a few hours, Callie emerged from the cabin, followed by Trudy, holding baby Libby. She hugged both and mounted her horse, heading back to Oak Hill.

Carswell grinned. So, her darkie friend had a baby and she was coming everyday to visit. Interesting. He would have to keep an eye on this. It could work to his advantage some day.

Raymond observed Callie for a week, marking the time she left Oak Hill, arrived at the Jones's, and headed back to Oak Hill. He checked out the road, terrain, and anything else he could think of. One just never knew when that information would be important. He stored it all in his devious mind........waiting for any opportunity.

* * *

After the birth of Libby, Callie was engrossed in wedding planning. The first item was to have Dinah alter Kathleen's wedding gown and Hannah's veil.

Kathleen's dress was a simple ivory linen, full skirted with long sleeves and high neckline. Dinah lowered the neckline somewhat and trimmed it with ivory lace. She took out the extra fullness of the skirt in the front, adding it to the back. There she draped the linen and caught it just below the waist, making a sort of bustle. An underskirt was sewn of the same material only it was filled with rows and rows of the ivory lace.

Callie and Mammy Sallie had been experimenting with hairstyles and finally decided on one. Ben liked Callie's hair when it was cascading down her back in its natural curls instead of corralled into a chignon, but that was not fashionable. A compromise was needed and Mammy Sallie provided it.

Mammy parted Callie's hair down the middle and then pulled Callie's curls to the crown of her head, anchoring them with the comb Ben had given her, and then let them fall past the nape of her neck. This style would work perfectly with Hannah's veil.

The veil was of a very open lace pattern, cathedral length, held in place with a coronet of fresh orange blossoms. Instead of the coronet, Callie wanted a headpiece that sat forward of the crown of her head where the curls were held. Dinah made a tiara out of lace, linen, and eventually fresh orange blossoms. The veil was then attached *under* the gathering of curls, showing them off. Callie thought it was perfect and something she had never seen before.

In fact, she thought her wedding ensemble was the most beautiful she'd ever seen, more than Susan's and definitely more than Laura's. More than beauty, it was the sentiment behind the dress and veil that made it so special to her. She and Kathleen shed many tears during her fittings, but all in happiness.

With the wedding attire done, Callie's attention turned to the festivities after the ceremony. She left it up to Belle to determine the menu for the wedding breakfast, as long as she fixed Callie's favorite cornbread, with lots of butter and honey, and crisply fried bacon. Belle's famous fried potatoes and onions were also a must. Kathleen, Beulah, and Belle decided what to feed all the hungry guests who would be staying at Oak Hill for the weeks before the wedding.

Ben's family, Samuel, Laura, and her father, and all the Savannah relatives would be arriving soon. The house and grounds had to be in their very best shape.

Every available room was prepared for guests. Even the old schoolroom had been turned into a bedroom. Several mattresses would have to be placed on the floors to accommodate so many people.

With everyone working, it didn't take long for Oak Hill to be gleaming as it did before the war. The weather even cooperated, opening the new spring buds on the azaleas, pushing the tulips and daffodils up out of the ground, and sprouting the tender green shoots of grass against the red Georgia earth.

Callie stood on the front veranda looking at all of Mother Nature's wonders. She inhaled deeply, closed her eyes, and smiled. Spring was here for her marriage to Ben. She exhaled slowly. She didn't think she ever felt more happy or content.

* * *

"But, Papa, I have to go to the train station to pick up Ben! I just *have* too!"

"Callie, I'm going to tell you this one more time, and then that's it. The carriage can only hold six people. There are four people coming from Illinois. I need to meet them and I want Kathleen there too. She can talk to Abigail better than I can. Which means there is no room for you. Besides, you and Ben will just stare at one another making the rest of us uncomfortable. You are staying here. You can wait a few more hours to see Ben. No more arguing. I'm firm on this, Callie."

Callie stuck out her lower lip, but she knew she wouldn't sway Nathan this time. He was adamant about taking Kathleen along and there really wasn't room for her. Kathleen didn't come to her aid either. She thought it was best for the host and hostess to greet their guests together.

Callie didn't agree, but she didn't disagree - only because she knew she would be spending the rest of her life with Ben and would never be apart from him again. She could wait a few hours until he arrived at Oak Hill.

* * *

Raymond Carswell watched as the Hill carriage headed for Swainsboro with only Nathan and Kathleen aboard. He wondered where they were going this time - without Callie. He had heard some talk about a wedding taking place at Oak Hill, but he didn't know whose it was.

He was rewarded when he heard a carriage on the road coming back from Swainsboro later in the day. It was the Hill's again and full of people - four additional ones. An older man and woman, and a younger man and woman. Maybe they were arriving for the wedding he'd heard about. He would have to investigate further. Maybe this could be his chance.

* * *

Ben had a hard time sitting still in the crowded carriage. He was very disappointed when Callie was not there to greet him at the train station, but now he understood.

"Ben, please quit squirming. You're wrinkling my dress."

"Yes, Emma, dear. I'm just excited."

Abigail smiled at her son. "Won't be long now, son. Just a couple weeks."

Kathleen turned to Abigail. "Callie was not very happy that she couldn't come along. She's probably pacing the floors now waiting for us." Kathleen laughed. "No, I mean she's probably waiting for *Ben*, not *us*!"

"I know what you mean, Kathleen. Benjamin has been mighty antsy waitin' for the time to pass."

"Ma, you act like I'm not sittin' right here. Yes, I've been very anxious. Weren't you when you married Pa? I can't wait to start my life with Callie. Wish the weddin' was tomorra."

"Yes, I guess I was ready to become your pa's wife. Been so long ago, can't really remember."

"Abigail, dear. Not that long ago. We're still young at heart!" Henry reached over and patted his wife's hand. "You haven't changed a bit."

Abigail smiled at her husband and then, embarrassed, lowered her eyes.

Nathan looked out the window and pointed some fields out to Henry to change the subject. He was still uncomfortable talking about the wedding because it meant Callie would be leaving and he was dreading that day.

Soon the carriage turned into the lane lined with the live-oaks, the Spanish moss dancing in the breeze. The house was in view.

Abigail's hand went to her throat as she inhaled loudly. "Oh, my goodness, Kathleen! What a magnificent home!"

"Thank you, Abigail. We think it's pretty special."

The carriage pulled to the mounting step where Callie was waiting impatiently. She had been on the veranda for hours waiting for the Chapmans to arrive. Now that they were here, she was nervous. She was very polite greeting Abigail, Henry, and Emma, but when Ben stepped out, she wrapped her arms around him tight and wouldn't let go.

Nathan shook his head and smiled at Kathleen. "Come on, folks. We'll get you to your rooms and then show you around. Looks like Ben and Callie will be 'busy' for a while."

The pair didn't even know the others had left. They were in their own special world.

The two families spent the next few days getting acquainted and reacquainted. Beulah and Mammy Sallie instantly liked Abigail, Henry, and Emma. Callie insisted Trudy, Caleb, and Libby come and meet them too. It was somewhat awkward for the Chapmans to meet former slaves, but they immediately loved baby Libby. They almost felt like they knew Trudy, for Ben had told them so much about her.

It was a time of visiting, eating, resting, touring, and preparing for the wedding. Every day something was planned.

Emma and Trudy had their bridesmaids dresses fitted and finished by Dinah. Victoria and Laura would have theirs done when they arrived later. The women were wearing white muslin, fashioned with long sleeves, tight bodices, and skirts that mimicked Callie's dress, then all were trimmed in pink ribbons. Fresh flowers would adorn their hair. Susan's twins, Carrie and Annie, and baby Libby were going to be flower girls. The twins were wearing white muslin dresses similar to the ones Victoria and Callie wore at Susan's wedding, only with pink, not blue, ribbon sashes and trim. Libby would wear a simple white cotton dress with pink ribbons.

* * *

"Ben, do you mind if I ride over to Trudy's? I just need to get away from here for a few minutes. I don't think I can make one more decision about food or hems or flowers. I need to clear my mind. Sam and Laura are coming shortly so I'll be back in time to greet them."

"No, I don't mind. Do you want me to ride with you?"

"I'll be fine, so no. I won't be gone long. I just need to get away for a little bit. You aren't upset, are you?"

"No, no.......I know what you mean. Don't worry. I'll make excuses for you."

"I knew there was another reason why I love you so much. Thank you." Callie gave Ben a peck on the cheek and headed for the stables to saddle up Daisy. Ben just smiled and thought, "What a wonderful woman I'm marrying."

Callie reappeared mounted, walking Daisy toward the lane. She laughed, waved at Ben, and then pushed the horse into a gallop. Again, Ben grinned. Then he walked back up the steps to the front veranda and entered the chaotic house.

* * *

Raymond Carswell had been waiting for just this moment. Every day he had ridden towards the Jones's cabin, hoping to find Callie there also. He had almost given up since he heard it was she who was getting married soon. He was angry that he hadn't acted sooner. He had to revamp his plan, but now he could put it in play.

He followed Callie, but far enough away that she was unaware of his presence. She was galloping her horse, her chignon loosened by the wind, curls flying now behind her. What a sight she was! Raymond felt a stab of desire in the pit of his stomach. Well, she wasn't married yet.

She arrived at the cabin and entered. He waited......and waited..... and waited. He was a patient man. After several hours, he saw her come out and mount her horse again. She said something to the darkie and turned back on the road. This was his chance. He waited until she was far enough away from the cabin and then he acted.

* * *

Laura Ricketts Hill got her first glimpse of Oak Hill as they entered the oak lined lane. It looked fairly affluent with its tall columns, white brick, and black shutters. The grounds were lavish enough and well kept. Maybe it wouldn't be too awful to stay here after all.

"What do you think, darling? Isn't it everything I said it would be?"

"Yes, Samuel. It's very nice."

"Wait until I show you around. It's amazing what we've done with the place since the war. All the outbuildings were burned, you know. It's taken years to replace everything."

"Your family deserves a lot of credit for persevering after the war, Samuel," said Mr. Ricketts. "Many planters left for other places. That's how all the carpetbaggers and scalawags acquired so much land."

"That's correct, Lester. In fact, the plantation we just passed is an example of that. Elijah Montgomery gave up most of his land to a carpetbagger who came through here about three years ago. Nasty man. He's been after Father and me to sell him some of our acreage. Threatened me one day and then apologized all nice the next. He's been a thorn in our side since he arrived."

Laura shivered. "Hope he stays away, Samuel."

"Don't worry, dear. Nothing will ever happen to Oak Hill. Father and I will see to that."

The carriage pulled up to the step and everyone came streaming out of the house to greet the newlyweds. Hugs, handshakes, and introductions fell on the travelers. Samuel looked around. There was Ben and his family, Nathan and Kathleen, Mammy Sallie and Beulah, but where was Callie?

"Where's my sister?" He finally shouted loud enough above all the din to be heard.

Ben walked towards him. "She went to visit Trudy. Had to get away from all of this for a bit. She should be back soon, though."

"Good. I'm glad she's taking some time for herself. Well, let's go in and I'll get my family settled. What do you think of *my* bride?"

"She's beautiful, Samuel. You look very happy."

"I am, Ben. I am."

Laura found Samuel and grabbed his arm. "Can we go inside? I need to freshen up from the ride. I'm afraid I'm getting one of my bad headaches."

Samuel frowned. "Of course, darling. We'll be in my old room. Your father will be down the hall in the north room." He led Laura and Lester into the house and up the stairs.

"This is a beautiful home, Samuel." Lester was looking around as he walked.

"Thank you. It's seen a lot in its day, but seems no worse for the wear."

After Samuel got Laura and Lester settled, he went back downstairs to talk to his family. It wasn't very long before Laura knocked on her father's door.

"Come in."

"Father, it's me."

"Yes, Laura. I thought you had a headache."

"No. But I would have if I'd stayed down there in all that clamor. What do you think of Oak Hill?"

"Looks like a prospering plantation to me. Think you made a good choice. Samuel hasn't denied you any money yet, has he?"

"No."

"Then, things are going as planned."

"Except I will have to live here now with all these people."

"Some of them will be leaving after the wedding, dear. You can handle it."

Laura gave her father a stern look. "Yes, *I* will handle it."

Lester looked away sheepishly.

* * *

Callie wasn't home yet and Ben was getting worried, but no one else seemed to be. Callie often stayed at Trudy's for hours playing with Libby or helping Trudy fix a meal. She'd be back soon.

Everyone seemed to settle in the back parlor where card games were started and conversation was rampant. Laura thought she had begged off long enough and didn't want Samuel to think she was avoiding his family, so she started down the stairs to join the others.

As she got to the last landing, there was a knock on the front door. She waited for a servant to come and open the door, but when no one appeared and the visitor knocked again, she went to the door herself.

She opened the door a crack. A man was standing there dressed in an old faded green and yellow plaid suit. His eyes were like little beads, his hair was greasy and uncombed under his old hat, and his unshaven face looked pock marked. He was smiling at her showing rotten decayed teeth. Laura almost shut the door, but he put his foot at the bottom preventing her from doing so.

"Yes....sir. May I help you?"

"Came to see Miss Callie Hill, ma'am. Heard she's gittin' married and I brought her a little weddin' gift. We're neighbors, you see. Don't recollect seein' you here before, ma'am. You here for the weddin'?"

"I'm Laura Hill, Samuel's wife. Yes, I'm here for the wedding. Callie isn't here right now. She's visiting a friend, I think. Do you want to see her fiancé?"

"Well, congratulations to you and Mr. Hill, ma'am. No, I don't need to see her betrothed. Would you just please see that she gets this? I'd be mighty obliged."

"Of course. Thank you. May I tell her who it's from?"

"Oh, she'll know when she reads the card. Thank you, Mrs. Hill. I'll be goin' now."

Laura thankfully closed the door, took the gift, which was a large envelope, laid it on the front parlor table, and reluctantly joined the others in the back room.

* * *

Ben walked over to Samuel. "Samuel, I'm really getting worried about Callie. She's been gone for hours now. I'm sure she didn't plan on staying this late. It's almost dark."

Samuel shared Ben's concern. He had been wondering what was taking his sister so long. Looking around, he saw uneasy looks on Nathan and Kathleen's faces too.

He walked over to where Nathan was sitting. "Father, don't you think we should go look for Callie? Maybe something happened along the way from Trudy's. We can at least go there and find out when she left. I know she would be here before now because she knew Laura and I were coming."

"Yes, you're right, Samuel. We should have gone before now, but I didn't want to worry everyone."

The three men started for the door when Kathleen asked, "Where are ya'll going?"

"We think Callie should be back by now, so we're just going to go check the road," Nathan answered.

"Oh, dear, it has been quite a while since she left, hasn't it? Hurry on then, find her."

Laura overheard the conversation. "Before you go, Mr. Chapman, a gentleman was at the door when I came downstairs. He left a wedding gift for you and Callie."

Nathan and Samuel looked at one another. "Laura, dear, what did this 'gentleman' look like?"

"Well, he was really disgusting. Old suit, oily hair, bad teeth, beady eyes. I didn't want to talk to him very long, so I just took the gift and he left."

"Where's the gift, Laura?"

"On the parlor table, Samuel. Did I do something wrong?"

"No....no.....it just sounds like the man was Raymond Carswell, the carpetbagger I was telling you about earlier."

"Oh, no."

Ben walked into the parlor and retrieved the envelope from the table and ripped it open. Inside was a dirty, grimy folded piece of paper. He opened it and became very pale, clutching the table for support. He looked at Nathan and Samuel with horror in his eyes. "It's Callie's handwriting," he uttered hoarsely. "I can't......you read it..."

Samuel grabbed the paper from Ben's outstretched hand feeling as though an icy hand had squeezed his heart. He read aloud:

"Papa, I'm all right for now. Mr. Carswell has me. He's telling me what to write. He wants the deeds to the property by the old mill and 500 other acres that we aren't using. He says Sam will know which ones. Also, $1,000 in cash. If he doesn't get them by noon tomorrow, he will hurt me. Bring them to the big flat rock on the east side of the road as you turn to go to Trudy's cabin, leave them in the tin he's placed there and then leave. Once he has the deeds and money, he will let me go. If you try to find me or report him to the sheriff, he will kill me. Please, Papa, do as he says. Callie"

"NOOOOOO! NOOOOOO!" Ben doubled over as the cry of despair escaped from his lips. "Not Callie.......noooooooooo!" He couldn't breathe.

Nathan had paled as had Samuel. Samuel stood there with the note in his hand momentarily stunned.

Kathleen, followed by Abigail and Henry, rushed into the foyer when they heard Ben cry out. She looked at the men and knew something was terribly wrong. Samuel handed her the note which she quickly read. She looked up at the ashen faced men, herself feeling nauseous.

"We have to find her, Nathan! We *will* find her! Look at me, people! Don't just stand there and wring your hands. We need action! A plan. Get yourselves together and let's think."

Ben rose up and stared at Kathleen. "Benjamin, pull yourself together. We will find her."

"But....Callie......not again, Mrs. Hill! Not again!"

"We'll find her, Ben, don't fret. Now, let's sit down in here and devise a way to get our girl back."

Everyone sat down, all still shaken; not wanting to think of what Callie was going through. Hoping she was still alive. Hoping she wasn't hurt. Hoping that Carswell hadn't.........

* * *

Callie couldn't believe what was happening to her. How could Carswell overpower her so quickly? He had pulled her off Daisy before she knew it and then had her hands tied to the horn of his saddle. He flipped her so her head and feet were dangling from his horse. Her hair trailed in the dirty road, all the blood rushing to her head. Somehow he had managed to tie her legs together too. She was rendered helpless in a matter of minutes.

Now she was in some dark, dank shed, lying in a pile of old, musty, decayed straw, still tied up and gagged too. When Carswell forced her to write the note to Nathan, he released one of her hands. The other he tied to a stud in the shed.

"Don't try no tricks with me, missy. Won't do you no good. You can't get away, so you might as well cooperate," he told her with a sneer. "If your papa does what I want, you'll be back home tomorra afternoon. If not, well, then you have a problem." Then he took his grimy hand and touched her brow, tracing the line of her jaw down to her neck. She'd flinched and tried to turn her head, but then he grabbed her chin and forced her to be still and he repeated the motion, slower. He laughed at her and then left.

Now she was all alone with her thoughts. The tears had stopped flowing. It did no good to cry. She needed to think. There must be some way she could escape. She tried to work her hands out of the rope, but it was too tight. She knew her wrists were bleeding from trying. There wasn't any way to undo her feet either. But if she could just get loose she might be able to force the locked door open and escape. She focused on freeing her hands, ignoring the pain.

* * *

It didn't take long for the Hill and Chapman families to plan how they were going to rescue Callie. They surmised Carswell abducted her on the way to or from Trudy and Caleb's cabin. First on the list was to visit the Joneses and see if Callie had arrived, and if so, when she left.

After learning that information, Nathan and Henry were going to search the area around the Jones's cabin. Ben and Samuel were going to ride to the Montgomery place and search it.

If that failed, they would widen the search area and everyone, including the women, on every available horse or mount, would scour the countryside looking for Callie. They would search the night through. If she wasn't found, Nathan would place documents looking like deeds and some cash on the flat rock and then they would wait until Carswell showed up to collect it. But it was vital they found her tonight. They all knew what Carswell could do to her.

"Everyone ready to go?" Nathan asked from his horse. They were.

"Bring her back, Nathan, bring her back!" Kathleen called as the men started galloping down the lane. She herded the women and Mr. Ricketts into the house towards the back parlor. Mammy Sallie and Beulah waited there. Mammy was sobbing heavily.

"Now, Mammy Sallie, you stop that. Callie will be found and she will be fine. Now, to make sure, let's all bow our heads and pray for her return." Kathleen looked around and then bowed her head, followed by the others.

The men arrived at Trudy and Caleb's shortly. A light was still shining in the small front room. Nathan dismounted and started up the steps when he was stopped by the sight of a rifle muzzle sticking out of the front door.

"Who goes there?" It was Caleb. "Name yourse'f 'fore I's shoots you."

"Caleb, it's me, Nathan Hill. Please put the gun away. We have a terrible problem. Open the door."

Caleb opened the door and stepped out into the dark night. "Sorry, Mista Hill, cain't be too careful wit Klan men runnin' 'round at night. What wrong?"

"Carswell has taken Callie. He's holding her hostage for land and money. We wanted to know if she was here this afternoon and if she was, when did she leave. He had to have taken her around here."

"I's gits Trudy. I's out in the field an' didn' sees Miz Callie t'days. Wait minute. She in bed wit Libby. Come on in outs of the night. Who wit you? Oh, Mista Ben an' Mista Chapman an' Mista Samuel. Comes in, comes in."

"Thanks, Caleb, but I think we'll stay mounted." Samuel looked around at Ben and Henry who nodded in agreement.

"Hurry, Caleb, get Trudy. We're wasting precious time."

"Yes, Mista Hill." Caleb turned and stepped into the little room he had added before Libby was born. Trudy was lying in bed with Libby in her arms. She looked up at Caleb with worried eyes.

"Sumpin wrong, Caleb? Ain't the Klan, is it? I's heard horses." She pulled Libby closer to her.

"No, Miz Callie missin'. Carswell gots her an' Mista Hill needs help. Can you gits up an' comes out to talk to him?"

"Miz Callie gone!! She been taken!! Oh, my Lawd! Here you takes Libby while I's puts my robe on." Caleb grabbed the infant as Trudy threw her robe over her shoulders and ran into the front room.

"Masta Nathan, Caleb say Miz Callie gone! What can I's do to helps you finds her?" Trudy was now weeping as she saw the look on Nathan's face.

"Trudy, was Callie here today?"

"Yes, sir. She comes this afta'noon. Says she needs some time away from all the peoples at Oak Hill. We talks an' she play wit Libby. Then she lefts."

"Thank you, Trudy. That means he must have been waiting for her on the road somewhere between here and home. Now we can start looking for some clues around here."

"Can I's goes wit you, Masta Nathan? Gots to help finds my Miz Callie 'fore that man hurts her."

"No, but y'all might want to go to Oak Hill and stay there until we find her."

"You needs me to go wit you, Mista Hill? I's be glads to search too."

"Not yet, Caleb. You go to Oak Hill. Take your rifle in case Carswell shows up there. Watch over everybody at the house."

"Yes sir, we gits ready rights now. Come on, Trudy. Gits dressed fast."

Trudy wiped the tears off her face. "You find her, Masta Nathan. You find her."

"We will, Trudy, we will."

* * *

Raymond Carswell couldn't be happier. His plan had actually worked perfectly! He was sure none of the Hills had any idea where he had taken their precious Callie. He knew he had plenty of time. That woman at Oak Hill, Samuel's wife, seemed not to care much about giving the "gift" to her new sister-in-law, so it would be a while before they all figured it out. Best of all, no one at Pine Wood had any idea what he had done. He had taken Callie to an old dilapidated shed by the old mill on their property, but far from the cabins where they were living. He'd gone the back way so no one had seen him. He would check on her after everyone had gone to sleep for the night. He thought he might have some fun with her.......she was a beautiful young woman............just ripe for the taking.

* * *

There was someone watching Raymond. Someone who had been watching him for weeks. Someone who knew when he left and when he came home. Someone who knew he rode out everyday the same time Callie Hill did. Someone who had good reason to watch him.

Someone was watching......watching....watching...and waiting.

* * *

Ben and Samuel were headed on the road to Oak Hill and then Pine Wood when they found Daisy. In their haste to get to Trudy, the men had ridden by the partially hidden horse.

"There's Daisy! Over there, Ben! By the ditch. She's tied to the tree." Samuel was the first to see Callie's horse.

"How did we miss her before?" Ben rode over to the horse, which whinnied gratefully to be let loose. Ben smacked her on the rear. "Home, Daisy, go home." The horse took off trotting down the road toward Oak Hill.

Henry and Nathan had started searching around the Jones's cabin, widening their circle each time around. They stopped at every little shack or lean to, praying to find Callie there. Each time they were disappointed. Their shouts of her name could be heard over the chirp of the crickets and the hoot of the owls. But no one answered.

"Not much here between Oak Hill and Elijah's place where someone would keep a person. No sheds or shacks. No caves or anything like that either," Samuel told Ben as they rode past Oak Hill.

"Do you think he might have her right under our noses at Oak Hill?"

"Never thought of that, but don't know how he could. There's always someone around here. They would have seen him. Besides, he would have taken her about the time Laura and I arrived and everyone was outside. We surely would have noticed something, wouldn't we?"

"Just a thought. Have to think of anything, but what's happenin' to Callie. She must be so scared. She has to know we're lookin' for her. I just hope she can hold out."

"Callie isn't as frail as everybody thinks. She's strong. She's been through a lot and it's made her stronger. If there's any way she can escape, she will, or if she has to hurt Carswell, she will. I know she's scared, but sometimes that makes her mad and when she's mad, she's all right."

"I hope so, Samuel, I hope so. Do you think the people at the Montgomery's will cooperate with us and let us search the premises?"

"Think so. I've talked to Lizzy and Jenny a few times since Carswell arrived. Elijah and Almina, too. Don't think they're overly fond of him. Probably sorry they let him stay on their land. You'd better not talk much, though. They'll know you're a Yankee and Elijah's son was killed during the war. Worse yet, if they find out you were with Sherman when he came through here and burned their place."

"Won't say a word, Samuel." Ben looked out at the cloudless night where the stars were sparkling and the moon was full. "I'll do anything to find Callie....and soon, before that Carswell hurts her........or worse."

"Don't think about that. Just think about finding her."

* * *

Callie kept struggling with the rope around her wrists until she couldn't stand the pain anymore. Tears were streaming down her face - she couldn't even wipe them off. Her nose was running, her arms ached, her wrists were throbbing, her bound feet were stinging, the gag in her mouth was hurting, she couldn't have been more miserable. And, always in the back of her mind was Raymond Carswell returning. She had to find some way to get loose before he returned. She had to!!

* * *

Raymond waited until he saw the lights go out of the girls' cabin and Elijah's. He snuck out and meandered around the back way until he arrived at the mill. The old shed wasn't far from there.

He smiled and rubbed his hands in anticipation. Yes, this was going to be worth the wait. He wanted the acreage and the money, but having Callie Hill would be the best twist of irony. Especially so close to her wedding day. He'd show those Hills. He would get what he wanted. Since the first day he saw her, he wanted Callie Hill.

* * *

Nathan and Henry weren't having any luck at all. They had searched as far around the little cabin as they thought Carswell would go. Nothing. Not one sign of Callie.

"I think he must have taken her the other direction, Henry. We're wasting our time here. Let's go join the boys."

"Whatever you say, Nathan. If she's around here, we surely would have found something. Let's hope the boys have had better luck."

Ben and Samuel arrived at Pine Wood to find it in darkness. A small fire still wafted smoke outside of Elijah's cabin, stinging their eyes as they went by. Other than that, there was dead stillness.

Samuel dismounted and went to the first cabin, Elijah's, and pounded on the door. "Elijah! It's Samuel Hill. Come out! We need your help!" He pounded again.

From inside he heard Elijah stirring around. The old man was slowly shuffling towards the door. Samuel was impatient. "Hurry, Elijah! We need your help!"

Elijah, in his nightshirt, finally opened the door and stood in the moonlight. "What on earth you poundin' on my door at this time of the night, boy? Just getting settled for the night. What so dang-burned important to disturb an old man?"

"I'm sorry, Elijah. It's just that your man, Carswell, has kidnapped my sister and is holding her somewhere. We think he might have her here on your property. Could we search for her?'

"What.....? Raymond took that little gal? You sure? Why would he do that?"

"We're sure. He sent a note saying he did just that. He wants some of our land and money in exchange for Callie. The note said if we didn't bring what he wants by noon tomorrow, he'd kill her. Do you think he would?"

"Hmmm....don't rightly know. He's an odd duck. Always nice to me....been workin' pretty hard here. Don't think the girls like him, though."

"We aren't going to waste any more time. Can we search?"

"'Course. Start with his cabin. I'd help you, but I don't move too fast anymore."

"That's all right, Elijah. We'll find Callie if she's here."

Samuel mounted his horse again and motioned to Ben. "Come on, Ben, let's start looking. Thanks, Elijah."

The two men walked their horses down the line of cabins, noting they were being watched by the Montgomery women out their window. Almina stepped out into the night air, clutching her dressing gown to her body.

"Mr. Hill? If you're lookin' for Raymond, he isn't here. I heard his door shut some time ago and he left."

"Which direction was he going, Mrs. Montgomery? Do you know?"

"Yes, he seemed to go out and around the direction of your place - where your land joins ours by the mill. He done something wrong?"

"He's got my sister, Callie. We're going to get her back."

"You watch yourself, Mr. Hill. He's a mean one, just ask my girls. Take care of yourselves. Hope you find Callie."

"Thank you for your help, Mrs. Montgomery."

Ben and Samuel started off towards the old mill, their hearts beating with hope of finding Callie and fear of what else they may find.

* * *

Callie heard the crunching of heavy feet approaching the shed and smelled the odor of her captor before he arrived. Chills of fear cursed through her body. Why was he back? What was he going to do with her?

She fought to keep herself calm. She didn't want to give him the satisfaction of seeing her upset. She braced herself as he arrived at the door and slowly turned the lock and opened the door, causing an eerie creak.

He didn't say anything until he lit a lantern he was carrying and placed it on the ground a few feet from Callie.

"Well, how's my star boarder doin'? Don' look too worse for the wear. Thought you might be hungry so I brought you some cornbread Almina made and some water. Want you to keep up your strength."

Even though Callie hadn't eaten anything since morning, she knew she couldn't force one bite of food down without being sick. She shook her head no.

"Come on, Miss Hill. I'll even untie your gag if you eat a little bit."

Maybe she could scream and someone would hear her. She willingly nodded in the affirmative.

"Now don' go thinkin you can let loose a yell. Won' do no good. Nobody any wheres close to this place. Still want something to eat?"

Callie dismally shook her head no as her body slumped in defeat.

"Now, now, gal, don' be so unhappy. Raymond is here and he's ready for some fun before tomorra when I have to let you go - if your papa comes through with the money and deeds, that is.

Callie immediately shrunk away further into the disgusting straw pile, her eyes wide with fear, her body convulsing in fits of uncontrollable shivering. It was the wrong reaction.

Raymond's beady eyes narrowed and his body tightened, ready to spring. "You too good to have fun with me, Miss Hill? Think you somebody special 'cause you live in a fine house and have fine clothes? And have thousands of acres of land? Well, I got land too. And someday I'll live in a fine house and have fine clothes. That day comes tomorra, little lady, when I get the money from your precious papa. Then you won't be tryin' to get away from me, you'll be beggin' for me."

"Hah! I think you're beggin' for me now. How'd you like to have a little taste of a *real* man, not that boy you be marryin'?"

Callie started squirming more, trying again to get the rope off her wrists, even though the pain was excruciating. Anything to get away from this man who was coming toward her with an evil, depraved glare in his eyes. Spittle was drooling out of the corners of his mouth which was twisted into a wicked grin.

"Yessir, think I'll be doin' that Yankee boy a favor, breakin' you in for him." Raymond was stooping over her now, reaching for her. Callie twisted and turned to avoid his filthy hands, but there was not much she could do, being tied up and gagged the way she was.

Raymond straightened up and laughed. "Hah! Got no place to go, do you missy? Guess you pretty much gotta do what I want. Hah! This might be too easy!"

Raymond reached down and grabbed Callie by both shoulders, forcing her to lie on her back. He climbed on top of her, sitting on her legs to keep her from moving them. He held her so she couldn't wriggle away and slowly, deliberately began to trace her face, then her neck, and then her breasts with his hand. He kept repeating this motion, each time moving his hand further down her body. His breathing became more and more heavy and his eyes were glazing over.

Callie couldn't move. She was frozen by fear and the weight of Carswell's body on hers. Tears were spilling out the corners of her eyes. She tried to think of something she could do to rid herself of this horrible, repulsive man, but her mind was blank. She was just trying to survive and take her next breath.

* * *

"Ben, did you hear something ahead of us?" Samuel stopped his horse to listen. Ben immediately did the same. They both strained their ears hoping to hear something unusual in the night. "Nothing. I thought I heard something, but I don't know what it was. Maybe just wishful hoping or my imagination."

"Samuel, are we getting closer to the mill Mrs. Montgomery talked about?"

"We've a little ways to go yet." Samuel straightened on his horse. "I sure thought I heard something a minute ago."

"Wish you did. Means we might be closer to Callie. Surely, she'd be screaming or something."

"Not if she can't." Samuel looked at Ben in the moonlight.

"Oh…..Let's go, we *have* to find her!"

* * *

Callie tried to scream with the gag in her mouth. Nothing came out except a strangled moan. It was enough to stop Raymond's hand.

"Like that, huh? Thought you would." Raymond started to touch her face again. She snapped her head away and again tried to scream. This only seemed to infuriate Carswell more.

"You might as well cooperate, Miss Hill. You might even enjoy yourself." He sat up straighter. Callie looked at him with terror. What was he going to do now?

* * *

Neither Callie nor Raymond noticed the door of the shed being slowly opened, carefully so the creak would not be heard. Nor did they hear the silent steps of a slippered foot enter the shed and stay close to the walls, away from the lantern. The cock of the shotgun was not heard either over Callie's suppressed whimpers.

* * *

Nathan and Henry entered Pine Wood and galloped up to Elijah's cabin. Elijah, still awake, met them in front of his cabin.

"Elijah, has my son, Samuel, been here this evening?"

"Yep, lookin' for your little gal. Said Carswell took her and is holdin' her somewhere on Pine Wood. He and the other fellow were headed towards the old mill last I saw. Haven't seen them since. They should be there about now. Hope they find her, Nathan. Hate to see that pretty little thing hurt."

Nathan nodded. "Thanks, Elijah, we'll head that way too. Come on, Henry. This way!"

Nathan and Henry hurriedly sped their horses in the direction of the mill, guided by the light of the moon and the stars.

* * *

Caleb Jones sat on the top step of the front veranda, his loaded rifle in his hands. He jumped when he heard the front door open and someone step out into the night.

"Caleb, you hears anything?" Trudy walked over to where her husband was sitting and joined him.

"No.....nuttin'. Don' think that Carswell man has Miz Callie 'round here. Bet he tooks her someplace on Pine Wood. Where's Libby?"

"She sleepin' in Mammy Sallie's arms. Jes' like a lil angel. Mammy cryin' for Miz Callie. Libby he'ps her some."

"How's the res' of the fo'ks in there doin'?"

"Pritty good. Miz Kathleen a strong woman, strong woman. She keeping everyone prayin'. Miz Chapman an' Miz Emma sure nice ladies. Miz Beulah wents to bed. Samuel's new wife wents to bed too, sayin' she had too much 'citement an' had a bad headache. Her papa wents afta her. She seems dif'erent to me. Not like Masta Samuel at all, but guess he loves her. She pritty, but not so nice."

Trudy shrugged her shoulders and leaned her head on Caleb's arm. "Sure hopes they's finds Miz Callie soon. She be so scared, Caleb. Bad 'nuf when she a girl an' that Mista Williams grabs her an' Ben shoots him, but now that bad man takes her somewhere. Don' knows what he doin' to her. She be so scared." Tears trickled down Trudy's smooth brown cheeks.

"Miz Callie strong, too, Trudy. She takes care o' herse'f. She be fine."

"Hope so. Don' know what's I's do if'n sumpin happin to Miz Callie."

"You's a strong woman, too, Trudy. Eve'ythin' turn out fine, you sees." Caleb leaned over and took his wife in his arms and kissed her gently on her lips. "You's gots me an' Libby fore'er, Trudy. Fore'er."

* * *

Raymond had a heinous look on his face as he stared down at Callie, helpless before him. "Look at the high and mighty Miss Callie Hill now!"

Callie looked back at that face hovering above her and finally decided it was time to take matters into her own hands…..somehow. Fueled by new found anger and with all the strength she could muster, she flew her bound body at him, knocking him off balance. She rolled over and over and tried unsuccessfully to get to her feet. Once again she angered Raymond who now was so enraged he stood up and yelled like a raging bull.

"You'll pay for that, girlie. 'Bout time I showed you who's runnin' this show!"

"Oh, no you won't!" The voice came from the wall inside the shed. "Let her be, Raymond Carswell, if you know what's good for you!"

A look of complete surprise was on Raymond's face and Callie's. He turned slowly towards the voice.

"Get away from her! Put your hands up above your head and walk towards the door. Do as I say. I've got a loaded shotgun and the bullet's got your name on it."

Raymond still couldn't comprehend what had happened. He started to walk toward the door.

"I said, put your hands up above your head! Now!"

Raymond slowly put his hands in the air. Recognition crossed his eyes and he smiled. "Lizzy? Lizzy, is that you? What you doin' here? You shouldn't be out here. I'm doin' a little business deal."

Raymond dropped his hands to his side and turned to face the voice by the wall. "Lizzy, girl, you get back to the cabins. You've no reason to do this."

Lizzy Montgomery laughed cynically. "Oh, yes I do. I've plenty of reasons, you low down, no good weasel."

"Now, Lizzy......calm down. Nobody's hurt here."

"Nobody hurt? Look at Callie. Look what you've done to her. Just like what you've done to Jenny and me and probably Ma too. And, that's just what you've done to us. Getting Grandpa drunk and makin' him sign away all that land to you. Takin' away our birthright. Yes, Jenny and I know all about that. We know lots about you, Raymond. We know what an awful, horrible man you are."

A frown creased Raymond's forehead. "What do you mean? I've done nothing but good for Pine Wood. And, haven't I been 'specially nice to you and Jenny and your ma? Little lovin' does everybody good, doesn't it?"

"Not when it's forced on you. Just like what you're tryin' to do to Callie. Well, you ain't gonna do it anymore, Raymond Carswell. I'm seein' to that."

Raymond laughed. "And, just what do you think you're gonna do, Lizzy? Little thing like you?"

"I got me a big gun, though. And, right now it's aimed right at your wicked, dark heart."

Raymond quit laughing. "Now, Lizzy........you don't mean ....no harm to me. You like me. I.......help...you.....you....know.....do things." He slowly started walking towards Lizzy as he spoke.

"Get back over there! Stay away from me! I mean it, Raymond. I'll shoot!"

"No....no...you won't. You won't shoot me. Now, Lizzy....... put the gun down. We can talk about this later. Right now I've got business to do with Miss Hill here."

"I will so shoot you! You untie Callie and let her go. Right now, Raymond!"

"Now.....Lizzy........."

Suddenly they all heard horses approach and Samuel and Ben

calling out Callie's name. Callie tried again to scream, but wasn't loud enough. Lizzy and Carswell looked at each other. In that split second, he lunged toward Lizzy to grab the shotgun away from her.

Lizzy saw Carswell leaping towards her and in defense, pulled the trigger. The blast echoed throughout the little shed and out into the night. Raymond looked in disbelief at Lizzy who had now dropped the gun. He dropped to his knees, then fell face forward onto the dirt floor. Blood oozed out of the large hole in his chest, staining the floor red as it trickled outward.

Callie, like Lizzy, was stunned. They just watched as the blood drained the life out of Raymond Carswell. It was as if they couldn't take their eyes off this evil man as he died. The pool of blood became larger and larger as the two woman watched.

"CALLIE! CALLIE! Oh my God, Callie!" Ben knocked the door down and burst into the shed. "Callie! Callie!" He stumbled over the dead body of Raymond Carswell, turned to look at Lizzy still standing there staring at the body, and then heard Callie moaning across the shed in the straw pile. He was quickly followed by Samuel, who at a glance knew what had happened.

"Callie! I'm here!" Ben went to Callie and quickly removed the gag from around her mouth. Then he gathered her in his arms and held her tight. "Are you all right?"

"My wrists..........."

"Of course..........sorry. Ben released her from his hold, turned her around, took out his knife, and sawed away at the ropes around Callie's hands. "My God, Callie! Your wrists are raw."

"Tried to .....get....loose......couldn't."

"There I got it." He tenderly took her hands in his and tried to rub some warmth back into them, being careful not to touch the bloody cuts.

"Feet......please."

"Right........." Ben then cut through the binding ropes around Callie's ankles and started rubbing her feet as he had her hands.

When she was finally free, it was then that Callie sobbed gratefully and wrapped herself around Ben. They sat there silently in the mucky straw rocking back and forth in each other's arms.

Samuel walked over to where Lizzy was still standing looking at the body of Raymond Carswell. "Lizzy? Lizzy, are you all right?"

Lizzy looked vacantly at Samuel but didn't say anything. Samuel tried again, this time touching her arm. She flinched and jumped backwards.

"Lizzy, it's Samuel. Everything is going to be all right. You're safe now. He won't hurt you any more. You did a very brave thing, Lizzy. Lizzy…..Lizzy. … It's all right."

Samuel touched Lizzy's arm once more. This time she looked vacantly into his eyes. "He was a mean man, wasn't he? He deserves to be dead, doesn't he? You don't know what he's done to me and my family."

"Yes, Lizzy. He was a terrible man and deserves to be dead. You saved Callie's life, do you know that? You did a good thing, Lizzy."

"But I didn't mean to kill him…..I just wanted to scare him so he would go away. I didn't mean to really shoot him…..The gun just went off in my hands when he came at me. I didn't really mean it…..I didn't really mean to kill him." Then Lizzy fell to the ground in a heap. Her body was wracked with heaving sobs. "I didn't mean…….. to….I…really….didn't………"

Samuel sat beside her, putting his arms around her. She leaned against him sobbing. "You had too, Lizzy, or he would have hurt Callie and you. It was self defense. You had to do it. Thank God you did, Lizzy."

Lizzy lifted her tear stained face up. "Really? Do you think it was a good thing? He would have hurt us, wouldn't he?"

"Yes, he was determined to hurt you and Callie. The world is much safer now, Lizzy. Much safer. Just think about Jenny, your mother, and grandfather. Y'all much better off without Raymond Carswell."

Lizzy laid her head back on Samuel's shoulder. "Yes, so much better off. I did a good thing. A good thing………"

* * *

Nathan and Henry heard the shotgun blast. They didn't think. They just spurred their horses into a full gallop towards the sound. Nathan's heart was beating so fast, he thought it would jump out of his chest. "Please, Lord, please, don't let anything happen to Callie…..please, Lord, please………"

Henry too was praying. "Lord, please let our children be safe. Please, Lord, don't let anything bad happen to them now as they are just about to begin their life together. Please, Lord………"

The two men pulled up at the shed, leapt off their horses, and ran in. There was Ben and Callie in one corner; next to the wall was Samuel and Lizzy Montgomery, a shotgun lying in front of them. And, on the floor in a pool of blood was Raymond Carswell….dead.

* * *

Caleb woke at the sound of the thundering horses racing up the lane. He leapt to his feet, rifle ready.

"Who there? Who there?"

"It's us, Caleb! We have Callie! Go inside and tell the women!" Nathan pulled up his horse and jumped off, sprinting over to Ben's horse, where Callie sat slumped against him.

Henry had also dismounted, and the two men managed to get her off the horse and carried her into the house, followed closely by Ben. Inside, the women, except for Mammy Sallie and Beulah, who were too slow to awaken, met the men at the front door.

"Oh, Callie! Callie, sweetie…..are you all right?"

"Yes, Mama, I think I am………my wrists are awfully sore……… but I think the rest of me is all right…..I just really want to …..take a bath…..and wash my hair……and………" Callie broke into sobs. "Oh, Mama,………he was so mean to me…….I don't know what…I ever did to him……He was so hurtful………and dirty…..and he put his…hands…..all…over…me…..Please…..I…need…….to be clean…..please……."

Kathleen gathered Callie in her arms. "Of course, dear, of course. We'll have Belle start heating some water right now. Trudy and I will take care of you, don't you worry." Kathleen looked up at Ben. His face was a mixture of sorrow, love, and hatred.

"He hurt her, Mrs., Hill. He hurt her bad. But he won't hurt her any more."

"What happened, Ben? Is Carswell dead?"

"Yep, some other girl shot him before Samuel and I could get there."

Kathleen's face showed relief. "I never want harm to come to anyone, but that man was evil. Where's Samuel? Is he still outside?"

"No ma'am. He stayed with the girl at her place. She's pretty upset too. Mr. Hill can tell you the details later. I think we'd better take care of Callie now. Look at her wrists. They need some attention right away."

Kathleen saw Callie's raw, bloody wrists and cringed. "Oh, Callie, you poor thing. Caleb, will you run down to Lenora's cabin and wake her up? Tell her Miss Callie is back and we need her."

"Yessum, Miz Hill. I goes fetch her."

Abigail and Emma had stayed in the background, but now came forward. "Kathleen, let's get her laid down someplace until her bath water is ready."

"Of course, thank you. Ben, Nathan, put her in the parlor on the settee for now. I'll go tell Belle to hurry and get things ready. Trudy, is Libby still sleeping?"

"Yes, ma'am. She nebber woke up with all the ruckus. What can I's do to helps?"

"Stay here with Callie until Lenora comes, then you can help me bathe her."

Callie was taken into the parlor, followed by all concerned. "I think there are too many people in here," Kathleen said, once Callie was lying on the settee. "Nathan, you take everyone out and you'd better go tell your mother and Mammy Sallie that Callie is back. Ben, you and Trudy stay here and I'll go help Belle."

The rest of the Chapmans gathered around Nathan where he and Henry told them what they knew about what had happened at Pine Wood. "That poor girl…..what she must have endured." Abigail sighed heavily. "I'm sure he is being punished in hell now for what he did to her……and that family. You know, Nathan, we will do all we can to help her……and Ben…..get through this."

"Thank you, Abigail. Callie is pretty brave, but I'm not sure exactly what he did to her yet. I know she will need all of our support to recover. Oh, here comes Lenora. She's our wonderful 'doctor.' She'll tend to those wrists and whatever else is wrong."

"Where's my Miz Callie? What did that bad, bad man do to her? Let me through, let me see my Miz Callie." Lenora plodded through the small group and went into the parlor where Ben and Trudy were sitting on the floor in front of Callie on the settee.

Callie had her eyes closed, but was jabbering to Trudy, reliving the past few hours. Ben had tears rolling down his cheeks listening to her. He kept stroking her hair, now filled with bits of straw and dirt.

"I's here, Miz Callie. Ole Lenora comes to takes cares of you. Don' you worry none. We gits you all fixed up, jes' like whens you was a lil gal. 'Members when you brokes your arm? Old Lenora sets that arm jes' right. Takes cares of you now, jes' likes that. Now, Trudy, you go gits me some warm water an' soap an' some clean rags for band'ges. Mista Ben, you goes 'long now. I's takes care of her, don' you worry none, but I's needs to do it 'lone."

"Are you sure, I hate to leave her like this."

"I's sure. You's has plenty time later. Rights now, she needs my helps."

Ben very reluctantly left Callie's side, but not without tenderly kissing her forehead and whispering "I love you," in her ear. She smiled faintly.

"Now, Miz Callie, we's gits to work fixin' those pritty wrists."

Trudy arrived with the warm water and soap and Lenora started to gently wipe the dirt and blood off the wounds. Callie flinched each time Lenora applied the water to her hands and wrists. Lenora nodded a knowing glance at Trudy.

"Miz Callie, you must has tried awful hards to gits loose. These pritty wrists looks rubbed raw."

"I did, Lenora….I tried so hard……but I couldn't….get away….He tied…..them…too tight…..I tried….I really did…."

"I's sees that. He ties you up anyplace else?"

"My feet…..and…around….my mouth…..so I couldn't….scream… I tried….to scream…anyway….but nothing…..came out…I tried….I tried.…"

"Trudy, you looks at her feets. I sees now, Miz Callie. You's lips cracked an' bleedin'. I's gots some oint'ent to put on them."

"Her feets don' look bads, Lenora. They's must been tied over her dress an' stockins."

"Good. Now, Miz Callie. Lenora wants you to tell her what that bad man did to you, 'sides tyin' you ups."

Callie opened her eyes wide. "What…do…you…mean, Lenora?"

Lenora looked straight into Callie's brown eyes with her own. "I's means, did he do to you what makes babies? Likes you an' Trudy an' I's was talkin' 'bouts 'whiles back?"

Callie sat up straight. "No….Lenora….he didn't do that. But… he…" Callie lay back down and started crying softly. "He…he… he…put his…dirty…hand…on my…face…and my….neck….and down….to my….bosom…and he….kept…doing it over….and over…and over…while….he was…on top of me. Over….and…. over. Then…he stopped….and stood up….and I think……maybe… then….he was…going to do…..you know…..try….to….make a baby…….but then…..Lizzy shot him.…"

"Thank the Lawd for Miz Lizzy," Trudy said, wiping her own tears away. "Yessir, thank the Lawd for Miz Lizzy," Lenora echoed. Callie nodded her head and reached with her wounded hands for the two women. They both embraced her and held her until her sobs subsided.

"Now, Miz Callie. You feels any better?"

"Yes…Lenora, I do….Thank you….for… making me tell you. My wrists don't really hurt that much any more….just my heart…. What….do you think…. Ben….. will think… of me…now?"

"What? What you sayin'? Mista Ben loves you no matter whats. You should've seen him takes off lookin' for you. If'n Lizzy hadn't shot that bad man, Mista Ben woulds. Your papa an' brudder too. They's all mad as hornets an' spends all nights lookin' for you. Lots people loves you, Miz Callie. We's all helps you. We gits you back on your feets jes' likes before." Trudy was standing with her arms akimbo looking down at her friend. "Don' you goes feelin' sorry for yourself now. You's gots a weddin' to go to."

Callie replied hesitantly. "That's if… Ben still wants…. to marry me. I feel…. like….. I've been tainted….. Carswell even…. said that. Said…. he was going to …'break me in'….for Ben."

"You get that notion right out of that beautiful head, Callie Hill. I love you and nothing that man did to you will make me love you less. I want to marry you even more now." Ben strode from the doorway over to the settee in one fluid motion, picking Callie up and holding her close to him. He gently kissed her cracked lips, her smudged cheeks, the tip of her nose, the lobes of her ears, and her forehead.

"Ahem! Mista Ben! I's tole you to stays outta here whiles I's fixes up Miz Callie! Now you's in here, kissin' her! How's I's 'posed to do my work?" Lenora chuckled at Ben and Callie as she shook her finger at Ben.

Even Callie had to smile. Ben looked at her sheepishly. "I'm sorry, Miss Lenora, but I just couldn't stay away when I knew she was hurtin' so bad. I'm glad I came in." He turned back to Callie. "I never want you to think I wouldn't marry you because some deranged man did things to you. None of this was your fault, Callie. None of it. Please remember that. You had no control over what happened to you. It was all Carswell. I'm just so thankful we found you in time. And, Trudy's right. I would have killed him, if Lizzy hadn't. I already saved your life once, I'd do it again." He kissed her cheeks softly.

"Oh, Ben, I do love you so." Callie closed her eyes and leaned her head against Ben's shoulder.

"Callie, your bath is ready," said Kathleen, as she entered the parlor. "Let's go get you cleaned up. You'll feel much better once you are out of those filthy clothes and get your hair washed."

Ben carried Callie into the kitchen where Belle had the bathtub filled with hot steaming water. Clean towels and Callie's nightgown and dressing gown were laid out on the chairs. Combs and brushes were waiting on the table.

"Now, you really do have to leave, Ben," whispered Callie quietly. "We aren't married yet."

"I'll let these women tend to you, but when you are out of the tub and dressed, I'm comin' back in."

Ben left as Kathleen and Trudy proceeded to undress Callie and get her in the hot soapy water in the tub. She sighed with pleasure as she soaked, letting the heat warm up her aching muscles. She submerged her head to wet her hair and Trudy began to shampoo it.

"Oh, Trudy….that feels so good….."

"Duck down again, Miz Callie, an' rinse off. Then we do it again."

"Look how dirty my water is! I can't stay in this!"

"Don't worry, dear, Belle has more ready. We'll just empty this. Stand up and we'll take it outside." Kathleen wrapped one of the towels around Callie and she and Belle drug the tub to the door and tipped it to drain the water. They immediately began filling it again with the kettles full of steaming water. Once again Callie stepped back into the tub and really relaxed this time. So much so that she almost fell asleep.

"Callie, we'd better get you done and out of here so you can go upstairs and go to bed, even though it's almost dawn." Kathleen shook Callie who nodded drowsily.

"She cain't go to bed wit a wet head, Miz Kathleen," Belle said. "She has to sit by the fire an' let that dry."

"You're right, Belle. I'll stay up with her. Trudy, you and Belle go to bed."

"Miz Kathleen, if'n Miz Callie all rights now, I's thinks me an' Caleb take Libby an' jes' goes back to our cabin. Wants to sleep in our owns bed."

"I'm all right, Trudy….you take Libby and go home…"

"Yes, of course, Trudy," Kathleen agreed. "I just hope Libby lets you get some sleep. If she doesn't, you bring her here and someone will watch her so you can get some rest. Promise?"

"Promise." Trudy bent over and kissed Callie's cheek. "You 'haves youse'f now, Miz Callie. Gits some sleep an' you be good as new."

"I will, Trudy." Trudy turned to leave. "Trudy?"

"Yes, Miz Callie?"

"Thank you……I love you."

"I's loves you too, Miz Callie. Good nights."

* * *

While Callie was being taken care of, the rest of the household was finally settling down. Beulah and Mammy Sallie had been told to just stay in their beds, as Callie was fine and in good hands. They didn't put up much fuss as they knew they weren't of much use anyway.

Laura and her father hadn't appeared when Callie arrived. Evidently, all the commotion hadn't awakened them, or they chose to stay away from the chaos. Either way the other families found it strange behavior. Wasn't Laura concerned about Samuel? Apparently not.

Laura was awake and heard everything going on downstairs, but she chose to stay in her room. Lester had come in, asking her if they should join the others. No, she wouldn't. She didn't really know any of these people and she didn't care what was happening. Samuel would tell her later. Lester had shrugged his shoulders and gone back to bed.

The Chapman family, except for Ben, was urged by Nathan to retire for what was left of the night. He assured them no one would wake them and for them to sleep as long as they liked. They all gratefully went to their rooms and were soon asleep.

Nathan and Ben sat in the library waiting for Kathleen to come so they could tell Callie good night. She soon appeared and informed them Callie would be up for a while longer so her hair could dry. They weren't sending her to bed with a wet head for fear of her catching a cold.

"Can I see her now, though?" Ben asked Kathleen.

"Of course. We moved her into the back parlor by the fireplace and Belle is brushing her hair, trying to get all the tangles out. We're hoping that will dry it faster. Nathan, you can go too. She's been asking to see you. Remember, she's been through a lot, but she seems to have weathered it quite well. She's achy and bruised. Lenora has her wrists bandaged. She's tired, but clean, which seems to have revived her spirits. I think she will come through this. I'm so thankful, Ben, that you are here. Your love will see her through. Now......why don't you both go tell her good-night and go get some sleep."

"I can't sleep, Kathleen! Not after what's happened!"

"I know, Nathan, but there's nothing for you to do now." Kathleen rubbed her husband's arm and said in a low voice, "Besides, dear, Callie has Ben now. She wants him."

"Oh......" Nathan looked into his wife's dark emerald eyes. "Oh.....well...then...I guess I'll just go tell her good-night."

"That would be the thing to do, dear." She turned to Ben after Nathan left the room.

"This is very hard for him, you know. Callie has always been his 'baby girl' and he's the one who's always looked after her, especially after her mother, Hannah, died. He'll eventually be fine, but tonight made it even worse."

"I understand. I know how much you all love Callie and how much you will miss her. I feel the same way when I'm not with her. Mrs. Hill, I don't know what I would have done if things turned out differently tonight. I've been praying to thank God for delivering her safely to us."

"Me, too, Ben. Me, too........Do you want to go see her now?"

"Of course!"

When Ben entered the parlor, Nathan was just leaving. "Take good care of her, Ben."

"Yes, sir, you know I will."

Callie smiled when Ben came in and opened her arms to him. Now he could fully embrace her, which he did ardently. Without saying anything, he released her, moved closer to the fire with her, picked up the hairbrush, and began brushing her long, flaxen curls. Callie sat in front of him, totally relaxed now as he brushed stroke after stroke.

Kathleen peeked in the door, saw the two of them and left, smiling. Callie was in good hands.

* * *

Samuel was in a difficult position. His wife was back at Oak Hill, but Lizzy Montgomery needed him desperately. Lizzy was much worse off than Callie, in fact. The realization of what she had done hit her hard as the men started dragging Carswell's body out of the shed. She started shivering and shaking uncontrollably, and when they turned his body over and she saw his open eyes, staring at her, she started screaming. The men didn't know what to do other than quickly remove the body and bury it, which they did. Samuel tried to calm her down, reassuring her it was self defense. He finally had to shake her by the shoulders to get her to stop screaming.

Lizzy had looked at him blankly and then started walking out of the shed and into the night. Samuel called after her, but she didn't stop and just kept going. He called after the others who were digging Carswell's grave. "Father, I'm going to go take care of Lizzy. She's not herself. I'm going to take her back to her cabins and then stay until I'm sure she's taken care of. It might be late, please explain to Laura."

"Lizzy, Lizzy….Wait for me…" Samuel ran after the lone figure walking silently in the moonlight staring straight ahead. He caught up with her and took her arm.

"Lizzy, let's get you home and into bed. I'll stay with you. Is that all right?"

She nodded her head yes and then looked at him, her chin trembling, her eyes seeing again and understanding. She let out a guttural cry and then collapsed into Samuel's arms. He held her tightly as she sobbed and heaved until the sobs turned to whimpers and then to silence. They sat down on the grass until finally there were no sounds, only her uneven breaths and the sounds of the night.

"Lizzy. Lizzy…..I think we'd better get you home now. You're exhausted and you need to be with your family."

She shook her head. "No……stay here….just a little longer…. please."

"All right. But I don't want you to take a chill. Here take my coat and wrap it around you. I'll be fine." He took off his coat and put it over her shoulders. She held it to her body gratefully and then enveloped Samuel's waist with her arms and laid her head against his chest. Samuel didn't know what to do and in spite of himself, he reacted to her embrace. He instantly felt very guilty and tried to disengage from her hold.

"Lizzy, I'm married now…..I can't do this….we must get you home.

Lizzy looked at him with eyes reddened from weeping, her full lips quivering. She looked so lost and forlorn that despite the consequences, Samuel bent over and softly kissed those lips. Lizzy didn't resist but instead pressed hers more firmly against Samuel's.

Suddenly Samuel jerked his head backwards. "Lizzy! What am I doing? Stop! I'm married! Laura is waiting for me at Oak Hill. Come on, we have to go!" He stood up and pulled Lizzy to her feet, but he didn't miss the faint smile on her face.

"I'm sorry, Samuel, but it was a nice kiss. Thank you. I know you have to get back to your wife, but do you think you could stay a little while at Pine Wood and tell my family what happened? They'll believe it if you tell them. Please? For me?"

Samuel couldn't refuse her. "Of course.....let's go."

When the two arrived at Pine Wood, everyone was asleep except Jenny. She knew her sister had left shortly before Ben and Samuel had arrived, but she didn't know why.

Lizzy and Samuel approached her cabin and when they opened the door, Jenny came quickly out to greet them. When she saw her sister, she immediately knew something was terribly wrong. "Ma! Ma! Wake up! Lizzy's here and something bad has happened to her. Ma!"

Almina slowly opened her eyes, trying to focus in the dark. "What? Lizzy?" She got out of bed, draping her bedraggled dressing gown around her, and went outside. Her two daughters were embracing while Samuel Hill stood and watched.

"Better wake up Elijah, Mrs. Montgomery, we've something to tell everyone." She nodded and started for Elijah's cabin. After several knocks, the old man came outside with her.

"What the devil's going on now? Thought you were lookin' for your sister, Samuel. Did you find her? Did Carswell have her? What's this to do with Lizzy? Why you cryin', girl?"

Samuel took them all into Elijah's cabin and proceeded to tell what happened in the shed, as he knew it. He was interrupted by sobs from Lizzy, especially at the point where she pulled the trigger.

Elijah, Almina, and Jenny sat silent and stunned for several minutes as they digested what Samuel told them. Then Almina stood up and paced the small cabin floor.

"Well, I, for one, am glad that no-good scoundrel is dead. He's been doin' bad things to us for a long while now."

"Like what?" Elijah asked. "I didn't see him do anything bad."

"That's because you weren't lookin', old man. Do you think for one minute he didn't come after my girls and force himself on them……and even me? After he got you drunk and you signed over the deeds to him, there wasn't anything we could do about it. Where else could we go? He owned the land and he owned us. That's what he used to say too. He'd say, 'don't tell anyone or I'll kick you off Pine Wood and you can fend for yourselves.' What choice did we have? I've been planning how I'd kill that man myself. Lizzy, you did a good thing…a real good thing."

"Did I, Ma? I didn't mean to kill him…..I just wanted to make him leave. But then…he looked like he was comin' after me…and the gun just went off. Next thing I know, he's dead and his eyes are staring at me…..accusing me."

"Yes, you did right, Lizzy. Look at how he was treatin' Callie. By the way….how did you know he was there with her in the first place?"

"I've been watchin' him for a long time. He always left a certain time of the day with no excuse and always went down the road toward Oak Hill. So one day I decided to follow him. I saw him waiting outside Oak Hill in the brush and then when Callie came ridin' out, he started following her all the way to Trudy's cabin. Then he waited in the thicket again and followed her back. I thought it was strange, so I figured he must be up to something. The day he took her, I was watchin' too, but I didn't know what he was goin' to do with her. Then he came back here without her, so I thought maybe he'd let her go, but when he left again that night, I followed him just to make sure. I took the rifle, thinking I could scare him if he did have her…..and he did."

"Lizzy, if you saw Carswell take Callie, why didn't you come and tell us then or try to help her?" Samuel looked bewilderedly at Lizzy.

"I don't know……I didn't really think. I guess I wanted to find out what he was up to first. I'm sorry, Samuel."

"I'll tell you why, Samuel," Almina said. "That man had my girls brainwashed. He controlled them somehow. I'm surprised Lizzy had the gumption to go after him."

"She had to, Ma," Jenny said quietly. "When he came back earlier, he grabbed me and took me to his cabin and........." Jenny looked down at her hands in her lap and tears fell from her eyes. "He..... did....what he usually did...only this time....he was hittin' me...... Lizzy heard him. I knew she followed him when Samuel and the other man came lookin' for Callie, but I didn't know where they had gone." She looked up. "If I'd known, I would have told you, Samuel."

Jenny looked at her grandfather. "Grandpa, that man was the devil and you let him into Pine Wood. You should've sent him on his way like the Hills did. So I'm glad Lizzy killed him, because if she didn't, I was goin' to somehow."

Lizzy looked at her family and sighed. "I guess we all suffered from Raymond Carswell.....the Hills too. Guess it's a good thing he is dead.......but I still wish I weren't the one who killed him." She shuddered and Jenny embraced her.

There was silence again in the tiny cabin, each thinking of what had occurred and how it affected them. Samuel finally spoke. "I feel that we haven't been very good neighbors, but, truthfully, we tried to stay away from Carswell. He kept coming over and wanting to buy land from us and we wanted to keep our distance. We had no idea what was going on at Pine Wood. I'm very sorry, Almina, Jenny, Lizzy, Elijah. Please accept my apologies for our entire family. Maybe if we had been more vigilant, none of this would have transpired. I guess one can never predict the future and hind-sight is the best, but I hope a lesson has been learned. Trust me, things will change."

Samuel stood up. "I think everything is in control here and it's almost dawn....I'd better be getting back to Oak Hill. I'm sure my wife is worried....this is her first visit and I'm sure it's one she will never forget." He smiled. "She thought country living would be very boring."

Lizzy stood up next to him. "I'll never be able to thank you for helping me, Samuel."

"No, it is I who thank you for ridding the world of Raymond Carswell and rescuing Callie. Good-night or, I guess, good morning to y'all. We'll be seeing you soon."

"I'll walk out with you." Lizzy started for the door. As they stood outside under the fading darkness with the sun emitting its first rays of light, Lizzy suddenly felt very shy. "Thank you, Samuel. I'll never forget what you did for me tonight."

"I think maybe you'd better, Lizzy. I certainly didn't act like a gentleman and I apologize for my behavior. It won't ever happen again."

As Samuel mounted his horse and turned to ride out of Pine Wood, Lizzy whispered to herself, "I hope it *will* happen again!"

* * *

Samuel arrived at Oak Hill when the sun was peeking out of the eastern horizon. Rays of magenta, orange, and pale yellow were streaking across the faint turquoise sky. The air was crisp for a mid-April morning, and Samuel missed the coat he had lent to Lizzy.

He wasn't tired. In fact, he felt invigorated. He took some deep breaths of the cool morning air and exhaled loudly. He wondered if Laura was waiting up for him. He hoped so. He needed to talk to her. To tell her of the night's events….omitting parts, of course. He felt himself blush suddenly. What had he been thinking? Why did he kiss Lizzy? Worse yet, he enjoyed it. Laura had never kissed him like that. Maybe she was too refined and inexperienced. Maybe she just…..he didn't want to think about it anymore.

There wasn't much activity at Oak Hill. Samuel saw smoke rising from the cabins' chimneys and heard Malindy's baby boy, Lincoln, crying. He dismounted and tied his horse to the hitching post - he'd take care of him later. Right now, he wanted to see Laura.

Assuming everyone was still asleep, he quietly opened and shut the front door and tiptoed into the foyer. As expected, he didn't see anyone, but checked all the downstairs rooms anyway.

Peeking into the back parlor, he had to smile. There sitting on the floor, leaning against one of the chairs by the fireplace, was Ben. His arms were encircling Callie, a hairbrush dangling in his hand. Both were sound asleep. Callie was even snoring a little, or maybe that was Socks, who was curled up at his mistress's feet.

Samuel thought, "Good. She's fine and obviously sleeping well.

Probably better than Lizzy is. Callie has Ben and all of us to help her. She will come out of this just fine."

He went back to the staircase and started up, careful to avoid the steps he knew squeaked. He cautiously opened the door of his room and let himself in. There was Laura lying in bed, turned away from him. He quietly undressed and slipped into the bed. She never moved. "Better not wake her," he thought. "She's probably had a long night, too." He lay on his back staring at the ceiling trying to relax. Soon he succumbed to sleep and his breathing became even.

Only then did Laura allow herself to change positions. She was very careful. She didn't want to wake Samuel. She laid there for several more minutes making sure he was in a deep sleep and then she slowly got out of bed and quietly began her morning preparations.

Once dressed she proceeded out of their room and down the hall to her father's room. Lester was already up and stirring. She went in and sat in a chair.

"What's wrong dear? Is Samuel back yet? How is his sister?"

"He just came back. I pretended to be asleep so I wouldn't have to talk to him. I guess his sister must be fine. It seems everybody else is still asleep."

"That's good. I still think we should have stayed with Samuel's family during this whole ordeal instead of coming up here."

"No, I couldn't stand it any longer."

"But, Laura, these are nice people. They have treated us very well."

"I know. I just don't want to be here. I don't want to be with Samuel. I don't want to pretend. I just don't want........." Laura put her hands to her face, holding back tears.

Lester walked over to her and, not knowing what to do, patted her on her head. "Now, Laura, you must be strong. You will eventually love Samuel, then everything will work out. Right now, we need his capital. Don't forget that. We still aren't solvent by any means."

Laura jerked her head away from her father's touch. "That's easy for you to say. You aren't the one who has to lie in his bed at night. You don't have to endure the touch of someone you don't love. You always loved Mother, even when she stopped loving you!"

Lester flinched. "Your mother loved me very much, Laura."

"You can think what you want, but I know differently. I don't want a life like you and Mother had. I want someone *I* love, and that someone is *not* Samuel Hill."

"Shh, dear, keep your voice down. Now, be sensible. You're already his wife. He has money. *Learn* to love him!"

"Oh, Father, why do I waste my time talking to you? I'm going downstairs and get some coffee."

* * *

Mammy Sallie had lain in her bed long enough. Her old bones told her it was time to get up and start moving. She sat on the side of the bed waiting for her body to catch up with her mind. She slowly rose, holding on to the nearby chair and struggled getting into her clothes. Finally, she lumbered out into the kitchen and set to making the morning coffee.

Mammy heard Callie come home, but Nathan had told her to stay in bed, there wasn't anything she could do. Her feelings were hurt, somewhat, because there was a time when she was the only one who could help Callie. But she did as she was told, and secretly, was glad for it. As long as Callie was fine, that's all that mattered. Things upset her more now and she didn't need the aggravation. She and Beulah discussed this often. They both felt useless sometimes, but decided it wasn't such a bad thing.

She sat in one of the old chairs by the table, waiting for the coffee to brew. Much to her surprise she heard footsteps - hesitant footsteps. Laura appeared in the doorway and jumped, surprised to see someone else up.

"Oh, excuse me. I thought I was the only one awake. Mmmm… that coffee smells divine. May I help myself?"

"Goes right aheads. Masta Samuel home yet? Masta Nathan says he stays wit Miz Lizzy. She the one shoots that bad Mista Carswell. I's knows that man was bad the minute I's lays my eyes on him. Nebber like the way he looks at Miz Callie, even when she a young gal. Glad he be dead."

"Yes, Mammy, Samuel is home. He's sleeping soundly now."

"You talks to him 'bout the shootin'?"

"No, I didn't want to wake him."

"Weren' you worried 'bout Masta Samuel? Thinks you wents to bed 'fore Miz Beulah an' I's did. Anybody comes tells you 'bout the shootin'?"

Laura looked down at her coffee cup, swirling the spoon around and around. "No, no one told me. I wasn't feeling well when I left to retire. That's probably why. I did awake when Callie was brought home with all the commotion, so I assumed everyone was fine, including Samuel."

Mammy Sallie looked at Laura, who avoided those dark brown eyes. "You's care, Miz Laura, what happins to Masta Samuel?"

"What......what....do you mean? Of course...I...care....He's... my...husband."

Mammy reached over and stopped Laura's hand from stirring the coffee. "Miz Laura, does you loves my Samuel?"

Laura looked at Sallie flustered and bewildered. She hesitated just a second, but it was a second too long. "Yes....of course...I love Samuel. Why...else...would I have married him?"

"I's don' knows, Miz Laura, but I's thinks it weren' for love. You sees how Miz Callie an' Mista Ben looks at each odder? An' Miz Kathleen an' Masta Nathan? They's *loves* each odder. Masta Samuel looks at you that way, but I's don' sees you lookin' at him like that."

Laura involuntarily flinched. She forced herself to steady her nerves and looked Mammy Sallie right in the eye. "I do love Samuel, Mammy Sallie......just not in the way....you are accustomed, I guess."

"You's bedder loves him, Miz Laura. I's nebber wants to sees my Masta Samuel hurt. I's raises him wit his mama an' then I's he'ps Masta Nathan raise him afta she pass. I loves him likes my own boy. Anybody hurts my Samuel will has to answer to Mammy Sallie. Yes ma'am.....has to answer to Mammy Sallie."

"I'll remember that, Mammy. But you don't have to worry about me." Then Laura rose from the table to get another cup of coffee.

* * *

Gradually, the other residents and guests of Oak Hill trickled downstairs to start their day. Livestock needed to be fed, chores had to be done, water had to be carried in, meals had to be cooked, life had to go on.

Ben and Callie awoke; embarrassed they had fallen asleep together on the floor. No one scolded them, though. Everyone was just happy that Callie was safe. Ben scooped Callie up in his arms and carried her upstairs where he deposited her on her feather bed. He tucked the coverlet under her chin and then sat by her side until she fell asleep once more. He watched her as she slept, marveling at her beauty and strength. Finding his own eyes growing heavy, he leaned his head back against the chair and slept.

Later in the day, Samuel and Nathan made a trip back to Pine Wood. As they approached the cabins, the Montgomerys gathered near the fire outside of Elijah's cabin. Like the Hills, they looked exhausted from the night before.

Nathan had hitched a cart behind his horse and the family was curious as to why.

"Elijah, Almina, girls. Samuel and I were talking this morning and we decided some action on our part was needed. If we had been more neighborly sooner, maybe the events of last night wouldn't have occurred." Nathan had dismounted and walked to the group around the smoldering fire. He had the Montgomerys' attention.

"First, I want to thank Lizzy again for saving Callie's life. Lizzy, I know you've paid a high price for shooting Carswell, but you did the right thing. We'll never be able to repay you, but maybe this is a start."

Nathan and Samuel went to the cart and started unloading boxes and bags. "We've brought you some clothing and food. And, after Callie's wedding, we will bring you a sow with piglets, some chickens, and a dairy cow with her calf. That should start building your livestock up again. I'll also send William over here to help you plow up land for a garden and provide you with seeds."

"But most of all, I want to extend an invitation for y'all to attend Callie and Ben's wedding next Thursday at ten in the morning. Don't worry about your appearances - there are clothes in there suitable for a wedding. Kathleen saw to that. We'll send the carriage for you around nine, so be ready."

The family didn't know what to say. Nathan had overwhelmed them with kindness. They murmured their gratitude and promised to attend the wedding.

Samuel, for the most part, was trying to ignore Lizzy. But he could feel her eyes boring into his body and he was forced to look at her. She looked so happy; her hazel eyes were sparkling in the late afternoon sun. She flashed Samuel a grin that came from her heart and went straight to his. She looked so fresh and innocent! It was hard to believe she had just killed a man. Samuel smiled at her, which made her eyes dance even more.

"I'll be talking to you again soon, Elijah. My brother-in-law from Savannah is coming tomorrow and I want to talk to him about maybe starting up your old sawmill again. Think we could invest in it - there's a great need for lumber again around these parts."

Elijah's mouth opened wide in surprise. "Yessir, Nathan. That would be a good idea. Wouldn't take much capital to get the mill up and running again."

"That's what I think. But we'll wait until after the wedding. Well, Samuel, we'd better head back home. Lots of work to be done there. See y'all next week."

Nathan and Samuel mounted their horses. "Thank you, Nathan and Samuel, for everything. You know we sure do appreciate it."

"Your welcome. Just sorry it's so late in coming."

* * *

"Here they come, Ben! Here they come!" Callie jumped up from the porch swing and ran to the veranda steps. She stood there between the two great white columns waving her hand in welcome. The Whitsons had pulled into the lane.

The relatives from Savannah arrived in a caravan. There were several carriages and a wagon loaded with people and baggage. Once the horses stopped, the adults and children started spilling out onto the front lawn, stretching as their feet touched the earth and then started for the house.

Ben had informed everyone inside the house the Savannah clan had arrived, so by the time the Whitsons and Norrises had brushed themselves off, most of the Hill family was ready to greet them. It had been nearly five months since they had seen one another so there were plenty of hugs and greetings. Introductions were made to the Chapmans, Laura, and her father and then everyone was ushered into the house.

* * *

"I just can't believe it, Kathleen! How on earth did that happen to our Callie?" Caroline shuddered and twisted her hands in despair. She looked at Victoria and Susan who had expressions of horror on their faces, shocked at the news of Callie's abduction and ensuing aftermath.

"I know, Caroline. It all seems like a dreadful dream now, but it is still very real to Callie. That's why she requested I tell you, and Nathan tell the men, so she didn't have to relive it all again. Please, don't dwell on it around her. It's fine to say something to her, but don't press her for details."

"Thank goodness she has Ben. He has been such a blessing. He hasn't left her side since she returned. We wondered if she wanted to postpone the wedding, but she was very steadfast about keeping it on Thursday. She didn't want Raymond Carswell to ruin her wedding plans, and we all agreed with her. Sometimes Callie has a strength that amazes me......"

"You know we will all support her, Kathleen. What that girl has been through in her young life.......it amazes me, too, how she's managed. But then......" Caroline looked at her daughters and Kathleen with a sweeping glance, "we southern women have all suffered these past years. I think it has made us all stronger."

"You're right, Caroline. We've had terrible things happened to all of us....and yet...here we all are.....to celebrate a joyous occasion. I guess that's just life."

"'We have to take the bad with the good,' my mother used to say, 'and hope the good outweighs the bad.'"

The women nodded their heads in unison and smiled.

* * *

The next few days at Oak Hill were organized chaos. Final preparations for the wedding were underway. Bridesmaid dresses had to be fitted, the lawn was prepared, cooking and baking was ongoing, rooms were cleaned. Throughout it all, Callie remained calm. Ben, too, as they counted the hours before they would be man and wife. They were never very far from one another and spent most of their time side by side.

Oak Hill was bursting at the seams. Every available bed, cot, and pallet was in use. Families doubled up and slept together, many on the floor. Belle enlisted the help of Mammy Sallie, Trudy, and Malindy, along with Kathleen and Caroline to assist in the kitchen. Constant cooking was needed to feed the hungry mouths of eighteen people, plus Trudy, Caleb, and Libby who visited frequently. It was a noisy, animated, energetic time. One which everyone thoroughly enjoyed.

Callie noticed Ben was absent at a certain time each morning and would be gone for an hour or so and then reappear. She also realized that Victoria and Trudy were gone around the same time. She didn't say anything; however, she was very curious as to what they were up to. But, she didn't have time to worry about it - her wedding day was almost here!

* * *

April 23, 1871 began as the sun rose slowly against the eastern horizon, sending shafts of pale light and pastel colors across the bluing sky. The evening stars became faint and the full moon began to fade away as the sun proceeded its climb. At Oak Hill it would be a glorious day.

Callie had been awake for several hours. She hadn't been able to sleep. She was too excited, not nervous or apprehensive, but eager for this day to begin. She lay in her familiar feather bed with Victoria snoring slightly next to her; Emma was mumbling in her sleep from the cot on the floor; Socks was breathing heavily beneath her. Sounds of sleep all around her.

She was smiling, so happy and content. All thoughts of the past week's turmoil erased from her mind. It was her eighteenth birthday *and* her wedding day! She sighed and turned over on her side, careful not to disturb Victoria. Then she grinned. This would be the last time she would ever have to sleep with Victoria. From now on, only Ben would be in bed with her. Chills of anticipation swept through her body. What wonders would she experience tonight?

Callie finally gave up all thoughts of going back to sleep, and as the first beams of the dawn's light reached her window, she crawled out of bed silently, put her dressing gown on, and tiptoed out of her room, shutting the door quietly. She padded down the hallway in her bare feet and then cautiously started down the stairs.

She really didn't want anyone to see her. "I'd probably scare them," she thought, reaching up to touch all the rags on her head, used to curl each tress. She couldn't help but giggle at the thought.

Without thinking, she headed to Mammy Sallie's room. The door was already ajar and she could hear Mammy shuffling on the other side. She whispered, "Mammy Sallie, are you dressed?"

Mammy smiled at the soft voice. "Yes, Miz Callie. Comes on in. I's jes' gots to puts my shoes on."

Callie quickly entered the room and softly shut the door behind her. She immediately went to Mammy Sallie and hugged her. Despite her euphoria, she felt tears spring to the corners of her eyes. In many ways, this day was bittersweet. She was now old enough to marry and..........leave home. She had told herself many times she wasn't going to think about telling everyone good-bye until the very last minute, but now that was hard.

Mammy Sallie hugged her back. "Happy birfday, Miz Callie. You's a grown womin now. I's glad I's still on this earth so I's can sees my lil gal all grown up an git' married! I's so proud of you! Your Mama Hannah would be too. I's knows she watchin' you today.......Now, now, lez not be sheddin' no tears. Today a happy day.....a happy day for this family."

"I know, Mammy Sallie. These *are* tears of happiness. But still...
...I try not to think about leaving Oak Hill and everyone here, but sometimes it just creeps up on me."

"I's knows, I's knows. But you big gal now an' you gots to live your own life. You's so lucky to has Mista Ben. He so good to you. He loves you so much….eve'ybody can sees that. You's goin' has a good life, Miz Callie…..has a family of your own wit Mista Ben. Today a good day….a happy, happy day."

Callie smiled at Mammy Sallie and didn't see all the deep wrinkles in that brown face, nor the white hairs escaping her kerchief. She didn't see the stooped back or the age spots on her arthritic hands. She saw the Mammy Sallie of her youth. The one who dressed her, brushed her hair, bathed her, calmed her fears. The one who rocked her to sleep singing lullabies. The mammy who had taken the place of her mother. The woman who raised her, along with Nathan, until Kathleen had arrived, and even after that.

Callie hugged the old woman again, tightly, fiercely, not wanting to let go of those memories of her childhood. "Miz Callie, you squeezin the breaf right outta me!"

Mammy Sallie started laughing as Callie finally released her. She put her hands on Callie's shoulders and looked her right in the eyes. "I's loves you too, Miz Callie. Jes' like my own chiles. We's always be parts of each odder, no matters where you lives. I's be there wit you." Sallie took her hands off Callie and put them on her hips, cocked her head, and grinned. "You's not gonna git rid o' your Mammy that easy, lil gal……Now, lez git you some breakfast so you's don' faint takin' them weddin' vows!"

"Oh, Mammy Sallie, I love you so much, so much! Thank you for everything!"

"You's welcome, lil gal. Did it all outta love……." Mammy stood there, arms akimbo staring at Callie. Then she laughed. "Well, Miz Callie, we best git them rags outta your hair 'fore someone comes an' sees you. You scares 'em to def!"

The woman and her mammy fell into each other's arms, giggling, once again, as in the past.

* * *

"Callie, you look absolutely stunning, just stunning." Kathleen was admiring Callie's reflection in the mirror. "I just can't believe how beautiful you are. I think it's the happiness radiating from your face."

Callie smiled broadly. "I *do* look pretty, don't I, Mama? I think Ben will like the way I look."

The bride and her bridesmaids had been getting ready for over an hour, each helping the other. Finally, Kathleen whisked Callie away into her bedroom for the final touches.

"Yes, sweetie, I think Ben will be very pleased with his gorgeous bride."

There was a knock at the door and in came Beulah and Mammy Sallie. "We've come to give some special gifts to you Callie...both wedding and birthday."

"Oh, Grandma, please, please come in. How do you think I look?" Callie turned a full circle to show Beulah the entire ensemble.

"You take my breath away, honey. I can't believe that skinny little girl turned into such a beautiful young lady. What do you think, Sallie?"

"I's thinks Miz Callie looks right pritty, but if'n we keeps tellin her so, she gonna git's a big head!!"

"Oh, Mammy Sallie.....you tease me too much!! I know how I looked this morning with all those rags tied in my hair!!"

"Hahahaha....wells, you does look mighty good, gal. Doin' your family proud. Me too."

"Speaking of doing the family proud, Callie, I have a gift for you that's very special to us Charlesworth women." Beulah pulled a black silk pouch out of her pocket and opened it as she spoke. She pulled out a single strand of perfectly matched ivory pearls. "These belonged to my grandmother, Beatrice. She received them from my grandfather, Samuel, who gave them to her for their wedding. Since then, all Charlesworth women have worn them on their wedding day. I've been saving them for you all these years. And, since it's also your eighteenth birthday, I want you to keep them. Then maybe someday you can give them to your little girl to wear for her wedding."

As she was speaking, Beulah placed the pearls around Callie's neck and fastened the clasp. They looked like they belonged there.

"Oh, Grandma! These are so so beautiful! Thank you so much. I will cherish them always."

"You're welcome, sweetie. You are very deserving of them. I only wish your grandfather was here today. He would be so proud of you - even if you are marrying a Yankee!"

Callie felt herself blush and she sheepishly lowered her eyes.

"Don't worry, dear, Preston would love Ben. They have much in common, you know, both being farmers.....and very good looking."

"Grandma!"

"I wasn't always old, Callie." Beulah's eyes twinkled with merriment. "Now, I think I'll go find my seat outside. Bless you, dear. I love you..........and I know Preston *is* with us today."

"I know so too, Grandma. Thank you again. I love you, too." Callie hugged her grandmother and kissed her on the cheek.

"Come on, Sallie, let's go outside."

"Jes' minute, Miz Beulah. I's got sumpin for Miz Callie too." Mammy Sallie pulled a pale blue cotton handkerchief from behind her back. "Your Mama Hannah gives this to me one Christmas long ago. Thinks she mades it herself. It gots some pritty em'bro'dren on it. She tol' me it's my name....Sallie. Would likes for you to carries it, Miz Callie, an' 'members your mama an' me."

Callie took the offered handkerchief from her mammy. "Mammy Sallie, it's beautiful. Thank you so much. I know it's very special to you. Oh, goodness, now I'm going to cry!"

"Not yet. I have something too." Kathleen walked over to her dresser and picked up a small box. "Here, you will probably recognize these. I wore them when I married your father. They were his gift to me."

Callie opened the box to reveal the pearl drop earrings Kathleen had worn at her wedding. She looked up, tears now flowing down her cheeks. "Yes, I remember these. I always thought they looked so beautiful with your dress." She put them into her ear lobes. "Perfect. They *still* look beautiful with your dress. Now…. I think I'm ready."

"There ya'll are! I've been trying to find you." Caroline burst into the room and then stopped suddenly. "Oh, Callie, aren't you just a vision! Oh, my dear, you are one of the prettiest brides I've ever seen. I love your hair….and the veil under it….and the tiara….oh, the dress is perfect….let me get a good look at you." Caroline walked all around Callie. "Perfect, just perfect, but I expect you are missing something."

They all looked at her and shook their heads no. "I gave her something old - my pearls." Beulah looked at Mammy Sallie. "I's gives her sumpin blue - my hanky." Mammy looked at Kathleen. "I gave her something borrowed - my earrings. Her tiara and her shoes are the something new….oh….we're missing the penny for her shoe!"

"Not anymore!" Caroline held up a bright shiny, new, copper penny, the color of Kathleen's hair. "Here it is! Put it in your shoe, Callie. *Now* you're ready to meet your groom!" Laughter suddenly replaced all the tears.

* * *

The bridesmaids, Victoria, Laura, and Emma, along with Susan and her twins, Carrie and Annie, who were the flower girls, were waiting in Callie's room for her to appear. Trudy had stepped out to nurse Libby before the ceremony.

"Victoria, since I hardly know Callie, maybe you could tell me why she has a darkie as a bridesmaid and her baby as a flower girl." Laura was standing in front of the dresser mirror adjusting the flowers in her hair.

"Well, it's because she and Trudy are very close. They grew up together. Trudy was Callie's only playmate as a child. They've stayed friends even after Trudy got married and had baby Libby. Why do you ask? Hasn't Samuel told you about Trudy and Callie?"

"Somewhat…I just find it very strange that she's in the wedding party. I was friendly to some of our slaves who were my age, but I wouldn't *think* of having them participate in something as important as my wedding. What do you think, Emma….as a Yankee….would you have a darkie in your wedding?"

"Well…..I'd never even seen a dar…..negro….until I came here. We just don't have any around Clayton Township. But I suppose if I had been friends with her all my life, then yes, I'd have her in my wedding. Besides, Callie can do whatever she wants….it's her wedding."

"Hmmmm……interesting. I guess I'm just not used to the ways of country people."

"Susan and I are *not* from the country! We are Savannah born and raised, *and* I might add, Savannah is a much older and cultured city than Atlanta!" Victoria pulled out her fan and started waving it furiously.

"I apologize…." Laura took a step back and bowed her head slightly and then walked to another part of the room. The others just looked at one another in exasperation.

* * *

Trudy had taken baby Libby to Mammy Sallie's room to nurse her. She didn't want her crying during the ceremony. Trudy still hadn't had a moment alone with Callie today and she was a little upset. Every time she thought they'd be by themselves, someone had interrupted them. She hadn't even had time to tell Callie how happy she was for this day. But, then, Callie already knew that. Maybe she could sneak a quick comment before they all left the house for the ceremony.

Trudy chuckled. For the first time, Callie had treated her equally in front of Victoria. In fact, Callie had informed the other bridesmaids that Trudy would be the one standing by her side during the ceremony.

Trudy hadn't missed the surprised expressions on the others' faces, especially Laura's. She giggled again at the thought. "Well, Miz Libby, I's guesses we'd bedder gits agoin' an' sees Miz Callie gits herse'f marrieds. You be a good lil gal an' don' cry, now." Libby looked at her mama with her big black eyes and gurgled with glee.

* * *

"Papa, are you all right?" Nathan had entered the room where Callie and the other women in his life had gathered. He was so taken aback by this lovely creature in front of him that he couldn't breathe.

"Nathan, darling, come sit down. You look rather pale." Kathleen took her husband's hand and led him to the chaise.

"No, no…I'm fine. It's just that….that….my God, Callie, you are so beautiful! I just can't….believe…this is my baby girl!" Nathan's voice cracked as he fought back the tears. He looked to Kathleen for help.

"She is spectacular, isn't she? But then, we've always known what a beauty she is - inside and out, haven't we, dear?"

Nathan just nodded his head and stared at his daughter.

"Come on, everyone, I think Callie and her papa need some time together." Caroline started guiding everyone to the door. "We'll see you when you come down the aisle!"

Kathleen came over and kissed Callie on the cheek, followed by Beulah and Mammy Sallie. "I love all of you. Thank you for your gifts," Callie called out after them as they exited the room. Then she turned to Nathan.

"Papa, I've never been so happy in my life. But I'm also kind of sad because marrying Ben means I'm all grown up and will be leaving you soon. But I want you to know……that I will be thinking of you every day…and will always have you here…" Callie put her hand over her chest. "Here…in my heart."

"Oh, baby girl. I know….I haven't been able to even think about you leaving, but the time will be here soon, won't it? But look at you. You *are* all grown up. Good heavens! With all the excitement of the wedding, I almost forgot about your birthday today!" Then Nathan's teary eyes started twinkling with mischief. "Almost! But you won't get your present until after the ceremony and reception are over."

"Oh, Papa, shame on you! You know now I'll be wondering what it is! You're just teasing me like when I was a little girl." Callie started laughing, but tears quickly filled her eyes. "I'm going to miss you so so so much, Papa!"

"I'll miss you too, sweetie. But as you said, we'll always be in each other's hearts." The two hugged and then wiped each other's tears.

"I think it's time we took that walk down the aisle to get you married to Ben. I've been told he's pretty anxious to become your husband."

"I've heard that too." Callie grasped Nathan's arm and started for the door. "Now, about that birthday present……"

* * *

The bridesmaids and flower girls, Kathleen, and Samuel were

waiting for Callie and Nathan at the bottom of the stairs. Samuel had not been allowed to see her before now. He had been with Ben, as he was one of the groomsmen.

Samuel was amazed at the transformation of his sister. "Callie, good heavens you are too pretty! What happened to my little sister who's usually running around here in pigtails and a calico work dress?"

"Same sister, Sam, just a little different outfit."

"Oh, by the way, happy birthday.....I understand gifts will be given later. We all know how patient you are!"

"You and Papa are terribly mean! You tease me all the time..." Callie burst out laughing. "Ever since I was old enough to know what my birthday meant, you have surprised me on my birthday....I expect that today too, but I'm not going to let my curiosity ruin my big day!"

"My, the little sister is all grown up." Samuel reached over and pecked Callie on the cheek and whispered in her ear, "You can't tell me you aren't just a little teeny tiny bit curious!"

"Sam! Of course I am!" Callie laughed again. "You'd better go back to my soon-to-be husband. We'll discuss this later."

Samuel picked up his sister's hand and brought it to his lips, noticing the long sleeves covered the bandages still wrapped around her healing wrists. "As you command, my dear. I'm on my way."

"It's time everyone," Kathleen announced as Samuel left. "Laura, you will go first, then Emma, Victoria, Trudy, and finally Carrie and Annie. I will see y'all outside. Remember to smile!" She gave Callie and Nathan a final hug, adjusting the blusher over Callie's face. "Now you are really a bride, dear. I can't begin to tell you how happy I am for you."

"I know, Mama, thank you."

Kathleen started out the front door, looking back to make sure everyone was in the right place. "Laura, when I'm seated, you start the procession."

Trudy turned around to look at Callie and Nathan. "Miz Callie, I's...we... .didn' gits...a...chan....."

"I know, Trudy, we don't need too. I know how you feel. I love you, too, you already know that."

Trudy gave Callie a huge smile. "Yessum, I's guesses I's does." Libby cooed in Trudy's arms. "Guesses, Libby does too!"

Callie chuckled and reached out to grab Libby's little waving hand. "Miss Liberty Caludy Jones, you behave yourself while I get married."

Libby smiled a big toothless smile at Callie and then gurgled with delight. "See, she listens to her Aunt Callie." Callie grinned at Trudy. "Always, Trudy, always, you will be my very best friend and almost-sister."

"Don' makes my cry, Miz Callie," Trudy sniffled. "Don' have no han'chief."

"Here, use the one Mammy Sallie gave me to carry."

Trudy quickly wiped her eyes when she realized Laura had exited the front door. The wedding was underway. She handed the handkerchief back to Callie. "Thank you, Miz Callie. Loves you."

"Loves you too, Trudy."

Each of the bridesmaids went through the front door, followed by the flower girls carefully tossed their rose petals along the aisle. Callie and Nathan stood there silently, waiting until all were in their places under the live-oak tree. Both took a deep breath. "Guess this is it, baby girl."

"Guess it is, Papa. I'm ready. Let's go."

"Don't forget to smile, sweetie."

* * *

As Callie and Nathan approached the veranda steps, everyone in attendance stood up and turned to see the bride and her father, each with their own thoughts. They were all looking at Callie, but she saw only one person - Ben. He had his back to her, but slowly turned to see her as the father and daughter neared the aisle.

He knew Callie was beautiful, but he was not prepared for what his eyes now saw. He suddenly had to choke back tears; he was so overcome with emotion. He blinked fiercely, bit his bottom lip, and held his breath. Nothing helped; the tears were there, waiting to flow down his cheeks.

Trudy was beaming, so excited for Callie. She glanced at Caleb, now holding Libby, and grinned at him. Callie and Ben loved each other as much as she and Caleb did, and she was pleased for her friend.

Kathleen thought of the little girl she had first encountered as a student. Now she was her grown up "daughter." Callie deserved all the happiness in the world and more.

Beulah was wishing Preston could see their granddaughter all grown up ready to start a life of her own with the man she loved. He would be as proud of her as Beulah was.

Mammy Sallie had tears running down her face. Both of her "chiles" were grown up and on their own. Callie was so special to her.

Abigail and Henry, who was Ben's groomsman, were thinking about the little boy they had raised so lovingly. He was so happy. Callie would be a wonderful wife for him. They welcomed her into their family with open arms.

Caroline and John were thinking how lovely Callie looked and how happy she was. They hoped she and Ben liked the surprise they had arranged for them later.

Victoria thought Callie looked stunning and wished it was her. But she was happy for her cousin, even if she was marrying a Yankee.

Samuel wasn't looking at his sister. His eyes were scanning the guests until he saw who he was searching for - Lizzy. There she was in the back row. She looked wonderful. Amazing what a new dress could do. He'd be sure to talk to her later and tell her how lovely she looked.

Laura was watching Callie walk down the aisle with her eyes fixed on Ben. Laura looked at Samuel. Why couldn't she feel that way towards him? He was looking at someone towards the back and smiling. She followed his gaze and saw the young woman return the smile shyly. Hmmmm…what was this?

Emma was so happy for her brother. Callie was beautiful and so nice. She was so delighted she was going to be her sister-in-law and live nearby.

Lenora nodded her head as Callie passed by her. She remembered taking care of her when she broke her arm. My, my, the time goes so fast now.....

Joseph, William, Malindy, holding baby Lincoln, Dinah, and Belle watched as their former mistress walked to meet her groom. Each had their own memories of Callie. Dinah thought she had done a wonderful job of updating Kathleen's dress.

Lastly, Nathan tried not to think at all. He concentrated on putting one foot in front of the other, but each step made him feel one step closer to losing his daughter. No....he wasn't losing her.....she would always be his baby girl no matter where she was. And, she was so blissfully happy - she was radiant. Ben was a good man. He'd take care of her.

As they finally reached the flower covered arbor under the old oak tree where Ben and the minister stood, Nathan took a deep breath and exhaled. "Smile, Papa," Callie said under her breath. "Smile."

Nathan couldn't help but grin until he saw Ben's tear streaked face. This man truly loved his daughter. Another man loved Callie as much as he did. This was hard to realize, but good.

Nathan lifted the blusher to completely reveal Callie's face. He bent down to kiss his daughter's cheek. "Love you, baby girl," he whispered, his voice catching. "Love you, too, Papa." Callie kissed Nathan on his cheek and smiled brilliantly. Nathan took her hand and Ben's and brought them together. "Take care of her, Ben."

"I will, sir."

The minister began, "We are gathered here today to witness the marriage of Callie Hill and Ben Chapman in holy matrimony." Callie and Ben looked at each other with love and wonderment and contentment.

The minister continued, "St, Paul, in First Corinthians, Chapter Thirteen, Verse Four, gives us the definition of love to follow as husband and wife: 'Charity suffereth long, and is kind; charity envieth not; charity vaunteth not itself, is not puffed up, Doth not behave itself unseemly, seeketh not her own, is not easily provoked, thinketh no evil; Rejoiceth not in iniquity, but rejoiceth in the truth; Beareth all things, believeth all things, hopeth all things, endureth all things. Charity never faileth.'"

"Ben, Callie, if you remember this, you will have a wonderful marriage. As all those in attendance who are married will tell you, if you have love, you will have happiness. Of course, there will be times when you will be tested, but if you truly love one another, a compromise will be met. Remember to keep God in your home and heart, and your life will be a blessed one." The minister smiled at both of these young people so obviously deeply in love.

"Now before God and these witnesses, you will take your vows of marriage. Please join your right hands."

Callie went first. "I, Callista Beatrice Hill, take you, Benjamin Henry Chapman, to be my wedded husband, to have and to hold, from this day forward, for better or worse, for richer, for poorer, in sickness and in health, to love and to cherish, till death do us part."

"I, Benjamin Henry Chapman, take you, Callista Beatrice Hill, to be my wedded wife, to have and to hold, from this day forward, for better or worse, for richer, for poorer, in sickness and in health, to love and to cherish, till death do us part."

Ben squeezed Callie's hand and grinned.

"Ben, do you have a ring for Callie?"

"Yes, sir." Ben pulled a plain gold wide band from his pocket.

"Place it on her finger and repeat after me: 'With this ring, I thee wed, in the name of the Father, and of the Son, and of the Holy Ghost.'"

Ben did as told, looking into Callie's large, luminous brown eyes as he slid the band onto her finger.

"By the power invested in me by God and the state of Georgia, I now pronounce you husband and wife. 'What therefore God hath joined together, let not man put asunder.'"

Ben and Callie looked at each other in amazement. "We're married, Callie, we're really married!" Ben whispered in his new wife's ear. Callie's smile was expansive, illuminating her entire face. The couple turned to face their guests. Everyone had tears of joy and were smiling irrepressibly. Ben and Callie started down the aisle nodding at people as they passed by them. When they reached the end of the chairs, Ben stopped. He gathered Callie in his arms and kissed her sweetly. "I'm the happiest and luckiest man on the face of the earth!"

"Oh, Ben, I do love you so." Callie tilted her head for a second kiss, but by this time the wedding party had caught up with them.

"No, no, no, Miz Callie…..no more kissin' til tonight!" Trudy chuckled as she went to her friend and hugged her tight. "I's so happy for you, Miz Callie…..so happy. Now lez gits into the house so you can receives your guests prop'ly an' then we cans eats Belle's scrum'tus breakfast."

* * *

"I have a surprise for my lovely daughter and her new husband," Nathan announced as he stood at the table. "And, I guess for everyone else that's here." He had everyone's attention now.

"Most of you know that today is also Callie's eighteenth birthday and, as she knows, Kathleen and I haven't given her a birthday gift yet." He looked down at Callie, who suddenly blushed. "It's been a tradition in our family to give Callie something very special for her birthday. This year was very hard - how do you top a wedding?" Everyone smiled. "But, my lovely wife thought of a very good idea, I think. Arriving very soon will be a photographer from Savannah who will be taking photographs of the newlyweds, the wedding party, families, and all our guests too, if you wish."

"Oh, Papa….that's wonderful! We can look at the photographs and remember what a happy, special day this is! Thank you so much - you too, Mama!" Callie had risen from her chair and gone to Nathan and Kathleen.

"You're very welcome, sweetie. That's exactly what we thought. Also, Belle has made your favorite pound cake, which we will all partake in right now!"

On cue, Belle entered with the cake, topped with white icing, and sat it in front of Callie. "There's you goes, Miz Callie. I's done made you eighteen bir'day pound cakes now. Hopes to makes you many, many more."

Callie grinned at Belle. "I hope so too, Belle." She turned to Ben. "Wait until you taste this cake. You will swear it's the best you've ever eaten."

"Well, then, let's slice it up and try it."

* * *

After the last slice of cake had been devoured, the attendees gathered on the front veranda. The photographer, Lewis Lockhorn, had arrived. For the next several hours, Callie and Ben stood, sat, and posed, by themselves, with their families, with the bridesmaids, with the groomsmen, with the flower girls, with the guests, with Socks, Daisy, and Rumpel, with anyone there.

It took forever for Mr. Lockhorn to get the right pose and then to take the picture. Everyone was beginning to get so irritable that Nathan and Kathleen were beginning to wonder if this was a good decision or not.

While the photographs were being taken, Samuel sought out Lizzy. He found her huddled with the rest of her family in a corner of the veranda, trying to be unobtrusive. They didn't think they should be in any of the photographs.

"There you are! I've been trying to find y'all. I'm so happy y'all decided to come to the wedding. I must say, ladies, you look very pretty, and Elijah, you look most handsome."

"Thank you, Samuel," answered Almina. "It was a beautiful wedding and reception. Your sister is a very pretty bride."

"Yes, I think she is too, but then I'm not very objective when it comes to Callie. Have you had your photograph taken yet?"

"No...no...We don't want to have no picture taken of us," Elijah said. "No reason too." He gave Samuel a look of disgust.

"I understand. I wasn't too happy to oblige either, but Father was adamant about it. Said we hadn't had any likenesses of ourselves since the portrait painter came when Callie and I were younger. Well, I guess I'd better get back to my family. Hope y'all are enjoying yourselves." Samuel turned to leave.

"Samuel! Wait." Lizzy stood up and smoothed her dress. "Can I talk to you...in private?" Samuel gave Lizzy a quizzical look, as did the rest of her family.

"Certainly, Lizzy. Let's go sit over here on the swing." Lizzy looked at the other end of the veranda where the swing was.

"No. Could we walk out to the garden?"

"Well….."

"Please, Samuel, it's important."

"All right." Samuel offered his arm, which Lizzy eagerly took. They proceeded down the front steps and around the house to the side garden where they could still be observed by the guests, but were by themselves.

"What is it, Lizzy? What did you want to talk to me about?"

"Oh, Samuel, I just wanted to thank you privately for everything you have done this past week for us. The clothes. The food. The invitation here. It's made a big difference in our lives. Especially mine. You saved me, Samuel, from a terrible thing. I have hope now. I think things will only get better from now on." Lizzy was looking at the ground all the time she spoke, but now she lifted her hazel eyes and Samuel could see they were rimmed with tears. Her chin started to quiver. She looked so vulnerable Samuel wanted to grab her and hold her close, but he remembered where he was.

"Lizzy……" He cleared his throat and took a step backward. "Lizzy….I'm glad we could help you. You don't need to thank me anymore." He looked around to see if anyone was watching them. Someone was - Laura. He caught her stare and quickly said, "We'd best go back to the others."

Lizzy followed his gaze and saw Laura looking at them. She smiled at her - a demure smile - then nodded her head in acknowledgement. Laura turned away. "Yes, I guess we probably should."

* * *

Finally, all the photography was finished. Everyone breathed a sigh of relief, but all concluded it would be a wonderful remembrance of the day.

People were sprawled all over the veranda and lawn lazing in the afternoon April sun. It was a beautiful day. The sun overhead shone brightly in the blue cloudless sky. The only shade was dappled under the live oak where the ceremony had occurred. Callie and Ben sat under the arbor now, exhausted.

"Don't you want to change and get out of your dress?"

"No, I think I'd like to keep it on forever. Don't you like it?"

"Oh, yes, I love it, Callie, you look so pretty in it. I just thought maybe you'd be more comfortable in something else."

"No, I'm fine, just tired. It's been a pretty hectic morning." Callie smiled. "But a wonderful one. I can't believe we're actually married, Ben."

"I know. It's a wonderful feeling, isn't it?" He leaned over and kissed her gently.

"Hey, hey, you two. There's you goes kissin' 'gin!" Trudy came up behind the tree laughing. She had Libby in her arms.

"Trudy Jones! Are you spying on us?"

"Uh-huh. Don' want you to spoils your weddin' night!"

"Trudy!" Callie felt herself turn red. "Stop that!" Ben began laughing at his bride's embarrassment, making her become even redder.

"Do you knows where you sleepin' tonight, Miz Callie?" Trudy put Libby up on her shoulder and began patting her back.

"Of course, I do. In my room. Where else would I sleep?"

"Mista Ben, you sleepin' in Miz Callie's room wit Miz Emma an' Miz Victoria?"

Ben looked at Callie and grinned. "I don't think so, Trudy. Miss Callie isn't either."

Callie looked at him perplexed. "Then where *are* we spending the night, husband?"

Ben's eyes twinkled with mischief. "It's a surprise. A birthday surprise. You'll just have to wait and see."

"Oh….you are as mean as the other men in my family!"

* * *

After enjoying a light late lunch, everyone started dispersing. The Montgomerys left for Pine Wood, the workers went back to their cabins, Trudy and Caleb went home with baby Libby, the relatives retired to their beds for a nap. Left on the veranda were Callie and Ben, Nathan and Kathleen, and Caroline and John. Callie still refused to change out of her wedding gown.

"What are your plans for the next few days, Callie, Ben?" Caroline asked.

"Well….we really haven't planned anything, Aunt Caroline. We are going to stay here for a few more weeks so I can get all my things organized to ship to Illinois. Ben's family is going home in a few days - so are all of you. I'll get things ready and then we will take the train, probably around the end of May in time for planting season there."

"Aren't you going to take some sort of honeymoon by yourselves before you leave for the Midwest?"

Callie and Ben looked at each other as if this was something they hadn't thought about. "No….I guess we never planned for that. Callie, do you want to go somewhere by ourselves?"

"I haven't really thought about it, Ben."

"Well, your Uncle John and your Papa and Mama and I have thought about it." Caroline's face lit up with excitement and anticipation. She was sitting on the edge of her seat just bursting to reveal her surprise.

"What, Aunt Caroline?"

"We are all giving you a honeymoon!"

"What?"

"Callie, remember when we were in Chicago and you were so amazed at the size of Lake Michigan? And, I was surprised that you had never visited Tybee Island on the ocean? Well, we," she gestured to John, Nathan, and Kathleen, who looked like they were about to explode, "we decided you should see the ocean - you and Ben. John and I built a cottage on the beach at Tybee. It's yours for as long as you want to stay there. It's all stocked and ready for you. All you have to do is bring clothes."

Caroline leaned back in her chair waiting for the couple's reaction. Callie and Ben looked at one another; their mouths dropped open in shock. Both were momentarily stunned into silence.

"Well, what do you think? Isn't that wonderful?" Kathleen stood up and walked over to Callie.

"I….we….I…Ben, what do you think?"

"I….I…think it's a very generous offer, Mrs. Whitson." Ben was at a loss for words.

"Please, call me Caroline. You know, Ben, Callie is very special to us and we wanted to do something grand for her birthday and her wedding. Please say yes. You both will have a wonderful time, trust me."

Callie and Ben stared at one another and at the same time said "Yes!"

"Of course, we will go, Aunt Caroline. Uncle John, Mama, Papa, thank you so much! What a wonderful surprise!" Callie got up to hug her family and Ben did too.

"We have another surprise, too, baby girl. An inn has finally opened up between here and Savannah, so Kathleen and I have made arrangements for you to stay there on your way to Tybee and back."

"We all stayed there on our way here for the wedding and it's a lovely little place, Callie. Not some roadside tavern, but a very pleasant inn," Caroline added. "But we also expect you to stay a couple days with us in Savannah so we can show off the city to Ben."

Ben looked downcast. "I've already been to Savannah, Mrs. Whi... Caroline. During the war."

There was a brief pause in the excitement of the moment, but Caroline was determined. "Well, it looks a lot different now, Ben, so the sights will be new to you."

Callie immediately said, "We'll be most happy to stay with you, Aunt Caroline. I'm sure there are many things that Ben hasn't seen - me either. Thank you."

"Oh, I'm so excited! Just think, Ben, the ocean! How wonderful!"

Ben couldn't contain his own eagerness either. He had glimpsed the Atlantic at Charleston, but not the open sea. Nor had he set foot on a sandy beach.

"Thank you again, everyone. I'm sure Callie and I will have a memorable time there. Maybe we can even get her to change out of her wedding dress before then!"

"Oh, Ben....I won't get to wear it ever again. Mama, didn't you feel that way when you wore it?"

"Yes, yes I did. I guess it has some sort of magic to it."

Nathan laughed, "I think it's just some sort of 'woman' thing."

"Maybe so, husband, but if Callie and Ben are as happy as we are since I wore that dress, then I consider it magical."

Nathan had to agree.

* * *

The sun started setting in the west, casting a palette of colors across the sky. It was becoming chilly out on the veranda where Ben and Callie were alone on the old swing. Callie had her head on Ben's shoulder, not quite asleep, but drowsy. Neither was speaking. Callie yawned and then sighed.

"You tired?"

"Yes, I guess I am. It's been a long day, but I don't want it to end yet." Callie sat up straight. "Aren't you tired?"

"Yes, I am."

Callie lowered her eyes and said very softly, "Well, then, hadn't we.....shouldn't we....go...to...bed?"

"Hmmmm.....I guess that would remedy our tiredness, wouldn't it?" Ben grinned, put his hand under Callie's chin, lifting it to meet his lips.

"Mmmmm....I'm *really* tired now, Ben. I think we *definitely* should go to bed." Callie looked Ben in his eyes and smiled mischievously. "The question is, where is our bed? No one has said a thing to me about where we will sleep tonight. Do you know, Mr. Chapman?"

"Mrs. Chapman, I *do* have an idea where we will sleep for the next few nights."

"Oooohhh...I like the sound of 'Mrs. Chapman!' Well, are you going to keep grinning like the cat that swallowed the canary, or are you going to tell me where we will be tonight?"

"I think maybe I'll just take you there. Ready?"

"Ready. Let's go."

Ben grabbed Callie's hand and pulled her off the swing. He headed down the veranda steps toward the live oak. Callie stopped.

"Ben, we aren't going to stay out under the tree tonight are we?"

"Well, we got engaged here, married here, why not spend our wedding night here?" Ben's eyes were twinkling with merriment, not missed by Callie, even in the dimming daylight.

"Oh, you are just teasing me again! It's too cold to stay here."

Ben started pulling her hand again, laughing. He began pulling her faster and soon they were both running through the grounds toward the former slave quarters.

Callie was concentrating so much on not tripping on her dress that it wasn't until Ben stopped in front of one of the cabins that she fully realized where they were. He stopped, apparently almost giddy over her confusion. He didn't wait for her to say anything. He scooped her up in his arms and carried her to the last cabin, pushed open the door, and went inside.

Callie looked around. It was beautiful. The walls had been recently whitewashed, new muslin curtains were at the window, clean rag rugs were on the freshly scrubbed pine floor. A small fire was burning in the fireplace casting a cozy glow to the room. The bed was in the corner with a soft new feather bed, covered with new sheets and coverlet. Fluffy pillows were at the head and another quilt was folded at the foot. On the wall across from the bed was a small washstand with an ewer and basin and clean towels. A worn pine table, on one side of the fireplace, held a hurricane lamp with a candle in it. Two ladder back chairs were pushed under the table. Hanging from the pegs on the wall were Callie and Ben's nightclothes and outfits for tomorrow.

Callie was speechless. Ben was smirking from ear to ear. "What do you think, Mrs. Chapman? Cat got your tongue?"

"Ohhhhh, Ben, it's perfect. But...how...did.....?"

"Trudy and Victoria helped me. I told them I wanted a very special place for us to stay after the wedding. Trudy came up with the idea of the cabin. From there it was easy. So, I'm guessin' you like it?"

"Very much. Put me down so I can take a better look." Ben deposited Callie on her feet and watched as she walked around the little cabin. "It's lovely, Ben, lovely. I knew there was a good reason I married you!" She walked over to him slowly and put her arms around his neck. "But I'm still *very* tired, Mr. Chapman."

"So am I," said Ben, but he took Callie's arms from his neck. "Let's sit over here for a minute first, please?"

"Certainly." Callie had a perplexed expression on her face. Ben pulled out one of the chairs, motioning for her to sit down. Then he went over to his clothes hanging on the peg and reached into a pocket.

Callie strained her head to see what he was doing.

He came back and sat in the other chair, holding two objects wrapped in muslin in his hands.

"In case you haven't noticed, I have yet to give you a birthday gift. I don't know if I can top all the ones you've received today, but I think this one will make you very happy."

Callie squirmed in her chair in anticipation, but she didn't say anything. Ben slowly took one of the items and placed it on the table in front of her. "Happy birthday, Mrs. Chapman. I hope you like it."

Callie eagerly started to peel the muslin away. She gasped. In front of her was a miniature house carved out of soft pine that fit in the palm of her hand. She loved it, but looked puzzled. Ben chuckled. "It's not a toy, Callie, if that's what you're thinking."

"No...no....but I am wondering. Did you carve this?"

"Yes, I did." Ben took the little house from Callie and held it in front of her. "This, Mrs. Chapman, is our new house. It matches the real one I built for us back in Clayton Township."

"Ben! You built us a house already! You built us a house? Why haven't you told me before now? I thought we were staying with your parents until you put up one for us."

"Yes, I built us a house during the winter, and I didn't want to tell you because I wanted it to be a surprise. But I couldn't wait until we got back there, so I carved this little one for you. I thought it would be pretty cramped in Ma and Pa's house, so I went ahead and built ours."

"See this front porch? It faces west so we can sit out there and watch the sun set. That door goes into a big room that has the kitchen on one end and the parlor on the other. I even got you a nice shiny new cook stove so you won't have to cook over an open fire. This window in the back is our bedroom. Back here is a tiny catch-all room. I put shelves in it so we can use it for storage and it has the back door."

"I know it's not at all what you're used to, it bein' so small, but I figure I can add on to it as soon as we start havin' babies and need more room. What do you think?"

Callie had been watching Ben as he explained the house to her. She saw the love on his face as he described it. She couldn't help it.

Tears started in the corners of her eyes and now spilled out down her cheeks.

Ben looked at her and saw she was crying. "Oh, no! You don't like it! I know it's small, just two rooms, really, but…."

Callie grabbed his face and kissed him passionately on his soft full lips, her tears wetting his face. She pulled back, looking directly into his teal eyes. "Ben Chapman, this is the finest, nicest, most thoughtful, most loving gift I've ever received. I can't wait to see it in person. You are remarkable! I'm the luckiest woman in the world to have you as my husband." She kissed him again.

Ben pulled away this time. "So, I guess you *do* like it. I can't wait to carry you over the threshold. But……." He placed the other wrapped gift on the table in front of her. "I hope you like this one too. It's your *wedding* gift from me."

Callie wiped her tears with her fingers. "I don't know if I can stand another surprise," she giggled, "but I'll try."

She unwrapped the other article to reveal a ruby red velveteen box. She looked at Ben. "You always give me wonderful things in small boxes." She opened the box and inhaled sharply. Slowly she took out the beautiful gold lavaliere pendant hanging from a delicate gold chain. She could see the face of a watch in mother-of-pearl. "Oh, Ben," she whispered. "It's exquisite."

"Turn it over."

Callie carefully turned the watch over and saw the back had been engraved. She held it to the light of the candle and read, "*To my Callie. Forever, Ben - April 23, 1871.*"

Once again, the tears flowed. "I don't know what to say….it's so beautiful…the house….I don't deserve all this."

Ben took her in his arms. "Don't ever say that. You deserve more than this, Callie, and I'll do my darnedest to give it to you."

"But, now I feel terrible because my gift to you is in my room. I thought we would be there tonight so I left it there."

"Doesn't matter. I don't need any gifts. I got you." Ben's voice cracked.

Callie said very softly, "Will you help me out of my wedding gown now? There's lots of little buttons in the back."

"So, *now* you want to get out of that dress! I've wanted you to change all day because now we don't have anywhere to put it. I know it bein' Kathleen's and all that you want to keep it pretty."

"So *that's* why you kept after me about the dress! Well, let's see...." Callie looked around the tiny room. "Can't hang it on one of those pegs, it would ruin it. No wardrobe to hang it in. Hmmmm...if it doesn't get very cold tonight, I think what we can do is spread that quilt out on these rugs and then fold up the dress on top of it."

"Very good idea! Let's try it!" Ben turned his bride around and started unbuttoning all the tiny buttons. Both of them suddenly got very still. With each button released their breaths came quicker. Finally, Callie stepped out of her gown, while Ben took the quilt and unfolded it onto the rag rugs. Callie carefully folded the dress and laid it on the quilt.

"There! Done!" She realized she was standing in front of the first man to see her in her petticoats, chemise, drawers, and corset. Ben was looking at her with a puzzled look on his face. "What's the matter, Ben?"

"Can't figure out why you women-folk wear so darn many clothes under your other clothes. Makes no sense to me."

Callie laughed. "It doesn't to me either. In fact when I was a little girl, I decided it was too hot to wear so many clothes so I took some of them off. Grandma and Mammy Sallie were so angry with me. I still remember the looks on their faces."

"I bet you were something when you were a little girl. Probably just as pretty as you are today." Ben stroked Callie's hair. She bent her head back, wanting him to kiss her.

Instead, he started taking off her petticoats, then chemise, then corset, then she stepped out of her drawers. Ben could barely breathe. Neither could Callie.

She started undressing her groom until both of them stood naked, the firelight reflecting on their bare skin. Without a word, Ben picked her up in his arms, walked over to the bed, laid her in it, and slipped in beside her.

* * *

"Miz Callie, Mista Ben! Miz Callie, Mista Ben!"

There was a rapping at the door to the cabin. Callie slowly awoke and stretched lazily like a cat. She grinned as she looked at Ben beside her.

"Miz Callie, Mista Ben! I gots you brea'fast!"

Ben murmured something incoherent and turned over on his side, squishing the pillow with his fist.

"Ben, Ben! Wake up! Dinah's at the door." Callie shook Ben.

"What?"

"Dinah is knocking on the door. She said something about breakfast. Go see."

"Hmm...right. Knockin' on the door. Breakfast. Get up." Ben sat groggily on the side of the bed and shook his head. He stood up and started for the door.

"Ben!" Callie burst out laughing.

"What?"

"You don't have any clothes on!"

"Oh, forgot." He reached for his pants and pulled them on, almost falling down in the process. Callie was holding a pillow to her face to keep from laughing.

"Miz Callie! Mista Ben! I's ain't standin' here much longers. Comes an' gits your brea'fast."

Ben padded over to the door, as Callie ducked under the coverlet, and opened it slightly. Dinah was standing there with a tray covered in a linen towel.

"'Bouts time. This food be gittin' cold." Dinah got a sly smile on her face. "You twos must be havin' a good time in there."

Ben smiled. "Who do I thank for the food.....Trudy?"

"Yessir. She mades Belle make Miz Callie's fav'rite an' made me 'liver it." Dinah tried to peek in the door to see Callie. All she heard was giggling. "Miz Callie, Belle done mades you cornbread an' bacon. Miz Callie, you ins there?"

A muffled voice answered. "Yes, Dinah, thank Belle and Trudy for me. Ben, take the tray from Dinah so she can leave. Good-bye, Dinah.

See you later."

"Bye, Miz Callie." Dinah looked at Ben and chuckled. "Think you twos havin' a fine time ins there. I's tell the odders to lets you alone." She turned to leave, chuckling as she went. "Havin' a fine time."

* * *

"Miz Callie, Mista Ben! Miz Callie, Mista Ben! I's gots your lunch! Come opens the door." Dinah knocked on the door again, harder this time. "I knows you ins there 'cuz nobody seens you yet today. Belle says you gots to has some lunch, so I's brings it. Now opens the door!"

Dinah heard lots of giggling and laughter on the other side of the cabin door. "Just a minute, Dinah. Ben's coming." More laughter from Callie. Finally, Ben opened the door a crack.

"Wells, you gots to open it more than that, Mista Ben. Cain't gits no tray through that tiny crack." Ben opened the door more and Dinah started to go in herself, but Ben blocked the door.

"I'll just take the tray, thank you." Dinah thought Ben looked very disheveled, more than he had this morning.

"Miz Callie," she raised her voice, "you all rights in here?"

"Oh, Dinah, I couldn't be any better. Just tell everyone we are enjoying ourselves and will see them at dinner tonight."

"Yessem, Miz Callie. I's do that." Ben took the tray and smiled sheepishly at Dinah. "You two havin' too much fun in this here cabin, Mista Ben. Too much fun." Dinah turned around smiling to herself.

* * *

Callie and Ben finally emerged from the cabin in time for dinner. They walked into the dining room, hand in hand, faces glowing. All through the meal they hardly took their eyes off one another. More than once they were caught whispering to each other and then snickering. All the others at the table just smiled, glad they were so happy.

When everyone was finished eating, Callie excused herself and went to her room to retrieve Ben's wedding gift. When she came back, Ben was waiting for her in the foyer.

"Good night, everyone. We're really exhausted so we're going back to the cabin to sleep. See you all tomorrow." Callie grabbed Ben's hand before he could say anything and raced out the door. The families stood staring at the door closing behind them, but it was Beulah who finally spoke. "Ah….young love. Isn't it wonderful?"

* * *

When the couple arrived at the cabin, Ben immediately started up the fire to take the chill out. Callie watched his face as the flames started licking at the logs and reflected in his eyes. He is so handsome! She felt her heart flutter and heat course through her limbs.

"Mmm…that feels much better. It's so cozy in here, isn't it? I hope our house will feel like this too." Callie sat in one of the chairs and motioned for Ben to occupy the other. "I have my gift for you now, Mr. Chapman. Close your eyes and hold out your hand."

Ben did as he was told and felt her place something metal on his palm. "Open your eyes."

In his hand was a gold ring. "I know it's not customary for a husband to have a wedding ring, but I have one and I wanted you to have one too. Besides, I want everyone to know that you are *my* husband." Callie smiled. "Look inside."

Ben turned the ring to the firelight. Engraved there was *Callie and Ben, always, April 23, 1871.* Callie took the ring from Ben and started slipping it on his finger. She looked into his eyes and said, "With this ring, I thee wed, in the name of the Father, and of the Son, and of the Holy Ghost. Forever and ever and ever. Amen."

"Oh, Callie…..it's beautiful and I *will* wear it always. Thank you." Ben picked up his bride and carried her to the bed.

* * *

They arrived at the Whitson's cottage on Tybee Island late at night and immediately dropped their baggage on the floor, found their room, and went to sleep.

Callie woke. She opened her eyes to see Ben sleeping soundly next to her. She smiled and reached over to brush the hair out of his eyes. No, that might waken him. From the east window she could see the first hint of daylight. She listened in the stillness and heard a sound over and over. Her ears pricked trying to determine what it was. The ocean! She was hearing the ocean!

She had to see it. Quietly she slipped out of bed and grabbed her dressing gown. On tiptoe she left the bedroom and went into the hallway, down the stairs, and out the front door. She stood there for a few minutes to get her bearings and then headed for the dune in front of the house. She stopped at the top of the dune catching her breath, for there spread out before her was the Atlantic Ocean. The sun was just peeking up on the horizon, casting pale yellows and pinks across the waves. It was beautiful!

Callie felt the pull of the waves and started down the dune to the water's edge. She glanced around her. She was in a very private and secluded area so she tossed her dressing gown on the ashen gray sand and went closer to the water. Boldly, she untied her nightgown and slipped it over her head and dropped it on the sand.

She walked to the lapping waves on the shore and stepped into the water. It was cold! She backed up. The waves seemed to follow her, beckoning her back in. She tried again. It wasn't as cold this time. She laughed out loud. Gazing out at the horizon and seeing nothing but water captured her spirit. She threw her head back and her arms out. The wind whipped her long hair about and the salty sea spray stung her bare skin, but she had never felt so alive. All the woes of her young life seemed to roll off her skin - never knowing her mother, the war, the Yankees at Oak Hill, James Williams, longing for her father and brother to return from the battles, losing her grandfather and baby brother, and mostly Raymond Carswell. All swept away by the wind and the salt spray.

She didn't know how long she stood there, but jumped and screamed when a hand caressed her shoulder. Ben draped her dressing gown over her and then wrapped his arms around her. He nuzzled her neck. "Mmmmm….you taste like salt."

"Ben, you scared me. How long have you been here?"

"Long enough."

"Why didn't you join me sooner?"

"I was enjoyin' the view."

* * *

The newlyweds spent the next several days enjoying the beach at Tybee. The Whitson's house was hardly a cottage. It was a two story large home with front and back parlors, day parlor, sun room, five bedrooms, and a wrap-around porch. The house was raised up on "stilts" so it had a clear view of the ocean over the sand dunes tufted with sea grasses. A separate kitchen was in the back where a cook, Leticia, came everyday and prepared their meals, otherwise, they rarely saw her. They had the house and the beach all to themselves.

They took long walks on the beach, picking up washed up shells as they went. They gathered scallops, conches, whelks, slippers, augers. Callie marveled at the abounding sea creatures as well. Crabs scurried away from them; sea birds stabbed at the sand to find morsels of food or dived into the waves for fish; gelatinous jellyfish were washed ashore; porpoises could be seen leaping out of the water for air. It was a magical place for the honeymooners.

Every morning they got up and walked over the dune down to the water and watched the sunrise. Then they would go back to bed, rising a few hours later for breakfast. In the evenings, they would sit on the porch listening to the crashing of the waves, eventually lulled into drowsiness and would then make their way upstairs.

Leticia cooked them all the delicacies from the sea, most of them foreign to Callie and Ben. They ate spicy she-crab soup, rich oyster stew, shrimp and grits, tasty crab cakes, sautéd scallops, steamed mussels, many different kinds of fish: striped bass, redfish, pompano, flounder. They tried it all - even raw oysters.

Every day they spent on Tybee was an adventure, something new. They chanced upon an old black fisherman, his skin wrinkled from the sea and the sun. He taught them how to wade out in the ocean with their fishing poles to catch a fish. Both were astonished when they did. They took them home for Leticia to fry up for dinner.

One morning after low tide, they found a cache of sand dollars - hundreds of them. Callie made a bag of sorts out of her skirt and they took them back to the house where Leticia showed them how to bleach them in the sun. She broke one open and told them the story of the doves.

Callie especially liked to stand and watch the pelicans swoop and dive into the water in perfect formation. Ben laughed at all the tiny sandpipers moving together as if they were choreographed. They both delighted in seeing the hermit crabs toting a shell bigger then themselves, the horseshoe crab with its armor, the smaller fighting conches inching along the edge of the waves waiting to be sucked back into the water.

But the time came when their idyllic honeymoon must end. They regretfully said good-bye to the beach and ocean and went back to Savannah. There they spent several days with the Whitsons who showed Ben and Callie many of the sights of their city.

They had picnics at Forsyth Park with its ornate water fountain; shopped at the City Market; toured the Cotton Exchange with John; watched the ships enter the harbor; walked along the river front. Ben saw the house that was the headquarters for General Sherman; the Marshall Hotel where some of his fellow soldiers recuperated when it was a Union hospital; Montgomery Square where his unit had been encamped. It was an unexpected cleansing experience for Ben as he relived his previous time in Savannah. He and Callie finally put away the ghosts of their pasts and were ready to start their lives anew - together - in Illinois.

* * *

"Nathan, are you ill?" Kathleen went to her husband's side with a worried expression on her face.

"No, not really." Nathan sat down on their bed and put his head in his hands. "I'm just having trouble, Kathleen. My baby is leaving in several hours. I don't know when....or if...I'll ever see her again."

"Of course we will see her again! Don't even talk like that, Nathan! You've known this was coming for a long time. I thought you had come to terms with it."

"I thought I had too. But, now the time is here. I don't think I can let her go."

"You don't have a choice, dear. She's going. You have to be strong for her. You know how hard this last week has been on her."

"I know....I'm trying...I'll be fine. Just don't stray too far from me. I need you."

Kathleen smiled, putting her arms around Nathan. "I'm not going anywhere. We will survive *and* we will see Callie again. You said yourself, the railroad is getting faster and more comfortable so we all can make trips back and forth. It's not like in the olden days." Nathan produced a wan smile and then buried his face in his wife's bosom.

* * *

Callie and Trudy stood on the front veranda holding each other and weeping. They didn't even try to stop. This was their last good-bye. Ben and Caleb, who was holding Libby, stood off to the side and let their wives cry. Socks lay at Callie's feet. Finally, the two friends could speak.

"Trudy, you have to take special care of Socks for me. He's going to be very sad at first, so give him lots of attention. I know he will be happy at your place after a while. Oh, I'll miss him so! I wish I could take him with me, but I just can't on the train. Then he'd be so mixed up once we got there, I'm afraid he would die. This is a much better solution, but please, please, take good care of him!"

"You knows, I's will, Miz Callie." Trudy was wiping her tears away with the edge of her apron. "Me an' Socks been 'gedder longs as you an' him has. I's 'members when Masta Nathan an' Masta Samuel brings him heres. I's real scared o' that jumpin' basket. 'Members, Miz Callie?"

Callie giggled, wiping her eyes. "Of course, I do. He was awfully cute then, wasn't he? Now he's an old dog. Hasn't been quite the same since that awful James Williams hit him in the head."

Socks sat up, knowing they were talking about him. He started panting nervously. Callie sat down on the floor and hugged her dog for the last time. She caressed him, kissed him, and murmured soft words in his ear. The panting stopped and Socks licked her tears away.

Callie took a deep breath. "Socks, you go with Trudy now, all right, boy? You be a good dog and watch over Libby."

Trudy, with fresh tears running down her cheeks said, "Guess we better be on our ways now, so you an' Mista Ben can goes to the train."

Callie stood up, once again embracing Trudy. "Oh, Trudy…I'm going to miss you so much! You know I will write to you ….and you do the same. You take good care of Caleb and Libby and I will be back to visit……I love you so much!"

Trudy was sobbing. "I's will, Miz Callie….I's will. You takes care o' Mista Ben, too. I's writes you letters…. an' hope you be back real soon to visit….I loves you too!"

Ben and Caleb looked at each other as tears streaked down their own faces. They had never witnessed anything quite like this before - it was heart wrenching. Each went to his wife. Caleb put his hand under Trudy's arm and gently pulled her away from Callie. He handed her Libby and took Socks' leash. They slowly went down the steps and out onto the grounds. Trudy looked back once and raised her hand in a feeble wave. Then they disappeared down the lane, Socks trotting obediently behind Caleb.

Callie collapsed into Ben's arms and sobbed tears of sorrow.

* * *

The passengers in the dark green carriage were very still. Each had red swollen eyes and bouts of weeping. Callie and Ben were on their way to the train station with Kathleen, Nathan, and Samuel. They had said their final good-byes to Beulah and Mammy Sallie. Laura decided to stay at Oak Hill.

Saying good-bye to Trudy had been very hard, but leaving Beulah and, especially, Mammy Sallie was worse than Callie thought it would be. They were both older and the prospect of never seeing them again was possible.

Bidding a final farewell to Oak Hill was surprisingly hard too. Callie never thought that a collection of buildings and land would be hard to leave, but these buildings and land were her home. The only one she had ever known. As the carriage started down the oak lined lane, she looked out the window and burst into more tears.

Ben felt terrible for his bride. He was blaming himself for all her anguish and told her so. It was then that Callie tried to be brave. She assured him she was anxious to start their new life, but it was just hard to say good-bye to everyone. Once they were on their way, she knew things would be better. However, now in the carriage, she realized the time was finally here when she would have to say good-bye to her father, mother, and brother. Each time she looked at one of them, fresh tears sprang to her eyes. She could hardly bear it.

Never did a carriage ride seem so long and so short at the same time. Mercifully, they arrived at the station in Swainsboro. There were no more words to be said. As they waited for the train, Callie sat between Nathan and Kathleen, holding their hands and leaning her head on their shoulders. Samuel and Ben sat across from them.

"Papa...."

"Shh....baby girl. I already know. *You* know. This isn't good-bye." Nathan felt a lump form in his throat and swallowed hard.

"Callie, we will be with you every day...in your heart...and you will be in ours." Kathleen squeezed her hand.

"I know...Mama." Callie sighed brokenly. She looked at Kathleen through a veil of tears. "It's just so hard..."

Kathleen brushed the tears away with her hand whispering in Callie's ear, "You must be strong, sweetie, for your father and for Ben."

Callie looked at her husband. He had a forlorn and guilty expression on his face. She nodded to Kathleen and took a deep breath.

Samuel came to her rescue. "Just think, Callie, you will have to cook and clean and do the laundry and tend the garden and kill the chickens and can the food....." He reached over and poked her in the ribs causing her to giggle.

"Oh, Sam...."

Ben also smiled. "She will have lots of help, Samuel. Ma and Emma will be close. And, me too."

"Ben, have you tasted any of her cooking yet?"

Ben shook his head. "No....?"

Samuel laughed. "You're in for a big surprise then!"

"Samuel Hill! I can cook.....well....I can make coffee and cornbread and beans. Belle showed me how to fry chicken." Callie had to laugh too. "We might have to eat at your parents at first, Ben!"

Ben chuckled. He didn't care if Callie could cook, he was just happy to hear her laugh today. He felt better.

The sound of the train roaring into the station chased away their laughter. Callie looked desperately at Nathan, clutching his hand.

"It's all right, baby girl. It's all right. Let's get you and that husband of yours on the train."

They all walked towards the train as it screeched to a halt, steam billowing out of the smokestack, the whistle piercing their ears. The passengers started boarding the car.

Callie and Ben waited as long as they could. Callie grabbed Samuel and hugged him hard, not worried about the tears any more. Then she engulfed Kathleen with her arms and sobbed. Finally, she went to Nathan who unabashedly was weeping. She hugged her father as hard as she could, stood on tiptoe to kiss him, and then snatched Ben's hand and mounted the steps to the car. Turning around on the top step, she managed a weak smile, mouthed "I love you," and then entered the car.

She couldn't see her way for the tears, so Ben took her arm and guided her to a seat by the window. After using Ben's handkerchief to wipe her tears, she saw her family huddled together, comforting one another. Ben knocked loudly on the window, finally attracting their attention. Callie waved furiously and blew them kisses. The train began to pull out of the station. She waved until she could see them no longer and then she fell over into Ben's lap, sobbing. They were on their way.

* * *

It was hot. The air was so laden with moisture it was difficult to breathe. The sun beat down on the small two room house situated on the northeast two acre corner that was part of the forty acres in the southwest corner of the Southeast Quarter of Section 34 Clayton Township, Illinois that now belonged to Mr. and Mrs. Benjamin Hill.

Callie sat on the small porch snipping string beans. She had on a blue calico work skirt, a white muslin blouse, and no shoes. Since no one was there to see her, she had on only her drawers and thin chemise as undergarments. She had her skirt pulled up over her thighs and her blouse unbuttoned to her waist. Still the sweat was pouring down her face. She wriggled her free toes and paused to wipe her face with the thin muslin apron she wore.

"And, everyone thought it was hot in Georgia," she said to the black and white cat lazing on the porch step. "This is worse, Thomas. I can't even breathe. It's even worse in the house. I don't know what Ben expects for supper tonight, but I'm *not* lighting that stove! We'll just have to have some bread and jam. It's too hot to eat anyway."

"Good thing his mother told me to plant tansy around here. At least the mosquitoes aren't so bad. Oh, Thomas, I'm so hot! I'm miserable! Wish Ben would come home."

Callie looked at the cloudless sky. "No, too early. He won't be home for another couple hours." She sighed. "Well, here I am talking to a cat, who's not even listening. Maybe the heat is making me crazy!"

She finished snipping the beans and stood up, stretching her arms high above her head. "Let's see, Thomas. I think I have most of my chores done so far. The chickens and hogs are fed. Gathered the eggs. The weeding is done. Beans picked and snipped. Cleaned the kitchen and tidied our bedroom. Brought the water into the house. Think that's it until Ben comes home. Think I'll bring my lap desk out here on the porch and write home. Yes, that's what I'll do. I wonder if it's as hot at Oak Hill as it is here. Don't bother moving Thomas, I'll be right back."

Callie went into the little house to get her writing desk, a wedding gift from Emma. She looked around the rooms and nodded satisfactorily. The front room was split between the kitchen and the parlor. The kitchen had a new wood burning stove, a dry sink, a pie safe, and a cupboard. In the middle was a drop leaf cherry table and four ladder back chairs.

The parlor end was still a little bare. On the wall opposite the front door was a captain's chair, and beside it stood a small walnut table holding a china lamp with lilacs painted on it.

By the window in the corner was an upholstered slipper rocker, which matched the captain's chair, along with a fern stand adorned by a lush Boston fern. Next to the window was the fireplace with an oak mantle.

On the mantle Callie displayed some of their wedding gifts - a small china teapot with painted pink roses on the sides and lid, a bisque figurine of a young girl that resembled Callie, a pine mantel clock painted black with gilded corners and columns, several books. Silver framed photographs of Callie and Ben with their families at their wedding also were on the shelf. A large photograph of just Callie and Ben, encased in a beautiful heavily carved gilded frame, hung above the mantle.

Callie stared at it now. That was such a happy day. She smiled at the memory. It seemed so long ago, but it was only a little over three months. How her life had changed since then!

She looked at the empty wall to the right of the door. It would be a while before they could afford a proper settee. All depended on the crops.

She crossed the room into their bedroom. Henry and Abigail had given them a bedstead, feather mattress, wardrobe, and small washstand. Callie brought sheets and quilts with her from Oak Hill. A bright red and white Irish chain quilt, made by Kathleen, adorned the bed now. Callie reached under the bed to retrieve her writing desk and, finding it, walked back out to the porch. Thomas was still stretched out on the step.

She sat back in her rocker, a gift to them from the Chapmans' hired men, and collected her thoughts. She pulled out a sheet of paper, unscrewed the lid to the ink, dipped her pen in it, and began writing:

July 30, 1871

Dearest family,

It is so very hot today that I think I am wilting like the flowers! I'm sure it is hotter here than I ever remember at Oak Hill, except maybe the July when Papa came home from the war.

Ben is out in the fields cultivating the corn. There's a saying here that the corn should be "knee high by the Fourth of July." Ours wasn't. Too little rain says my farmer husband. We do need some rain soon or everything will be dried up. I've been warned about the prairie thunderstorms and twisters they call tornadoes. Hopefully, we will just get a gentle rain so it can soak in.

Mama, I'm very proud of my little vegetable garden. All those days after the war of tending the garden have paid off. In fact, I just finished picking and snipping some string beans. We won't be having them for supper, though. I've decided it's too hot to light the stove! We'll be eating a cold meal tonight.

I haven't met too many of our neighbors yet, but Ben says when the cultivating is done, we will be going to a social at one of their houses - the Robinsons, I think. We will take Emma - she needs to find a beau! Also, the Lutheran church several miles from here, St. Peter's, is having an ice cream social in a few Sundays. I'm anxious to see what that is like. Abigail assures me I will enjoy it.

I'm very pleased with our home. It is small, but cozy. It is filled with love. Thank you for shipping all the wedding photographs. They are on the walls where I can look at them all the time. I can't wait until you can come and visit and see our home. Ben said next spring he will add another room so we will have room for guests or....maybe a baby. We do so want a baby! How do you feel about becoming grand-parents and an uncle? I can see your faces now. No, we are not expecting... yet. I will let you know if and when.

I hear from Trudy rather regularly. She keeps me updated on Socks. Guess he's happy there now. She said he loves to play with Libby - let's her pull his tail without complaining.

Well, I'd better get my beans in the root cellar before they get too hot. I love getting your letters, so please keep writing. Samuel, I haven't heard much from you and Laura. Don't forget me, dear brother!

As always, I love you and miss you, but I am very happy here with Ben. Please don't worry about me. I'm very content.

Love to all,

Callie

She reread the letter. Satisfied, she put it in an envelope, sealed it, and stamped it. They would mail it whenever they went to a town. She had several others waiting to be mailed. Ben assured her they would be going to Minonk or El Paso soon to get other supplies.

"Thomas, I think I'll try to get presentable before my sweet husband comes home and then figure what we will have to eat. Let's see....we have some pie Abigail gave us.. and bread. I must learn to make the bread soon. Oh, butter and jam….some cornbread…some carrots I picked yesterday. I guess that can all be made into a meal. Bye, Thomas, I'm off to become beautiful." Callie laughed as the cat stood up arching his back and stretching. "You'd better make yourself useful, Thomas Cat, and go find some mice." Thomas just yawned indifferently. Callie went into the house to clean up.

She emerged a few minutes later, still sweating, but in a clean skirt and blouse. Her hair was pulled back into a bun. Ben liked it loose falling down her back, but it was just too hot today to have it down.

She sat on the rocking chair, fanning herself, gazing down the dirt lane watching for Ben to return home for the evening. She soon rocked herself to sleep, her head falling forward.

* * *

"So this is what you do all day? Sleep on the porch while I'm off workin' hard?" Ben laughed as Callie's head snapped up. She blinked several times trying to focus her eyes. She saw her husband's beautiful smile and his adoring eyes. She returned the smile.

"Of course. I have a fairy who comes after you leave to clean, cook, garden, and wash the clothes. All I have to do is sit back and wait for you, my prince."

"Ah, a fairy. Well, princess, your prince is hungry. Has the fairy cooked anything for supper tonight? I don't smell anything comin' from the house."

"Hmmm….well. The princess decided it was too hot today and told the fairy to take the afternoon off. There will be no cooking tonight as the house is already cooked."

Ben looked at her skeptically. "Really, Ben, it's too hot to light the stove. I've been burning up all day. There's not a breath of air, even out here, and the house is even stuffier. I decided we can eat a cold meal tonight. That's all right, isn't it?" Callie lowered her eyes, then began blinking her lashes furiously, giving Ben a very demure look.

"Somethin' in your eyes, Callie?" Ben reached over and tilted her chin up with his hand. He kissed each eye softly, then tenderly kissed her waiting lips. She eagerly encircled his neck with her arms and pulled him closer to her.

"Mmmm….Mrs. Chapman….our cold supper….is it ready?" He murmured into her ear.

"Uh….no….not yet….let's kiss some more first. You aren't really that hungry, are you?"

"Not for food, Mrs. Chapman." Ben picked her up and carried her into the house and laid her on the Irish chain quilt.

* * *

The hot, sultry days of August led to cooler, less humid days in September and October. Rains in early August had rescued the corn crop which was now drying in the fields. The wheat and oats had already been reaped and threshed.

Callie worked alongside Abigail and Emma to can and dry the vegetables from their gardens and orchards to put up for the winter. Countless jars of vegetables, fruits, jelly and jams were put on their pantry shelves.

On a brisk late October day, butchering took place. Callie still found this a disgusting but necessary process. Everyone worked furiously to preserve every part of the hog. A few days later, the beef cattle were butchered. The families feasted on the fresh beef. Some was hung in the smokehouse with the hams, some was salted down, and the rest was canned.

The root vegetables were dug and packed away in the root cellars, as were some apples and pears. Henry and Abigail shared their bounty with their son and new daughter-in-law, but Callie's garden had produced enough for her and Ben too. Unless it was a really hard winter the Chapman families would have plenty to eat.

Word reached the township in mid October that a fire had consumed the city of Chicago on the 9th. Three hundred people lost their lives and over 18,000 buildings burned to the ground. Callie remembered her visit to the city and wondered if any of the places she visited were still standing.

In late November, the Chapmans gathered at Henry and Abigail's to celebrate the Thanksgiving holiday, proclaimed by President Lincoln in 1863 as the final Thursday in November.

The table was laden with two wild turkeys that Ben and Henry shot and Abigail dressed and stuffed. All sorts of side dishes were served, along with homemade dandelion wine and apple cider.

However, Callie didn't feel much like eating. Lately, her stomach had been upset often and she was very tired. Ben was getting worried about her as she looked pale and thinner. Sometimes she got very dizzy and had to lie down before she fell down. On this Thanksgiving Day, though, she was feeling fine and was enjoying herself despite her lack of appetite. She had an idea what might be wrong with her, but she wanted to be sure.

The one thing about Illinois Callie was looking forward to was the snow. Except this year, so far, they had only experienced several dustings since the temperatures had been mild.

She was also anticipating her first Christmas with Ben. He went to the closest timber and cut down a white pine tree and drug it back to their house. They both exploded in laughter when he brought it into the house, for it filled up the entire parlor. Much trimming was needed to get it down to size. Then they both decorated the tree on Christmas Eve. Callie had strung popped corn and dried berries, which they now draped on the tree. She had purchased some ribbons on their last trip to town and made bows. Ben gathered pine cones and hedge balls which they slipped into the branches. They stood back and admired their work. No candles this year adorned the branches, maybe next year.

They spent the evening curled up in front of the fireplace, gazing at their tree.

"I have something important to tell you, Benjamin," Callie said quietly.

"Is it about my present?"

"Somewhat."

"Well...?

"I'm going to have a baby."

Ben was stunned into complete silence for several seconds. Callie looked at him and grinned.

"WOOOOOHOOOO!" He suddenly yelled, scaring her. He pulled her up and putting his arms around her, picked her up off the floor and twirled around and around, finally setting her back on her feet. "Are you sure? Is that why you haven't been feeling so well the last couple months?"

She nodded her head, laughing at his exuberance. "I guess you're happy about it?"

"Am I happy about it? Of course, I'm VERY happy! Aren't you?"

"Oh, yes! I can't wait to have our baby."

"Oh, Callie, I have to get to work on the extra room. Do you know when it will come? Are you scared? Do you think we'll be good parents? You'll have to see Doc Slemmons. Wait until we tell Ma and Pa! And, your Mama and Papa! They'll surely want to come and visit. Emma and Samuel will be an aunt and uncle. Your Grandma Beulah will be a great-grandmother. Have you told Trudy? Have you told anyone else at all? I'll have to plant extra acreage in the spring so we have more money." Ben was rattling away, all the time pacing back and forth across the little parlor, running his hands through his hair.

Callie sat calmly in the chair, with a loving grin on her face, watching him going back and forth. Catching her eye, he finally stopped, went over to her, got down on his knees, and laid his head in her lap. She stroked his hair, brushing it away from his face.

"I haven't told anyone else - you are the first, of course. I think the baby will come in late spring or early summer. We have plenty of time to tell everyone else. I want it to be our secret for a while longer. Just think Ben, we've made a baby with our love."

Ben put his hand on her stomach and stared into those big brown eyes he loved so much. "In there, Callie, is our child. What a miracle! We *have* made a baby with our love."

Tears came to both of their eyes as they sat there on Christmas Eve in their little parlor in their little farmhouse in Clayton Township, full of love for each other and their unborn child.

CHAPTER 7
1872

The wind started howling in late morning. Callie could feel the little house shake and rattle with each increasing gust. She looked out the parlor window into the western sky and saw nothing but gray ominous skies.

Ben had gone to his parents earlier this morning to help Henry repair some of their machinery and tend to the cattle. Before he left, he fed the hogs, the two horses, Clayton, his stallion, and Georgia, Callie's mare, and the dairy cow and her calf.

Callie stood at the window for several minutes wishing for Ben to come riding up the lane. The weather was making her antsy. Thank goodness she had already done her outside chores. She was in the midst of trying to bake bread, after waking up from a short nap.

The oven and the fireplace were keeping the little house snug, but occasionally she felt a draft through the window that made the curtains stir. She shivered now and moved away from the window.

"Nothing I can do about the weather, but wait," she said aloud. In her mind, she thought, "Good thing I'm having the baby in the spring and not now."

Her pregnancy was finally showing. She loosened several of her skirts and could no longer close the bottom buttons on her blouses. Ben took her to Dr. Slemmons in Minonk who examined her and confirmed her pregnancy.

He agreed with her the baby would arrive in late May or early June. He told her to take a nap when she was tired, eat even when she didn't feel like it because the baby needed nourishment, get fresh air every day, and not do anything too physically strenuous. He would deliver the baby if he was available and got there in time, but Marie Parker, who lived south of them in Greene Township, was a midwife and had delivered many babies. She was much closer and could arrive faster.

The Chapmans had hitched up Georgia and Clayton on a crisp clear mid January day and driven to the Parkers. Callie immediately liked

Marie who reminded her of Lenora. She was all business, but very nice. Callie knew she would feel comfortable with Marie delivering the baby if Doc Slemmons couldn't make it.

Callie went to the window again as another gust of wind blew against the house. She hadn't seen clouds like these since she moved to the prairie, and they were making her very uneasy.

She went back to the stove where her bread dough was supposed to be rising, but it wasn't. She still hadn't gotten the knack of using the yeast right. Poor Ben! He almost broke a tooth on the first rolls she tried. But he dipped them in his milk to soften them and didn't say a word. The last batch she made had been better, at least they were edible. She chuckled now at the thought.

Another blast of wind brought with it the sound of something peppering the house. It was a different sound than rain. Once again Callie ran to the window. Tiny pellets of ice were bouncing on the porch floor. Now the house sounded like a symphony of pings. Callie held her hands over her ears trying to drown out the sound. She was afraid.

She looked at the mantle clock. It was almost noon. Ben should be home any time now for lunch, but how could he ride in this weather without hurting himself and Clayton? He would have to stay at his parents until it passed.

"Come on, Callie. Be a big girl. It's just a storm. It'll be over soon." She placed her hand on her belly. "Don't worry, little one, I'll get calm in a minute." She took some deep breaths and went back to the stove. She took an egg out of the pantry and decided to have it for lunch. At least she was competent at frying eggs.

As she sat down to eat her egg, the pinging stopped. "Good, it's over. Guess I got all afraid for nothing." She finished her lunch and tidied up the kitchen after popping the bread in the oven.

Another gust of wind rattled the windows. She looked outside to see…..nothing. Everything was completely white. She strained to see the lane, but couldn't see a thing. Snow was blowing horizontally - a blizzard. How could that have happened in just those few minutes? She looked at the clock again. It was one o'clock. Where was Ben?

Callie got a sinking feeling in the pit of her stomach. What if Ben had started home, worried about her, and gotten caught in the storm? What if he'd stayed at his parents and she would be here all by herself in the middle of this blizzard?

She had to, had to hope Ben would stay put. It would be too dangerous for him to try to make it home. She had to prepare to ride out the storm on her own. "Think, Callie, think. What has Ben told you about surviving a blizzard? Be prepared. Well, too late for that. Wait. He piled up logs on the porch last night. If I run out of wood in here, it's close by. I have food. I gathered the eggs this morning and there's the pantry that's full. Plus, my bread." She made a wry grin. "Guess I could eat it even if it's hard. Mainly, I just have to keep the fire going. Maybe I should go get some wood in now before it gets worse."

Finally deciding action would be better than worrying, Callie went and got her wool cape, put it on, then wrapped her shawl around her head, found her new mittens Emma had given her for Christmas, and put those on too. She headed for the door.

She was surprised when she couldn't open the front door! She pulled and pulled, but it wouldn't budge. "The ice pellets! They must have frozen the door shut. Well, I have to get out!"

She took off her outerwear and sat in one of the chairs, thinking. "Aha, maybe I can get the teakettle going and the steam will melt the ice." She put the kettle on the stove and soon it was whistling merrily. She carried the steaming pot over to the door and held it against the jambs, all the time pulling with her other hand. She thought it was giving a little, and quickly reheated the water again. But the door had refrozen in the meantime.

After several attempts, Callie finally got the door open using the steaming kettle and prying with a knife. However, she was unprepared for what happened when the door eventually opened. The blast of wind and snow sent her reeling back into the house.

Quickly donning her cape, shawl, and mittens, she went out the door into the blizzard. It was like nothing she'd ever experienced before. The wind drove the snow into her eyes, nose, and face. It was so fierce, she couldn't catch her breath. She found by putting the shawl over her nose and mouth, she could at least breath normally.

As fast as she could, she found the pile of wood on the porch and started dragging the logs into the house. Her fingers rapidly grew numb, as did her uncovered forehead and eyes. "I've got to keep going. This may be my only chance."

After what seemed like hours, the pile of wood was now inside the house next to the front door on the parlor side. Callie gratefully shut the door tight and sank into the kitchen chair. She rested several minutes and then began peeling off her frozen garments.

She realized by having the door open so long, the house had cooled down considerably. She fed the fireplace and the stove. "Oh, my bread!" She pulled it out of the oven, burnt to a crisp. She didn't know if she should laugh or cry. She did know she was exhausted. Looking at the clock she saw she had been carrying the wood in for almost half an hour. It seemed much longer than that, but at least she would be warm.

* * *

Ben was frantic. "I have to get home, Ma! I can't have Callie there all by herself in this storm, expectin' our baby!" He was pacing back and forth in Abigail's kitchen.

"Now, you know, you can't go out in this storm, Benjamin. We all know what happens to people when they're out in a blizzard like this. They're found frozen. Callie will be fine. She's got shelter, fire, and food. She'll be fine. In fact, she's probably hopin' you're stayin' put. Isn't that right, Henry?"

"Your Ma's right, Ben. Callie will be fine as long as she stays in the house, which I'm sure she'll do. Storm should be over by morning and then you can head out."

"I should have left here when the sleet came."

"No, Ben. The snow came up too fast after that. You would have been in trouble. Can't see anything out there but white. You just settle down, son. Your bride is a strong lady and a smart one. She'll know what to do." Henry leaned back in his chair and lit his pipe.

"What about my animals? She can't go out to feed them, or at least she'd better not."

"They'll survive for a night, Ben. Quit worryin' 'bout things you can't control. You're just goin' to have to wait it out. Now sit down and drink your coffee before it gets cold."

Ben sat down, but he didn't drink his coffee. He put his head in his hands and berated himself mentally for leaving Callie. Then he prayed that she and their baby would manage through the night. Ma and Pa were right. There was nothing, absolutely nothing, he could do without risking his own life. Callie was smart. She'd been in worse situations and come through them. She'd have to do the same now. It was going to be an awfully long night.

* * *

Callie soon realized she was going to have to ration the firewood. There was no way she would make it to the woodshed to bring in more, so this was going to have to last her through the night and into tomorrow.

She decided to eat a quick supper and then let the fire in the stove die out. She would put on more clothes and burn less wood in the fireplace. With that plan, she went into the pantry and dug out some pork sausages from a crock and a potato from the bin. She fried the meat and the potato, drank a glass of milk - fortunately, she had milked the cow this morning - and then went and put on extra layers of clothing, including her cape and shawl. She grabbed several quilts from the wardrobe and took them into the parlor. She pulled the slipper rocker directly in front of the fire, took a book from the mantle, and tried to read. She couldn't concentrate. The wind was howling and the snow was pelting against the house, shaking it like a rag doll.

She tried writing a letter to Trudy, but she didn't have much luck with that either. Finally, she resigned herself to sitting and staring at the flames. Before one log completely burned up, she went and retrieved another. She calculated she had enough until morning when, hopefully, Ben would come home.

As she was sitting in the rocker, wrapped in quilts, her mind wandered. This was something like.....no....nothing like when Carswell had her locked in the shed. Callie shook the thought out of her head. She pushed it to the place in her mind where she kept the things she never wanted to think about. Once in a while they surfaced as nightmares, but she had Ben to comfort her.

She took a deep breath and said aloud, "Come on, girl. You can do this. You're not helpless. You're smart. It will be all right. Just get through the night. Surely, this storm can't last longer than that."

She became drowsy and was just about asleep when she felt something inside her move. Her head snapped up. What was that? She reached under the quilts and clothes until her hand touched her bare belly. She felt it again. Something must be wrong with the baby! No, maybe it was just the sausage not agreeing with her stomach. But she felt fine, not sick at all. There it was again. She even felt it against her hand.

Suddenly, Callie smiled as she comprehended what was happening to her. To the fire she said, "I'm feeling my baby! I'm feeling life! Our baby! She's alive and kicking me!"

To her baby she said in a soothing voice, "It's all right, sweetie, Mama's going to take good care of you. Don't you worry. I won't let anything happen to you."

She got up and put two logs on the fire. "Think it's time for Mama and baby to get a little sleep." She sat in the rocker and drifted off into a light sleep with a contented smile on her face.

* * *

Callie awoke several hours later, shivering. The fire was almost out. She put another log in and glanced at the mantel clock. It was four o'clock in the morning. She looked out the window and could see nothing. Snow drifts were piled up against the glass, blocking everything out. She went to the bedroom and looked out the east window. It was etched in frost on the inside, but after scraping away a little hole near the top, she could just barely see out. All white.

She listened. The wind was not howling anymore. In fact it was very still. Maybe the storm had moved on. Daybreak would be here soon; maybe Ben would be able to come home. She went back to her rocker and was soon back asleep.

* * *

"CALLIE! CALLIE! Are you all right? Open the door!"

Callie woke with a start from the banging on the door. It took her a few seconds to gain her senses. Ben!

She threw off her quilts and ran to the door, trying to pull it open. "I'm here, Ben! I'm fine! Push on the door when I pull. It must be frozen shut again."

Between Ben pushing and Callie pulling, the door dislodged and flew open. Ben rushed to embrace his wife, but realized he was a frozen mess. Callie was astonished at his appearance. He had on several coats, scarves, and hats all covered with tiny particles of ice and snow. The only part of him she could see was his eyes and there were little icicles hanging from his lashes and brows.

In spite of the seriousness of what they had both experienced, Callie couldn't help but laugh at her husband. He was shocked. "Why are you laughing, for heaven's sake? This isn't funny, Callie. I rode all the way from Ma and Pa's this morning the minute the sun came up and the wind stopped. I lost my way twice because everything is covered with drifts. Good thing Clayton has a nose for his home. I've been worried sick about you and here you are laughing!" Ben frowned and began to take off the outer layer of his garments.

"I'm sorry. But you look like some kind of…kind of….I don't know…mountaineer or snow person. You just look funny to me. Here, let me help you get out of those wet things." Callie giggled again as she started to unwind one of Ben's scarves.

"Callie! This is not funny! I've been through hell coming here for you. Stop laughing!"

But now Callie had the giggles and couldn't contain herself. Soon she was laughing so hard tears rolled down her cheeks. Ben stood staring at her, confused by this reaction.

Soon her laughter was spent and she sat down in the kitchen chair wiping her eyes with a towel. "I'm so sorry, darling. I don't know what's come over me. Thank you so much for coming this morning. I think maybe I'm a little 'off' from lack of sleep. Anyway, you know I'm grateful, don't you? Now, come on, let's get the rest of your clothes off so you look like yourself again and not some foreign mountain trapper." She smiled and then quickly looked away so Ben wouldn't see it.

"Hmmppfff....I guess I just expected to get a better welcome than this. Wait, I've got to take care of Clayton and the animals in the barn. You surely didn't go feed them last night, did you?"

"No, but I did bring the wood in from the porch. That wore me out. I figured the animals could manage a night without food. It was a good thing you brought that wood onto the porch, though. Otherwise I would have been in quite a pickle."

"I'm going back out now and do the chores and bring some more wood in. Do you have enough to fire up the stove and make me some coffee and breakfast? I ate a little at Ma's, but I wanted to get on my way."

"It will be ready when you get back. Oh, Ben, I have something marvelous to tell and, hopefully, show you. Hurry back." Ben started for the front door, but stopped and turned around.

Both of them said "I love you" at the same time.

* * *

When Ben returned, they both ate breakfast and compared their experiences during the blizzard. Ben was impressed how calmly Callie had handled being alone, and she was equally amazed at her husband's journey to rescue her. A proper welcome was soon withcoming.

* * *

"What did you want to tell me, Callie? The 'something marvelous?'"

"Oh, well, it hasn't happened again just yet."

Ben was brushing her hair by the fire. "Can't you just tell me?"

"I was just about asleep in the chair here last night when I felt a fluttering inside me. I thought maybe I was sick, but I wasn't. Then I thought something was wrong with the baby. When I felt it again with my hand against my belly, I knew what it was."

"What was it? Is something wrong?"

"No, silly. It was the *baby*! The baby was moving *inside* me! Isn't that a miracle? I could feel the baby turning."

Ben's features softened and he said in a low voice. "You mean...

our baby was moving around inside your belly?"

"Yes! Life. I was feeling life. Just like Trudy did with Libby. She used to let me feel her belly when Libby was turning around in there and that's what I felt. Oh....wait!"

Callie quickly grabbed Ben's hand and placed it on her stomach. "There...did you feel that? It's like a little punch."

Ben's face lit up. "I do! I feel it! Our baby! Callie, our baby's in there!"

Callie laughed. "It is amazing isn't it? Oh...there she goes again!"

"She?"

"Well, I think it's a she. It's easier than to say 'it.'"

"I hope it's a she. And, I hope she looks just like her mother."

Ben moved his face down to Callie's belly. "You hear us, little girl? You look like your Mama. Mama and Papa love you already. You know that? We're goin' take real good care of you. Your Mama already is. Don't you go kickin' her too hard, now. She's goin' to need her rest."

Callie stroked Ben's hair. She loved him so much. And their baby. What a life they would have!

* * *

By January of 1872, the Georgia State Assembly was under the control of the Redeemers, the state's resurgent white conservative Democrats. Samuel Hill was not one of the Redeemers, as he opposed their tactics of terrorizing the black legislators to strengthen their rule. One black expelled assemblyman, Abram Colby, was pulled out of his home and given one hundred lashes with a whip. His colleague, Abram Turner, was murdered. Samuel wanted no part of that.

From his short time as a state senator, and the fact he was a Confederate veteran and married to Senator Rickett's daughter, he had gained much respect from his fellow assemblymen, but on this treatment of the blacks, they differed; however, the Redeemers left him alone and did not pressure him to join them. For this, Samuel was grateful, because he heard enough about it from his wife and father-in-law at their home in Atlanta.

Lester Ricketts believed whole-heartedly in the Redeemer

movement and tried to convert his son-in-law. But Samuel would not budge. He didn't feel this was the direction Georgia should be taking. They were going backwards instead of forward. The Klu Klux Klan had already tarnished the state's reputation in the North; they didn't need to further antagonize Congress in Washington, D.C. After all, the Reconstruction Act was still the law of the land.

Therefore, Samuel was looking forward to the end of this session of the Assembly so he could retreat to Oak Hill and let his home soothe him as always. The minute he would pull into that oak lined lane, his troubles would vanish and he would heave a sigh of relief.

As the Assembly was recessed until next year, Samuel could not contain his excitement of returning to Oak Hill. Despite all the tribulations in Atlanta, he had decided to run again in his district and wanted to start campaigning early because this time he had an opponent, an avowed Redeemer, and he wanted to beat him.

He was packing his things away and wanted to check on Laura in her bedroom to make sure she was doing the same. He knocked on her door.

"Come in."

Samuel opened the door to his wife's bedroom, a place where he was not welcomed. Laura was sitting in front of her vanity mirror. "Are you getting ready to go home, Laura?"

"I am home."

"No, I mean to Oak Hill." Samuel looked around. He saw no evidence of someone getting ready to take a journey.

"I'm not going." Laura stood up and turned around to face Samuel, who had a confused look on his face.

"What do you mean? Of course, you're going. The Assembly is recessed. I have to get back to Oak Hill for planting season."

Laura stood straighter and sighed. "I'm not going to Oak Hill or anywhere else with you, Samuel. I want a divorce."

"WHAT? I...I...don't understand!" Samuel looked astounded.

"There's nothing to understand. I want a divorce."

"Why? What has happened?"

"Nothing has happened. I don't love you. I've never loved you. I hate Oak Hill that's out in the middle of nowhere, and where everyone watches me like a thief, especially that nasty old mammy of yours. I no longer want to be your wife."

"But…" Samuel sat down on the edge of Laura's bed, his head spinning. "What about our family….our children?"

Laura burst out in a haughty laugh. "Children? Children? Why do you think I've banned you from my bed? I don't want any children… especially yours."

Samuel could not believe what he was hearing. He looked forlornly up at his wife. "Then why on earth did you marry me in the first place if you didn't love me?"

Laura stared into Samuel's eyes with a smirk on her face. "Think about it, Samuel. The taxes are paid on this house now with money left over. Father and I won't lose it."

Samuel jumped up and walked over to just inches from Laura's face, his own face reddening as the truth occurred to him. In a low strained voice he said, "Do you mean you married me for *money*?"

Laura was silent for a few seconds, letting the idea sink into Samuel's mind. She held on to the back of the chair and then smiled devilishly, drilling her hazel eyes into Samuel's. "Yes."

Samuel reeled in front of her, staggering once again to the bed. He sat with his head down. He couldn't think. He must have married a monster. All this time….what a fool he had been! Had he missed all the signs? Did anyone else know? Lester! Of course, he knew. Well…..

"I want a divorce and I want it right away." Laura walked over to the fireplace and toyed with one of the figurines on the mantel.

Suddenly Samuel jerked his head up and looked at this stranger before him. He realized she had manipulated him all along. He had been too smitten with love to see it. His mind was clear now. If Laura wanted a divorce, then he would give it to her…..gladly. Surprisingly, he suddenly felt free. He always felt he was walking on eggs around her trying to please her. Not upsetting her so she wouldn't get one of her "headaches." Worrying that her lack of affection was due to his prowess as a lover. Giving her everything she asked for to make her happy. Now that would be over.

He walked to the door and turned around. "I'll see my lawyer right now and get the process started. He'll be in touch with you, as I'm headed *home*." He opened the door and walked out.

"Oh, Samuel." Laura cried out. He stopped. "You make sure I'm provided for or I'll make sure you'll never be able to marry little Lizzy."

Samuel walked through the door and slammed it shut. He stood there for a few seconds and then went down the stairs and out the door.

When Laura heard the front door slam, she sat back down at her vanity and looked at herself in the mirror. She smiled wickedly and said to her reflection, "Now....*that* was rather enjoyable."

* * *

Ben came home for lunch one early April day to find Callie at the kitchen table sobbing, her head in her arms. He immediately assumed the worst and rushed to her side.

"Callie! Is it the baby?"

Callie looked up with swollen red eyes. She shook her head no and handed Ben a piece of paper, then began crying again. Ben took the paper - a letter - and began reading. It was from Trudy.

"*Miss Callie,*

I afrade I has bad news. Socks is ded. He dyed yesturday morning. I got up like I do and went to let him out, but when he did not moove, I thout he was ded. I screemed and Caleb came and tryed to shake him, but he was gone. He must have dyed in his sleep, Miss Callie. I so sorry. I mis Socks so much. Libby duz too. She keep looking for him on the flor and then looks at me and crys. Even Caleb is sad. Socks used to go wit him when he did our chors. But Miss Callie, we both no Socks had a good long life and he was always happy. We took him to Oak Hill and Masta Nathan put him in the graveyard there and marked his grave wit a stone. He tol me to tel you. He sad too. Socks was a good dog, a very good dog. I sorry agin, Miss Callie. No you going to be upset. Tel Mista Ben to take care of you.

Love you,

Trudy
March 1, 1872"

"Oh, Callie. I'm so sorry." Ben put his arms around Callie and held her.

Finally, she could speak. "He…he…was..*my* dog, Ben. *My*..dog… and I..wasn't even..there..when..he…..died!" She started crying again, her tears wetting Ben's shirt.

"I know, darlin', but you not bein' there wouldn't have made any difference. It was just his time. He was an old dog….older than most. He had a happy life and a good life. You and Trudy gave that to him."

"Yes…but..I….should..have…*been*..there!"

"Callie, you couldn't have been there. Not with the baby comin'. Here, take my handkerchief. Wipe your eyes and blow your nose. There….now, listen to me. I know how upset you are, but there's nothing you can do but remember the good times you had with Socks. He was a very lucky dog to have you as a mistress."

"Remember how you told me you talked your father into letting him be in the house? And how mad Mammy Sallie and your grandmother were? If you hadn't done that, he would have been a barn dog and never had all that extra attention. See how lucky he was to have you?"

Callie blew her nose again and leaned against Ben's shoulder. She knew he was right, but it was so *hard* to know Socks wasn't on this earth anymore. She sniffled some more and then took a deep broken breath.

"I'll be fine, Ben. It just was something I hadn't expected. But I guess he was old. I got him for my seventh birthday so he would be twelve. That probably is old for a dog."

Ben held her tight until she felt better. "I guess I'd better get lunch started."

"Don't worry about that. I'll do it. Let's just have some sliced ham and bread."

"All right. I'll get some pickles and some of that corn relish your mother gave us."

* * *

Callie was now in her seventh month of pregnancy and it showed.

Her movements were slower and she walked differently. Ben told her she waddled like a duck, but he also told her she was beautiful. And, she was. Her face glowed with impending motherhood and the added weight made her body curvier.

She still felt well and performed all the chores around their little house. She even put in an early garden with Ben's help. It was hard for her to bend over now. Already, the tiny radishes and lettuce leaves were peeking up from the loamy black soil.

Emma came over once a week and helped her do the heavy cleaning and laundry. The two developed a very good and easy friendship. Emma was also teaching Callie how to bake bread. She was doing a little better, but still had some disasters. In fact, her cooking overall was improving. She was enjoying being the mistress of her and Ben's household.

Once the cold days left, she and Ben took more rides in the buggy. They would hitch up Clayton and Georgia and take off. Ben showed her all around the township and beyond. Sometimes they would drive as far as Metamora and do some shopping.

Callie was receiving packages from Oak Hill containing baby clothes, afghans, and diapers made by Kathleen and Beulah. Abigail and Emma had also been busy in the winter making clothes, blankets, and quilts for the baby.

Ben had started construction on the extra room as soon as the snow melted and now only had to finish the inside. The room fit behind the parlor and against their bedroom. The door into it was from their bedroom so they could get to the baby easily. Ben also made a door from the parlor so when the Hills visited they could have more privacy. The room was fairly large so it could accommodate a crib and a bed.

As soon as it was done, Callie was going to put all the baby's things in a chest in there. Henry had made them a cradle and they were going to use Ben's old crib. As of yet, they still didn't have a bedstead or mattress.

The arrival in early 1872 of the Chicago, Pekin, and Southwestern Railroad through Woodford County spurred growth in all the townships. Now there was a rail connection between Peoria, Bloomington, and

Chicago. The inhabitants of Clayton Township were thrilled.

In Clayton Township, J.M. Schmitt and his brother constructed a mill patterned after the old style Dutch mills. It received power from four great wings propelled by the wind. Each was forty foot in length and consisted of lattice work on which canvas was stretched. The blades turned great wooden wheels which ground the wheat.

The Chapman families visited the mill when it was finished and marveled at the grandness of it. They would bring their wheat to Schmitt to be ground into flour. They used most of what they ground themselves, but if there was any extra, it would be put on the train at the depot and sold. They felt they finally had joined the modern world having a railroad so close.

* * *

April 23rd arrived during a week of warm spring weather. The air smelled of fresh earth, early daffodils, and growing grass. The prairie was coming to life again in all its glory. There had been no violent storms, just gentle rains. The farmers were getting antsy to get out in their fields, but they knew it was still too early. Many remembered April blizzards from years past.

Callie was sitting on the porch enjoying the fresh air and the warm sun on her face. She was knitting a pair of booties and matching bonnet for the baby. She put her needles down and just let the sun and the breeze caress her face.

Today was her birthday - her nineteenth - and her first anniversary. She couldn't believe how fast this year had gone. Yet, it had been slow in the fact she hadn't seen her Oak Hill family for almost a year. Yes, letters had arrived regularly, but it wasn't quite the same as talking to and seeing them in person. She closed her eyes. She tried to picture them all in her mind and to remember their voices. She got up and walked into the house to look at the wedding photographs once again.

Ben found her there wistfully touching her loved ones faces and placing a kiss on their likenesses. He knew she was more homesick now that the birth was getting closer. He thought maybe he had the right present to cheer her up.

"Callie."

She jumped at the sound of his voice. "Ben! You scared me! I guess I was daydreaming."

"Are you going to get ready to go to Ma and Pa's for our celebration?"

"Yes. I was just enjoying the weather outside, then came in for a few minutes. All I have to do is change and fix my hair. How about you?"

"Yep, goin' to get cleaned up right now. What do you think they have planned for us?"

"I don't know. Emma was pretty secretive when I asked."

"Hmmm…Pa wouldn't tell me anything either. Just to make sure we were on time."

"Well, then I guess we'd better get ready so we're not late." Callie started for their bedroom.

Ben grabbed her. "Wait. I don't think I've received a proper anniversary kiss yet."

Callie smiled. "I don't think I've received a proper birthday kiss yet."

"Well, then we'd better take care of that, don't you think?"

Callie put her arms around her husband's neck. They both laughed as her protruding stomach prevented them from being as close together as they used to be. Ben reached over and kissed his wife tenderly on her waiting lips. "Ouch! There she goes again! Now our little girl is kicking *me*!"

He placed his hand on Callie's belly. "Whoa, she's really busy in there today."

"Yes, she knows it's a very special day and she wants to be a part of it."

"Next year she will. Just think, Callie, next year she may be walkin' around here."

"I know. It's a miracle, isn't it?" Callie reached for Ben's lips again. "I do so love you, Ben. Thank you for such a wonderful year. I've loved every minute of it."

"I know you've missed your family…..still do."

"Yes, but I've got you, our house, and soon our baby. I'm very happy, Mr. Chapman. Very happy."

"So am I, Mrs. Chapman. So am I."

They walked arm and arm into their bedroom to get ready for the celebration.

* * *

The three mile trip usually took them around twenty minutes, but today, they let Clayton walk at his leisure since it was such a beautiful day. They chatted about this and that and everything else.

When they finally pulled up at the Chapmans, they were surprised to see several other buggies there. Then they were even more surprised when everyone started pouring out the front door onto the porch and yelled, "Happy anniversary and happy birthday, Callie."

Ben helped Callie out of the buggy and both went to the porch to greet everyone. "Since we really never had a party to celebrate your wedding with all of our friends, we decided to wait until your first anniversary." Henry was smiling ear to ear. "You never had a proper chivaree either, but we aren't going to do that now."

Ben and Callie started mingling with the many guests: John and Elizabeth Forney and daughters, Joseph and Louise Harms, John and Barbara Weast and family, Thomas and Sarah Backer, George and Mary Fritz and sons, Henry and Anna Wilke, Jacob and Sally Kindig and family, and of course, Henry's hired men, Gus, his wife, Eunice, Slim, and Ed.

Abigail loudly announced all the food was ready and for the anniversary couple to come and eat first. Callie was really overwhelmed by the generosity of all the neighbors towards her and Ben. Everyone had brought their favorite dish and Abigail and Emma had made a "wedding cake."

After all had eaten their fill, the guests showered them with gifts. Callie couldn't believe it. They received household items, canned goods, baby things, tools, bedding. It was amazing.

"Us folks in Clayton stick together. Have to in this place. Sometimes Mother Nature makes it mighty hard to make a livin' here, so we all need to be neighborly and help one another. All of us here know how hard it is to start out on your own - specially with a little one comin'."

Jacob Kindig was talking to Ben and Callie who were still in shock from all the attention.

Callie turned to Ben and poked him in the ribs. "Say something to them all, Ben."

Ben cleared his throat and stood up. "Callie and I just want to thank you all for everything here today. We thought we were comin' to dinner at Ma and Pa's and sure didn't expect anything like this. But it's a real nice surprise. We hope we can be more neighborly in the future - we're pretty much settled in now - and repay all of you for thinking of us. That's all I got to say, except thank you so much." He sat down realizing his face was burning.

Everyone applauded and then set to cleaning up and heading for their homes. It was a lovely day on the prairie of Illinois.

* * *

When the Chapman families were finally alone, Ben took Callie's hand. "Let's go for a short walk." He led her towards the little barn. "I've got somethin' to show you."

They reached the barn and walked inside. It took Callie a few minutes for her eyes to adjust to the dimmer light. Ben left her side and went deeper into the barn. "Just stay there, Callie. I'm coming right back." She stopped where she stood wondering what he was doing.

Ben returned with a silly grin on his face and led her back outside in the light. His belly looked as big as hers and it was moving! She looked at him, eyebrows raised. "What on earth do you have inside your shirt?"

At that moment, she saw a little black nose wriggle out between the buttons, followed by a black eye and a white ear.

"A puppy! Is it a puppy?" Callie clapped her hands in delight. "Let me see, oh, let me see!"

Ben opened his shirt and there was a tiny, black and white spaniel puppy, his little pink tongue sticking out.

"Let me have him!" Callie took the pup from Ben and held him up to her cheek, where he started licking her. "Oh, Ben, he's so adorable! Who does he belong too?"

"You. He's yours. Wilkes had a litter several weeks ago, before Socks died. I had them save the male for you. The pups were just weaned last week, so Pa brought him here so I could surprise you. Thought you could get him trained before the baby comes. Happy birthday."

"Oh, Ben. You are too good to me. He's perfect! I think he likes me." Callie giggled as the puppy licked her neck and ear. "He smells just like I remember Socks smelling when he was a puppy. Thank you so much."

"Do you know what to name him?"

Callie held the little pup away from her and looked him over. "That's easy. He's Patch. Look at the black patch over his left eye."

"Funny, that's what I've already been callin' him. I guess we must be thinking alike. Must be an "old" married couple already!"

"Benjamin! We will never be an "old" married couple! We're always going to be young! Uh-oh….look….Patch is wetting." Callie immediately put the puppy down on the grass. "There, that's where you go little Patch." Patch looked up at her with his dark brown eyes and wagged his tail so hard, his whole rear end shook. Callie and Ben broke out into laughter. "He's so cute, Ben. I love him. Let's take him home."

"We'd better go tell Ma and Pa and Emma thanks for the party. Ma wants us to take some of the leftover food with us too."

"All right. Then let's get this little boy back to our house where I can spoil him!"

* * *

May can be a fickle month on the Illinois prairie. It can bring cold, wet, damp days or warm, sunny, breezy ones. It can be chilly with frost or it can be as hot and humid as in mid-summer. This year, May was indecisive. The early part of the month was dreary and rainy. The last half of the month was exceptionally hot and dry.

The farmers in the area were working furiously to get their crops planted now that the weather was hot and the fields were finally dry. Ben was gone from the house most of the day and into the evening hours. He sent Emma to stay with Callie in case the baby decided to arrive. Emma had strict orders to find him as soon as Callie started labor.

Callie was heavy with child and the hot, dry weather was making her miserable. Even little Patch couldn't raise her spirits, although she was very thankful to have him. She became very irritable and missed Ben. When he came home, he was bone tired and after cleaning up, went straight to bed, exhausted. This went on until the last day of May when the planting was finally finished.

Two days later, on the second of June, Ben told Callie he had to go to the new train depot close to the Schmitt Mill, and pick up a delivery.

"Can I go with you? Please, I need a change of scenery. Patch can go too. We can take a picnic lunch and stop by the creek on the way. Please say yes, Ben, please."

"Callie, you know you can't go. What if you start havin' the baby? What if the wagon ride hurts you? No, you can't come. I'm sorry, darlin', but you have to stay put until our baby comes. Emma is comin' here to stay with you. I'll be back as soon as I can."

Callie pouted and stuck out her lower lip, but she knew Ben was right. She couldn't endanger their child. "All right, but hurry back. I've missed you."

Emma arrived and Ben left with the wagon. Callie didn't even ask him what the delivery was he was getting. She just assumed it had something to do with the farm.

She and Emma sat out on the front porch, Patch sleeping at Callie's feet. Emma was embroidering a pillowcase as a gift for Abigail.

"Emma, have you seen any more of Eugene Miller?"

Emma blushed. "A little. He came over before the plantin' began and we went for a ride in his new buggy."

"Is he your beau?"

"I don't know. He's awfully quiet and never says much. I'm not sure what he thinks of me."

"Is his sister Josie still angry with Ben for marrying me?"

Emma giggled. "She's still mad as a wet hen. Doesn't know why Ben went and married a Rebel. She can't see how happy he is with you."

"Hmmmm…I guess I should be really nice to her the next time I see her. She was at the Wilkes at the last social and she was staring at me all night. I just smiled sweet-like and ignored her. That was before this baby made me as big as a cow! I don't think I'll ever be thin again!"

"You look just fine, Callie."

"Thank you, but I do have a mirror over the dresser and I know I don't look fine. I'm fat and ugly and I wish this baby would decide to enter the world very soon."

"What did Marie say the last time you saw her?"

"She said any day now. The baby has turned into the right position and could come anytime. Emma, I feel like I'm sitting on an egg just waiting for it to hatch!"

Emma laughed so hard, she dropped her embroidering. "Oh, Callie! Stop it! You are making me cry!"

* * *

It was close to sunset before Callie and Emma heard the rattle of the wagon come up the lane. They had already eaten their supper and were sitting in the tiny parlor. Ben's meal was warming in the oven.

"Sounds like my big brother is coming home."

"Emma, you spend the night with us. It's too late for you to be riding back."

"Thanks, Callie, but if I leave right now, I can make it before it gets too dark. Liza Jane is a fast little filly and she knows the way with her eyes closed." Emma stood up and started for the front door. As she opened it, she saw Ben and the wagon lumbering towards the house. Except the wagon wasn't filled with anything to do with the farm - it was filled with people and trunks and boxes.

"Callie! I think you'd better come here."

Callie managed to struggle out of her chair and plodded over to the door. "What is it, Emma? Isn't it Ben?"

"Look."

Callie peered out the door. The wagon was just pulling up to the porch and Ben was getting down. In the evening light, she saw three people stand up in the wagon and climb out. She squinted her eyes and then let out a long shriek and started waddling as fast as she could to the wagon.

"Mama!! Papa!!! Trudy!!! Mama!! Papa!! Trudy!! Libby!!"

The three ran to her and they all fell into each other's arms, hugging and crying, laughing. Ben walked up to the porch where Emma was watching. "Think Callie likes my surprise."

* * *

Callie woke up, stretched, and smiled. She heard someone in her kitchen. She lay back in bed and shortly Trudy arrived with a tray full of fried eggs, sausage links, and buttered toast. Libby was toddling right behind her, followed by Kathleen.

"How's the mother-to-be this morning?" Kathleen went around to the other side of the bed and sat down. Libby crawled up on Callie's side and eyed the toast.

"Here, Miss Libby, you take a piece of this perfectly toasted bread." Callie held out a half piece and Libby looked at Trudy.

"You's can has it, baby."

Libby grabbed the toast out of Callie's hand and immediately stuck it in her mouth.

"What's you tells Miz Callie?"

"Tank you."

Callie laughed. "You're welcome, Libby dear." She reached out and poked Libby in the stomach, making her giggle.

"Now, Miz Callie, you eats your brea'fast an' I's goin' to tidy up the kitchen."

"No, Trudy, you sit here with me, too. I can't get enough of all of you. Stay here."

"All rights."

"Tell me again about your train ride here."

"Oh, Miz Callie, it was sumpin! That train car was goin' fas' an' the lan' jes' sped right by. Then we's even *sleeped* on that train! Me an' Libby cuddled right up. Masta Nathan an' Miz Kathleen had their own place. An' we eats on it too. Food pritty good, too." Trudy's eyes kept getting wider as she remembered her first train ride.

Callie smiled. "You're way ahead of me. When Ben and I came here, we had to sleep sitting up in our seats or stop at a hotel."

"Yessum, that what Masta Nathan says."

"It was a most pleasant journey, Callie. The sleeper and diner cars make all the difference in the world. Plus, we got here much faster."

"Well, Mama, I'm just so happy ya'll are here. It was a wonderful, wonderful surprise. Ya'll going to spoil me, though. Breakfast in bed? I never got that unless I was sick!"

"You's needin' your res' now, Miz Callie. I's knows. Takes lots of work to git that baby out. Mista Ben dids a good thing havin' us come he'ps you."

"Yes, he did. He's a remarkable man, isn't he?" Callie smiled. So did Kathleen.

"You really are very happy here, aren't you, Callie?"

"Mama, I feel like the most blessed person on the earth. Yes, I'm very, very happy. Once this baby comes, our family will be even more blessed. I can't wait to meet her."

"Her?"

"Yes, I'm sure it's a girl."

"Hmmm…we'll just have to wait and see, I guess."

* * *

Callie finished her meal and then got up and dressed. Meanwhile, Trudy and Kathleen straightened up the kitchen and the parlor. Nathan and Kathleen were sleeping in the new room and Trudy and Libby were in the parlor. Libby was in the baby's crib and Trudy had a mattress on the floor, which they put away in the mornings.

Libby quickly adjusted to her new surroundings. At first she was very shy around Callie and Ben, hiding behind Trudy's skirts, but they both eventually won her over. Callie would take her by the hand to the chicken coop to gather the eggs and let her hold the new baby chicks.

Libby also loved Patch. They both romped together on the floor of the parlor. Patch let Libby tug at his tail and his ears. Then he would jump on her and lick her face. She giggled with glee.

Nathan went with Ben to help with the chores, and then sometimes they would ride to Henry and Abigail's to see what new farming techniques Henry was using. They would come back with freshly baked goods or a big bowl of chicken and noodles or sauerkraut and spare ribs for supper. Otherwise, Kathleen and Trudy insisted on doing the cooking, while Callie entertained Libby. They all treated Callie like a "lady of leisure."

One night the families all had dinner at Callie and Ben's. The tiny house was bursting at the seams with laughter, talking, and eating. It was a very happy occasion.

* * *

"Oh my! I think something just happened." Callie was standing by the kitchen table talking to Trudy, who was washing dishes.

"Whatcha means?"

Callie looked down at the floor where drips of water were running down her legs.

"I'm leaking!"

Trudy followed her gaze. "Oh, Miz Callie! You's water jes' broke! That baby comin'! We gots to gits you in bed."

Callie's eyes were wide. "But I feel fine, Trudy. It must be something else."

"No, no, that's what it is. Happin to me. Then the pains starts. Hurry, gits your nightgown on an' gits in bed. I's go gits Miz Kathleen an' tells her. She knows hows to gits Masta Nathan an' Mista Ben. I's be rights back. Gits in bed!"

Trudy ran out the door to the chicken coops where Kathleen had taken Libby to see the baby chicks. "Miz Kathleen! Miz Kathleen! The baby comin'! The baby comin'!"

Kathleen and Libby peeked out of the coop. "What, Trudy?"

"The baby comin'! Miz Callie's water jes' broke! Go git the men! I's goin' back inside an' he'p her. Tell Mista Ben to gits that Marie lady. Miz Callie have that baby too quick to git the doc'or! Take Libby wit you." Trudy ran back towards the house and Kathleen left with Libby and headed to the barn where Nathan and Ben were.

"Ben! Ben!" Kathleen ran into the barn, out of breath from carrying Libby. "Ben, hurry, the baby is coming!"

"What?"

"The *baby*! Callie is having the baby! Go get Marie. Hurry!"

Ben quickly saddled up Clayton and took off for the Parkers. He spurred the horse to go even faster.

Nathan took Libby from Kathleen so she could catch her breath. "Our grandchild is about to be born, Kathleen?"

"It seems so. Her water broke and that's the first sign. Could be fast or could take hours."

Nathan had a worried look on his face, which Kathleen easily detected.

"Don't worry, Nathan. Callie is young and strong. She will have an experienced midwife to help her. She won't be like Hannah. The baby won't be like our Nathaniel. Mother and baby will both be healthy."

"You don't know that, Kathleen."

"Yes, yes, I do. I feel it. Come on! Let's go back to the house. I'll have to help Trudy. You can entertain Libby."

"Shouldn't someone go tell Henry and Abigail and Emma?"

"Yes, of course. Here, I'll take Libby. You ride over there on Georgia. Hurry up! You don't want to miss meeting your new grandbaby, do you?"

"I'm on my way!"

* * *

Several hours later, everyone had descended on the tiny farmhouse. Ben brought Marie back with him and she was attending to Callie. Trudy and Kathleen took turns holding Callie's hand and wiping her brow with cool water. Libby had settled down for a nap. Henry, Nathan, and Ben were sitting out on the porch looking at each other. Abigail and Emma were cooking in the kitchen in case anyone felt like eating. As labor progressed, more moans were heard coming from the bedroom. At each one, the men tensed up. Finally, Ben could no longer stand it. He jumped up and started pacing the length of the porch. "What's taking so long? I thought this would be over by now."

"Settle down, son. Never know how long it takes. Babies come at their own time." Henry reached up to grab Ben's arm. "You took over fourteen hours, but Emma came in three."

"Well, I'm just going to go in there and see what's happenin'."

"I wouldn't do that, Ben." Nathan smiled. "Women get testy when someone is giving birth. They'll just shoo you away."

"I don't care. I'm the father. I have a right to know what's happenin'."

"Go on, then. But don't say we didn't warn you."

Ben opened the front door and started for the bedroom, where he could hear Callie groaning. His mother stopped him. "Where do you think you're going?'

"To see Callie."

"No you're not. No men are allowed in there until that baby is born."

"Ma! I want to see my wife. You can't stop me." Ben strode across the little kitchen and went into the bedroom. Callie was on the bed, drenched in perspiration; Trudy was wiping her forehead; Kathleen was rubbing her hand and arm; Marie was sitting on the edge of the bed.

They all stared at him like he was a ghost. All except Callie. "Oh, Ben! I wanted you here, but no one would get you. Sit over here. Ohhhhhhhh.......!"

"Was that a strong one, Callie?" Marie asked.

Callie nodded her head.

"Callie, how bad is it?" Kathleen left so Ben could sit down by Callie. He grabbed her hand.

"Bad, but I know what we will have in the end, so I'm thinking about that and not the pain.....ohhhhhhhhh......"

"Another one?"

"Yes, Marie."

"They're coming faster. Think it's about time. You'd better leave, Ben."

"NO! I want him to stay!"

"Miz Callie, mens ain't 'posed to see birthins. They ain't strong 'nuf. Lenora says they passes out."

Ben looked at Trudy and she confidently nodded her head at him.

"I don't care! Ben, you stay here! If I have to go through this, then you can too. It's *our* baby, not mine!"

Ben looked a little pale. "I don't know, Callie. Maybe all these women are right. Maybe this isn't a place for men."

Callie glared at Ben just as another pain gripped her. "I have to push, Marie! I have to push!" She grabbed Ben's hand and dug her fingernails into his palm. "Ben, you *are* staying! Don't you *dare* leave me now!"

Ben knew he was in a predicament and there was no way out. He swallowed hard and concentrated on Callie face, ignoring what was happening at the foot of the bed.

"Ohhhhhhhhh........ohhhh........"

"That's good, Callie. Now push like that again when the next pain comes."

"Ugggggghhhhhhhh........ohhhh....."

Ben held on to Callie's hand and stared into her eyes. "Come on, Callie. You can do this. Come on little mama."

Callie gave him a look of disgust. "Easy for you to say, Benjamin. Ohhhhh.....uggghhhhh..."

"Good! I can see the head. One more Callie. Just one more!"

"Uuummmmmmmmmmmm.....ohhhhhhh...."

"It's out! It's a girl! A beautiful girl!" Marie held up the newborn for her parents to see just as the baby let out a cry. Callie started sobbing and Ben realized he too had tears running down his cheeks. He also felt very weak in the knees. Kathleen quickly saw his paleness and slipped a chair under him.

"I just have to cut....the....cord...There..." Marie gave the baby to Trudy who had wet cloths to wipe her off. She wrapped the little girl in a new blanket and laid her in Callie's arms.

"Put her on your breast, Callie, and let her nurse right away. I believe that gets your milk started and it's good for the baby." Marie said.

Callie was exhausted so Trudy helped her. The little baby greedily started suckling right away. Callie had to smile. "She came out hungry."

By this time Ben had recovered enough to wrap his arms around his wife and daughter. "You did a good job, Callie.....a good job. A girl....just like we thought...and she does look like you, except look at all that dark hair. She got her papa's hair."

Marie finished up and walked out to the porch where everyone else was now waiting. "It's a girl - a good sized one too. Mother and daughter are just fine. No complications. An easy birth. The father is a little green, but he'll be fine too."

Henry and Nathan clapped one another on the back and opened a bottle of whiskey they had handy to celebrate the birth of their first grandchild. Kathleen and Abigail joined them on the porch, but sipped some wine instead.

"I think Ben might need some of that whiskey," Kathleen smiled. "He held in there, but he got awfully pale."

"We told him not to go in there, but he insisted." Nathan laughed. "Now he knows why."

Kathleen didn't laugh with her husband. "I think it was very nice that he took part in the birth of his child. Callie was much better too after he was there. Maybe it does a man good to see what women have to go through to give birth and they will appreciate their wives and children even more."

"Here, here, Kathleen. I agree completely." Abigail raised her glass.

Nathan and Henry looked sheepishly at their wives, who quickly hugged them and toasted, "To Callie, Ben, and Baby Girl Chapman!"

* * *

Ben soon joined the festivities on the porch while Callie slept. Trudy was sitting with her in case she woke and needed anything. The newborn was sleeping quietly in Callie's arms.

"Well, son, congratulations!" Henry grasped Ben's hand and pumped it hard. "A new Chapman has joined the world."

"A new *Hill*, too," added Nathan who was beaming. "When can we see her?"

"They're both sleepin' right now. When they wake up, I guess. Marie's gettin her things together and will be wantin' a ride home soon. Guess Callie did so good, she won't be needed any more."

"How'd you do, son? You feelin' better?" Abigail reached up and brushed Ben's hair away from his face. "Heard you got a little pale in there."

"Yes, Ma, I did, but I'm sure glad I stayed. Seein' that little girl born was a miracle I won't ever forget."

"Who does she look like?" Nathan went over and sat down in one of the rockers and sipped his whiskey.

"Kind of hard to tell right now, but I'd say Callie. Except she's got lots of dark hair. Can't tell what color her eyes are, she hasn't opened them yet. Hope their brown, like her mama's."

"Does this precious little thing have a name yet, Benjamin?" Abigail asked her son. "Yes, Ma, she does. But I ain't sayin' what it is until Callie can tell you all. She's the one thought it up and I agreed. We've had it picked out for a while now. Well, think I'll go back in and check on them. Just can't get over it - *I'm a father!*" Ben shook his head and left the group to rejoin his wife and daughter.

The new grandparents and aunt sat on the porch and talked about the baby and what plans they had for her. Each was longing to see and hold her. All were anxious to see Callie. They marked June 7, 1872 as a day they would always cherish.

* * *

"I think it's time we go inside and eat somethin'. Sun's about to set - be dark soon. Surely, Callie will be awake and hungry by now." Abigail looked out at the western sky with her arms akimbo. "Come on, Emma. Let's get a meal on the table."

"Let me help, too, Abigail." Kathleen rose and joined the other two women. "Maybe Callie is ready to see us all now and we can get a peek at that baby."

"You ladies go on in. Take your turn and then let us know when it's time for us grandpas to come. We'll stay out here and enjoy the sunset while you're fussin over that new one." Henry leaned back in his chair and smiled.

"All right, husband. That's what we'll do. Then while you're 'fussin' we can get supper done."

The women went into the little house hoping the new mother and daughter were awake. Trudy saw them from her chair in the bedroom where she sat with Libby on her lap. "Comes on in. Miz Callie feedin' baby girl now, but she wants to see y'all." Libby squirmed in her lap. Trudy set her down and she toddled over to Kathleen and raised her chubby little arms to be picked up. Kathleen immediately complied.

Before the new grandmothers and aunt entered the little bedroom, Trudy and Ben left to join the others on the porch. It was getting hot in the little room, even with the window open.

"Welcome everyone. I'd like you to meet someone very precious. This is your beautiful new granddaughter and niece." Callie pulled the baby off her breast and turned her around for them to see. "Isn't she just beautiful?"

"Oh, my goodness. Look at that hair. Just like Ben's. And, that nose. So like yours, Callie."

"Oh, Callie, sweetie. She's just as precious as you. Has she opened her eyes yet? Look at that sweet mouth. Oh, Nathan will swoon when he sees her. How are you feeling?"

"I'm fine, Mama. Just tired. Marie said I did really well considering it was my first baby. I'm supposed to take it easy for a few days until I feel like myself again. I'm really glad y'all are here to help Ben and me. Where are Papa and Henry?"

"They're still on the porch. We're taking turns so as not to bother you too much."

"Well, go get them. I want to introduce the newest Chapman to them."

Kathleen left with Libby to get the rest of the family. Nathan and Henry came in very quietly until they saw their new granddaughter. Then Henry let out a whoop of joy.

"Henry! You'll scare that little girl!" Abigail scolded her husband.

"Sorry, just got excited."

Nathan went over to the other side of the bed for a better look. He leaned down and kissed Callie on her forehead and took her hand. "Thank you, baby girl, for this wonderful child. I can't believe you are a mother with your own 'baby girl.'"

"I know, Papa, it's a miracle, isn't it?" Callie turned to all the others and motioned Ben over by her. "Don't y'all want to know what this tiny baby's name is?"

They all nodded and waited anxiously.

"Ben let me choose the name if it was a girl and I had a lot of time to think about it. I hope y'all like it."

Callie beamed. "Let me introduce you to Miss Kathleen Abigail Caludy Chapman, who will be known as Katie."

"Oh, Callie......" Kathleen started crying. "Are you sure? Oh, my....I don't know what to say.....thank you."

"Me neither," said Abigail, wiping her own eyes. "Thank you both."

"Thought that'd make you happy, Ma. Emma, makes you connected to her too, since that's your middle name."

"Yes, thank you so much, big brother, and Callie. I'm very touched."

"Caludy? I don't understand that one." Henry was frowning. "Who is that?"

Callie held out her hand and Trudy came over and took it. "'Cal' is for Callie and 'udy' is for Trudy, Caludy, friends forever. It's Libby's middle name too. Trudy came up with it then and I thought it was perfect for my little Katie, too."

Trudy smiled through her tears and rubbed Callie's hand. "You knows, how happy I's am 'bout that, Miz Callie. Our girls be bes' friends too - likes us."

"It's a beautiful name, baby girl. It fits her too. Just look how content she is. Oh...look....she's opening her eyes!"

Katie had big dark eyes, shaped just like Callie's. She gazed up at her mother and waved her little fists as if to say, "Here I am!"

"I can't stand it any longer, Callie....please let me hold her." Kathleen gave Libby to Trudy and went to Callie's side.

"Of course, Mama. Here....got her? Oh, she likes her grandma." Katie looked at Kathleen somberly and then stuck her hand out. Nathan, next to Kathleen, grabbed her little hand. She held on to his finger. Both grandparents were radiant as they cooed and talked to their little Katie.

"All right....you have to share her now." Henry and Abigail came over and Katie was passed to Abigail, who held her up to her cheek.

"I've forgotten how good a baby feels. Oh, my, little Katie, aren't you somethin'?"

"My turns. Let me has that lil gal." Trudy took Katie and squatted on the floor so Libby could see her too. "This here Miz Katie, Libby. You an' her goin' be bes' friends."

"Fends," said Libby as she tentatively touched the baby's hand. "My fend."

"That right, Libby, your friend. Jes' like me an' Miz Callie."

Libby grinned and then ran to Callie and tried to get up on the bed. "Fend."

Ben picked her up and sat her next to Callie, who hugged her and said, "Yes, Libby, friends."

* * *

The next few days were filled with feedings, changing diapers, and all the things that come with new babies. No one allowed Callie out of bed, except to use the chamber pot; until she was frustrated enough to finally join the others at the kitchen table to proclaim she felt fine and didn't need to be bedfast anymore.

Abigail, Henry, and Emma came almost every day to hold and coo over Katie.

"I swear, I haven't heard this child let out a peep yet. Does she ever cry?" Abigail was holding Katie, who was just looking up at her with her deep brown eyes and waving her little hands.

"Well...we don't let her," said Callie with innocence. "Why would she cry? If she looks like she's going too, I just nurse her, and if that doesn't satisfy her, I change her. Otherwise I just hold her, or someone else does, and we talk to her."

"You'll spoil her, Callie."

"You can't spoil a little baby, Abigail. And...well...I don't care if we do. She seems content. She eats, she sleeps, she's alert when she's awake, she's happy."

"I must agree with Callie, Abigail," said Kathleen as she reached over to touch Katie's little smooth cheek. "Whatever we're doing, it must be working. I've never seen a child so satisfied."

"I remember, Callie, you were nothing like that. You cried all the time. 'Course it was a bad time after losing your mother, but even Mammy Sallie couldn't get you to stop. She even rubbed whiskey on your gums to calm you down."

"Nathan! Really! That's awful!"

"I guess that's what mammies used to do, Kathleen, when babies had the colic."

"Well, our Katie will never need any old whiskey. She's got her mother's milk to keep her happy." Callie walked over and picked up Katie from Abigail's lap. "And, this mother can tell it's time for a feeding now. So, if y'all excuse me, I'm going to tend to that in the other room. Then you can have her back."

* * *

One afternoon while Katie and Libby were napping, Kathleen, Trudy, and Callie were enjoying the fresh, early summer breezes on the front porch. The smell of a morning rain still hung in the air. A small flock of robins had descended on the front lawn, looking for earthworms. Thomas, the cat, was stretched out on the bottom step, eyeing the birds. Patch laid at Callie's feet sound asleep, snoring slightly.

"I know we have all been avoiding this subject, Mama, but you must tell me about Sam. In his letter, all he said was that he and Laura were getting a divorce. How can that be, Mama? I didn't think anyone *ever* got divorced. Why would Sam? I know he loves Laura very much. Did he do something terrible? Did she?"

Kathleen and Trudy exchanged glances. "Laura asked....no, demanded, for the divorce, Callie." Kathleen squirmed in her chair. "We don't know all the details, but from what Samuel told us, she married him for *money*, not love, and now that she has all the money from him she needs, she no longer wants him. She also never enjoyed Oak Hill. According to Samuel, she detests it."

"That's about all we know, except Samuel is mortified, so we don't speak of it much. He helped with the planting and then did some campaigning. You know, your father and Uncle John invested in the Montgomery mill, so Samuel has been going there to oversee its reconstruction. He spends a lot of time there, as a matter of fact."

Again Kathleen and Trudy exchanged glances. Callie saw this look between the two of them.

"All right, what *aren't* you telling me? There's more, isn't there?"

Kathleen sighed. "Yes, there is. We think....no, we know, Samuel has been seeing Lizzy Montgomery."

"What? Lizzy Montgomery?" Callie sat there stunned. "Hmmmmm....that's interesting. Well, I suppose Sam can see whoever he wants now that he's no longer married. But I'm.....was he interested in Lizzy *before* he and Laura divorced?"

"We're not sure. We know he spent time with her after the...the.... Carswell shooting. Other than that, we don't know. But I don't think Laura divorced him for that reason...if it was a reason. I think she really did marry him for the money. In fact, she's making him pay her now."

"What! Can she do that?"

"Apparently. He has to give her a monthly stipend until she dies or marries again. And, it's not a small one either." Kathleen was fidgeting with her wedding ring. "I think she'll never marry again, just to spite Samuel."

"Mama! Is she really that cold?"

Kathleen looked Callie in the eyes. "Yes, I think she is. I think she's a cruel, calculating woman who took advantage of our Samuel. In fact, I'm glad he's rid of her even if it is a disgrace for him. I never did like her, and I tried, I really did. But she was always so cold and aloof and never joined our family. And, if he is happy with Lizzy, then, I say, let them be together. Samuel needs someone to love him, just like the rest of us do."

"Well...that's very true." Callie sighed heavily. "I wish there was something I could do to help him."

"I think he's recovering, sweetie. And, like I said, he really doesn't like to talk about it - it embarrasses him. So don't write anything to him about it - wait until he approaches the subject himself. Don't say anything about Lizzy either, please. I don't want him to think we're gossiping about him."

"Oh, I won't, Mama. I'll just fill the pages of my letters with news about Katie. I hope he gets to meet her soon. Mammy Sallie and Grandma, too. Are they both doing all right?"

"They've both slowed down considerably, but are still going. I think they're doing wonderful for women in their seventies, don't you, Trudy?"

"Yessum. Mammy Sallie slow, but she still sassy. Miz Beulah still look like a strong South'n lady, toos."

"Be sure to tell them all how much I miss them and love them. I will make sure Katie knows who they are. Thank goodness we took all those photographs at the wedding. Now she can *see* what her relatives look like."

"I'm so glad too. It was very tedious that day, but I'm so thankful we did it. We look at those photographs every day."

"Me, too. Maybe when Katie is a little older, Ben and I can have a family portrait taken. I think he went to Peoria to have the one taken that's in my locket. That's only a day's ride over."

"I think that would be a lovely Christmas gift, Callie. Do try to do it sometime. But, also, try to come and visit. I know it will be harder with the baby now, but it can be done. Isn't that right, Trudy? Libby was a very good traveler."

"Yes, Miz Kathleen. Weren't hard at all to git here wit Libby. She a good lil gal."

"I know we will, Mama. Just depends on the crops, weather, and livestock. I would want Ben to come too. Don't think I could manage the baby by myself."

"Oh, definitely. No, it wouldn't be good for you to travel alone with Katie. I meant for Ben to come too."

"Uh-oh. I's hears my Libby. Guess nap time over. Gots to gits my gal 'fore she wakes up lil Katie."

"I'd better be checking on her anyway. Come one, let's go get our girls."

* * *

After staying at the Chapmans for over a month, the Hills finally had to bid good-bye and head back to Oak Hill. It was a sad, sad, parting, full of tears and long hugs. Callie didn't go to the station with

Ben. She said her good-byes at the house. Once alone with Katie, she cried some more and then some more, finally wiping her tears, resolving to visit her family before another year went by. She would write to them everyday to keep them updated on their granddaughter's life. She vowed Katie would know them as if they were still here in the house with them.

Callie's life as a farmwife and mother fell into a routine. On Mondays she generally did the laundry, which took the entire day. Tuesdays were reserved for ironing and mending. Wednesday was bake day. Callie still struggled with baked goods, but she was getting better. In fact, her pies were very good. On Thursdays and Saturdays, the house was given a thorough cleaning. Friday was again a baking day. Sunday was a day of rest, after completing the everyday chores.

She was also responsible for getting three meals on the table daily, hauling the water into the house from the well, keeping the fire burning in the stove, sewing clothes for herself, Katie, and Ben, preserving the bounties of her vegetable garden, and tending to the poultry.

In between doing all these chores, she took care of Katie, nursing her, changing her, and holding her. Callie was very fortunate because Ben helped her with many of her chores. He took care of the livestock and helped in the garden. He also was an active father who looked after Katie while Callie was cooking or baking.

Even though she was often exhausted at the end of the day, Callie made sure she and Ben spent time with Katie. Katie had moved into the new room recently and seemed to really like her new surroundings. She also let her parents sleep almost the entire night. She usually woke up around three o'clock in the morning for a feeding and then went right back to sleep.

After daybreak when Callie and Ben arose, she would lay in her crib awake, but just cooing and entertaining herself. When Callie went to pick her up, she would award her mother with a grin and a gurgle. Callie would then remind herself what blessings she had in her life. Her family was perfect.

* * *

In the fall, the country once again elected Ulysses S. Grant as its president over the Democrat's candidate, Horace Greeley. As the women in Callie's family learned, Victoria Woodhull was the first woman to be nominated as president, but she never appeared on the ballot because she was too young and did not meet the constitutional age requirement. Frederick Douglas, the former slave, was her vice presidential pick.

Susan B. Anthony and other suffragettes were arrested for attempting to vote in Rochester, New York, as women finally decided men shouldn't be the only ones to cast their ballots in elections. When news of this reached Clayton Township, all the farmwives secretly, and openly, as in Callie's case, applauded the suffragettes' protests. They worked equally as hard as their men did, and they felt they should have the right to vote too. Women were coming into their own.

Also this fall, a horrible horse virus reached epidemic proportions, killing over four million horses, mainly in the East and the South. Cities, such as New York and Boston, were crippled by the epidemic, where horses were used for shipping and transportation. In Boston, two hundred horses a day were dying, stopping all freight and most commerce.

Scientists were baffled by this "horse flu" and couldn't find a cure. Finally, in December, it abated as fast as it appeared. Only then was it learned the virus was carried by mosquitoes, which were killed by the freezing weather.

Fortunately, the virus didn't reach the Midwest so Clayton and Georgia and the other horses owned by the Chapmans remained healthy.

* * *

Before the weather turned too cold, Ben and Callie decided to take Katie and make a trip to Peoria to a studio photographer. Since it took around six to seven hours to make the thirty-five mile trip, they borrowed Henry's carriage and hitched up Georgia and Clayton. They packed their bags for a two night stay at the Jefferson Street Hotel.

They left early in the morning, bundling Katie up against the cold. Off they went to the city by the river. It was a gloriously crisp November day with the sky clear of clouds. Most of the leaves had dropped from the trees, but there was still a little color left for them to enjoy. Callie and Katie were in the enclosed carriage with Ben driving. Katie quickly went to sleep.

When they arrived on the outskirts of Metamora, Ben pulled the carriage over to a grassy area and Callie brought out the basket of food she had prepared. They both enjoyed fried chicken, hard boiled eggs, biscuits, and cider. It felt good to walk around and stretch their legs. The day had warmed so Katie joined them on the quilt they spread out on the grass.

After nursing Katie, Callie climbed back into the carriage and Ben hoisted himself up to the driver's seat and they resumed their journey. By late afternoon they finally saw the wide Illinois River ahead of them. The team of horses cautiously started to cross the plank bridge over the river.

Ben seemed unconcerned, but Callie was somewhat nervous. However, seeing the steamboats going up and down the river and all the hustle and bustle along the shorelines made her apprehension turn to excitement. Her nostrils were soon attacked by the distinct smell of fishy, muddy water which caused her to hold her handkerchief over her nose. Katie didn't seem to mind the smell at all. She was gurgling and looking out the window at the sights.

They finally crossed the bridge, making Georgia and Clayton much more relaxed, even if the traffic did increase. Ben steered the pair carefully and then turned onto Jefferson Street. They hadn't gone too far when they pulled up to the Jefferson Street Hotel. Ben tied the horses to the hitching post in front of the building and went inside to get them a room. Callie was entertaining Katie when he shortly reappeared.

"Got us a room, Mrs. Chapman. You and Katie get out here and I'll drive the carriage around back. Just stay in the lobby and I'll find you, but just in case, we're in room number 220."

Callie, Katie, and their luggage went into the very nice open lobby and waited for Ben to take care of their carriage and horses. The man behind the desk asked Callie if she wanted to go to her room, but she declined, deciding to wait for Ben. He soon was at her side and with the help of a bell boy, they went to their room.

It was a nice sized room with a window overlooking the street. Ben looked around the room. "I asked if they could get us a crib for Katie, but the man said he didn't think they had one, but if they did, they would bring it."

"It doesn't matter, Ben. She can sleep with us. She does at home sometimes, why not here?"

"I guess. Looks like we won't have much choice. Let's get our things unpacked and then we can go out and find a photographer and make an appointment for tomorrow. The manager gave me several names of studios near here."

The young family ventured out into the street and presently stopped in front of a furniture store. Displayed in the window was a beautiful little settee upholstered in rich, dark red velvet. The back was separated by a carving of an urn with flowers and the arms, legs, and the top of the back were ornately carved also.

"Oh, Ben, isn't that settee pretty? It would look so good in our parlor. The red would go well with the dark blue already on the two chairs too." Callie lingered at the window sighing over the settee.

"Do you really like it, Callie?"

"Yes, of course. Don't you?"

"I guess. You know I don't know much 'bout this sort of thing. But if you like it, let's go in and see how much it costs."

"I'm sure it's too much, Ben. Look at all that carving, and I know velvet is more expensive. No, I'd rather not know."

"Well…..I was savin' it as a kind of surprise….but the crops did real well this year, so did the hogs and cattle. Pa gave us a sort of bonus. So….if you *really* like it and it isn't *overly* costly, we could get it as a Christmas present to ourselves."

He didn't get another word out before Callie and Katie disappeared into the furniture store. In another few minutes the settee was purchased for $5.00 with instructions on how to deliver it before Christmas. Callie was beaming.

They found the Erler Photography Studio and made an appointment for the next morning. Then they walked into a tiny café and ordered supper. Callie had ham with sweet potatoes and Ben had roast beef and mashed potatoes. Katie got a little taste of both potatoes. After the meal, they strolled around for a while longer and then it was back to the hotel and bed. Katie slept between them as she often did at home.

After breakfast at the café again, they went to the studio where they posed and waited and posed and waited. Katie had to be distracted, fed, and changed before they got her to sit still enough for the photographs. Ben, too, was getting restless and was happy when the session was over. Mr. Erler promised to get the photos done in time for Callie to send them to Georgia for Christmas.

They spent the rest of the day walking by the riverfront and at one of the nearby parks. After another night in the hotel, they were ready early the next morning to start their journey back to their farmhouse. Callie was very pleased. They had accomplished their mission of having their family photograph taken and, as bonuses, they had enjoyed their trip and purchased the settee.

* * *

"Kathleen! Kathleen!" Nathan shouted as he bounded up the front steps of Oak Hill. He flung open the front door. "Kathleen! Mother! Mammy Sallie! Look what I have!"

The women came out of the back parlor, Kathleen leading the way. "What is it, Nathan? Show us!"

Nathan pulled out a flat box and opened it with a flourish. The women were very curious and crowded closer to him. He pulled out a stiff piece of paper and turned it around. They all gasped. There was Callie, Ben, and little Katie right before their eyes.

"Let me see my great-granddaughter closer, son." Beulah hobbled over to the photograph and took it gently in her hands. She walked over to the front door where the light was better. "Oh, my, she's absolutely beautiful. Looks just like Callie, except for the dark hair. Look at those eyes and that sweet mouth. Oh, my, what a wonderful gift. Look, Sallie."

Mammy Sallie waddled over to the photograph. "Hol' it back some so's I's can sees it, Miz Beulah. You knows my eyes ain't that good no more up close." Beulah did as instructed. "Oh, you's right, Miz

Beulah! Look what our Miz Callie has! Nebber seen such a pritty lil baby gal, 'cepts maybe Miz Callie. Looks jes' like her mama an' Miz Hannah, too. My oh my. Nebber thoughts I's see this day." Mammy Sallie looked at the photograph, her eyes wet. "Miz Callie lookin' mighty fine, too. Mista Ben givin' her a good life. I's knows it. He a good man. He lookin' pritty good, too. Goodness. Ain't this sum'thin', Miz Beulah? We seein' Miz Callie an' her family right here an' they far, far away. My, I's miss my lil gal. Hope I's gits to sees her agin."

"Of course you will, Mammy Sallie. I expect they will come sometime next year. Callie said so when we were there. Now, let me look closely at my little granddaughter." Kathleen took the photograph and Nathan joined her. "Precious, just precious. She's really changed since we were there, hasn't she? Still looks like Callie, though. What a wonderful Christmas present."

* * *

Callie and Ben spent Katie's first Christmas quietly in their home. Ben chopped down a smaller tree this year - one that would fit in the parlor. They put it in the middle of the room, now that the new settee took up the empty space on the wall.

Katie would stare at the tree and then laugh out loud. Callie and Ben were perplexed, but decided she liked it.

The family was sitting on their new settee admiring the tree and gazing at the burning logs in the fireplace when Callie glanced out the window. "Look, Ben, look! It's snowing!"

They carried their daughter to the window and the little family watched the enormous white snowflakes float gently to the ground.

"It's a Christmas snow, Callie. A very special snow. For our very special family." Ben put his arms around his wife and child, while Callie leaned against his chest.

"We are very lucky, Ben. I love you and Katie so much. I love my life with you. It's been a wonderful year and I think the next one will be even better." She turned her head and Ben's lips found hers.

CHAPTER 8
1873

Change was coming to Clayton Township. With the advent of the Chicago, Pekin and Southwestern Railroad, more traffic was coming through the township. It was soon realized this would be a good place for businesses to develop.

On February 20, 1873, on property owned by John Weast, thirty-eight acres were laid out on the west side of the railroad tracks by the county surveyor. A town was born.

Soon businesses started popping up in the new village. The first store, carrying a stock of general merchandise, was opened, and before long so was a drug store. Another building erected on a corner was also a general store.

The post office was in the office connected with the drugstore. A hotel was even established when the owner moved a house from Greene Township into the town. Dr. Slemmons moved his office from Minonk to the new town. The Schmidt Brothers flour mill was still grinding wheat. Soon more businesses joined the others: a lumber yard, hardware store, millinery shop, jewelry store, agriculture implements store, harness shop, and a wagon maker. Also, the Catholic congregation in the area built a new church, St. John the Evangelist.

The township had been settled almost twenty years ago so some farmhouses were now not far from the new town, including the Chapmans, both Henry and Ben. Callie could easily ride Georgia into the newly created village for supplies.

"Ben, what is going to be the name of our new town?" Callie asked as she was preparing breakfast for Ben one early March day.

"Talk is it will be called Benson, after S.H. Benson, the general freight agent."

"Hmmm….Benson. Sounds kind of nice, I guess. It's an honor to Mr. Benson, that's for sure. Benson…..Benson, Illinois. It has a nice ring to it. Now I can tell people I live near Benson in Clayton Township in Woodford County, Illinois. Sounds impressive, doesn't it?" Callie grinned as she finished her coffee.

Ben grinned too. "Think you're bein' highfalootin' now, Mrs. Chapman."

"Highfalootin'? What's that?" Callie smiled. "Is that good or bad?"

"In your case, it's good. Everythin' is good with you, my sweet Callie. Everythin'" Ben stood up and bent over to kiss his wife. "Too bad I've got to go do chores, but gotta earn a livin' and keep food on the table for you and Katie."

"That's right, Mr. Chapman, but when Katie takes her nap after lunch, you might want to stay for a bit and 'rest.'" Callie coquettishly lowered her eyes and began batting her eyelashes.

Ben laughed, startling Katie in her high chair. "There you go, battin' those eyes of yours, but, yes, I think I could use a 'rest' after lunch. See you then, my love." Ben put on his coat and hat and went out the door. Callie sighed deeply. "Your papa is an amazing man, Katie dear….amazing." Katie smiled and babbled, "Dadadadada." Callie chuckled.

* * *

Dear Callie,

I'M ENGAGED TO BE MARRIED!!! I'm so excited, I couldn't wait any longer to write and tell you. Daniel proposed last night. It was so romantic. He took me to Forsyth for a picnic in the late afternoon and then just as the sun was setting and we were packing to go, he took my hands and got down on one knee and asked me to marry him! Well, he said a lot of other personal things too, but now I'm going to be his wife! Can you believe that? I was beginning to think I would be an old maid until Daniel came back into my life.

I know you fancied him at one time and I don't know what happened - probably Ben - but I'm very glad you were no longer interested. He's really grown up since then, Callie. Has his law degree now and is setting up an office with Joseph Smythe, Fannie's brother. So, I will be a lawyer's wife. I'm just so happy I could fly! Oh, I almost forgot. He gave me his grandmother's ring. It's a HUGE pearl surrounded by tiny diamonds and rubies. It's so beautiful. I just keep staring at it.

We have talked to Mother and Father about the wedding and all decided November would be best. I know it's a tradition in the South for brides to marry in April, but November just works out best for all of us. We really don't want to wait another whole year.

Callie, I really, really want you to be my bridesmaid. PLEASE say yes!! It would give you a good excuse to come home. Besides, we haven't seen you or Ben since your wedding and goodness, we haven't seen little Katie at all! Let me see, how old will she be then? Maybe she could be one of my flower girls. Let me know. But back to you - please, please say yes and be in my wedding. I so want you to be there.

Mother and I are planning a trip to New York City to purchase my gown and trousseau. I want a gown that is MEMORABLE! (and expensive!!) Father said whatever makes me happy. The railroad has been very good to us!!!!

I'll write later and tell you the exact date in November - we haven't talked to the minister yet about the church. I just want you, Ben, and Katie to come so badly. I want to make sure you have plenty of time to plan your trip.

Much love to your family. I can't wait to meet my new cousin. Write back soon to tell me you will be in the wedding.

Happily,
Victoria
March 18, 1873

Callie sat with Victoria's letter in her hand grinning from ear to ear. Poor Daniel! He doesn't know what he's getting into with Victoria. Well, maybe he does, and that makes him happy. She hoped so. She really wanted Victoria to have a happy life, like she did.

Now, she just had to convince Ben that they needed to go to Oak Hill and Savannah in the fall to attend the wedding. It shouldn't be too hard. He knew she needed to go there to see Sam, Grandma, and Mammy Sallie. They all needed to see Katie too. Ben would completely understand.

* * *

The blizzards that plagued the northern Midwestern states that winter eluded central Illinois. In fact, the farmers were concerned there hadn't been enough moisture to replenish the soil. However, the months of March and April more than made up for the lack of snow, as almost daily rains saturated the ground.

Even Callie felt depressed by the constant rains and clouds. Katie was cranky too, but then, she was cutting her molars, which made her fussier than usual. Even Patch wouldn't go outside until he absolutely had to.

April 23rd happened to be one of those rainy, dark, gloomy days. On the morning of her twentieth birthday and second anniversary, Callie rose early and started her morning chores, as usual. Ben was also up working already. Katie was fussing in her crib, waiting to be changed and fed.

Callie came back into the house after collecting the eggs just as Ben arrived from feeding the livestock. They both were soaking wet and muddy, Katie was crying in her crib demanding attention.

Callie quickly shed her coat and took off her muddy shoes, Ben did the same. They toweled off near the fireplace, welcoming the heat from the fire. Then they both glanced up at the same time seeing the framed photograph of their wedding hanging above the mantel. They looked back at one another and both immediately broke into laughter, causing their daughter in the next room to stop crying.

Then Ben grabbed Callie, wet clothes and all, and held her close in a tight hug. She laid her head against his chest, smiling. He loosened his grip and she turned her head upward. Ben slowly and passionately kissed his wife. They stood there lost in the kiss for several minutes, before Katie once again let her parents know she was hungry.

"Happy birthday, Mrs. Chapman."

"Happy anniversary, Mr. Chapman."

"Remember last year when I said we'd have a little one to help us celebrate? Well, I think she wants to join us."

Callie laughed, "No, she wants out of her bed and something to eat. I guess we'll have to postpone our 'celebrating' for later. Right now I have to go fix breakfast."

"Oh, no you don't. It's your birthday. Today I'm makin' breakfast. You know I'm pretty good at fried eggs, sausage, and potatoes. You go tend to Katie and get out of those wet clothes and I'll have food on the table in no time. Scoot!"

Callie looked at Ben with her dark brown eyes filled with love. "Ben, you are too good to me, but I love it!" She quickly kissed him again and went into Katie's room.

* * *

There was no real celebration for the young family this year. The road between their farm and Henry and Abigail's was mired in mud and almost impassable. Besides, the rain was still coming down. So, Callie and Ben spent a quiet day in their little house with their baby daughter just enjoying one another and their life.

* * *

The rains finally gave way to sunshine around the second week of May. The farmers were fretting about being behind in their planting. It would take at least two weeks for the fields to dry out. Such a late planting time would make a big difference in the crops - a short growing season was not desirable.

Henry and Ben had all their equipment ready so they could immediately get into the fields the first day the ground would let them. In the meantime, they spent their time caring for the livestock and doing other chores.

In all this tension, Katie started walking. She had been walking around the chairs and tables and holding onto Callie's finger, but she still hadn't ventured off on her own.

One morning while Callie was making cornbread, she gave Katie two pan lids to bang together. When she bent over to put the cornbread in the oven, she noticed the banging had stopped. Turning to see what had happened, she saw Katie standing almost beside her, holding the lids for balance with a look of accomplishment in her eyes and smiling broadly. "Mamamama" she jabbered.

"Oh, Katie, look at you! You're walking all be yourself!"

Suddenly aware that she was standing alone, Katie's smile vanished and she plopped back down on the floor and raised her arms up towards Callie. "Mamamama."

Callie chuckled. "Oh, you little sweetie pie. You can get up by yourself now. You do it. Go on. Stand up for Mama."

Katie smiled again and crawled over to the chair where she pulled herself up and then let go, toddling over to Callie with her arms outstretched. When she reached her mother, Callie lifted her up, hugging her. "Oh, my big girl! So brave! Look at you! You're a big girl now. And not even a year old yet. Wait until Papa sees you. He will be so proud."

Callie covered her chubby cheeks with kisses and then hugged her some more. Katie grunted and pointed towards the floor. Callie put her down by the chair and she once again took off walking, toddling and gurgling all around the kitchen.

* * *

By the time of Katie's first birthday, the farmers were still in the fields, desperately trying to get their crops in the ground before the rains came again. Henry and Ben even took lanterns and worked in the dark. Everyone was bone tired and not in the mood for any celebrating. Their life blood had to be planted to ensure feed for the livestock and cash for themselves. Callie, Emma, and Abigail were busy also planting the big vegetable gardens that would feed their families through the winter.

But in all this frenzy, Katie was not forgotten. Callie and Ben decided to wait until the planting was finished and then host a birthday party to celebrate Katie's first year and the end of the planting season. After all, Katie didn't realize her birthday was on June 7th.

* * *

Dear Miss Callie,

I is going to has anoder baby! Caleb and me is so happy. I hope this time it a boy for Caleb. Lenora say maybe in October the baby wil be born. I feels good, jus git tired. Libby real good. Talking all the time now. Always ask why. Wants to no everything.

I hears from Masta Nathan you coming to Oak Hill for Miss Victora weding in Novimber. I can't wait! You will git to see my new baby and I will git to see how much Miss Katie has growed. He said you staying until Christmas so we will has much time togeder, I hope.

Imagin Miss Victora wil has a reel fancy weding. But it won be as nice as yours and mine. I thinks bout that when I go to Oak Hill and see the front poch and the big oak tree. Happy, happy days. Now we both mamas! You and Mista Ben thinking bout hasing anoder baby? Hope so. My lil boy need someone to play wit. Libby has Miss Katie.

Well, Miss Callie, Libby pulling on my skirt telling me she hungry so gess I best stop riting and take care of her. You be good and tell Miss Katie I loves her. Loves you too.

Trudy

Callie jumped up from the table, the letter still in her hand and ran out on the porch to find Ben. He was just coming in from the barn.

"Ben! Ben! Trudy is having another baby and it will be born in October so I will get to see it when we go back home."

"Whoa, Callie, slow down. I didn't catch any of that. What about Trudy?"

"She's having another baby in October, so I will get to see it when we go back home for the wedding."

"Well, good for her. Does Caleb want a boy this time?"

"She said she thought he did. Is that important to you husbands?

Ben shook his head. "Not that I wouldn't like to have a son, because I would, but I'll take as many daughters as you can give me if they are like our Katie."

"Oh, Benjamin, you are something else! How did I get so lucky to marry you?"

"Don't know, just fate, I guess. Awful glad it happened though." Ben took Callie in his arms and hugged her.

Callie returned the hug and then looked Ben in the eyes. "We do want another baby, don't we? I know Marie told me I wouldn't get pregnant as long as I was nursing Katie. Maybe I should stop so we can have another child."

"Yes, we want another child. But don't stop doin' what's good for Katie. She's only a year old. She eats other food, but your milk must be makin' her as healthy as she is. You'll know when it's time to stop." He picked Callie up and swung her around and then put her back down on her feet.

She laughed, gasping. "What was that about?"

"I'm just so happy with my two girls! Got the crops in, livestock is good, weather is finally good, got the new town....life is so good, Callie!" He picked her up again and swung her around, both of them laughing.

* * *

The corn was finally a little over a foot high by the Fourth of July, not nearly close to being "knee high," but the farmers weren't too worried. The hot, humid days of July and August could make the corn grow right before their eyes. The oat and wheat crops looked good too, considering their late planting.

The town of Benson decided to hold a Fourth of July celebration on the new Front Street. The wives of the township worked for days frying chickens, baking pies and cakes, emptying their shelves of pickles, relishes, beets, and other canned goods. Men put boards on sawhorses in the street where all the food was placed and then shared with everyone.

There were games for the young children, and older adults amused themselves with checkers and card games. There was plenty of beer, brewed by the German families, to be enjoyed by the men. Some of the young boys had acquired fireworks and were setting them off trying to scare the young girls.

Callie noticed that Emma and Eugene Miller were spending the day together, talking and laughing. She smiled to herself. Eugene was a fine man. He would be a good catch for Emma. But they both were so shy! She chuckled to herself. No one could say that about her and Ben.

She sought her husband in the crowd now. He was with a group of young farmers talking by the beer table. She was with some of those farmers' wives sitting outside the general store. Abigail had Katie in her lap.

Callie tensed. Josie Miller was walking toward her, her hips swaying, but she directed all her attention to Abigail, completely ignoring Callie. "Why, Mrs. Chapman. How are you today? Isn't this just a wonderful day? My oh my, is this Benjamin's daughter? What a cutie! Looks just like her papa."

Abigail cleared her throat, "Well, actually, we all think she looks just like Callie, except for the hair color, of course. But, yes, we think she's the prettiest granddaughter anyone could have."

Josie hadn't yet acknowledged Callie. "Well, I think she looks like her papa. Probably has his disposition too. She's just so precious!"

Callie had had enough. She said very sweetly, as she reached over and picked Katie out of Abigail's lap, "Yes, she is very precious. Ben and I are so grateful to have her in our lives. But, then, she is just the first of all the children we will have *together.* Won't be much longer before you have some brothers and sisters, will it, Katie?" Callie looked up at Josie. "Ben and I are very very happy, Miss Miller. Now, if you'll excuse me, I think I'll go find him. It's getting time for us to go home to *our* house."

Callie stood up and glared at Josie, then turned and walked toward Ben. Josie muttered something under her breath and went the opposite direction. Abigail and the other women burst into giggles.

* * *

The sultry, muggy weather of July did indeed make the corn grow. Some said they could "hear" it growing in the fields. Ben and Henry were very pleased at how the crops were coming along after such a late start.

The humidity did nothing for Callie's spirits. She hated it. She felt like she had to gulp to get any air into her lungs, it was so oppressive. Even happy little Katie became cranky and fussy. There were days when Callie dressed her only in a diaper, wishing she, too, could wear less clothing.

The gnats, flies, and mosquitoes were vicious, biting the minute one stepped outdoors. All the windows inside the little house had to be closed to prevent the insects from invading, thus making it unbearably hot. At night, Ben strung netting over their bed and Katie's crib to keep the bugs out so they could open the windows and air out the house.

All this dampness resulted in several strong thunderstorms with streaking lightning, followed by roaring thunder. They were brief, but the rain offered no respite, only making it wetter and more humid.

One afternoon the bright sunny sky began to cloud. Callie was gathering the clothes off the clothesline, muttering that they were once again damp even though they were in the sun. She glanced up when she realized the sun was gone.

Huge dark clouds were scurrying across the sky looking very ominous. She sighed. Another storm. She waited for the lightning followed by the thunder. It would probably wake Katie from her nap. Ben was cultivating the corn in the northeast quarter. He would be stuck in the mud if there was a downpour.

She picked up her clothes basket walking back towards the house, looking over her shoulder at the sky. For some reason, she shivered. She had an eerie feeling.

Once in the house, she laid the damp clothes on the bed, checked on Katie, and then went back on the porch. She was surprised by the sudden drop in temperature. Again she looked at the dark, gloomy clouds rushing by. Why no lightning, thunder, or rain yet? It certainly looked like it could. She sat down on the porch, anxious, unsettled.....watching.

Suddenly, there was a gust of wind causing Patch to come running from the side of the house. Callie stood up. Another blast and Patch was at the front door scratching to go in. She looked up. It was darker now, and getting darker. She could barely see the barn.

The wind was tugging at the loose bun at the nape of her neck, whipping her long hair across her face. She had to struggle to stand up as she made her way to the door. The force of the wind made opening the door an effort, but she succeeded and was now in the kitchen. Patch was pacing back and forth between the kitchen and the parlor, whining. The hair on the back of his neck was standing straight up.

Callie realized this was not going to be a normal thunderstorm. Ben had told her about the tornadoes that could happen on the prairie and she wondered if this was one of them.

She moved quickly, picking up a still sleeping Katie, wrapped her in a sheet, yelled at Patch to follow her. She started to the door to make a dash to the storm cellar Ben had dug about sixty feet from the north side of the house. It was too late.

When she went to open the door, a blast of air slammed it shut, and then chaos ensued. Chunks of ice were falling from the sky. She heard the window glass in the parlor shatter, saw divots made in the porch floor. Pieces of ice hit the fireplace hearth after hurtling down the chimney, bouncing onto the parlor floor. She could hear the roof being pelted.

Katie screamed. No that was her own voice. Katie was crying. Patch was howling. They stood there in the kitchen surrounded by the din of the storm. It was as if the world was crashing around them, rattling the house, trying to knock it down. Callie's ears popped with the pressure. She remembered back to the twister at Oak Hill when Mammy Sallie and Beulah had pushed the children under the furniture.

Holding Katie, she ducked under the kitchen table and yelled at Patch. He came instantly. They sat there for what seemed like hours, but was only a few minutes and watched as the rain and hail, along with other debris, blew into the parlor, knocking over the chairs. The wedding photograph above the mantle began to sway. "No!" screamed Callie. She put Katie on the floor and ran to the photograph, taking it down and bringing it to safety under the table.

Tears were streaming down her face as she picked up Katie, holding her tight and trying to calm her down. She had to keep her safe.

Miraculously, the roof held. The hail had stopped, now the rain started. A downpour. She couldn't even see out the kitchen window, but she could see the rain running into the parlor through the broken window. Again she put Katie down under the table and ran to pull the settee and chairs toward the kitchen away from the water. She grabbed the other photographs on the mantle before the rain ruined them. In fact, in only a few minutes, she had moved the parlor into the kitchen.

By this time the wind had finally died down. Then the rain lessened. Finally, it was just the sound of a gentle rain falling. And, then that too was gone, and the sun broke out from the clouds.

Callie was afraid to leave the shelter of the table, but when the sun was streaking through the broken window, she came out. She uttered cries of anguish as she surveyed the damage done to the little parlor.

Even though she had managed to move the furniture away from the window, it was still wet in places. The china teapot had blown off the mantle and lay broken on the floor. The figurine fell, too, its head broken off. The fern was lying on the floor, dirt everywhere, coupled with all the debris that had blown in. Leaves and grass were plastered on the wall and floor. The flooring would be ruined, the rugs soaked and dirty.

She went into the bedrooms to see if any damage was done there. They were fine, as the storm came from the west, damaging that side of the house.

She clung to Katie, and Patch was right at her heels when she went out to check the outbuildings. The porch floor and walls were pitted where the hail had struck and were covered with debris.

The chicken coop was minus its roof and the chickens were running around in circles. The west side of the barn was pitted and many shingles on the roof were missing. The necessary was tipped over on its side. The hogs had taken shelter in the barn, so the livestock seemed all right, only skittish. Everywhere were leaves, limbs, twigs, and dirt.

Callie went to her vegetable garden and gasped. There was no longer anything there. The hail had stripped all the plants, shredding the leaves. Only the root crops would survive.

"Oh, Katie, what will we do? Where's your Papa? He must have been caught in the storm unless it weakened before it got to him. I hope so! What would he do if he was caught out in the open in that hail?"

"Dadadada?" Katie looked at her mother and then smiled. "Dadadada." She turned her head and searched for Ben.

"No, sweetie, no Dada yet. We'll just have to wait for him to show up. He surely was safe. He has to be safe." Callie sighed heavily and again surveyed all around her. "Well, I guess I'd better get to work. Let's go back in the house, Katie, and see if we can fix things."

* * *

The mantel clock had somehow survived. Callie watched it now as the minutes turned into hours and still no sign of Ben. The sun was starting to set as she went to the front porch for the upteenth time, staring down the lane wishing Ben to appear.

This time she was rewarded. She saw a shadowy figure walking far down the lane. "Ben! Ben! Is that you?" she yelled as loud as she could while she ran towards the figure. There was no answer. She slowed down. Maybe it wasn't Ben after all.

As a cloud left the setting sun and the lane brightened a bit, she saw that indeed it was her husband. She ran faster towards him finally catching up, but stopping dead in her tracks when she reached him. It was if she was looking at a ghost. Ben didn't look at her, but past her. His face streaked with dirt, his hands trembling.

"It's gone, Callie. It's all gone." He still stared off into the sky.

"What's gone, Ben? What's wrong with you?"

Ben finally turned to her, his eyes tearing as he spoke. "The crops. The crops are gone. No crops. The hail stripped them."

"Everything?"

"Almost forty acres. Gone."

"What about Henry's?"

"Pa still has some standin', but not much."

Callie looked around. "Where's Clayton and Georgia?"

"Don't know. They took off. Thought they might be here."

"No, not yet." Callie reached up and put her arms around Ben's neck. "We'll be all right, Ben. We'll manage. Can't you replant?"

"Maybe. Oats. Wheat. Not corn." He shook his head and his body jerked.

"Callie! Did the hail hit here?"

She nodded her head. "Yes, but Katie and I are fine. We went under the table. The west parlor window broke. I've been cleaning up the mess in there. The chicken coop roof is gone, the necessary blown over, and some damage to the barn. Nothing that can't be fixed."

"Good." They stood in silence. Behind them, they heard the beating of hooves. Here came Georgia and Clayton trotting down the lane. They were covered with leaves and dirt. Ben sighed heavily then turned toward the horses. "You get Georgia, Callie, and let's get them back to the barn and cleaned up."

324 Kathy Meismer Darding

The couple led the horses towards the barn, now barely visible in the fading light. A few stars popped out in the now darkening skies, twinkling at them, mocking them, as if to say, "See how fickle the prairie can be?"

* * *

The land that lay in the path of the "Hail Storm of '73" in Clayton Township never really recovered that summer. Some replanted oats and wheat. The vegetable gardens were replanted with fall crops: turnips, beets, lettuce, onions, radishes, beans, cabbage, carrots, peas, pumpkins, and squash, but the yield was sparse.

Callie witnessed first hand what havoc a summer storm could wreck on people's lives and the consequences of it. No corn crop meant no feed for the livestock and no grain for sale. Late oats and wheat meant very little flour for use and none for sale. When the farmers counted their pennies, the new businesses in the little town suffered and so did their families.

Luckily, the hailstorm had not affected the entire township, so neighbor helped neighbor to recover. Henry and Abigail had less acreage affected so they helped Ben and Callie as much as they could.

Adding to the uncertainty were events occurring in the nation. In late September Jay Cooke and Company, an investment bank that was the principal backer of the Northern Pacific Railroad, started another transcontinental line and went bankrupt. The New York Stock Exchange closed for ten days and all credit dried up. The Panic of 1873 had begun.

It really started with the Chicago fire in 1871, the equine flu epidemic in 1872, and the demonetization of silver in early 1873. Railroad companies had been popping up at a high rate, glutting the market with more than 364 by 1873, too many for creditors. After the financial collapse of Cooke and Company, 89 of the railroads also declared bankruptcy. Nathan and John's Georgia Central did not.

Many farmers who relied on credit from banks lost their land, unable to make payments. The Chapmans, Henry, Abigail, Ben, and Callie did not. They had been settled there long enough to own their land out right. But that didn't mean the families weren't affected.

Farm prices fell to new lows, meaning the farms became more self-sufficient than ever. Whatever livestock or grain that was sent to market made very little profit. Sometimes, it was better to keep it for themselves. Abigail and Callie made do with what they had - no new clothing, furniture, or dishes were purchased.

Callie was afraid Ben would cancel their trip to Georgia in November, but he never mentioned it. Nathan had already made all the arrangements and insisted on buying the tickets as he received a large discount, but there would still be some expense for them. Ben knew how important this trip was for her....and the Hills.

* * *

"They's comin'! They's comin'! Miz Beulah, Mammy Sallie, I's sees them turnin' into the lane!" Trudy was jumping up and down, calling to Beulah and Mammy Sallie who were waiting patiently on the porch swing for the arrival of the Chapmans. Nathan and Kathleen had left early this morning to pick them up at the station in Swainsboro.

By the time the two elderly women rose and walked to the top step of the veranda, the carriage had stopped and the door opened.

"Grandma! Mammy Sallie! Trudy!" Callie came running out of the carriage and up the top step, her arms opened wide. She embraced all three women, who were now all crying with joy. She broke the hug and then turned to each of them for an individual hugging.

"Let me look at you, Callie." Beulah held her at arm's length and looked her up and down. "Yes, I'd say married life and motherhood definitely agree with you. I've never seen you so radiant."

"My's turn." Mammy Sallie made her turn around. "Uh huh....mmm...you shore lookin' good, gal. I's knows Mista Ben takes good cares of you. You lookin' mighty fine. Now where's that lil baby gal? Where's our Katie Chapman?"

"Here she is." Kathleen had hold of Katie's small hand and they were walking slowly to the steps. Katie was watching Callie.

"It's all right, Katie. Mama's right here."

Kathleen and Katie walked up the steps to where the three women stood.

"Grandma, may I introduce you to Kathleen Abigail Caludy

Chapman, your great-granddaughter."

Tears streamed down Beulah's wrinkled cheeks. "Oh, my, Callie. She's precious. So like you." Beulah bent over to touch Katie's cheek. Katie looked at her with her big brown eyes and smiled.

Kathleen picked her up so Beulah could see her better. Katie took her little hand and reached out to touch Beulah's gray hair, then she laughed. "Oh, I could just eat her up!" Beulah took hold of that little hand and kissed it. Katie gurgled gleefully.

"I think she likes you, Grandma."

"Yes, I think she does. Oh, if only Preston were here to see her. Another generation. He would be so proud, so proud and happy…as I am. Thank you, Callie, for bringing her. You just made an old woman very happy."

"Lez me see that gal, Miz Callie." Mammy Sallie crept closer to Kathleen and Katie. Katie suddenly was very serious. She looked at Mammy Sallie for several minutes. Then she started laughing and reaching out to her.

"Guess she decides I's not so bad!" Mammy chuckled. "You's a good gal, Miz Katie, jes' like your Mama. Looks like your Mama, too, 'cept she had them light blonde curls. Miz Callie, you an' Mista Ben done good…..real good. Makes this ole mammy happy to sees your chile. Nebber thought I's would. Thank the Lawd for this day when I's sees your chile." Mammy Sallie took the end of her apron to wipe her tears away. "Yessum, thanks the Lawd for this day."

"Amen, Sallie."

"Why don't you two go sit down on the swing and I'll put Katie between you. You can entertain her while I catch up with Trudy. Callie looked around. "Where is Libby and baby Freeman, Trudy?"

"Libby nappin' at the cabin. Caleb goin' brings her when she wake up. Freeman sleepin' inside in the parlor in your ole cradle. Miz Kathleen had ole Joseph an' Caleb fix it up for me so's I's can bring him heres. He so sweet, Miz Callie. Such a good boy. Hardly nebber cries."

"Should we all go inside, or is everybody happy out here on the porch?" Kathleen looked around her. "It is a beautiful day for

November. Oak Hill welcomes you back, Callie, with blue skies and sunshine."

Callie stood, closed her eyes, and breathed deeply. "Yes, I swear, the air does smell differently here." She looked at Ben lovingly. "I do so love Illinois, husband, but Oak Hill is.....well.....Oak Hill....is...home!"

* * *

After unloading the carriage and wagon, Nathan and Ben joined the women on the porch. "Where is my brother? Why isn't Sam here? Didn't he know what time we were coming?" Callie looked around at the now smug faces.

"Samuel will be coming soon. He has a surprise for you." Beulah glanced at Kathleen and nodded.

"A surprise? Hmmmm....he knows how I love surprises, so it must be a good one."

"Oh, it is. It's a wonderful surprise." Kathleen grinned.

"Don't tease me like that, Mama. Just tell me!"

"No, Samuel left instructions that we were not to tell you, no matter how hard you tried to find out. Oh, here comes Trudy with baby Freeman."

Trudy came across the porch, holding a small bundle in her arms.

"Oh, Trudy, he's so tiny! I forget how small Katie was. May I hold him, please?"

"Heres Miz Callie. I's jes fed him so he should be happy."

Callie took Freeman in her arms. "Look, Katie, see the baby?"

Katie grabbed one of Freeman's tiny hands in her own. "Baaab," she said as she smiled at Callie.

"Yes, that's right. Baby."

Katie looked very proud of herself as she said again, "Baaab."

"Trudy, I think Freeman resembles Caleb more than you, don't you think?"

"That's what eve'ybody says, Miz Callie. But my Libby looks like her mama. Cain't wait for her to gits here. You be s'prised see how much she growed. Jes like I's s'prised to see Miz Katie so big. Can I's holds you, Miz Katie?"

Trudy held out her arms and Katie went right to her and sat on her lap. "I's thinks she 'members me from her birthin'." Trudy and Callie laughed.

As they were reminiscing about Katie's birth, a buggy turned into the lane, stirring the red dust. Soon the roan horse stopped at the hitching post and the passengers got out.

"Sam! Sam!" Callie cried from her chair. She immediately gave Freeman to Kathleen and ran down the steps to greet her brother. It had been over two years since she last saw him. She almost knocked Samuel over in her excitement.

"Whoa, little sister!" Samuel held her at arm's length. They both had brilliant smiles on their faces as they laughed and then hugged one another.

"It's just so good to see your face and hear your voice again, Sam. It's been too long."

"I agree. I...we will have to make a visit to Illinois to see you. I need to check out the town you write me about."

By this time Callie finally noticed Lizzy Montgomery standing behind Samuel patiently. "Lizzy, I'm so sorry. I was so excited about seeing Sam that I didn't see you. How are you? I'm glad you came to welcome us back."

"I'm fine, Callie. In fact, I'm better than fine, thanks to your brother."

Callie looked to Samuel and raised her eyebrows. "Does this have something to do with the surprise I've been told about?"

Samuel suddenly became tongue-tied and blushed. "Yes....yes...it does." He took Lizzy's hand. "Lizzy and I are going to be married on Christmas Eve. We waited until you would be here to celebrate with us."

Callie's hands flew to her face as her eyes widened. "Oh, Sam... Lizzy....I'm *so* happy for you!" She hugged them both. "Ben, Ben! Come here! Sam and Lizzy are going to be married while we're here! Isn't that wonderful?"

Ben came down the steps. "Congratulations, Samuel...Lizzy. I only hope you will be as happy as Callie and me." He shook Samuel's hand and gave Lizzy a peck on her cheek.

"Do you have a ring, Lizzy? Or is my brother too cheap?"

"Callie! Of course, I got her a ring."

Lizzy held out her left hand and there was a large pearl surrounded by tiny blue stones on a gold band. "Isn't it beautiful, Callie? I told Samuel it was too pretty for me, but…he….said I was worth it." Lizzy lowered her eyes, looking at the ground.

"It is just right for you, Lizzy. Sam, you make me proud. I'm so happy for you!!!"

Callie once again hugged her brother and his fiancée. "Now, I have someone I want you to meet….your niece. I've been telling her stories of her Uncle Sam and she's very anxious to see you. Oh, now she will have an Aunt Lizzy! Wonderful! Come, come and meet Katie."

* * *

The carriage and wagon were once again pulling up to the familiar red brick Georgian style mansion in Savannah. There was a bit of a chill in the November air, but the sun was shining and the sky was clear of clouds.

Laughter spilled out of the carriage as the occupants began one by one to leave the carriage via the mounting step. The huge front door swung open and the home's mistress came out to greet her guests.

"Aunt Caroline! I'm so happy to see you! It's been too long. Oh, my goodness, you never change." Callie embraced Caroline, noticing several strands of gray hair now amongst the black ones. She also saw the extra wrinkles around Caroline's bright eyes. But those almost black eyes still danced and sparkled as they always did.

"Look at you, Callie Chapman! My, motherhood has made you even more beautiful."

"That's just my happiness showing, Aunt Caroline. Please, come meet our little angel."

Ben walked up holding Katie. "Here she is, here's our Katie."

Caroline beamed. "Callie, Ben, she's absolutely adorable." Katie hid her face on her father's shoulder. She just had gotten used to the strangers at Oak Hill and now she was faced with more.

"She's a little shy, Aunt Caroline. Lots of strange faces. She'll make up to you after a while."

"I know, dear. Susan's twins were the same way at that age. Well, all of you, come on in. I'm sorry Beulah couldn't make it, Nathan, but I completely understand."

"Yes, Mother was very disappointed, but it's just too much for her anymore."

"Samuel! Samuel! Oh, my goodness, it's good to see you!"

"Hello, Aunt Caroline, it's good to be here too! I have so many pleasant memories of being here in Savannah. I'm anxious to show Lizzy around the city. Oh, where are my manners? Aunt Caroline, this is my fiancee, Miss Lizzy Montgomery. Lizzy, Caroline Whitson."

"Lizzy, I'm so happy to meet you. I think I remember you from Callie's wedding. You were there, weren't you?"

"Yes, Ma'am, I was."

Caroline leaned into Lizzy's ear and whispered, "You are a very lucky lady to be marrying Samuel, you know. He's very special to us since he lived with us all those years while he was going to school. It looks like you've made him very happy."

Lizzy blushed. "Thank you Mrs. Whitson."

"Caroline, please. Mrs. Whitson sounds too old!"

"Caroline, you will never be old and you know it!"

"Kathleen! Well, I hope not. I have to stay young to keep up with my children and grandchildren."

"Me, too. Aren't grandchildren so special?"

"They certainly are. I told Nathan we'll miss Beulah. Who's watching Oak Hill?"

"Caleb and Trudy and William and Malindy. We have complete trust in them. Caleb and Trudy are staying in the house with Mammy Sallie, Beulah, and Belle. Libby and Freeman entertain the older ones."

"Much different than the 'old' days isn't it?"

"Yes, but better, I think. Well, where's John, or did I miss him?"

"No, he's still at the Exchange, but he should be home shortly. Come on in. Victoria and Daniel are due home any minute from his parents. Let's get all of you settled and then we can really catch up on all the news."

* * *

Victoria burst through the front door, dragging Daniel in behind her. "Oh no, I thought we'd get back before y'all arrived! Hello, hello, hello everyone!" She proceeded to hug everyone standing in the grand foyer, leaving Daniel to himself.

Daniel immediately went to Callie. "Callie Hill...."

"Chapman now, Daniel. It's nice to see you again."

"You have only grown in your beauty, Callie." Daniel grabbed both of Callie's hands. "I think of you often out there in the middle of nowhere - Illinois - stuck on some tiny farm, as Victoria says."

Ben moved towards his wife and possessively put his arm around her waist. Daniel dropped Callie's hands. Callie smiled. "It's not 'in the middle of nowhere,' Daniel, and I love it there. Ben and I and our daughter are very happy. Oh, Daniel, this is my husband, Benjamin Chapman. Ben, Daniel Moore, Victoria's groom."

"My pleasure, Mr. Chapman. Your wife looks radiant. You must make her very happy."

"Thank you. She does the same for me. We hope you and Victoria have a marriage as wonderful as ours."

"Callie!" Victoria came rushing up to Callie and grabbed her hand. "Come with me! I have something to show you." Victoria pulled her towards the stairs. Callie gave Ben a helpless look and followed Victoria.

They went into Victoria's room. Callie stood in the doorway surveying the lovely room. "Victoria! Where are all the rosebuds?"

Victoria laughed. "I finally pestered Mother enough that she consented to redecorating my room and now I'm moving out!"

"It's lovely, but I still like the rosebuds. I remember thinking it looked like a fairy land."

Callie entered the room and looked around her. The walls were now covered with a big floral print of gold, burgundy, and ecru glossy wallpaper. The rich satin bed covering and the plush oriental carpet picked up the same colors. The new furniture was a dark stained walnut with elaborate and intricate carvings. The room looked entirely different, but very inviting.

"I like it, Victoria. It's more....more...grown up, I guess. It suits you."

"Oh, I know. Now...look at this!"

Victoria had gone to the wardrobe and withdrew a voluminous silk gown which she now held up for Callie to see.

"Oh, my, that's lovely. I've never seen such a pretty color."

"It's violet - very regal and royal. It's your bridemaids dress."

"What? I thought we were wearing white muslin." Callie walked over and ran her fingers over the delicate silken fabric.

"No. While Mother and I were buying my gown, the bridal consultant said the newest rage in weddings was *color* for the bridemaids. That way, the bride really stands out in white and all the attention is focused on *her*. Isn't that wonderful? I can't believe no one thought of that before. Anyway, I just loved this color and style. It will make my wedding the talk of Savannah because no one has ever dared to have the color of royalty on *anything*! Oh, and Callie, wait until you see *my* dress! As pretty as this is, mine is magnificent!" Victoria laughed and then so did Callie.

"Leave it to you, Victoria, to have the latest and the best."

"Well, of course, dear. I've been planning this wedding forever. I just had to find me a groom!"

* * *

The wedding day quickly approached and the bride and her maids were ready. Victoria was correct when she said her dress was magnificent. The silk crepe white gown had a bodice with tiny pleats and pearl buttons down the front, a high neckline, adorned with Caroline's cameo brooch, bell sleeves that just reached the wrist, and an intricate skirt of water-like folds and drapes over a bustle with a full court train. Her headpiece was a coronet of wax orange blossoms, as fresh ones were not available in November. A full length cathedral tulle veil finished her ensemble.

As Callie walked down the aisle in her violet silk gown, all heads turned. The gown showed off her figure and hair, enhancing her beauty even more. Ben couldn't take his eyes off his lovely wife, thanking God that Daniel had kissed her without asking and she had found her way to him.

After the late morning ceremony, the guests left the church for the Whitsons' home where a wedding luncheon was held. It was a beautiful day, not too hot or too cold, so the reception was held outside, just as Susan's was so many years before.

Ben was amazed at all the food presented at the reception. "Your Uncle John must be more well off than I thought to put on a feast of this kind, " he whispered into Callie's ear. "Evidently, the Panic hasn't hurt him."

"Uncle John has always been a good investor and Papa said the railroad isn't his only holding. It's a good thing, too, or Victoria would have been crushed!"

They both laughed as they watched Victoria and Daniel interact with their guests. "I kind of feel sorry for Daniel," Ben said. "He has a lot to live up to." Callie nodded her head in agreement, her eyes twinkling.

It wasn't long before Victoria changed into her traveling suit and the couple departed for their honeymoon. "Are they going to the cottage at Tybee like we did?" Ben asked Callie as they waved good-bye to the couple.

"Oh, no. Victoria said she wouldn't be caught dead going to that 'shabby' place. She and Daniel are going on the Grand Tour of Europe. They will be gone for a month or more - London, Paris, Rome...."

"Well, they can't have as nice a honeymoon as we did on Tybee. In fact, I'm rememberin' it now....my wife out by the ocean...naked.... hair blowin' in the wind...."

"Benjamin!!" Callie looked at her husband with exasperation on her face and then impulsively kissed him passionately on his soft lips in front of all the guests at Victoria's wedding.

* * *

Exhausted from their activities in Savannah, the Hill and Chapman families returned to Oak Hill to rest. Callie related all the details of the wedding to Trudy who decided Victoria's wedding was "too fancy" for her tastes.

Lizzy was still in awe over the lavish production and couldn't stop talking about it. She and Samuel had done some sight-seeing on their own, as Lizzy hadn't visited Savannah since she was a child. Although she enjoyed all the hustle and bustle of the city and the wonderful sights, she, along with everyone else, was glad to be back to the slower pace of plantation life.

Callie and Lizzy were sitting on the porch swing with Katie on Callie's lap, enjoying some late November sunshine.

"Lizzy, I remember so clearly the day you rode up here to tell us the Yankees were coming. I remember Trudy and I were so frightened. Little did we know what would happen next. Who would have ever thought I would find my husband among those Yankees? Life is odd in some ways, isn't it?"

Lizzy nodded her head in agreement. "If that awful Raymond Carswell had never come to our place and then took you, I'd never found Samuel. Strange how our lives have been connected, isn't it, Callie, and we never really knew each other."

Callie reached over and squeezed Lizzy's hand. "I still can't thank you enough for saving my life that awful night." She smiled. "Now, we're going to be sisters-in-law. You'll be Katie's Aunt Lizzy. Amazing." She took a deep breath of the cool fall air. "I guess we have no control over our future, just our present. Living on the prairie has taught me that. Just when you think everything is wonderful, a blizzard, or hail storm or something else comes along and whoosh…. it's all gone."

"I heard Samuel say your crops were ruined this year from the hail. How are you and Ben doing?"

"We're fine. He replanted some of the wheat and oats and we harvested enough to feed us and the livestock. Henry had some corn that survived so he's shared with us. I replanted my garden with fall vegetables and between mine and Abigail's we had enough to put up for the winter. I think we'll be all right, but it was a setback, that's for sure. The people in the township are wonderful. If someone has extra, they share."

"Sounds like a friendly place." Lizzy paused and seemed to

struggle with herself. "I haven't said anything to anybody 'bout this, Callie, but I'm scared 'bout going to Atlanta with Samuel and being the wife of a state senator. I'm not sure if I know what to do. I know we'll be going to dances and balls and dinners and I've never done anything like that." She looked down at her hands, twisting them. "I sure don't want him to be embarrassed and have people say he really 'married down' from his first wife."

Callie turned to face Lizzy, who now had tears rolling down her cheeks. "Lizzy…Lizzy…look at me." Lizzy forced her head up and looked into Callie's brown eyes, brimming with kindness. "Lizzy, Samuel loves you, that's very obvious. He's not marrying you because he needs a wife to adorn his arm to impress the folks in Atlanta. He loves *you*! Don't ever think of yourself as being below Laura. I knew from the start she wasn't right for Samuel and she turned out to be a witch! We are so glad he's rid of her. So get that thought right out of your pretty head."

"Now, as far as mingling with those so-called 'fancy folks' just follow Samuel's lead or watch some of the other wives. That's what I had to do in Benson. The customs there are much different than I was used to here. Just watch and learn."

"But I don't even have anything to wear to those things! I'm gonna stick out like a sore thumb."

"No you won't. Let's see…well, you can wear the dress you wore to Victoria's wedding. That was very nice. And, isn't your wedding dress one you can wear later?"

"Yes, but I don't have a *ball* gown and I don't want to ask Samuel for one 'cause I'm not sure we can afford it."

"Hmmm….." Callie's face lit up as an idea popped into her mind. "Lizzy, you can have my bridesmaid's dress! The color will be perfect on you. We're about the same size….I'm sure Dinah could alter it for you. Oh, that's perfect! I'll never have any reason to wear it again. It'll just take up extra space in my trunk. It's just the perfect solution for both of us!"

"Oh, Callie, thank you….but…I couldn't take your dress. Surely, you want to keep it. It's so beautiful."

"No, I don't want to keep it. There haven't been any balls or fancy dances in Benson since I've lived there and I doubt if there ever will be. Even if there is, the women wear better calico or poplin dresses. *I* would look out of place in a violet silk gown! So, the dress is yours, if you want it."

Lizzy's face lit up in a grateful smile. "If you're sure, then yes, I'd very much like to have it!"

Callie reached over Katie's head and hugged Lizzy. "Wonderful! Let's go try it on now!" She picked up Katie, put her on her hip and with her other hand grabbed Lizzy's and pulled her up out of the swing. "This will be fun!"

* * *

"Belle, I swear, I've tried making your pound cake, but it never tastes the same. What am I doing wrong?"

Callie was in the kitchen with Belle and Malindy, who had taken over most of the cooking duties as Belle declined with age.

"Well, Miz Callie, I's puts lots o' love in that cake. You doin' that?"

"Of course, I am, but it still lacks something. Show me again what you do."

Belle slowly got out of her chair and went to the pantry. Callie followed her as the aged cook pulled out the flour, sugar, baking powder, and salt. "Malindy, you's goes down in the cellar an' gits me six eggs an' a poun' o' butter an' some cream. We's gonna makes us a poun' cake for Miz Callie."

Belle started measuring out the dry ingredients. "Poun' o' flour, poun' o' sugar, lil powder, lil bit o' salt. Now we's sift that flour four times, Miz Callie. You do's that?"

"No, I only do it twice."

"Gots to do it four times." Belle sifted the flour and then added the sugar, baking powder, and a dash of salt. Malindy came up from the cellar carrying the other ingredients.

"Now's we adds the eggs, six of 'em or a poun', an' a poun' o' butter, an' some cream."

"Oh, Belle, I always used milk, not the cream. I didn't think you used cream."

"Miz Callie, ev'ry poun' cake I's ever made for you, I's use the cream, not the milk. I's thoughts I's tol' you that." Belle frowned at Callie. "Maybe you's wasn' lissenin'."

Callie smiled. "Maybe not. Go on…show me how you mix it all together."

"Firs' makes sure you's butter is sof'. An' I's always uses a wooden spoon. Mix careful, not too much. Now we's puts it in the pan - makes sure it greased good - an' pops in the oven. It be done when the top is brown an' it don' shake. Sometimes I's sticks a knife in it an' if'n it come out clean, it be done."

Callie stood up and hugged the old cook. "Thank you, Belle, for the lesson. I'll try it when we get back, but I'm sure it will never be as good as yours. I can't wait to eat this one tonight for dessert."

* * *

After dinner was served in the dining room, Malindy brought in the freshly made pound cake for dessert. Belle had iced it with white butter cream frosting. Callie had the first piece and couldn't wait to taste it.

"Mmmmmm….this is *so* good! It tastes like heaven. I hope I can make one like it when we get back home, but I don't know. I still think Belle sneaks something special in it."

Belle, who was standing at the doorway heard her and said, "I's don' tol' you, Miz Callie, it love. I's puts love in that cake." Then she laughed and shook her head as Callie had her mouth full of the delectable cake and couldn't answer her.

Ben was savoring his piece. "This sure is good, Belle. My compliments. But Callie's is good too."

Callie looked at her husband, "Why, thank you, husband. Just don't tell them how I almost broke your teeth with my first attempts at bread and rolls."

Ben chuckled and then related the story to the others who also laughed at Callie's futile attempts at bread making. "But she's got it down pretty good now," Ben concluded. "In fact, my wife here is a darn good little cook and baker. She can make a really good apple pie - melts in your mouth and her fried chicken is better than Ma's."

"She learned that from me," said Belle. "I's showed her how's to make that fried chicken."

"Well, you did a fine job of teaching her, because it's very very good."

Callie beamed at her husband. "Thank you, Ben."

Kathleen whispered in Nathan's ear, "Isn't it wonderful how much in love they still are?"

"Just like us, dear. Just like us." Nathan reached under the table and squeezed his wife's hand.

* * *

Samuel found Callie in the back parlor with Trudy. They were playing with their girls while Freeman slept in the cradle. "Callie, let's go for a ride. I haven't had much time to spend alone with you. It's beautiful outside today - just right for an invigorating ride. Maybe we could ride to the Montgomerys and I'll show you the new mill."

Callie turned to Trudy, "Do you mind, Trudy? I can take Katie with me, if you want to do something else."

"No, no, Miz Callie. You goes wit Masta Samuel. I's watch Miz Katie so she an' Libby can keeps playin'. When it time for they's naps, I's puts her down wit Libby. You goes rides on Daisy likes you used to."

"All right then, Sam. Let me change quickly and I'll meet you in the stables."

Callie soon appeared at the doorway to the stables, searching for Samuel and Daisy. He came out of the barn leading her horse and his new jet black stallion, Beaumont. When Daisy saw Callie, she immediately whinnied and tossed her head.

"I think she remembers me."

"Of course, she does. Horses are smart. How do you like Beaumont? I just bought him a few months ago at a sale in Atlanta."

"Very handsome. Very *large*. He's a lot of horse."

Samuel laughed. "Don't worry, I can handle him just fine. Now, mount and let's go."

Daisy was a little larger than Georgia so Callie had to adjust somewhat, but soon was galloping beside Samuel. It was exhilarating to feel the wind rush through her hair and tingle her cheeks. They galloped for about a mile and then slowed down to a walk to rest the horses and talk.

"Sam, you and Lizzy *must* come to visit us in Illinois. The train ride is very pleasant now and Lizzy would enjoy it. I have so much to show you at our house. It isn't big, but we love it. And, I know Ben wants to show off the farm and Henry's equipment."

"We'll see, Callie. I'm pretty busy with Oak Hill, the mill, and the state senate."

"Samuel Preston Hill! You are never too busy to visit your sister! I know for a fact that Lizzy really wants to come and there is time. How will Katie ever get to know her aunt and uncle if she only sees them every two to three years? I won't take 'we'll see' as an answer."

Samuel looked at his hands holding the reins loosely. "Callie...I don't know...I...I...I...still feel uncomfortable about being in the North."

Callie's mouth dropped open. "What? Sam, the war has been over for... what... eight years? Eight years, Sam! Surely by now, you've come to terms with that. Besides, it's a different country now."

Samuel stopped Beaumont and Daisy too. He gazed into Callie's eyes. "I never spoke much of what happened to me in Illinois, and I don't want to now. Just take my word that it wasn't a pleasant experience. I've also never told anyone about my journey back to Oak Hill, which was through the Midwestern states. It also was not something I want to experience again. I know the war has been over for a long time, but it is still in my head and will be until I die. I know you don't understand, Callie. You have no idea what it took for me to accept Ben as your husband - a Yankee who was with Sherman's army!"

"But you have, haven't you? Ben is so wonderful, Sam. Surely, you have forgiven him?"

"Yes, but it's taken a while. I can see how happy he makes you."

"Then you need to come to our house and see the rest of the picture. It could help you get over this...this...war thing you have. The people there are so nice, Sam. They have accepted me even though I'm a

'Rebel.' You know, the North suffered too during the war. Many of Clayton Township's young men died on Southern soil doing what they thought was right too."

"I know." Samuel started walking Beaumont again. "I'll try, Callie. I'll try. That's the best I can do. Maybe marrying Lizzy will help me forget those horrible days. I'm sorry, 'we'll see' is still the best I can do....at least for now."

"Well, it's still not good enough, but I think I will be seeing you at the Chapman farm next year. I think Lizzy will make you whole again, Sam. Just let her."

Samuel nodded his head then smiled, "Race you to the gate of Pine Wood!" He spurred Beaumont and Callie did the same to Daisy.

* * *

Finally, December 24th arrived. It was a frosty day, but the sun was shining brightly against the cloudless azure sky. Everyone at Oak Hill was bustling around in preparation of Samuel and Lizzy's wedding that evening.

Christmas decorations adorned the house, especially in the front parlor where the wedding was going to be held. Pinecones, evergreen boughs, hedge apples, red velvet ribbons, and small sparkly glass ornaments covered the mantle and the Christmas tree in the corner. It looked beautiful.

Nathan and Samuel were carrying in large urns filled with blooming camilleas and placed them on either side of the fireplace.

"There, that looks nice, just like Kathleen said it would. Are you nervous son? Wedding's getting closer."

"No, Father. This time, I'm just anxious to have Lizzy as my wife." Samuel adjusted one of the flowers. "I feel so much better than when I married Laura. I should have known something wasn't quite right. But now I know *everything* is right. I love Lizzy more than anything and can't wait to start our life together, and, if we're so blessed, have children."

"You know I want a wonderful future for you and Lizzy, Samuel. I think you've found the right woman this time." Nathan grasped Samuel's arm and then gave him a hug. Samuel was surprised to see tears in his father's eyes as Nathan let go of him.

Nathan wiped his eyes with the back of his sleeve. "Sorry, son. Tears of joy, not sadness. It's so satisfying to see both of my children so happy. Overwhelms me at times."

"I understand, Father. No need to apologize. It makes me happy too."

Nathan patted Samuel on the back. "Maybe we better find Ben and go get ready. The women have been primping all day and we've done nothing." He laughed. "Can't let them outshine us, now, can we?"

"Afraid we'll lose on that one, Father. They'll *always* outshine us."

"Very true, son. Guess that's the way it's supposed to be anyway."

* * *

"Oh, Lizzy! You look so pretty!" Jenny was eyeing her sister from head to toe. "Just beautiful."

"Do you really think so, Jenny?" Lizzy was gazing at her reflection in the mirror. She saw a young woman in a stiff taffeta bronze colored dress with lace trim. The high neck had three rows of intricate ivory lace in a vee shape from each shoulder, the point ending just below the bust. The same lace adorned the sleeve cuffs. Six hand covered buttons shaped like hearts were lined up on the front of the bodice. Lizzy turned sideways to admire the back of her dress. There were flounces and heavy bronze fringe around the bottom of the skirt that flowed from the bustle.

"Oh, yes, Lizzy. Samuel will be so pround of you."

"Well, it isn't a fancy white wedding dress like Callie's or Victoria's, but I thought I should be more practical. This is something I can wear again, especially in Atlanta."

"I think it's a beautiful wedding dress, even if it's not white. The color looks so good with your eyes and hair. Oh, here comes Ma."

Almina entered the room where her two daughters were getting ready. The Hills had been so kind to let her family have rooms at Oak Hill to prepare for the wedding. Samuel and Lizzy bought Jenny and Almina their dresses when they were in Savannah at the same dress shop Lizzy got hers. Almina felt her eyes fill up with tears as she looked at her daughters. They had all been through so much since the war, but their lives were finally turning around, thanks to the Hills and especially Samuel.

"My, my. Look at my girls! Don't you two look grand!"

"You, too, Ma. We just got to put some of these flowers in Lizzy's hair, then she's all ready. Want to do it?"

"Of course." Almina took the offered camilleas and placed them in Lizzy's curls. "There…you're ready to meet your groom."

"Is everybody in here ready?" Kathleen was in the doorway. "Oh, Lizzy, you're breathtaking." She went to Lizzy and gave her a hug, careful not to muss anything. "I think we can start anytime now. The men are in the parlor waiting for us."

"Where's Callie?"

"Right here, Lizzy. I'm coming," Callie called from the hallway. "I just had to give Katie to Trudy. I'm ready."

"Is Grandpa ready to walk me down the aisle?"

"He's waiting at the bottom of the stairs, dear. Wait until he sees you! He is so happy for you." Kathleen smiled.

"All right, then, let's go get married!"

* * *

The ceremony in the parlor was short, but tender, as Samuel and Lizzy became husband and wife. Samuel thought his bride was stunning in the candlelight - her bronze dress glowed, as did her face. Both the bride and groom were calm and confident as they recited their vows, knowing their love was strong and secure. Everyone attending also sensed the strength and rightness of this marriage. Happiness was bounteous.

After enjoying a simple wedding dinner complete with Belle's pound cake, the newlyweds left to spend the night in the same cabin Ben and Callie stayed in for their wedding night. Callie suggested it, as she and Ben had such a wonderful time there.

The next day, Christmas, was anticlimactic after the wedding, but was still enjoyed by everyone. Katie was the receipient of many gifts. She was overwhelmed and chose to play with the ribbons instead, which amused the adults. Samuel and Lizzy appeared after breakfast to cheers and applause. They both looked tired, but very happy.

Callie looked around the circle of people gathered in the front parlor by the trimmed tree and sighed. She was so fortunate to be part of such a family. She reached over and grabbed Ben's hand. He looked at her wondering what was wrong, but saw the contentment on her face and smiled.

"Merry Christmas, Mrs. Chapman."

"Merry Christmas, Mr. Chapman."

Katie toddled over to her parents and laughed as she piled ribbons in Callie's lap. "'erry 'ismas, Mama. 'erry 'ismas, Dada."

They picked her up and placed her between them, nuzzling her neck. "Merry Christmas, Kathleen Abigail Caludy Chapman. Merry Christmas."

CHAPTER 9
1874

"Oh, it's so, so, *so* good to be back home!" Callie put Katie on the floor and she immediately ran for her room. Callie began snatching the dust covers off the furniture in the parlor.

Ben was watching her with a peculiar expression on his face. "Are you *sure*?"

"What was that, darling?"

"Are you sure you're glad to be back here?"

Callie looked astonished. "What on earth do you mean, Ben? Of course, I'm glad to be in our home. Why wouldn't I?"

"Well, there was certainly a lot of cryin' and sobbin' and wailin' when we left Oak Hill, especially by you."

Callie folded the dust covers and put them on the kitchen table. "Yes. I was sad to leave my family. I don't know when I'll get to see them again. And, every time I leave Grandma or Mammy Sallie, I think it could be the last time I'll *ever* see them. I miss Trudy too. I don't have any close friends like her here. But that all doesn't mean I don't love my home here."

"Hmmmpfff. Seemed like you didn't want to leave there and come back here. We were there a long time, Callie."

"Yes, yes we were. But I thought after we got there and found out Samuel and Lizzy were getting married, we would stay for the wedding. Didn't we agree, Ben?"

"Guess so. Just seemed like we've been away for quite a spell. I'll go get the rest of the trunks."

"Wait, Ben." Callie tugged at his coat sleeve. "What's really bothering you? It isn't our visit to Oak Hill. You enjoyed it too, I know you did. What's wrong?"

Ben's hands hung by his side and he looked down at the worn floor of the tiny kitchen where they were standing. He took a deep breath, avoiding Callie's eyes.

"I know I'm bein' stupid, but I can't help but feel I'm letting you down, Callie. Oak Hill is so grand and here all I can give you is this little shack, hardly big enough for one person, let alone three. No servants around to help you out. No one to watch Katie for you. No cook. I feel like I've failed. I'll never be able to give you a place like Oak Hill. And, when I see you there, all happy and such, I get to feelin' like someday you won't want to come back here with me." He looked up and met Callie's brown eyes, now squinted and filled with fury.

"Are you finished, Benjamin Chapman?" Ben nodded his head, afraid to speak any more after seeing her eyes. "Good, then it's my turn."

"First: Oak Hill is where I grew up, so it's natural for me to love it. Second: I love my family there, just like you love your family here. Third: I miss seeing my family, yes I do. I'd love to be as close to them as we are to Henry and Abigail. Fourth: not all my memories of Oak Hill are good ones, remember that. Fifth: it doesn't matter what *size* of house I live in. It matters *who* is in the house with me. Sixth: I don't need cooks or nursemaids. I'm perfectly capable of doing things myself, in fact, I prefer it. Lastly: I LOVE *you*, Ben Chapman! And Katie. And my life with you. We could be in Mexico or England and I'd still be happy if you were with me. My life is with YOU, no matter where you are. Do you understand, or is that too much for your brain to comprehend?"

Ben sheepishly grinned and put his hands in his pockets. "Guess not. Guess I just needed to hear it. Still can't believe a beautiful Southern 'belle' like you loves a lowly Yankee farmer like me."

"Well, believe it. Now get over here and kiss me, you 'lowly Yankee farmer.'"

"Happy to oblige, Ma'am."

* * *

Callie wasn't feeling well. She was tired, nauseated, and overall lethargic. At first she blamed it on something she ate. Then on the weather. Next was "female problems." Finally, she concluded what she thought all along - she was expecting a baby again. She was elated. Now, she just had to tell Ben.

She was trying to prepare supper, but kept going outside to be sick, so Ben told her to go lie down in bed, he would finish. After he and Katie ate, and he put Katie to bed, he came into their room and sat on the side of the bed.

"Callie, I think you'd better go see Doc Austman, the new doctor in Benson. There has to be some kind of medicine he can give you."

Callie smiled weakly. "I think I'd better go see Marie instead, Ben."

"Marie? Why Mar.......oh, Callie! Are you sayin'....are you.... another...?"

"Yes, Mr. Chapman. You're going to be a father again!"

"Yippeeee!"

"Shhh. You'llwake Katie!"

"Oh, Callie, love, I'm so happy! But you're feelin' so bad."

"It will pass, just like it did when I carried Katie. It's going to be a boy this time, Ben. I know it."

"Well, you were right 'bout Katie, but you know I'd like another daughter too."

"We have time to wait. I think maybe October or November. A fall baby this time."

"Can't wait to tell Ma and Pa - Emma too. You wrote your folks yet?"

"No, and we're going to wait a while to tell everyone, especially Katie. She'll expect a baby brother the next day."

"Guess I can keep a secret, but won't be long before everyone will be able to *see* our secret!"

"I know. We'll tell them before that happens. I don't want everyone to think I'm just getting fat!!"

"Oh, Callie, I love you so much! You make me so happy!"

"You know I feel the same way, Ben. Lay down here with me."

"Yes, Ma'am."

Callie laid her head on Ben's chest and was soon sound asleep. Ben watched her as she slept. She was so beautiful. He brushed a curl away from her face. He didn't know what he'd do without her. Tears threatened to run down his cheeks. He shook them away. He was so happy.

* * *

This pregnancy was different. Callie had no energy, no appetite. She was losing weight instead of gaining. It took all her efforts just to perform menial chores. But she kept Ben from having anyone help her; she still wanted to keep the baby a secret.

Emma came for a surprise visit and immediately saw something was wrong. The house was in disarray, the laundry hadn't been done, dishes were piled in the dry sink, Callie was in bed with Katie.

"Callie! Where's Ben? What's going on here?"

"Hello, Emma, I'm in here. Ben is looking at the crops. Sorry the place is such a mess, I haven't been feeling well. Katie, go see Aunt Emma."

Emma picked Katie up and gave her hugs and kisses. "Down." Katie ran into her room to get a book for Emma to read her. "Read."

"Please, Katie. Please read." Callie corrected her.

"Peez, read."

"Maybe later, Katie. I'm going to help Mama. You can help too. Let's go do some of those dishes and pick up the house, all right?"

"I good help." Katie ran into the kitchen on her chubby legs. "Come, A'nt Em, come!"

"Thank you, Emma, that will be so nice. Ben has been trying to keep up, but he doesn't always have time."

"You mean this has been going on for a while? You've been sick and haven't told us?"

"Not that long. I'm feeling better. Just tired."

"Well, I must tell you, you look awful, Callie."

"Thanks, Emma," Callie said with a wry smile. "Nice to know that."

"You know what I mean. Have you seen the doctor?"

"No, don't need too. I'll be fine. Just need some rest."

"A'nt, Em! *Come!*" Katie was standing impatiently in the doorway. "Help!"

"Coming, Katie. Callie, why don't I take Katie back with me for a few days and you can rest more? I'll clean up here and then pack her a few things. She loves it at our place and then you can recuperate."

"That would be wonderful, Emma, thank you so much." Then Callie turned over on her side and immediately was asleep.

* * *

Later that night, Callie was awakened by a stabbing pain in her abdomen. She got up and used the chamber pot, but that didn't seem to help. She laid on her side, then her back, then her other side. The pain was intensifying until it took her breath away.

"Ben! Wake up! I think something is terribly wrong!"

Ben slowly opened his eyes. Callie shook him. "Ben, I….I….I can't…." She cried out in pain. "Help me! Oh, no………."

Ben jumped out of bed. There was only light by the moon streaming into the little room, but he could see his wife's face. It was twisted in pain. Then she whimpered softly, so softly, he could barely hear her. "Get Marie. I think I'm losing the baby. Hurry!"

He jumped into his clothes and started for the door. "Ben, wait. It's too late." Ben saw the blood stained sheets under his wife. "Callie, what can I do?" She started sobbing. "I don't know. Help me."

Ben got some water out of the ewer on the washstand and a clean cloth and started washing the blood off her. Then he made her drink some water. The blood appeared again. "Callie, I have to go get help. I'm riding into Doc Austman's - he's closer than Marie."

"Hurry, please….." Callie said weakly.

Ben ran out of the house, quickly saddled up Clayton and galloped the two miles or so into town. He pulled up to the doctor's office, jumped off Clayton, and ran around to the back where the doctor lived. He pounded on the door and yelled as loud as he could. Presently, Dr. Louis Austman, a man of about forty, opened the door cautiously. He was dressed in his nightshirt, carrying a lit hurricane lamp.

By now Ben was out of breath. "Hurry, Doc. Callie is in trouble….. she thinks she's losin' our baby."

"Let me get dressed and get my bag. You go saddle up my horse and I'll meet you in front."

The two of them left the little town just before dawn racing to the Chapman farmhouse.

* * *

Callie was lying in her own blood, rapidly losing consciousness. She knew she had to stay awake. Ben was getting help. She had to stay awake. The doctor was on his way. He would help her. She had to stay awake. Keep her eyes open. Think of Katie. Think of Oak Hill. Think of Trudy. Stay awake. Help was coming. Stay awake, Callie. Stay awake.

She lifted her arms above her head and grabbed onto the spindle of the headboard as another wave of pain wracked her body. She felt another gush of blood. Oh, God, please, please help me. She screamed in the near dawn light. "Help me…help me! God…please…..help me!" Then all went dark.

* * *

"Callie, wake up. Come on, darlin', wake up." Ben shook her slightly and looked at Dr. Austman.

"She'll be fine, Ben. She's sleeping now. She's lost a lot of blood, but everything else looks good. Good thing you got to me in time. She would have hemorrhaged to death. She's a strong, healthy woman, though. Should be up in a week or so, good as normal."

"Are you sure, Doc? She looks awfully pale."

"Once she gets some rest and some food back in her, she'll come around real fast. Oh, don't worry about her not being able to have more children. Like I said, everything looks good. She can have a bunch."

"What happened then? Why did she lose our baby?"

"Don't know. No one does. Something wasn't right and that child just wasn't meant to be. Nothing she did or didn't do. Just happens. I've seen women have ten babies just fine and then lose two or three in a row. Then have a couple more. Just never know."

"I know Ma lost a couple, then she had me and Emma."

"Well, there you go. Happens all the time."

Callie stirred slightly and then slowly opened her eyes. She tried to focus. Ben grabbed her hand.

"Callie, Doc Austman's here. He says you're goin' to be fine. Right, Doc?"

"That's right, Mrs. Chapman. I'm sorry to say you lost the baby. I stopped the bleeding and cleaned you out. Now you just have to rest and regain your strength."

Callie looked blankly at both of them, still trying to bring them into focus. She frowned and rubbed her eyes. Then she winced in pain.

"Callie, are you hurtin'?"

She nodded her head grimacing. "Doc, what 'bout her pain? Can you give her something?"

"I'd rather not if she can stand it. It'll pass soon. She'll be uncomfortable for a few days, but the worst is over." He spoke to Callie, "Is it too bad, Mrs. Chapman?"

Callie shook her head. "No. Can take it."

"There, what'd I tell you, Ben. She's a strong one. Well, I think I've done all I can do here. If you have any problems, come get me. I'll be back tomorrow to check on her. If the bleeding starts again, which I don't think it will, come get me quickly. You probably should get your sister or mother over here to stay with her, Ben. She'll be in bed for a few days."

"Thanks for everythin', Doc. Sure do appreciate it."

"You're more than welcome. Mrs. Chapman, you take it real easy now and let people wait on you. I'll see you tomorrow. No need to see me out, Ben. Bye now."

Callie waited until the doctor had left the house, then she turned to Ben with tears trickling down her cheeks. "Our baby, Ben.....our baby. Where is he? I want to see him."

Ben was startled. "Callie, he was way too little, not even a real baby yet. There's nothing to see."

"I want to see my baby!"

"Callie, you're not thinking right. Doc cleaned you up, there's nothing to see. Now, you close those pretty brown eyes and go back to sleep. When you wake up, you'll feel much better. I'm gonna sit right here and watch you, then while you're sleepin', I'm gonna make you some tea. Doc said you got to eat something to get your strength back."

Callie looked at him with dead eyes. "When I wake up, I want to see my baby boy. Get him ready." Then she closed her eyes and was instantly asleep. Ben put his face in his hands, not knowing what to do. He fell asleep.

* * *

Callie felt better physically in a few days, but she was lost in the world of grief over her unborn child. Abigail came and talked to her, telling about her four miscarriages. Emma sat with her while Ben did the chores. Katie lay in bed with her mama, not knowing why Mama was so sad. Nothing seemed to bring her out of the doldrums.

Ben wrote to Nathan and Kathleen explaining what had happened, suggesting a visit might cheer up Callie. He received a letter from Kathleen telling him it was impossible for them to leave Oak Hill as Beulah and Mammy Sallie were both ailing. But she thought maybe she could talk Samuel into taking Lizzy on a trip that would end at Benson. He would do almost anything for his sister. In the envelope was a separate smaller one addressed to Callie and marked "personal." Ben was curious, but decided to give it to Callie; maybe Kathleen had written something to help her.

Callie took the envelope reluctantly and opened it. In Kathleen's beautiful penmanship was a five page letter. Callie started to read:

"I know exactly how you feel, Callie dear. You don't understand why this happened to you. You wonder what you did wrong or what you didn't do that you could have done. Why would God allow a baby to die before he's even born?

Yes, I know. I asked myself all these questions and more when Nathaniel died at birth. You remember, don't you, how sad I was? Well, I have found that time helps heal the wound, but it never goes away. You will always remember the day you lost him. You'll always think, 'oh, he would be three today, or seven......' You will wonder what he looks like - whose hair color, eyes, would he have. What would he love to do - run, read, write, ride, dance, laugh, tease? Would he have his father's sense of humor, his mother's tenderness? It goes on and on in your mind.

But, Callie, it does get better. It's there, but it's not as big. The hole in your heart will be there, but it grows smaller. You can bear it. Others need you, especially Katie. And, luckily for you, Ben said you can still have other children. Not that they will replace him. He will always be a part of you, of your being, but life goes on, sweetie. We have to accept what God gives us and move on. Think of the rest of your family. They want you back. Go back to them, Callie. He will always be there with you.

You know how much I love you and it breaks my heart that you have to go through this. But you aren't alone. Ben and Katie, Ben's parents, and Emma will help you because they love you too. Let them. Take each day at a time. Believe in life again, Callie, it still beckons you. Live it. Embrace it. Your son would want you to.

I hope this helps you some. I wish I could be there with you, but Grandma and Mammy Sallie are both feeling poorly, so I'm nursing them both. We all want you to be well, you know that. Please write when you can. I love you.

Kathleen

Callie lay back on her pillow and started sobbing, heaving sobs. Ben rushed into their room when he heard her. She waved him away. "Let me be. Shut the door. I'll be fine."

He did as he was told, but he stayed on the other side of the door listening to his wife cry. Just when he thought she was done, fresh sobs came from behind the door. Finally, silence. Maybe she had cried herself to sleep. He carefully opened the door so as not to wake her.

"It's all right, Ben. I'm awake." Callie was composed sitting up on the bed. Her eyes were red and her face tear-stained, but she seemed normal. "Come here."

Ben went to her, gathered her in his arms and held her tight. "Ben, Kathleen's letter helped me. Now that I've had a good cry, I think I'm better. I know our baby will always be a part of me, even if he wasn't born. But I can bear the sorrow. Just like I bear what Williams and Carswell did to me. Eventually, it becomes like a dream. What I have forgotten is that you lost a baby too. In all this I've only been thinking of myself, not you. I'm very sorry about that, Ben."

"Callie, I have to tell you.....and I feel so ashamed about this...." Ben lowered his eyes, he couldn't look at her. "All I've been thinking about is what I'd done if I'd lost you. When I saw all that blood, I wasn't thinking about the baby, I was thinking about you. I haven't thought about the baby yet - just you."

Callie was surprised. "But, Ben, you so want a son."

"No, you *think* I so want a son. Doesn't matter to me. What I want is *you* - a healthy you. Of course, I want other children, but not at the expense of your life, Callie. Don't you know that yet? You *are* my life." His voice became choked as he blurted out the last words. He blinked back the tears, but the minute Callie cradled his face in her hands, the tears came. No words were necessary.

* * *

Oak Hill was teeming with activity in readiness for the spring planting. The red clay soil was plowed, eager to accept the seeds of cotton, corn, wheat, and oats that would furnish the family with food and cash. The kitchen garden was tilled and planted with early spring vegetables that would grace the table and be devoured by hungry Hills anxious for fresh foodstuff. The livestock were delivering offspring daily to further enrich the coffers of the plantation. The country might be experiencing a Panic, but the inhabitants of Oak Hill would be eating well.

News of Callie's miscarriage put a damper on the cheeriness of the home. Kathleen particularly was bothered. It brought back too many memories for her. She hoped her letter to Callie had helped, but it had distressed her to write it - even more so that her beloved step-daughter had to experience the grief she herself carried. But, as usual, life on the plantation continued.

The family was gathered around the dining table in the evening enjoying some of the fruits of their labor. Beulah was not present, feeling unable to come downstairs. This was becoming a common occurrence.

"Samuel, I really think you and Lizzy should consider a trip to Callie's this summer. Your sister needs you and it would be good for you and Lizzy too."

Samuel turned toward his step-mother, chewing slowly, then taking a sip of water before he answered. "I know, Kathleen, but I'm just not sure I can get away from my duties here and then there will be campaigning again this year."

"You most certainly can get away from 'your duties here'," Nathan said. "Caleb, William, and I can take over for a month or so. As far as campaigning, you're running unopposed again, aren't you? You have no real excuse, Samuel. Kathleen's right, Callie needs you. That should take precedence over anything else right now. You know we'd go, but I'm worried about Mother. Mammy Sallie is doing better, but Mother seems to be failing. I can't leave her."

"I've been trying to tell him that, but he won't listen." Lizzy spoke and then blushed, realizing she had revealed too much, and looked down at her plate.

"I know I should go to Callie's. I just don't think this is the right time."

"Will there ever be a 'right time', Samuel?" Kathleen asked. "I know how you feel about going north, but I think it would be good for you to face your demons. I know our first trip helped your father in that respect, didn't it, Nathan?"

"Yes, it did. Son, Kathleen's right. You should give this very serious consideration. Put aside your feelings and think of Callie.... and Lizzy. Lizzy, you'd enjoy a trip north, wouldn't you?"

"Oh, yes! I've never been out of the state. I'd love to go see Callie...and Katie. She's my niece, but I've only seen her once. She won't even know who Aunt Lizzy is."

"Well, Samuel......" Nathan stared at his son.

"Well......I guess I'm outvoted. But I won't go until July and I'm NOT going to Chicago!"

Lizzy clapped her hands in excitement. Kathleen smiled and nodded in approval. "Nathan, better get the tickets and hotels lined up. Samuel and Lizzy are headed north!"

* * *

Benson was growing. In April, an addition of 27 acres on the east side of the tracks was laid out and known as Weast Addition, as John Weast was the original owner of the acreage. This brought the town even closer in proximity to the Chapman farms.

John Forney built a new hotel, which was greatly needed in the growing town, but the mainstay of the town, besides the railroad, was the grain elevators. By this time three elevators had been built and between them had the capacity of over 50,000 bushels of grain and handled over 300,000 bushels a year. Also more than 4,000 head of hogs were shipped a year. Benson was a busy place along the Chicago, Pekin, and Southwest Railroad.

Even in the midst of the Panic, the farmers of Clayton Township were prospering and growing. Crops planted that spring would provide for the farms and the surplus would provide for the nation.

* * *

"Well, Miss Kathleen Abigail Caludy Chapman, are you ready to help Mama make your birthday cake?"

Katie nodded her head and grinned at her mother. She was so happy her mother was feeling better. She didn't like it when she had been in bed all the time.

Callie found it hard to believe her baby girl was two years old. She was such a pretty little girl with her dark brown hair curling around her face, big brown eyes framed with long dark lashes, a little stub of a nose, rosy cheeks, and full lips. She considered herself a "big girl" now and liked to use the word "no" often to her parents. But both Ben and Callie had the patience and the sternness to correct her when she misbehaved, which wasn't very often. Katie was a happy, healthy, very much loved child.

"All right, baby girl, let's get the ingredients for the pound cake and we'll put lots and lots of love in it just like Belle."

Katie followed her mother into the little pantry to retrieve the flour, sugar, and baking powder. Then they went outside to the root cellar to get the eggs, cream, and butter.

Callie brought the ingredients, the bowl, and the utensils to the table and picked Katie up and put her in her high chair which was then pulled up to the table. "There, now you can help Mama bake."

She measured out the flour and then showed Katie how to shake the sifter over the bowl. "We have to do this four times, Katie. Count for Mama."

"One..........two.............free.............four."

"Good girl! Now we have to mix the rest. Here...you help stir it while I break the eggs."

"We puttin' love, Mama?"

"Oh, yes, Katie, dear, we are putting lots of love in this cake. It's your special cake, you know. When I was a little girl like you, Belle made me this cake on my birthdays and other times too because she always knew it was my favorite."

Callie stopped with one of the eggs in her hand and smiled as she remembered her birthdays at Oak Hill. She realized what a spoiled little girl she had been. Not too many children received a pony or a piano on their birthdays. But the best gift she was ever given was Kathleen. She remembered the day her teacher arrived. What a blessing she was!

"Mama! Done." Katie broke her reverie.

"I'm sorry, darlin', Mama was dreaming."

"What 'bout?"

"Old times, baby girl. Old times. When you get a little older, I'll tell you all about when I was a little girl growing up at Oak Hill."

"Well, you did a good job stirring. Let's get the eggs in and put this lovely cake in the oven. Then tonight when Grandma and Grandpa Chapman and Aunt Emma come for dinner, we will have it for dessert. Are you excited about opening your presents?"

"Uh-uh. Hafta wait?"

"Oh, yes. You have to wait for everybody to get here, especially Dada. He should be coming home for lunch soon. Maybe you can open just one of your gifts then since you've been such a good helper. Would you like that?"

"Yes! Open one!" Katie clapped her hands and her eyes shone like diamonds. Callie laughed and picked her up out of her high chair and swung her around and hugged her. They both fell on the floor giggling and laughing.

* * *

That evening the little farmhouse bubbled with a merriment that had been missing for a time. After a delicious meal of fried chicken with all the trimmings, Katie's cake was served. All proclaimed it scrumptious - better than Belle's. She received a rag doll made by Callie, books from Emma, a tortoise shell comb and hairbrush from Henry and Abigail, and a china doll from Ben and Callie.

A package arrived from Oak Hill containing several new dresses from Nathan and Kathleen, an old gold locket of Beulah's, books from Samuel and Lizzy, another soft doll from Trudy, Caleb, Libby, and Freeman, and an embroidered handkerchief from Mammy Sallie. At the bottom of the box was another flat box. Callie was even more curious than Katie. Inside the flat box were two framed photographs. One was of Nathan, Kathleen, Beulah, Samuel, and Lizzy and the other was Mammy Sallie, Trudy, Caleb, Libby, and Freeman.

The note inside said: *"We don't want our darling Katie to forget what we look like, so a traveling photographer took these photographs for us. We hope she likes them."*

"Oh, Katie, look! There's Grandma Beulah and Grandma and Grandpa Hill and Mammy Sallie and Trudy and Libby….oh goodness, what a lovely present for you!"

"For you too, Callie," Ben said as he walked over to look at the photographs.

"Yes, me too."

"Like," said Katie as she picked up the photographs and planted a kiss on each of the faces.

"Maybe we should have a photographer take our picture, Abigail. Our grand-daughter seems to like that."

"Guess maybe we should, Henry. Maybe the next time we go to Peoria."

"I think that is a wonderful idea. Then we can have all our families' photographs on the mantle where we can see them always," Callie said. "Isn't this new time wonderful? Just think of the new things Katie will see in her lifetime."

* * *

"Callie, you have a package from Oak Hill," Ben shouted as he dismounted from Clayton. Callie was carrying a load of wet laundry to the clothesline to hang out, Katie was toddling behind her.

"What? What did you say Ben?"

Ben walked toward her holding a small box. "You have a package from Oak Hill. F.D. brought it to me while I was in the dry goods store."

Callie put the basket of clothes down on the ground. "That was nice of him. I think I'll save it until I get these clothes hung up so they dry. Think the breeze is picking up."

"I'll put it on the porch. I'm gonna put the supplies I bought in the house. You can put them where you want them."

"I won't be long. It's not a very big load."

"Katie, you want to come in the house with Dada?" Ben asked his daughter.

"No, stay with Mama. Help." She picked up some clothespins. "See, Dada, help Mama."

"That's a good girl, Katie, darlin'. You're a good helper for Mama." Ben turned around and walked to the porch, setting the package on the chair. "Don't forget the package, Callie."

"I won't."

* * *

Ben ran out of the house when he heard Callie cry out. She was sitting on the porch, Katie at her feet petting Patch. He immediately saw her grief stricken face, tears streaking down her cheeks.

"What is it? What's wrong?"

"Grandma! Grandma died! Oh, Ben!" Sobs caused Callie's body to shake. Ben ran to her and picked her up.

"Dada...Mama sick 'gin?"

"No, baby girl, you take Patch and go in the house and play with your doll. Mama's fine. She's sad."

"Come, Pat, go house." Patch obediently followed Katie into the house, looking back at his distressed mistress.

"Callie, tell me what happened."

"Here, read this."

She handed Ben the letter from Nathan dated June 17. Ben read aloud:

"*Dear Callie,*

It is with a very heavy heart that I write to you. We have very sad news. Mother died on the 14th. She went very peacefully in her sleep with a slight smile on her face, so she never suffered. I like to think she saw Father.

She hadn't requested breakfast that morning as she usually did, so Kathleen went to check on her and found her as such. She had not been complaining of any ailments lately, but had been slowing down.

Callie, we laid her to rest beside Father in the cemetery where I'm sure she will be happy. We mourn, but also celebrate a life well lived. She was truly a great Southern lady, as you well know. The house does not seem the same without her in it.

Mammy Sallie is taking it particularly hard. I guess we just didn't realize how close those two were. Mammy has taken to her bed in grief and just keeps saying "Miz Beulah....Miz Beulah..." We've all been trying to comfort her, but so far it's not working. Maybe time will help. Maybe you could write a special letter and Trudy could read it to her. Even Samuel can't break through to her. It's like she's given up.

We've gone through Mother's things and found a box with your name on it. It contained several pieces of family jewelry and other trinkets, all labeled. Due to their value, I'll send them with Samuel when he comes. But also in the box were these two items. I don't know the significance, but Kathleen said you would. She also said they showed Mother's wonderful sense of humor and that you would appreciate them.

Callie, I know how much you will miss your Grandma, but please remember she's happy to be back with Grandpa, your mother, and little Nathaniel. She had a long life, filled with sadness, but also great joys - you being one of the joys. She was so happy to spend time with you and your family again last fall, especially with Katie.

You are a lot like her - strong, resilient, caring, brave. She left her home to go with Grandpa to start Oak Hill, just like you left here with Ben to start your home and family. Remember that Callie as you mourn her. Be well, baby girl."

Fresh tears sprang to Callie's eyes as Ben finished the letter. He wiped them away with his fingertips. "Callie, I'm so sorry. Miss

Beulah was truly a great lady. I have to admit, she scared me at first, but she really was so nice. I will miss seein' her at Oak Hill."

Callie nodded, and then smiled through her tears. "She used to scare me sometimes, too, until I knew it was all an act. She tried to appear very stern, but underneath she was so loving. I wonder what she sent me. I didn't get that far in the letter."

Ben picked up the box on the floor and handed it to her. Callie opened it further and pulled out an empty perfume bottle and a full one. She burst into tears of laughter.

"Oh, Grandma! Just like you!"

"What do they mean, Callie?"

"When I was, oh, I think around ten or eleven, Socks got sprayed by a skunk. Trudy and I washed him off good, but he still stunk. So I got some of Grandma's good perfume and put it on him. I used more than I thought so I filled the bottle up with water to disguise it. Of course, she knew. It was during the war and the blockade prevented her from getting any more so she was disgusted with me. But, Grandma being Grandma, she turned my punishment into a learning lesson. That's when I learned to sew, knit, tat. I made Trudy do it with me, and she was much better than I, so it became a competition of sorts. This is just Grandma's sense of humor, but also, she knows I will think of her every time I smell this perfume. It was the only scent she wore. Open the bottle."

Ben carefully opened the full bottle. Callie held it to her nose and inhaled. "Yes, there she is." She closed her eyes. "I can see her coming down the stairs in her dark green dress, her grey hair perfectly arranged, jewelry on, back erect, a smile on her face ready to start her day as mistress of the plantation. Yes, it's definitely Grandma." She put the lid on the bottle. "It's a wonderful gift."

Callie laid her head on Ben's shoulder as new tears trickled out of the corners of her eyes. "I only wish Katie got to know her better. She was some lady. Thank goodness we have the photographs."

"What about Mammy Sallie? Sounds like she's hurtin' bad."

"Poor Mammy Sallie! She was Grandma's best friend, even though she was her servant. She'll be lost, but she'll be taken care of."

"You gonna write her a letter like Nathan asked?"

"Of course. I'd do anything for her; she's like a mother to me." She looked up at Ben. "I've been so lucky, Ben. My Mama Hannah gave birth to me, Grandma and Mammy Sallie raised me, and Mama Kathleen has been my real mama. Four wonderful women in my life."

"They sure made you wonderful, Callie." He reached down and tenderly kissed her quivering lips. She wrapped her arms around him and ardently returned the kiss. They were lost in their own world until they heard a crash in the house.

"Uh-oh, Katie's gotten into something. We'd better go check." Callie picked up the letter and perfume bottles, and went looking for her daughter.

* * *

Callie was so excited about Samuel and Lizzy's visit that she could hardly stand it. It gave her something to think about other than the baby she had miscarried and Beulah's death. She was definitely busy. Besides all her normal chores, she now was cleaning the house with a vengeance. Since she had been ill, spring cleaning had been neglected and now the little home was being thoroughly cleaned. The weather had even cooperated, with warm days and cool nights - rare for July in Clayton Township. The farmers wanted humid, hot conditions for the corn to grow, but Callie was very happy with the unusual circumstances.

Soon the windows sparkled, the floors glowed, the curtains and bedding were brighter, the furniture shone with polish, and the walls were scrubbed to look like new. Everything smelled with the scent of freshness and cleanliness. Katie's crib was moved into Callie and Ben's room so the Hills would have her room to themselves. Everything was ready for the visitors who were expected in a few days, except the cooking and baking. That would be done in the days left until their arrival.

* * *

"Whew! I'm exhausted." Callie sat down at the kitchen table after setting a plate of ham in front of Ben.

Ben looked at her worriedly. "You been workin' too hard 'round here. Samuel doesn't care how things look."

"I know, but I want to show him and Lizzy what a good homemaker I turned out to be. I'm showing off, Mr. Chapman. Let me have my fun."

"But you're getting too tired, Callie. You've still not fully recovered."

"Oh, physically I have. And, all this keeps my mind off the baby. So it's really good for me. Eat your ham."

"I just don't want you getting sick again from over doing it. Neither would Samuel and Lizzy."

"I'm not. I know my limits. Want some peas from the garden? I creamed them with some of the new potatoes. Katie likes them, don't you, sweetie?"

"Peas, good. More."

"More, please."

"More, peez."

"Thank you."

"Tank you."

"That's my girl."

* * *

The Samuel Hills arrived in the midst of a typical July thunderstorm. With the skies dark gray and lightning streaks across the sky, followed by loud bangs of thunder, the wagon approached the little farmhouse. Just as they climbed out and ran to the front porch, the skies opened up in a downpour.

Ben and Samuel ran furiously back and forth to unload the wagon while Callie ushered Lizzy into the house out of the pelting rain. Callie was beaming as Lizzy stood in the doorway and surveyed the house.

"Callie! This is just wonderful - so cozy and inviting. I love it! It's you and Ben for sure….oh, Katie, sweetie how are you? Do you remember me?"

Katie nodded her head, "A'nt 'izzy." She stayed by Callie's skirts, though, too shy to venture towards Lizzy.

"Give her a few minutes, Lizzy, then she'll be your best friend. How was your trip? Did you enjoy every minute of it?"

"Almost, every minute. We hit a bad storm comin' through the mountains, but other than that, it was wonderful. I sure got to see some things I've never seen before. Especially when we crossed the Ohio River and stopped in Cincinnati. Samuel said that's the way a lot of the runaway slaves came north. I wondered if any of ours ended up there. Oh, here come the men."

Samuel and Ben opened the door just as a gust of wind blew, spraying droplets of water into the house. The men were drenched and shook off the rain like dogs.

"Go back out on the porch and do that! You're getting my nice clean floor all wet and dirty!" Callie shouted above the wind.

"Is that any way to greet your brother after a long journey to come and see his baby sister?" Samuel grinned, but like Ben, moved back to the porch and shook off the rain.

Callie laughed. "Come here, big brother. I guess I can greet you properly even if you are soaking wet." She went to Samuel and gave him a big hug. "Here, dry yourself off with this and then come see our house."

* * *

The young couples sat around the kitchen table catching up on all the news while enjoying a delicious lunch of soup beans with ham, topped with onions from Callie's garden, cornbread with sweet butter, cabbage fried in bacon grease, and tart apple pie for dessert.

"I can't believe it! This lunch is amazing! Everything tastes so good. What's more amazing is my little sister cooked it!" Samuel winked at Ben.

Callie smacked him on his upper arm. "Sam Hill! You're terrible! Of course, I've learned to cook; otherwise we'd starve to death here. I've been told I'm a very good cook and that my pies are really good." She smiled at Ben. "Even Abigail is impressed.....sometimes."

"Well, I must say, I'm enjoying this immensely. Much better than any of the food we've had on the trip."

After the pie was served and Katie had awakened from her nap, Lizzy and Callie cleared the table as the men retired to the little parlor.

"Come over here, Callie. I brought you some surprises from Oak

Hill I think you'll like. I'll get them." Samuel walked into Katie's room and came back with a very large crate. Then he left again, this time returning with a smaller box.

"Oooo...you know how I love surprises. Katie, you like surprises too, don't you?"

"Uh-uh." Katie was investigating the large crate. "What in here?" She asked looking up at Samuel.

"Well, let's open it up and see. Ben, do you have a hammer handy to pull out these nails?"

"Be right back."

As Samuel began pulling the nails out of the crate, the suspense mounted between Callie and Katie. As the last nail popped off, the sides of the crate fell back.

"Oh, my goodness!" Callie laughed and clapped her hands in joy. Katie looked confused.

"Lil house, Mama?"

"Yes, Katie, dear. Look, do you know what house it is?"

Katie looked very close but shook her head no.

"It's Mama's old house, it's Oak Hill - a little Oak Hill." Then she turned to Ben. "It's my old dollhouse. I got it for my, I think, fourth birthday. Is that right, Sam?"

"Yes, I think so. There's a letter in there from Trudy which explains things. I think she and Kathleen found it in the attic."

Callie found the letter and scanned it quickly, smiling as she read.

"Well, aren't you goin' share?" asked Ben. "I'm kind of curious."

"Oh, certainly. I'll read it exactly as Trudy writes it."

"Dear Miss Callie,

I hopes you feel beder. I so sorry to heer bout your baby." Callie paused for a second to regain her composure. She continued, *"Miss Kathleen an me thot this mite cheer you up. We were lookin in the attik for old skool books. I been teechin Libby ledders and Caleb too. Anyways, we saw the doll house in the corner. We thot Miss Katie wood like to play wit it. So we had Ole Joseph fix it back up. Caleb help to. Member how it was reked whin the Yankees come heer? They work and work and now it look like new agin. Hope you like it.*

Freeman is crawlin all over and pulls up to chares. He will be walkin soon, I think. Libby growin like a weed. We all miss Miss Beulah." Again, Callie's voice cracked and she paused. *"Oak Hill don seem the same with her gone, but she an angil now. Mammy Sallie beder now, but stil so sad. Miss Lenora feelin poorly, too. She teechin me how to help sik peeple. So I help her whin somebody gits sik an that way I lern. She sade somebody has to be a heeler at Oak Hill since she gettin old an sloin down. Gess that be me. I hope I git to see you soon. Love, Trudy"*

Ben cleared his throat. "Your dollhouse was wrecked by our soldiers?"

"Yes."

Ben looked at his hands, fingering his wedding ring. "I'm sorry. That's about all I can say. I didn't take part in any of that."

"I know." She turned to Samuel who was holding the smaller box. "Sam, what's in that box?"

"These are the items Grandma wanted you to have that Father wanted me to bring to you instead of ship them. Some of them are pretty valuable, I think."

Callie took the box and opened it. "Oooooh, my! Look at this! I don't remember Grandma ever wearing this set." She pulled out a gold chain with at least ten rubies surrounded in diamonds dangling from it, a brooch in the same settings, earrings, and a ring. A tag was attached to the necklace stating: *"These belonged to my great-aunt Beulah, for whom I was named. I was always afraid to wear them because they are so valuable. Keep them for Katie."*

Also in the box was Beulah's gold wedding band, several earrings, brooches, and rings, each labeled with who they belonged to and why they should be passed on to the next generation.

"Goodness! Grandma was very kind. Did she give anything to you, Sam?"

"Yes, I received most of Grandpa's watches and a few jewelry pieces for Lizzy."

"Our treasures were all taken by the Yankees. What did y'all do with yours when they came?" Lizzy asked Callie.

"I know Grandma and Mama were busy even before you came and warned us the army was coming. I remember them taking a strong box to the stables with Joseph. After we learned the war was over, she had me and Trudy go to the burned out stable and dig under Rumpel's stall, and there was the strong box. I guess all these things were in there."

Ben shifted uncomfortably in his chair. Lizzy continued, "I guess we weren't smart enough to do that. When we learned the Yanks were at the Norton's, we real quick-like put our treasures under the floor board of the attic."

Ben interrupted quietly. "That's one of the first places they always looked." The other three stared at Ben as he spoke. "I was told to look in the furniture first, then the attic floor boards, and then to stick our bayonets into the ground outside. Lt. Hague also liked to poke around the cemeteries to see if there was any sign of fresh diggings. Cellars were checked too." Ben sighed. "Luckily, I avoided all of that, but many of the men told of finding troves of riches, which they kept for themselves or distributed amongst us.......Excuse me." Ben jumped out of his chair so fast he almost knocked it over and ran out the front door, slamming it as he left.

"What's wrong? What happened?" Samuel turned to Callie.

"I don't know, but I'm about to find out." She walked outside to find her husband leaning over the porch rail, gripping it with his hands, taking deep breaths.

"Ben, what on earth is the matter? Are you sick?"

He shook his head. "No.....Yes....." He took more deep breaths and shuddered. "I'm sick of a secret I've been keeping for a long time......Think it's time to get rid of it."

"Secret? What secret?"

Ben turned around and faced his wife, grasping her shoulders. "Callie, there are lots 'bout the war I never told you....never told anyone.....'cause I'm ashamed. I'm ashamed of things I did.....or didn't do."

"You saved my life, that's all I need to know."

"That was the only good thing." Ben reached up to caress her face.

He sighed heavily.

"Well, it can't be anything *that* bad. I know Sam has struggled with his memories, even Papa."

"I know. That war changed all of us. It made some stronger, some weaker, and some did things they never would have done elsewhere. That's me. I did something wrong. Something I regret. Something I try not to ever think about. But Lizzy reminded me. I have something to give her and I've got to do it now. Please don't be disappointed in me."

"You can't disappoint me, Ben, you know that. What would you possibly have to give to Lizzy?"

Ben took her hand and led her back into the house into their room while Lizzy, Samuel, and Katie watched. He went to the blanket chest where they kept the quilts and linens. In the very bottom was his old Union jacket. He rummaged in one of the inside pockets and withdrew a handkerchief wrapped around something. He stood up, again taking Callie's hand, and walked into the parlor.

"Lizzy, I have something for you that's yours, I think. It doesn't belong to me and I'm very sorry I have it. After we burned your plantation, and while we were camped before we went to Oak Hill, one of my buddies told me to take a souvenir home to my folks. He gave me a pretty brooch for Ma, a pocket watch for Pa, and a necklace for Emma. Said he found them in the place we just burned. Said they were the 'spoils of war' and ours for the taking. I didn't want them, but then he said we all deserved something for all the fightin' we'd done and, well…..I just took them and put them in my pocket and forgot about them."

"Later after all the commotion at Oak Hill, I still forgot them, until I got back to my unit. I tried to give them to another guy, but he wouldn't take them - said he didn't want no secesh souvenir, even if was worth money. So I stuck them in my haversack and ended up bringin' them home. But I was so ashamed and knew Ma would be real angry, that I never showed them to anybody and just hid them in my old uniform. I didn't think about them when Callie got kidnapped and Samuel and I went to your place, because I was too worried about her to think of anything else. Didn't cross my mind again until we got to Oak Hill this fall and then, of course, I didn't have them with me."

"Now's the time and I'm still so ashamed to even admit I have them. Will you forgive me, Lizzy?" Ben looked into Lizzy's eyes imploringly as he handed her the handkerchief. He held onto her hand.

Lizzy met Ben's eyes and hesitated only a second. "Yes, Ben, I do. You Yankees ruined my home and made our lives miserable. I hated you for a long time. But, now I've got Samuel, and Ma, Jenny, and Grandpa are fine. Most of our problems, after the war, happened when Grandpa let Raymond Carswell into our lives, which had nothing to do with the Yankees. Time does heal some wounds." She let go of Ben's hand and carefully opened the handkerchief.

"Oh!" she sucked in her breath. "Oh, my goodness! This is my pa's watch. See, it's inscribed on the back from Ma. She gave it to him on their weddin' day. The brooch - yes, I remember it too. It belonged to Grandma. She used to wear it at her throat every day until she died. And, this necklace is Ma's. She and Pa went to Savannah one time and he bought it for her. That was right before the war."

"Oh, Ben, thank you!" Tears rolled down Lizzy's cheeks as she caressed the objects in her lap.

"No, no, no.....don't ever thank me. I did wrong, real wrong, and I'm so sorry. I knew better, but I…I don't….I don't know why I didn't listen to myself."

"Dada sad? A'nt 'izzy sad?" asked Katie.

They had all forgotten about Katie's presence. She had been playing with the dollhouse.

"No, sweetie, everything is fine. Now, at last, everything is fine. Right, Dada? Right, Aunt Lizzy?"

Ben and Lizzy nodded their heads, "Yes, Katie, everything is fine - better than fine, even."

"Good. Don' like sad."

* * *

The Hills' visit sped by rapidly. An evening was spent at Henry and Abigail's where they enjoyed Abigail's famous pork ribs, sauerkraut, mashed potatoes, head cheese, pickled beets, and buttered carrots.

Callie brought her pound cake for dessert.

Ben took Samuel all around the township to various farms, showing him what Midwestern farmers did differently than southern ones. Samuel was impressed with the advanced equipment and techniques.

Callie took Lizzy shopping in the little town of Benson where she purchased some calico material to make some work skirts, a sun bonnet, and a new petticoat. They also bought some horehound candy to savor later. Katie got a peppermint stick which she enjoyed immediately, turning her lips, chin, and hands into a pinkish sticky mess. Callie and Lizzy were having so much fun; they just laughed at her and found a near-by pump to wash her off.

Unfortunately, all the farm work didn't stop when visitors arrived. Chores still had to be completed, work had to be finished. Callie put Lizzy to work helping her make sauerkraut out of all her cabbages. It was a hot, messy job, but the two made it fun. Laundry was also a shared job, giving Lizzy a chance to wash her and Samuel's clothing from their trip. Callie's clotheslines were full.

Samuel helped Ben with the livestock and the cultivating. They both discussed and drew up plans for an addition to the farmhouse if another bedroom was ever needed.

All the chores were finished by nightfall and then the two couples could sit on the front porch and visit. Katie was put to bed and the evening was theirs. Sometimes the discussions were lively, sometimes there was just silence. Often, stories were told of their youth, life on the plantations, life on the farm. The war was not discussed. There was still too much friction between the Yankee, Ben, and the Rebel, Samuel. It was better to stay on safer topics.

Callie had a chance to speak to Samuel alone many times. He expressed his sorrow for the loss of her child. She managed to pry from him that the trip to the North wasn't so bad after all. He shared his and Lizzy's desire for a family, hoping maybe it would happen while they were traveling. The brother and sister cried together grieving over their grandmother's death, then laughing over joyous memories of her.

Ben could see Callie getting stronger and happier each day the

Hills were there. Samuel was the medicine she needed - he was very thankful Samuel put aside his feelings about the North and came to their farm. Ben and Lizzy made peace over his part in the destruction of Pine Wood. After all, it was war time. Now they were part of the same family. It was best to look towards the future, not back at the past.

The day finally arrived when Samuel and Lizzy had to leave. Callie had been dreading it, but knew it was coming. As their wagon left loaded with their trunks, she stood on the porch shielding her eyes from the sun with her hand, and watched her brother and his wife until she could no longer see the tiny dot that was their wagon. She sighed and wiped away some stray tears. Ben had already gone to the barn. Katie was playing with Patch in the yard. She sighed and turned back towards the house.

"Mama?"

"Yes, Katie."

"Miss A'nt 'izzy an Unc' Sam."

"Me, too, sweetie, me too."

* * *

The tepid weather of July turned into a boiling inferno in August. The late summer sun was blazing hot causing the landscape to shimmer with waves of heat. Every drop of rain that fell was a blessing, but as soon as it hit the ground it evaporated. Adding to the discomfort was a scorching, constant wind, whipping up the fine inky black dust. Then came the dreaded humidity, drenching the air with heavy moisture making it nearly impossible to breathe.

The little farmhouse was stifling, unbearably hot. In the evenings the Chapmans moved their bed and Katie's crib out onto the porch in order to get some sleep. Callie had purchased netting to drape over the beds to keep out the mosquitoes, which buzzed constantly looking for fresh flesh to pierce.

"Whew! It hasn't been this hot for a long time," Ben said as he came in from the fields. He quickly washed up, and then took a long drink from the dipper in the pail holding the cool water from the well. "Look at Patch, even he isn't moving."

"I know, poor thing, he's so hot. He only moves to find a cooler spot on the floor or get a drink of water."

Patch knew he was being discussed and started thumping his tail, but didn't budge an inch.

"Pat hot, Mama. Katie hot too."

"I know, baby girl. Everybody's hot. Here, Dada, wash her face with a cool cloth."

"Seep out 'gin in bed?"

"Yes, I think we will, Katie. At least until it gets a little cooler. Do you like sleepin' on the porch?" Ben went over and pushed back Katie's sweat drenched curls with the water soaked rag.

"Yes. Fun."

"Lunch is ready you two. Let's take it out on the porch and have a picnic. Would you like that Katie?"

"Yes! Like p'nics."

The family carried their plates of cold fried chicken, cabbage slaw, string beans with bits of ham, and fried potatoes. Callie went back in to get their glasses of milk. Then she spread an old quilt on the floor of the porch and they sat down and enjoyed their meal.

* * *

"Callie I think I'm goin' over to Jake Kindig's to look at a new horse. He's got a stallion he wants to sell. Pa said it's a good horse, just a little skittish, but I think I can calm him down. 'Bout time we added to our stables. I can breed Georgia with him. Clayton's getting older and doesn't need to work so hard any more. We should just keep him for ridin'."

"If you're going there, take this peach pie I just baked. I heard Sally wasn't tolerating the heat too well and had taken to her bed. She was so nice to bring us food when I was sick."

"Is this the only one you baked?"

Callie laughed, "No, silly, I made another one. Don't worry, y'all get your share of peach pie!"

* * *

That night, the humidity was even higher and the air was suffocating, even out on the porch. Katie was sleeping soundly in her crib at the foot of their bed. Ben was breathing evenly. Callie was restless. No matter which way she laid, she was uncomfortable and hot. Finally, not wanting to disturb Ben, she quietly crawled out of bed and went to the porch railing. She stood there, willing a breeze to come and cool her. She gulped in the night air with deep breaths, but nothing helped. In desperation, she found the hem of her nightgown and lifted it off her body. She stood there in the darkness, naked. Still she felt the perspiration trickle down her neck and between her breasts. The small of her back was wet too, as was the nape of her neck. She lifted her mass of curls off her back and held them on top of her head. A cloud scurried across the full moon and suddenly the landscape was illuminated with moonlight. A breeze blew ever so slightly, but enough to feel. Callie turned to catch the full force, feeling it cool the perspiration from her body. Her full breasts, rounded hips, taut stomach were silhouetted against the moonlit sky,

"Come here!" Ben whispered. His voice was raspy.

Callie jumped, dropping the curls which cascaded down her back.

"Come here!" Ben's whisper was full of passion. He raised his finger to his lips and then pointed to Katie. "Shhh. Come to me." He held out his hand.

Callie moved quietly over to the bed taking his hand and crawled in beside him. Before she could say anything he covered her lips with his, stopping only to mutter, "My God, you are so beautiful! I love you so much, Mrs. Chapman!"

She murmured into his ear, "And I love you, Mr. Chapman." And then their bodies melded together and the sweltering heat was forgotten.

* * *

"Will this heat ever end?" Callie was cooking sausage for their breakfast, ready to fry the eggs. Her face was beet red and perspiration was dripping off the end of her nose.

"Let me do that….you go outside and cool off."

"But, Ben, dear, it's hot there too!"

"Yes, but not as bad as in here. Shoo….I can fry eggs."

Callie didn't need to be told twice - off she went through the door, taking off her apron as she went. Ben was right. It was a little cooler outside, and there was a breeze today. She faced the slight wind, closed her eyes, and thought of snow. It didn't really help.

"Eggs ready! I'm bringing them out - Katie's coming too."

Katie came toddling after her father, carrying her little plate with a fried egg and piece of sausage. She grinned at her mother. "I help."

"Mmmm...this looks good. Let's eat, I'm hungry."

They ate their breakfast, occasionally turning their faces to the faint puff of air coming from the west.

"Callie, I've decided to buy that stallion from Kindig. He's a beauty. Strong too. Make a good plow horse. Gonna get him before the harvest so I can get him used to pullin' the wagon with Georgia. I'll give Jake fifty dollars down and the other fifty after harvest."

"Sounds fine to me.......ohhhhh....I'm so tempted to take off some of these clothes so I can get cooled down."

"Well, why don't you. Ain't nobody here but us."

Callie looked at Ben with her eyebrows raised and a lopsided grin on her face. "I tried that once when I was younger and got in big trouble with Grandma and Mammy Sallie."

"Well....they ain't here now. Never have understood why you women folk wear so many clothes."

"Me, either, especially in weather like this. Hmm....you know, husband, you just might be right. Who would see me other than you and Katie if I didn't wear my skirt and blouse? Do you think I would be naughty if I work in my drawers and chemise?"

Ben's eyes twinkled, "maybe a *little* naughty."

"I'm going to do it! I don't care! This is ridiculous to suffer in this heat when I can be more comfortable."

Callie left, ran into their bedroom, and shortly returned in only her drawers and chemise. She had lost some of her bravado. She smiled at Ben and twirled around.

"It's cooler, but ....I don't know, Ben. It just doesn't seem right. What if someone did come here? They'd think I'd turned into a floozy or something. Be just my luck, today would be the day Josie Miller would visit!"

Ben laughed out loud. "I doubt very much that Josie would visit us, since she hasn't ever been here."

"Well, today might just be the day. No….I think…I guess….I'd better put my clothes back on and just suffer. Besides, I want to set a good example for Katie."

Ben chuckled again as Callie returned to the house for her clothes. "My little Southern belle……Beulah, you taught her well!"

* * *

The sizzling heat continued the rest of August, the only relief being occasional thunderstorms. The rains were welcomed, but then the ground steamed, producing even more humidity. Finally, finally, in mid-September the heat wave broke and cooler temperatures arrived. Everyone was in a much better temper, as the scorching weather had taken its toll.

There was a gathering at Henry and Abigail's to celebrate the now tolerable temperatures. The neighbors of Clayton Township and the town of Benson brought food and drink for the festivity. Adults visited, some of the ladies brought needlework to share, children played games, men had arm wrestling contests, and all ate and drank and enjoyed the day.

There was also an announcement that day of the engagement of Emma Abigail Chapman to Eugene David Miller. They had been courting for several years and Eugene had finally asked for her hand in marriage. The wedding was planned for next month - the middle of October. They decided there was no reason to wait any longer. Much to Callie's chagrin, Josie Miller would now be Emma's new sister-in-law and be considered as part of the family.

* * *

The weather continued to grow cooler and finally in early October, the first frost arrived. The leaves on the maple trees suddenly were a kaleidoscope of yellows, golds, oranges, and crimsons against their dusky bark. The large oaks were russet and deep burgundy.

Callie could stand on her porch and look out at the corn ripening in the fields, the stalks turning from green to brown, the ears hanging heavy with their plump kernels hidden in the husk.

Her vegetable garden was harvested, canning was almost done, and jams and jellies already in the pantry. It had been a fairly good year. The heat had stunted some of the plants, but they still yielded produce. The potato crop was very substantial, so they would be on the menu everyday at the Chapmans.

By the time of Emma's wedding, most of the harvesting had been done, except the corn. It was going to be nice to have a chance to relax and enjoy the ceremony and reception, if only for a day.

October 14th was a spectacular autumn day. Crisp, sparkling, fresh air with a brilliant blue sky, multihued leaves gently falling from the trees, and a soft mild breeze blowing, was the setting for the outdoor ceremony.

Callie and Ben were the attendants for the couple and Katie was the flower girl. She was so happy to have a pretty new dress that she just kept twirling around and around, making the skirt stand out. Callie wore her best calico and Ben his one suit.

Emma looked striking in royal blue poplin, trimmed with heavy ivory lace. The dress was beautiful, but practical. She could easily wear it again.

Henry unabashedly cried as he walked his daughter down the make-shift aisle to meet her groom. The ceremony was simple, but sweet, and Emma became Mrs. Eugene Miller.

Afterwards, the food was set out on tables on the lawn and the feasting began. Callie and Ben mingled with their family and friends, showing Katie off, and having a wonderful time. Callie and Josie did a very good job of avoiding one another.

Soon Emma and Eugene left for his house, which was about three miles away, to start their married life.

"Now the fun will begin," Ben said to Callie as they waved good-bye to the couple.

"What do you mean?"

"Didn't Ma tell you? We're goin' to chivaree them tonight! 'Member I told you 'bout that on our first anniversary?"

"Oh, yes…No…Abigail didn't tell me."

"She must have forgot with all the weddin' plans she was doin'.

We're all meetin' again tonight at Miller's house 'round midnight. Should be lots of fun."

"Do we bring Katie too? Get her out of bed?"

"Sure, she'll probably just sleep through it. It's goin' be a nice night. We'll just bundle her up and take her with us. You'll see, Callie. It's real fun."

"Probably not for Emma and Eugene."

"That's the idea!" Ben laughed.

* * *

Emma and Eugene had just gotten to sleep when they were awakened by a loud banging of pots and pans, singing, and general shouting. Eugene jumped out of bed with a start, grabbing his pants, struggling to put them on.

"Dang it! They're givin' us a chivaree, Emma!"

Emma giggled. "Didn't you half way expect it, Gene?"

"Guess so. Dang! That's loud. Come on, we'd better go to the window, or they'll keep it up all night."

Emma grabbed her dressing gown and, with Eugene, opened their bedroom window and poked their heads out and waved. The crowd assembled outside cheered and made even more noise. Then they started bringing food out of their wagons and settled down to eat. The newlyweds waved again, shut the window, and went to bed, but not to sleep.

* * *

"Ben, I need to go into town and get some muslin to make Katie some pantalettes. Now that she's a 'big girl' she needs some. I need to do some other errands there too. Could you hitch up Georgia for me?"

"You're goin' have to take Clayton instead. Kindig's bringin' over the new horse any minute and I need Georgia. I want those two to get used to each other pullin' the wagon."

"All right. It doesn't matter to me. I shouldn't be gone long anyway. I'm anxious to see the new horse. Have you named him yet?"

"Yep, he looks so noble, I think I'll call him King. See what you think when you see him. He sure is pretty. Never had a dun horse before."

"Well, can you hitch up the buggy for me now? I want to get back in time for Katie's nap."

"At your service, Ma'am. Have him pulled up here right away so my girls can go shoppin'."

Ben left and soon returned with Clayton and the buggy. "You two have a good time in town. Don't rush."

"Oh, we'll be back in time for lunch. See you then, Mr. Chapman." And, off trotted Clayton with Callie and Katie in the buggy.

* * *

It wasn't long before Callie and Katie arrived in Benson where she parked the buggy and wrapped the reins around one of the hitching posts in front of Jourgen Harms' dry goods store. Katie loved going into the store - there were so many things to look at, and Mr. Harms always gave her a peppermint stick.

Callie went straight to the muslin and ordered the yardage, conversing with Mr. Harms as he cut the correct amount and rang it up. She was eyeing a new sunbonnet for herself and a smaller one for Katie too. They both tried them on and Callie decided to buy them.

From there they went to the post office connected to F.D. Learned's drugstore to mail some letters to Oak Hill. Callie spent some time discussing the timeliness of the postal delivery system with F. D. until Katie started pulling on her hand to leave.

They walked by Barbara Weast's millinery shop, stopping to admire the pretty bonnets in the window. Then on to Charles Lauenstein's jewelry store, newly opened. He was adjusting his window display as they went by, beckoning them into the store. Callie waved and walked on by. Jewelry was not in her budget today.

"Callie! Callie!" Someone was shouting at her from behind. "Wait a minute."

Callie turned around and there was Sally Kindig. "I thought that was you and Katie. You out shoppin' too while our husbands do some horse tradin'?"

Callie smiled. She liked Sally very much. "Yes, it seems so. This must be some horse we're getting. I'm glad to see you're feeling better, Sally."

"Oh, I think the heat just got the best of me….that and 'female problems.' My, Katie certainly is grownin'. Just as pretty as her mama."

"Thank you. Yes, she's a 'big girl' now, so I got some muslin to make her pantalettes."

"My, you trained her early, didn't you, Callie?"

"Not really. She was two in June."

"Well, my gir………." Sally stopped in mid-sentence and turned toward a commotion near Dr. Austman's office. Callie did too. A man on a horse was galloping toward there and then pulled up sharply, leapt off, and ran into the office shouting for the doctor.

"My goodness, I think that looked like my Jacob."

"I think it was too, Sally. I wonder what's wrong."

Callie grabbed Katie's hand and they quickly walked to the doctor's office and waited outside. It wasn't long before Dr. Austman, followed by Jacob Kindig burst out the front door. They both stopped dead in their tracks when they saw Callie and Sally. Each looked at one another. "Doc, you get goin'. I'll take care of this and be right behind you."

"What's wrong, Jacob? Why are you here?" Sally asked her husband.

Jacob ignored her and went to Callie. He took her hands in his and stared into her now very worried brown eyes. "Callie, be strong. Ben's been hurt….bad. The horse I brought over kicked him while we were hitchin' him up to the wagon. He's unconscious….I couldn't get him to come to, so I left him to get Doc."

Callie dropped his hands, picked up Katie, and ran to her buggy. She quickly backed it up and flicking the reins yelled at Clayton. "Come on, Clayton, we've got to get home fast! Giddyup! Hold on tight, Katie! Dada needs us."

* * *

Jacob passed her on the way, his horse at a fast gallop. Sally was behind her in the Kindig's buggy. By the time Callie and Katie arrived at their house, the men had moved Ben onto the bed. Callie carried Katie out of the buggy and told her to play with Patch on the porch.

Shortly, Sally arrived and watched her.

Before Callie went into their bedroom, she took a deep breath and steadied herself. She quickly stepped into the room where Dr. Austman was examining Ben. Ben was lying very still on the bed, blood covering his face.

Dr. Austman knew she was there and started giving her orders. "Callie, go get a basin of water and start washing this wound. I know I'll have to stitch it up. Find something we can use as a bandage too - an old sheet, petticoat, anything that's clean."

She did as she was told, her movements automatic and stilted. She pulled a chair up to the side of the bed and carefully washed the crusty blood off her husband's face. Immediately, new blood poured out of the wound.

"Put pressure on that, Callie! Hold it down hard. Got to stop that gushing."

She pushed harder on the cloth, turning paler by the minute. "Doctor, why isn't he awake?"

"Don't know. Guess the blow was so hard it knocked him out. Might have a concussion of the brain. Seems like he should be coming to soon, though."

"Jake," Dr. Austman yelled over his shoulder. "Come here, please."

"What you need, Doc?"

"Can you tell me what happened so I have a better understanding what to examine?"

"Well, me and Ben had hitched up Georgia and were gonna put the harness on King. Ben went to him real slow and careful 'cause I'd told him he was skittish of the bridle. But King just bent his head and the bridle went right on. Getting the bit in his mouth was a problem. Ben kept tryin' real easy like, but then all of a sudden King reared up on his back legs and his hoof hit Ben in the head. The rest happened so fast, I'm not sure I got it right. But when Ben fell to the ground, King kept stompin' on him until I got hold of the harness and led him away. Think he might have hit Ben's shoulder and arm, maybe his back....not sure. I tried to revive Ben, but he didn't respond. Too much blood for me, so I just jumped on my horse and got you."

Callie had been listening quietly as she held a cloth on Ben's head. "Thank you, Jacob, for getting help so fast. You're a good friend, Sally too."

"No need to thank us, Callie. Ben would do the same for me. If it's all right for me to leave now, Doc, I'm gonna ride to Henry's and tell him and Abigail. Sally will stay with Katie, Callie."

"Go on, Jake, go to Henry's."

"Thank you, Jacob." Jacob left and Callie soon heard his horse's hooves thundering away.

"Take the cloth off now, Callie, and let's see if the bleeding has stopped." She carefully removed it. No new blood gushed out.

"Good, now I can sew that gash up. Then we'll get some smelling salts and see if we can wake him up. I don't feel any broken bones or internal injuries. So maybe if we get him stitched up, we can work on getting him to wake up."

"Whatever you say, Doctor. Just bring Ben back."

Dr. Austman looked at Callie, who had silent tears running down her cheeks.

"I'll do my best. Think you can handle watching me sew him up?"

She nodded her head. "I can do anything for my Ben."

* * *

Attempts to revive Ben had failed. He laid very still, his chest barely rising with shallow breaths. Dr. Austman had successfully closed the wound on his forehead and bandaged it. He again checked Ben for other injuries, finding only bruises on his shoulder and upper arms.

Henry and Abigail had arrived and shortly thereafter Emma, who took care of Katie. Sally and Jake left as the little house was becoming too crowded.

Abigail and Emma both tried to get Callie to leave Ben's side and rest, but she wouldn't hear of it. She sat at her husband's side, holding his hand, brushing the hair from his injured forehead, and whispering in his ear. She warily watched his chest rise with each breath and felt his faint pulse on his wrist.

Dr. Austman sat on the other side, occasionally listening to Ben's heartbeat and feeling his pulse. Several times he held smelling salts under his nostrils with no reaction - something that deeply disturbed him. He knew concussions were unpredictable and the brain would have to heal itself. All they could do was wait.

"Well, Callie, there's not much else I can do, so I think I'll leave to check on some other patients. You've enough help here. We just have to keep him comfortable and wait until he wakes up. Nothing much else we can do.....except pray."

Callie knew the seriousness of Ben's injury - she had already been praying. "Thank you, Doctor. I'll take good care of him, don't worry. He'll wake up soon, I just know it."

"I'll be back later this evening to see if there's any change. If you need me before that, have Henry come to my office."

When Dr. Austman left, Abigail took his seat on the other side of the bed. She, too, spoke to her son in whispers, stroking his arm. "He'll come out of this, Callie. Ben is a strong man with lots to live for. He'll make it. He comes from strong stock. I remember my brother got kicked by a horse one time....bad kick on the head. He lay for a week like this, then one day, just woke up and wanted bacon and eggs! Same will happen with Ben....just wait and see."

"I hope so, Abigail....I hope so. Is Emma with Katie? I should go see her and explain what's happening."

"Emma already has. Everything's fine with Katie. She's playing with your dollhouse and then Emma will put her down for her nap. Don't worry about her."

"Thank you."

* * *

Three days after the accident, Ben was still unconscious. Dread had settled into Callie's heart. What if he never woke up? How could she live without her Ben? She never left his side except to see Katie. The Chapmans and Emma took turns staying the night so Callie could get some rest. Other families in the township brought food.

On the fourth day, Dr. Austman was once again examining Ben. "Callie! Good news...his reflexes have returned. Watch." The doctor tapped Ben's kneecap and his lower leg moved. "That's a good sign."

"Will he wake up soon? What else can I do?"

"Just what you've been doing. Keep talking to him. Keep bathing him. Try putting a little water on his lips. That's about it for now. We just have to wait. He's not worse, which is a good thing. The wound looks good, keep it clean."

"All right, Doctor. I just think he should be waking up." Callie looked at Dr. Austman with tears welling in her eyes. "He *will* wake up, won't he?"

The doctor averted his eyes. "He should. But…" He stared into those glistening brown eyes. "There's always a chance he won't. Ben's strong and he's being well cared for, so I think he will recover, but there's always a chance….and I just want you to know it. One can never tell with head injuries. We just have to think positive, Callie… and pray."

The tears spilled over onto Callie's cheeks, but the eyes were determined and her chin was set. "He *will* recover, Doctor. He *will*. I'll *make* him."

* * *

After Dr. Austman left, Callie undressed down to her chemise and drawers and crawled into bed next to her husband. She molded her body against his and laid her head on his shoulder, her arm across his chest. She began talking in a soft, quiet voice telling Ben what was happening around him, the weather outside, all their friends helping them, what his parents were doing, how everyone had come to visit. Then her conversation turned more personal, how much she loved him, needed him. Finally, she lifted her head from his shoulder and pushed herself until her mouth was by his ear. "Benjamin Henry Chapman, you must come back to me. You see, I have a secret that I have not told anyone. I wanted to wait until I was positively sure and now I am. You are going to be a father again, Ben, and this time I feel so good. I haven't been sick at all, so I know everything will be fine and we'll have a healthy baby. I'm going to talk to Dr. Austman the next time he comes and have him examine me just to be sure. I think the baby will be here sometime in May. But, Ben, I can't do this by myself. I desperately need you…Katie needs you. You have to fight to come back to us. I know you can hear me, Ben. You must fight!"

Callie raised her head and stared at Ben's closed eyes. "Benjamin! You must fight to come back!"

Callie drew in a sharp breath. It looked like Ben's eyelids had moved! She blinked to clear her own, thinking she had imagined it. "Ben, open your eyes!" Again the lids fluttered and then were still. "Try, Ben, try again, please, please, darling." Nothing. Callie sighed and laid her head back on his shoulder. "It's all right. You're fighting, that's all that matters. You're still in there, I know that now. You will be back soon. Rest now, Ben. Rest." She closed her own eyes and was soon asleep.

* * *

Callie awoke with a start, sitting upright. Something was wrong. It was now dark, but the full moon spilled its light across their bed. She looked around the room, then at Ben beside her. Ben! His chest wasn't rising with breaths!

"Ben!" She quickly straddled her husband and without thinking, whacked his chest.

"Help! Help! Abigail, help!" Again she hit his chest with force. Instinctively, she opened his mouth and put hers over it and blew into it. Then she breathed into his nostrils. She repeated this several times, each time feeling his chest. She felt his wrist and could detect a slight pulse, but it was erratic.

"Callie.....what...oh, my goodness, what's happened?"

"He's not breathing! I can still feel a pulse and hear his heart, but it's very faint."

Once again she repeated blowing into his mouth and nose and hitting his chest.

"Let's prop him up a little more, maybe that will help." The women grabbed some pillows and quilts, putting them behind Ben's back. "Now check his pulse."

Callie laid her finger on Ben's wrist. After several seconds, she smiled at Abigail. "It's stronger!" They both watched as Ben's body suddenly jerked, then was still. His chest began rising again at regular intervals. A sigh of relief escaped both women's lips.

"I think he's resting now, don't you?" Abigail asked her daughter-in-law.

"Yes, he seems peaceful."

"Good thing you were right here or we could have lost him."

Callie began shaking. She couldn't control the tremors. "Callie, lay down. You're body's reacting to what just happened. It will pass." Abigail covered her up with a quilt and rubbed her arms and legs until the shivering stopped. "Let me go make you some tea." Callie nodded.

After Abigail left, Callie reached over, placing her hand on Ben's chest, reassuring herself that his breathing was once again normal. She inhaled slowly, then exhaled trying to relax her muscles, willing them to stay still. She mustn't fall apart. She needed all her strength to get through this. She had to remain strong for Ben, Katie, and the new baby. The baby! She hadn't let herself think about it much. She was afraid to. But she felt so good! This had to be a good sign that everything was all right this time. Telling Ben had made it real.

She lay on her back, placing her hand over her stomach. "Mama will take good care of you, little one. You grow and be safe. By then, Dada will be able to take care of you too."

Abigail returned with a cup of tea. "Any change? You feelin' better?"

"No, no... change in Ben. Yes, I'm feeling much better. Thank you, Abigail."

"Well, he's my son, you know. I don't want to lose him, Callie!" Then Callie comforted her mother-in-law, who broke down in tears.

* * *

Dr. Austman arrived in the morning, surprised to find Callie asleep in the bed and Abigail snoring in the chair. Emma was feeding Katie her breakfast.

"Shh, Doctor. I thought I better let them sleep. They were up during the night with Ben. I'm not sure what happened. I stayed with Katie. Would you like some breakfast?"

"Just some coffee, please, Emma."

Shortly, Abigail woke herself up with a loud snore and heard talking in the kitchen. She stood up, straightened her dressing gown, and went out of the bedroom, closing the door quietly.

"Oh, good morning, Doctor. Apologize for my appearance. It was a rough night." Then she proceeded to relate what had happened.

"Hmmmm.....Good thing you two propped him up. And, good thing Callie hit his chest and gave him air. I told her, head injuries are funny, you never know what's going to happen. Is Ben still breathing regular this morning?"

"He seems to be. I just watched his chest for a few minutes before I came out."

Suddenly, there was a scream from the bedroom. Not a terrifying scream, but a delightful scream. Everyone ran from the kitchen into the bedroom.

There was Callie sitting up in bed, smiling from ear to ear, tears of joy running down her face. "Look, everyone. Look!"

Ben, still propped up, had his eyes open! He was staring vacantly, blinking, trying to focus. Dr. Austman rushed to his side. "Ben, Ben... look at me. Ben, can you hear me?"

Ben's eyes narrowed as he sought the doctor. "Ben, wait." The doctor took Ben's hand. "Ben, if you hear me, squeeze my hand." Dr. Austman grinned as he felt a slight pressure on his hand. "Excellent! Now, if you can see me, squeeze again." Nothing. "Someone get a wet cloth so we can wash out his eyes." Abigail ran to the washstand and proceeded to wash Ben's eyes with a damp cloth.

"Now, Ben, squeeze my hand if you can see anything at all, even if it's fuzzy." Again the doctor smiled. "Good! Ben, my boy, I think you turned the corner. Would you like something to eat?" Slight pressure on the doctor's hand indicated he would.

"Abigail, how about getting your son some broth? I think he needs liquids."

"Gladly, oh, gladly. Benjamin! You're back, son!" Abigail rushed to her son and hugged him, followed by Callie and Emma, then little Katie.

"All right, let's not tire him out. Feed him a little broth or tea, then he has to rest. And, I mean rest. No disturbances." He looked directly at Callie. She nodded. He turned to leave. "I'll be back this afternoon to check on him."

Callie spoke up. "Doctor, may I speak to you in private?" Dr. Austman stopped, looking at her curiously. "Of course."

"Come, Emma and Katie. Let's go make Dada some tea. Katie, you can help."

They left the room. "What is it Callie? Ben's going to recover. I'm sure of that now."

"No....it isn't about Ben....it's me."

"Yes? Go on."

"I think I'm expecting again....no, I *know* I'm expecting. I just want you to examine me to make sure everything is all right this time. I haven't even felt sick, so it's all different to me."

"Of course. Right now?"

"If you could."

Doctor Austman proceeded with the examination. "Yes, you are definitely expecting and I think you're right about the birth date.... sometime in May. Everything looks normal too. You just make sure you get plenty of rest. When Ben's sleeping, you sleep. Others can take care of Katie for a while. Make sure you eat well too. Got another mouth in there to feed now." He chuckled. "I'm really happy for you, Callie.....Ben too. We just have to make sure both of you are taken care of. Well....if that's all, I think I'll head on out. Be back later today."

"Thank you so much, Dr. Austman, for everything."

"Hmmmppffff....you're the one who saved your husband, not me."

* * *

In the next few days, Ben started spending more time awake, taking liquids, seeing better, but still not speaking. Callie and Abigail massaged his legs and arms and moved them back and forth and up and down to prevent atrophy. His color was much improved and so was his breathing. For the most part, he rested and slept - with Callie by his side. Katie, also, started taking her afternoon nap with her "Dada."

It was a clear, crisp November morning when Callie, who was

tending Ben, heard a commotion outside the front door. She had been oblivious to the goings on at her home since she spent her days and nights in the room with Ben, and occasionally with Katie in her room. All the chores, laundry, cooking, and cleaning were being done by Abigail, Emma, and other neighbor women.

But this noise sounded different. It was time for Dr. Austman's morning visit, but he just slipped in and out. Who could be making such a racket? Her curiosity got the better of her and she left Ben to see what was happening.

Before she could open the front door, it swung out and in burst Kathleen and Nathan! Callie rubbed her eyes to make sure she wasn't seeing things.

"Callie, sweetie, it truly is us!" Kathleen went to her and hugged her tight. Callie started sobbing and virtually collapsed into Kathleen's arms. Nathan ran to hold his daughter and wife.

"Come, come, baby girl, sit down. Your mama is falling over!" Kathleen moved with Callie and they sat on the settee together.

"I...I...I...just can't...can't...believe you're here. How...how... did you know?"

"Henry telegraphed us right after the accident and it's taken us this long to get here. He said you would need us, so here we are. We thought he had told you we were coming. We didn't mean to surprise you so." Nathan held Callie in his arms, comforting her.

She started sobbing again. "I...I....I'm....*so* glad you....are here. Oh, Mama...I've...I've....been so...scared....I..thought...Ben... would never wake up...but he did."

"Oh, Callie, sweetie. Of course, he would wake up. He has you and Katie, his parents, Emma....he has much to live for. I know you've been taking such good care of him, too." Kathleen reached over to wipe Callie's tears.

Callie tried to compose herself, but to no avail. The tears flowed again. They were tears of relief, tears suppressed since the accident, tears of seeing her parents, tears of love, tears of frustration, tears of thanksgiving. Nathan and Kathleen exchanged looks of doubt as to what to do next. They just let Callie cry until she was done.

"I'm…I'm so sorry. That's not any way to welcome you. It's… it's just that seeing you two triggered something in me." She took Nathan's offered handkerchief, wiped her eyes, and blew her nose. "I feel much better, though. Goodness, I still can't believe you are sitting in my parlor! I'm so happy you are here!"

"So are we, baby girl, so are we. When we got the telegram from Henry, we just decided to let everyone else take care of things at Oak Hill and we got here as fast as we could."

"Trudy really wanted to come too, Callie," said Kathleen, "but she just couldn't this time. With the children and the harvest, she just couldn't leave, but she wants you to know how much she loves you and that she is sending prayers your way. She's been taking care of Lenora and Mammy Sallie too, who send their love and are praying for Ben to get well. Samuel and Lizzy also are praying for Ben's recovery."

"How is Ben?" asked Nathan.

"Come and see for yourself. He's still not speaking much - it's an effort, but his wound is healing and he's moving a little more by himself. His eyesight is improving too."

Callie took Nathan and Kathleen's hand and led them into the bedroom. "Ben, look who came to see you!"

Ben squinted his eyes and raised his hand to beckon them closer. His face lit up with recognition. "Naathaan…..Kaatthhleen……. haaapy."

"Not as happy as we are to see you, Benjamin," said Nathan. "It looks like the horse almost won the battle."

Ben smiled and shook his head. "Stillll goood hoorseee."

"I know what you mean. Not the horse's fault. He just wasn't trained yet."

Ben again shook his head. "Yeesss."

"You are looking much better than I expected, Ben," said Kathleen. "I was prepared for much worse. But, then, you've had excellent care with Callie and your family."

"Yessss. I haave besssst."

"Dr. Austman has been so good too, Mama. He still comes every day to check on Ben. We're lucky to have such a good doctor in this little town."

Ben grabbed Callie's hand. "Teelll yeett?"

"Tell what?" asked Kathleen.

Callie blushed and smiled broadly. I think what Ben means is we have some other news. Is that right, Ben?"

"Yeesss."

Callie took a deep breath, keeping her parents in suspense. "Well, you are going to be grandparents again! Katie will be a big sister next May."

Nathan and Kathleen both gasped in surprise. "Oh my goodness, this *is* a *surprise!*" Kathleen finally managed to speak. She went to Callie and embraced her. "How are you feeling?"

"Wonderful! I haven't been sick at all this time. Dr. Austman said it's a perfectly normal pregnancy. I've already felt life too, which is a really good sign that everything is fine. Papa, what do you think? Maybe a grandson this time?"

"I don't care what it is as long as you and the baby are healthy, Callie. What wonderful news! No wonder you're getting better so fast, Ben, you have to be ready to welcome that new baby. By the way, *where* is my granddaughter?"

"She's at Emma and Gene's. Everyone has been so helpful. I haven't done anything but take care of Ben. I'm afraid I'll get lazy!"

"Well, you can be lazy for a few more weeks, because we will take care of things around here, too." Kathleen smiled at Callie. "I'm so happy for you, dear, so happy. Now, we'll unpack our things in Katie's room and you two just rest. We sent Abigail and Henry home, so I'll make the meals today. I still know my way around a kitchen."

"And I still know how to do chores," Nathan added.

Ben and Callie just shrugged. "Fine. Make yourselves at home."

* * *

Kathleen and Nathan brought much news with them. Mammy Sallie was still feeling poorly, but she had finally accepted Beulah's death. Everyone at Oak Hill felt a vacancy with Beulah gone, but time was healing them. Lenora and Joseph also were slowing down and not leaving their cabins much. Trudy was learning from Lenora, and Caleb was taking over the carpentry work. Libby and Freeman were growing and were so smart and precocious. Malindy was doing most of the cooking, as Belle, too, was aging. Several new people had been hired to help at Oak Hill and the lumber mill at Pine Wood, which William now helped Samuel manage.

Letters from Caroline were filled with chatter. All the Savannah relatives were fine and prospering. Victoria and Daniel were building a lavish new home near Forsyth Park in the new Queen Anne style - lots of turrets and brick-a-brack.

Samuel and Lizzy had nothing but good things to say about their visit at the Chapmans. It seemed Samuel finally exorcized his demons from the war after visiting several battlefields on the way home, although Kathleen thought it was Lizzy's love that cured him.

After relaying all this news, Kathleen asked Callie, "Have you not heard from Victoria or your brother lately?"

"Probably. I have a stack of letters somewhere, but I just haven't taken the time to read them yet. Why? Do you know something else?"

"Well….." Kathleen looked at her husband, who was beaming. "We are going to be grandparents again, and not by you, but your brother. Samuel and Lizzy are expecting in April!"

Callie's hands flew to her face. "I'm going to be an aunt! I'm going to be an aunt! Hurray for Sam and Lizzy! Katie and the baby will have a cousin! Oh, this is so wonderful! How has Lizzy been feeling?"

"Just tired, otherwise fine. Samuel is like a proud rooster, strutting around, telling everyone he sees that he's going to be a father. I'm sure he has written to you."

"I will have to write soon and tell them how happy I am for them. Sam told me while they were here that he was hoping for a baby. This is so exciting! Anything else I need to know?"

"Well, Victoria and Daniel are building that big house because they also are going to have a child! Pretty soon, too. February, I think Caroline said. Of course, everyone there is thrilled."

"Victoria a mother! I guess I can see that…..maybe." Callie laughed. "I'm sure she will have lots of help, so she can still be a 'society matron!' Goodness, I have a lot of letters to answer. I can give them all advice on raising children." With that, Callie started laughing along with her parents. When she finally stopped, she giggled again, "I will have to see Victoria with her child to believe it, but I'm sure she will be a good mother. I *know* Lizzy will - she was wonderful with Katie."

"Calllliiiieee"

"My patient is calling. We'll talk some more later........Coming, Ben."

* * *

Ben couldn't vocalize yet what was going on in his mind, but he was worried. He wasn't healing fast enough. Now that another baby was coming, it was imperative that he get back on his feet to take care of his family. And, right now was the start of the corn harvest. Here he lay in bed while his crop stood in the field. He tried to tell Callie, but she just ignored him and said everything would work out. She was enjoying the Hills' visit. Well, he couldn't ignore it. Several times he tried to get out of bed on his own and failed. True, each day he was getting stronger, but his legs were still weak. It took all of his strength to get from the bed to the chair. He still hadn't left the bedroom. It weighed heavy on his mind.

Callie was worried too, even though she tried not to show it. She discussed the situation with Nathan and Henry. They told her to leave it to them. She had to take care of Ben and they would take care of the harvest. She knew Henry had acres and acres to do himself, along with the hired hands. This year, Emma would be helping Eugene at their farm, making one less field hand. But, she *did* have more to worry about than the harvest, so she turned her attentions towards getting her husband back on his feet.

* * *

Callie had barely woken up when she heard quite a din coming from outside. Ben heard it too as he turned to her with questioning eyes. "Whhhaattt thaaat?"

"I don't know, but I'm going to find out."

She quickly dressed and opened their door, only to run smack into Kathleen who was also on her way to check outside. They both opened the front door and stood there in amazement.

Before them were wagons, carriages, and buggies. Out of the vehicles came the people of Clayton Township - farmers and town people, young and old, men, women, and children, each carrying a dish of food or an implement.

"Howdy, Mrs. Chapman!" Jacob Kindig stepped forward, followed by Sally. "We thought we'd all pay you a little visit. Maybe do a little work while we're here, too, like get that corn crop out of the fields. We've got many hands, so it shouldn't take too long. Womenfolk got lots of food to share, too. That all right with you?"

Callie was speechless. She just stood there with her mouth wide open. Finally, Henry came to her rescue, putting his arm around her. "I guess my daughter-in-law is too surprised to talk - something new around here! But I know she and Ben more than appreciate what you good people are willin' to do. God bless you all."

"Then let's get to work!" Jacob shouted. Everyone cheered and scattered to the fields. Some of the women stayed behind where tables were set up and large amounts of food were placed on them. Then they too started for the fields where every available hand was needed.

Sally and Abigail went to Callie, who was still in a state of shock. "Callie, I believe Jacob told you when you first came here that we all have to take care of one another. We weren't about to let you and Ben suffer because you couldn't harvest. It didn't take long to organize all the neighbors. Every one of us has had troubles and needed help. Someday you can repay someone in need too."

Callie just nodded her head, as tears of gratitude started flowing. "Oh, Callie." Kathleen held her tight, whispering in her ear, "You are so fortunate to live in a place where people care so much for one another." Again Callie nodded.

Wiping away her tears, she hugged all three women at once. "Let's go tell Ben. I'm sure he is wondering what on earth is happening."

* * *

The day sped by fast as the corn was picked and husked. A team of horses was hitched to a wagon that had a high bank board on one side.

Following the horses at a steady pace, the pickers would walk the rows, grab the ear of corn, husk it by hand, and then toss it against the bank board into the wagon. If the ear missed the bank board, children trailed behind to gather them up. Often, cries were heard from those closest to the wagon. "Dang it, Louise, that's the second time you've hit me! Throw harder and higher!"

At noon everyone congregated at the farmhouse for lunch. The women of Clayton Township were good cooks and liked to outdo each other at these "pot luck" meals. Variety abounded and no one left hungry. After a short rest to "digest" their lunch, it was back to the fields. The same process was repeated for the evening meal.

As darkness approached, the last people straggled in from the fields. They were exhausted and dirty, but felt very satisfied that they had helped their neighbor. Many lingered outside in the yard and on the porch, visiting with one another.

"Callie, we got most of the corn in, still a few acres to go, but think Henry and his men can finish it easy enough." Jacob and Sally were sitting with Callie on the porch.

Just as Callie was about to thank everyone, a cheer arose amongst those facing the house. Callie and the Kindig's turned to see why. Wrapped in a blanket and wearing a smile as wide as his face, came Ben. He was supported on each side by Nathan and Henry. Callie ran to him. Loud cheers rose from the yard, followed by applause.

Nathan and Henry helped Ben into one of the chairs and everyone hushed. "Cann'tt thaannk youuu alllll eeenough. Looove allll oofff yooouuu." He reached for Callie's hand and smiled again through his tears. Once again applause erupted.

"Ben, you know we're happy to do it," Jacob said. "You'd do the same for us."

Ben shook his head yes. "Sooo niiccee tooo haaave ssuuch goood ppeooplee foor neeighbborrs."

"Now, all we ask of you is to get well. We don't plan on doin' this next year, do we folks?"

Everyone shouted "no" and laughed, Ben and Callie along with them. "Woon't haappenn aaagggaiin. Donnn't wwwooorrry."

"I'll see to that, believe me!" laughed Callie. "I intend for him to be back working very soon." Then she reached down and kissed Ben tenderly. More cheers from everyone followed.

"It's been a long day, but a good one. Let's all go home now and let this family rest. Thanks, everybody for all your help." Jacob turned to the Chapmans. "Think we better get Ben inside, don't want him to catch cold."

Callie threw her arms around Jacob and then Sally. "We can't begin to thank you for this day. I don't know what else to say."

"Just get that husband of yours up and goin' again. That's payment enough."

"You can count on that, Jacob. We've got plenty of reasons to get Ben healthy again." Her brown eyes sparkled even in the dimming light.

"I detect a secret there, Mrs. Chapman. 'Spect to hear something in due time."

Callie just smiled and hugged them again.

* * *

The days flew by like hours and it was soon time for the Hills to return to Georgia. Ben had made great strides during their visit. He could now speak much better, his eyesight was perfect, his appetite was back, and he was moving more. Although, still a little unsteady on his feet, he was determined to walk.

Kathleen and Nathan felt confident he would keep improving and Callie would be able to manage without them. The neighbors were still bringing in food and helping with the chores, along with Ben's family, so she would be well taken care of for a while longer. Besides, they wanted to return to Oak Hill before the winter weather arrived.

Callie urged them to stay until after Christmas, but she knew it was important for them to get back to their own home. She was encouraged by their promise to return in May when the baby would be born.

Many tears were shed on the day of their departure. Henry and Abigail were there to take them to the train station. Callie couldn't stop crying.

"I…I…don't know why I'm crying so…this time. I…just…

can't…seem..to stop."

"It's because you're expecting, dear."

"No…it's because..I..will miss you so…..much, Mama."

"We'll miss you too, baby girl," Nathan said as he hugged his daughter tightly. "But you have to take care of Ben and Katie and that new little one, and we have to get back to Oak Hill to take care of everyone there. We'll be back in the spring, God willing. Have to meet that new grandbaby, you know."

"Oh, Papa! I…love…you and…Mama…so…much!"

"We know, sweetie. We know." Nathan wiped a stray tear from the corner of his eyes and cleared his throat. "Well, Henry, let's get going or we'll miss our connections."

One last hug from Callie, a farewell to Ben who was sitting up in bed, many kisses from Katie, and they were on their way. Callie stood on the porch waving until they were a speck on the landscape. She sighed deeply and wiped her tears with her apron.

"Mama sad?"

"Yes, Katie, darling. Sad now, but I'll be happy again soon. Let's go in, it's getting cold out here."

They went into the house. Katie sat on the floor, petting Patch. Callie walked over to the fireplace and stared at the photographs on the mantel. She stood there as a wave of homesickness washed over her like she had never experienced before.

She saw Oak Hill at the end of the oak lined lane, standing proud and welcoming - it's tall columns and black shutters against the whitewashed brick walls - the Oak Hill of her childhood, before the war. She saw the live oaks with the gray Spanish moss swaying in the breeze, sometimes so long it touched the ground. She saw the front veranda with Preston and Beulah on the swing and Mammy Sallie and Trudy coming down the steps. She saw Nathan and Kathleen come out the huge oak front door to go riding on Daisy and Chester. She saw Socks and Rumpel running to meet her as she clapped her hands in delight. Samuel was galloping up the lane on Ivanhoe with a huge grin on his face.

She closed her eyes and smelled the honeysuckle in bloom, it's almost sickening sweet fragrance assaulting her nose. She touched the magnificent azalea blooms, vibrant with color. She felt the soft red earth oozing up between her toes after an early morning rain. She heard the darkies singing from the Quarters getting ready to start their trek to the cotton fields. She ran to the big oak tree in the front yard, spread a quilt on the ground, and laid on it, staring up at the leaves and the moss, petting Socks who sat beside her, soon joined by Trudy.

Callie blinked her eyes, now filled with salty tears. She blinked again. It was gone, all gone. Instead she saw her own little farmhouse, with its tiny parlor. She looked out the window to her "veranda"- her own porch with its few chairs. She saw the newly harvested fields, worked by the many hands of people who cared for her family. She heard her child, her daughter, on the floor by the fireplace, singing a silly tune to Patch, her dog.

"Callie!" She turned as she heard her husband, her Ben, call from their bed. She felt the new life stir in her womb, automatically placing her hand on her belly and smiling. She went to see what Ben wanted. He was sitting up in bed smiling at her. She smiled back, her eyes still glistening with tears. He didn't say anything. He opened his arms. She ran to them, and he enfolded her in an embrace and held her tight. This was *her* home. Ben, Katie, and the new baby, they were *her* home. She *was* home. She was *home*.

Would you like to see your manuscript become a book?

If you are interested in becoming a PublishAmerica author, please submit your manuscript for possible publication to us at:

acquisitions@publishamerica.com

You may also mail in your manuscript to:

**PublishAmerica
PO Box 151
Frederick, MD 21705**

We also offer free graphics for Children's Picture Books!

---

www.publishamerica.com

CPSIA information can be obtained at www.ICGtesting.com
Printed in the USA
LVOW100055031112

305477LV00003B/3/P